Simply PROTOCOL

Nicole Sharp

The Simply Trouble Series:

Big Trouble in Little Italy
Simply Protocol
Worth The Trouble
A Simple Avalanche

Standalone Books

The Italian Holiday
La Bella Luna
Surviving Thirty

Novellas

Let It Snow
The Museum Guide

For my sister Katie:
Who cut all my Barbies' hair and broke a lot of
my toys when we were kids...I still love you.
(Cuz Mom said I had to)

Simply PROTOCOL

Chapter One

"**M**om, I told you everything I know," Cassie hissed into her cell phone. She tiptoed down the hall to the back room of her two-bedroom apartment and peeked around the door, making sure her sister, Jessica, was still asleep. She pulled the door shut, all the while her mother continued to demand answers and action. "Cassandra, put your sister in the car and come over here. To this house. Right now!"

"No," Cassie whispered as she slipped into her flip-flops, and again, angrily berated herself for answering the phone in the first place. *And* for thinking it was a good idea to part with the information that her sister was calling off her wedding.

Why the hell did she think she needed to part with that information?

It couldn't have been because her mother continually gave convoluted details of how stressed Jessica's wedding plans were making her. Such as, trying to decide if the candles for the centerpieces should be tapered or tea lights; if the flower girl should wear a wreath or a bow in her hair; and if the bridesmaids should all do their hair the same way. The diatribe was so long that Cassie decided to interrupt her mother by announcing that Jessica had canceled her wedding, thinking it would release her mother from all the stresses; not inadvertently open a can of fucking worms.

Cassie grabbed a discarded headband off the entry table and pushed her unruly shoulder-length golden brown hair into slight submission. After shutting the door and locking her sister safely inside, she pocketed her keys and marched out of her second floor apartment, taking the stairs while her mother continued to list her demands.

Cassie should have found relief in the deep breath of Southern California's overcast afternoon. The slight smell of salt in the air and breeze from the ocean blowing her hair was normally calming. But not now, there was only one thing she could concentrate on at the moment.

"Barbara!" Cassie interrupted, using her mother's name now that she could speak at full volume. "We're not moving in with you. For God's sake, Jess is thirty-two and I'm thirty-five! She *just* called off her wedding, it isn't the end of the world. It's the end of her fiancé, Thomas, and good riddance."

"What does that mean?"

"Just that he wasn't...a good guy."

"Cassandra Leigh Dodd, I know when you're lying to me. I knew it when you were in high school and snuck out of the house, and I know it now."

Cassie pinched the bridge of her nose and blew out a frustrated breath. Sneaking out of the house was one thing, this current situation was completely different.

You're so dumb, she thought to herself, then shook her head. No she wasn't. It was the situation that was ridiculous. The announcement should have been simple: Hey mom, Jessica called off her wedding. She isn't in the mood to talk about it. Give her a few days and when she's ready, she'll come around and tell you everything.

That's all Cassie was really trying to say. But her mother was next level when it came to nagging and getting information out of Cassie.

"What happened in Italy?" her mom challenged.

"Jessica had a little trouble, that's all."

There was an eerily long pause, the kind Cassie knew as the calm before the storm. She removed the phone from her ear, allowing the weight of the situation to pull the phone down to her side as she muttered, "Two days, you went two days without answering her calls. You fucking moron!" She curled the phone back up.

It wasn't like Cassie told her mother about the special agents sitting in an unmarked car across the street from her apartment, working in the capacity of 'protective surveillance'. She shuddered at the thought of what a disturbance *that* announcement would cause.

"It's really nothing. Jess has jet lag. I promise, give her a few days to get some sleep and then I'll make her talk to you."

That should have been the end of the discussion. But no, Barbara Dodd was 'Special Forces' trained when it came to intuition and her daughters. There was a muffled sound on the other end of the phone; Cassie heard her mother yell at her father, "Walter, get in the car!"

"Mom," Cassie tried to sound calm and nonchalant, "it's a little heartbreak. Let her shake it off." She bit her lip the moment the words were out, worried that her mother's interpretation would be that her 'baby' was broken and the only person who could fix it was Barbara.

Cassie was not only angry at herself; she was also pissed at her sister.

Two days ago, Jess texted their mother that she was back in town; she had some news she would share at a later date; and she was going to be staying with Cassie for a while.

And that was it.

The little shit sent that text and then - radio silence. Which meant for the past two days Cassie had taken the brunt of calls and texts from their agitated mother. Messages which alternated between wedding planning questions and demands for Cassie to make Jessica call her.

The fact that their mom had not shown up on Cassie's front step was a testament to the woman's attempt to let her daughters live their own lives. And that was the only thing keeping Cassie's calm in check; because if her mom *did* show up, she would see the reason the CIA were sitting across the street. Jessica was still sporting stitches in her right eyebrow, a faded yellow bruise that encompassed her entire eye, and an arm in a cast. Not to mention the way she carefully carried herself as she walked, a result of fractured ribs. If their mother saw Jessica in this state, all proverbial and literal hell would break loose.

So whatever you do, don't mention the CIA surveillance, Cassie instructed herself for the hundredth time as she arrived at the unmarked car.

Her mother interrupted her thoughts, "Do you know what the best thing is for a heartbreak, Cassandra? The comfort of your parents' home. Don't you remember when you had the big break-up in college and you came home to lick your wounds? Heck, when I was in college, I remember how heartache ruined me..."

"Jesus Christ Mom..."

"Language," her mother bit, then continued her tirade about heartache and healing.

Cassie punched the mute button. "Fuck me." She pounded on the darkly tinted passenger side window of the nondescript car with her fist.

Nothing happened.

She gave a determined snarl, "I know you're in there and if you don't talk to me, our mother will be over here pounding on the window next. You think *I'm* making a scene right now? I learned from the best."

The window opened revealing a scowling agent. "Miss Dodd."

"Look pal, Jess has been asleep for...ever..." she glanced at the phone to make sure the mute function hadn't magically stopped working, "she cries when she *is* awake, and she hasn't been in the mood to explain anything to me yet. I'm really worried and I don't think you would be out here if everything was fine."

"Cassie?! Are you listening to me?"

She unmuted the phone, "Give me a second, I need to talk to someone..."

Mute.

"I am talking to you right now, whoever that is can wait!" her mother yelled.

Cassie lifted the phone toward the agent as if to solidify her need for information. "This is the tsunami I am trying to hold back."

"Cassandra!" Cassie ignored her mother's command.

She leaned closer to the agent. "I get that I should have ignored her phone call, but she's called twelve times. *Today!* And I really should be rewarded. I didn't say anything about Jess's current situation, but this woman has superpowers. And up until twenty minutes ago, she was still planning a wedding. And that's on me. I shouldn't have told her the wedding was off. But I did. And now I'm dealing with the consequences. Which means, she thinks I need to take Jess to our childhood home so she can recuperate. But if she sees Jess-"

"Cassandra Leigh Dodd!"

Cassie shook the phone. "Three names. She only uses three names when she's really pissed."

Unmute.

"Mom," she took a deep breath, "Jessica is asleep. In twenty-four hours, I will bring her home so you can see her for yourself, and she can tell you what happened in Italy." She knew it was all the time she could conceivably buy. She frowned at the agent, who winked at her, causing her frown to became a snarl, as she waited for her mother to agree to the terms.

"Fine."

Cassie's legs wobbled with relief. "Okay."

"Just tell her we love her."

"I will."

"And Cassandra, if she doesn't show up, in this house, twenty-four hours from now, I'm coming to your apartment."

"I know."

"Okay. I love you. Thanks for taking care of your baby sister."

"She's only three years younger..." Cassie closed her eyes, this was not the time. "It's no problem. I'll talk to you tomorrow." She punched the end call button, then waited several seconds to make sure the call had really ended.

"Okay pal, you gotta help me out. You *have* to tell me what the hell is going on. My mother thinks Jessica got home two days ago. Because that's when Jess texted the woman she was back in town." Cassie gestured between herself and the agent. "We both know it's been over a week now. And I've waited long enough for answers." She took a shaky breath. "C'mon buddy, throw me a bone here."

The agent exchanged a glance with the man in the driver's seat. After an unspoken decision, the passenger opened his door and climbed out. He held out his hand. "I'm Agent Stills, I believe we've talked before."

Cassie frowned and shook his hand as she studied him. Tired eyes, rumpled clothing. Black Dockers, cotton blend polo; nice enough for a casual meeting, but easy to move in, just in case situations got physical. He radiated overworked exhaustion and stale deodorant.

Cassie dislodged her hand from the lengthy shake.

Stills gestured toward the building. "Let's go into the apartment, it would be better if we talked there."

She rolled her eyes as they walked and sarcastically asked, "Why, do you have it bugged and need our conversation to be on the record?"

"Something like that," he answered calmly.

She stopped. "You have my apartment bugged?!" Her incredulous question echoed off the front of the apartment building.

Stills gave an unconcerned glance around, making sure no one had overheard the comment.

"Shouldn't someone have told me they were bugging my apartment?" Cassie asked angrily.

"Your home isn't bugged," he said softly and gestured for her to continue walking.

Cassie glared at him. "Then why would you say—"

"I was trying to calm you down by catching you off-guard," he offered.

She gave another eye roll and began walking again, not about to tell him that the flash of anger had helped.

The keys shook in her hands as she fumbled to unlock her door. It was a mix of the current adrenaline and worry. And Stills taking up too much space next to her.

"Your hair has red highlights when the sun hits it," he said.

"What?"

"There's some red in your hair, I suppose that's why you have a fiery side."

A wave of anger heated her cheeks, and she turned her full attention to him, trying to think of something snarky to say. But being this close, and getting a good look at him, shocked her into silence.

He was a head taller than her five-nine, maybe six-three. Definitely in shape. He had a nice build, and the way his polo shirt tucked flat against his abs into his Dockers shouldn't have been alluring enough to make her lose her train of thought, but it did. And that reaction was confusing and troubling to Cassie. He had short, auburn brown hair, a strong jaw and a furrowed brow. But his eyes were the most distracting; liquid amber eyes that flickered with the secrets they held.

"What's your first name again Agent Stills?" She tried to stop herself from studying him and his stupid eyes.

"Benjamin." His voice lowered on the introduction and he held out his hand for her to shake again as he reminded her, "We spoke on the phone."

"Yeah, we did." She looked at the offered hand then back into those amber eyes. He indeed had secrets hidden there, but there was also a hell of a lot of confidence and control. And he had done it again, tried to calm her down by distracting her with the 'fiery' comment. She forwent the second handshake. "Listen Benji—"

"Benjamin," he corrected.

Cassie laughed and went back to working on the door, opened it and waved him in. Once the door was closed, she squared off against him and tiredly demanded, "Benji, what the fuck is going on?"

He nodded toward the kitchen. "Do you have any coffee?"

"What?"

"I've heard it's customary to offer a guest a beverage before you both sit down and have a conversation about CIA dealings."

She shook her head, *was this guy for real*? "Are you trying to handle me, Benji?"

"Yes," his mouth twitched, "and I need some coffee."

She stomped to the kitchen, off the dining area, and went through the motions of making a fresh pot of coffee. She turned her attention to find Agent Stills leaning against the doorjamb.

She leaned against the sink and crossed her arms over her chest. "You know, Benji, three weeks ago my life was great. As far as I knew, my sister was engaged and in Italy on a romantic getaway with her fiancé, my mother was in heaven planning a wedding and I was...just fine."

"What happened three weeks ago?" he asked.

She snarled at him and he held up his hands. "I suppose that would be around the time your sister called you from Italy," he verified.

Cassie took a deep breath and admitted, "It's strange how one phone call can upend everything in a person's life."

Chapter Two

T hree weeks ago, Cassie was at dinner with Mark. Mediocre Mark. A work colleague had set them up. There'd been a handful of obligatory dates which led to some unexceptional romps in the sack, but nothing mind blowing. And Cassie and Mark really didn't have much in common. After the third date, he became a friend with benefits. After the fifth date, Cassie was ready to ditch him.

She decided to try one last date. Mainly because Mark asked her if she wanted to go to the Santa Monica Pier for fish tacos. And she did.

Within the first five minutes, he was over explaining the upcoming mock drafts he and his friends were running before the pre-season of his fantasy football league kicked off.

Cassie played soccer in high school and college and was part of a group that had pickup games the second Saturday of every month. "I wonder if the Europeans have fantasy futbol leagues," she teased.

"I'm sure they do." Mark frowned, not getting the joke. "Like I was saying, this year, everything kind of hinges on my first-round pick."

"Oh my God." That was the moment Cassie decided to put herself out of her misery, their quasi relationship wasn't worth her time.

She picked up the second half of her taco, pushed the plastic basket into the center of the table and stood up. "Mark, I gotta go. I'm pretty sure this thing has played itself out."

"What?" Mark was shocked.

Cassie exhaled. "Listen, I really think there is some girl out there that will love football as much as you, and everything else you like. But that girl is not me."

"Oh." He looked down at his basket. "Can I call you if...one night...like..." he raised an eyebrow.

"I think we should go cold turkey, cut everything off, you know?"

He scratched his cheek. "I suppose..."

"Mark." Cassie patted his back with her free hand.

"I'm okay. I get it," he nodded, "have a good life."

"You too, Mark," Cassie smiled, "and I really mean that."

With nothing more to say, she left and finished her taco on the way to the car.

The closer to home she got, the lighter she felt and realized she had indeed made the right decision. Mediocre sex with someone you didn't really like was a waste of time.

Once home, she changed into comfortable clothes and settled herself in front of her TV. She was opening a beer when her cell phone rang. She picked up the phone and studied the number. It wasn't anyone she knew. In fact, it was a rather long number, Europe maybe. She thought about not answering it, but then figured she didn't have much else going on tonight and maybe it would be an entertaining call.

"Hello," she said brightly.

"Cassie! Oh, thank God, Cassie!"

It was her sister. "Jess?"

"Listen okay? Listen really carefully Cassie—"

"You know, it must be nice to go on vacation to Italy last minute with your fiancé and not tell anyone." Cassie muted the TV and took a swig of her beer as she swept her legs under her, arranging herself more comfortably on the sofa.

"Cassie, I need help!" The screamed sentiment froze Cassie's whole body. She narrowed her gaze on nothing. "What's going on? You sound weird."

"No time. I'm on drugs..."

Cassie thought her sister was living it up in Italy, but this was not how she thought Jess would do it. Cassie's mouth was dry, she swallowed several times to find her voice while her mind swirled with which questions she needed to ask first, but the only thing she could think to do was repeat her sister's declaration, "You're on drugs."

"No...yes...listen I don't have time. I need help and it's hard to focus."

"Because you're on drugs," Cassie verified. "What drugs?"

"Morphine and, I think, cocaine," Jess said questioningly.

"What the hell?!" Cassie stood up and began to pace. This didn't make any sense. Jessica didn't mind the occasional social drinking, but she wasn't into wild parties that ended with morphine and coke.

"The doctor gave it to me. I have broken ribs and a broken arm. And something's wrong with my side but it didn't hurt all the organs. Organs gans, gans...does that sound right?"

The floor beneath Cassie's feet fell away. She stood still, her mouth a desert, her heart slamming against her ribs... "Jessica," she demanded calmly, "what the fuck is going on?"

"Listen, just listen. I need help. I need you to find Stacie's phone number." Jessica referred to a college roommate she had years ago, "I need you to find Stacie so I can find Parker. Stacie is the only person who has Parker's phone number." Her hysteria was palpable though the phone.

Cassie looked around her apartment as if she could make these people appear, but she didn't understand what her sister was asking of her. "Jess, I don't like this. You sound crazy. What's going on?"

"Cassandra, get online right now. Look up Stacie and Amadeo Lazzaroti. They live in Long Beach. Looonnnng Beach."

"What?" Even though she didn't understand, she was making her way to her laptop.

"Look it up. Now! Please. Before I forget what I'm trying to do," Jess begged.

"Okay, okay. Settle down..." Cassie tried to make her own voice sound calm, which was difficult, because every cell in her body was attempting to change her temperature, heart rate, and ability to comprehend signals from her five senses. She clicked open a browser then opened her email because she couldn't concentrate on what she was trying to do. The flood of emotions made focusing severely difficult. She took as deep a breath as her stressed lungs would allow and pulled up the white pages' website. She typed the names Stacie and Amedeo Lazzaroti in the search bar. "Tell me what's going on."

"Thomas is a bad guy. Mafia. He killed Luigi. I need to find the CIA," Jessica said.

"Who...Jessica...." Ripples of fear were wreaking havoc with the task at hand, the computer screen flickered and blurred, morphing into fuzzy distractions.

"Cassandra...please! No, wait, I should focus. I can't focus."

"Jessica, it's okay." Cassie pursed her lips as she cross referenced the information she found for Stacie and Amedeo in Long Beach with another website.

"Cassie, oh thank God! I need you to help me. I can't really focus. I need you to find a phone number for Stacie Lazzaroti."

"I'm looking the number up right now." Cassie fought to keep her voice steady, "Where are you?"

"In a cab." Cassie listened as her sister asked someone, "Where am I?" After a muttered interaction, Jessica announced, "Rome? Wow, I'm in Rome."

"Rome?" Cassie's mom told her that Jessica's fiancé, Thomas, had taken them to Florence. But now he's a bad guy and her sister was on drugs and the mafia were involved? "What are you doing in Rome?"

"Cassie! Oh, thank God, I need your help..."

Fear wrapped itself around Cassie – she shook her head to stop the threatening tears, this wasn't the time. "I know, I know kid, I'm right here," Cassie soothed as she checked the number against one more website to make sure it was correct. "Okay, I found the number. Are you ready?"

"I can't remember anything...wait...wait...hey guy! Hey Mr. Taxi Driver? Do you have a piece of paper? I need you to write this number down."

Cassie zoomed her computer screen in on the number and read it slowly, nodding her head when she heard Jessica repeat the number to the cab driver.

"I got it!" Jess said and then quickly added, "I'll call you later, okay? Don't worry."

"Don't worry?!" Cassie screamed and began pacing her apartment. "You said your life is in danger, Thomas killed someone, and you're on drugs!" A tear slipped then.

"I know but Parker can save me."

"Who the fuck is Parker?" The walls of the apartment were closing in on Cassie, and when she thought she couldn't take any more devastating announcements, her sister said, "My husband."

Cassie's voice shook, "Jess, seriously. What is going on?" She never got a reply, Jessica had hung up.

Cassie's legs buckled, so she let herself slip to the floor. Her sister's words and frantic voice echoed through her head and bounced around in her body. Helplessness cloaked Cassie. How the hell was she supposed to help her sister in Rome while she was in Southern California? Cassie was too far away to help.

She could hop a plane and try to get to Jess, but how would she find her? All she knew was that she was in Rome. And would Cassie even be able to get there in time to do anything?

Forming a plan, much less a coherent thought, was difficult. Sanity floated past her, unwilling to ground her.

"Stacie!" she shouted. She would call Stacie.

She would call the number she gave her sister and demand to talk to this Parker guy. But first she needed to give Jess time to get whatever information she needed. Cassie settled on twenty minutes. She'd give Jessica twenty minutes and then call Stacie. If she didn't get an answer, she'd call every ten seconds after that.

It wasn't a great plan, but at least it was something.

Cassie scrutinized the clock on the wall opposite her. The problem was how to keep her own panic in check for the next twenty minutes, because as the second hand counted out ten seconds, an entire lifetime passed.

Chapter Three

At the International arrivals area of the Los Angeles airport, Cassie paced and mindlessly chewed her way through a bag of overpriced Swedish Fish she'd purchased as she waited for Jessica. She wished the pacing would release the build-up of tension, but all it managed to do was make her feel like a caged animal.

Her attention fluctuated between studying the arrivals board and her cell phone to make sure she had the right flight and the right time. As if at any moment either of those things would be changed or her memory would fail.

From what Jess had told her, when she was finally able to call Cassie and explain a few things, she was headed home with a CIA escort. Jess would be the last one off the plane and then would have to go through customs, but she would meet Cassie right here. The Los Angeles Airport International arrival area.

So that's where Cassie was. Waiting and watching the mass exodus of travelers walk up the worn, shiny tiled ramp from some underground world that emptied into the greeting area.

Cassie would have loved to ask anyone for information. Actually, that wasn't true. She wanted someone to yell at. She wanted someone she could demand answers from regarding Jessica. But there wasn't anyone to question or yell at.

Where was the secret CIA arrival information desk when you needed it? If she could find such a fictitious place right now and scream the questions plaguing her she would feel better. She'd start with the question: Where the hell is my sister?

What if something had gone wrong on the plane? What if Jess had complications due to her injuries and there wasn't a doctor on board? What if something had happened in customs? Since both the mafia and CIA were involved, what if one of those organizations had a 'man' on the inside? A rogue employee at the airport that abducted Jessica again?

Cassie ground her teeth together and sarcastically thanked Hollywood for setting up such unrealistic thoughts. At least she hoped they were unrealistic.

Her teetering mirages of reality fell to the ground, becoming a pile of rubble when she caught sight of Jess walking up the ramp among a new surge of arrivals.

Cassie's joy rose and fell in the same inhale.

Holy Fuck.

Cassie swallowed the comment she wanted to mouth, because she wasn't ready to see her sister like this. The last time she'd seen her was the happy occasion when everyone gathered to help her pick out her wedding dress.

This woman limping up the ramp was a shell of her sister.

Her right arm was in a cast, her shoulders slumped forward slightly. And even from this distance, Cassie could see the drawn look on her face.

Cassie dropped the bag of candy on the floor and began waving. "Jess! Over here." She made a beeline for her. When Jess saw Cassie, she stopped; unable to continue anymore.

Cassie shoved her way through a few people to meet Jessica halfway. She pulled Jess in for a bear hug, not caring about the pain she might be causing because in that moment she was desperate to be sure of her sister's physical presence.

Jess buried her face in Cassie's neck and began sobbing, clinging to her older sister.

Cassie's spine straightened. A flash of memory punched. It was the moment her mom had put a baby in her chubby three-year-old arms and said, "You're going to help take care of your baby sister, right?"

At the time, Cassie had nodded her agreement to the task, but the weight of the promise never hit home until this very moment.

Jess wasn't the kind of person that 'needed' anyone to take care of her. Cassie had been a teacher, friend and confidant more than anything else.

Sure, there had been the usual 'older sister' protection against immature boys and gossiping girls. But Jess was strong and sassy and a veritable force of nature.

This shadow of a woman wasn't her sister.

Cassie silently renewed her three-year-old vow in that moment, and an animal-like protectiveness sent shockwaves through her bones and skin, which she attempted to infuse into Jess through the hug.

Nobody was going to fuck with her sister ever again.

"It's okay Jess. You're okay now. I got ya. I promise, everything is going to be okay." Cassie's throat ached around the promise.

When they were able to finally part, Cassie nodded and looked Jess over, her heart hurting with how much worse she looked up close.

Cassie narrowed her gaze and brushed a stray strand of hair behind Jess's ear. "Okay kid, we've got this. Let's go home."

She never let go of Jess's good arm as she steered her through the crowded airport. Cassie's head was on a swivel as she tried to shield Jessica from an unforeseen threat, all the while trying to keep her from noticing the frowns of concern other people aimed at them as they walked past. The other element Cassie didn't want Jess to see was the normal stereotypical happy travelers: suntanned, grinning tourists; grandparents squealing with delight over babies; and girlfriends buried in romantic kisses with boyfriends.

They walked out the sliding doors into the warm June Los Angeles evening and stood at the crosswalk. Jessica shielded her eyes from the golden sun and stepped closer to Cassie as the buzz of airport drama filled her senses. Cassie slipped her arm around Jessica's shoulder and gave a reassuring squeeze as they continued to the car.

Once settled Cassie started her red four door sedan, while vigilantly watching Jessica out of the corner of her eye. Cassie didn't want to ask anything that would upset her but at the same time, she wanted to demand Jessica explain everything right then.

Jess rolled her window down and took a deep breath as Cassie paid for parking. The breath seemed to go so well, she took another one.

"Cass, can we drive through In-N-Out?"

"Hell yes. Cheeseburger, animal fries and a chocolate shake?" Cassie rattled off her sister's favorites, and didn't miss the stray tear that slipped.

"Cass..." Jessica gave an exhausted sigh, "I'm so tired of crying."

"Listen, we aren't going to worry about anything today. We'll talk tomorrow, and if you don't want to talk then, we'll talk next week. I figure greasy food, a really good cry, a hot bath and then bed. Not necessarily in that order. Rinse and repeat as many times as needed."

Jess held up her arm with the cast. "It's hard to bathe with this."

Cassie shrugged. "We'll wrap it in a trash bag. I have lavender scented ones."

Jess laughed; it didn't completely reach her eyes, but at least it was something.

Cassie glanced in the rearview mirror as she pulled into traffic and saw the large black SUV following them. "So the goon squad is going to follow us everywhere we go now?" It was more of a statement than a question.

Jessica looked in the passenger mirror. "That's Agent Stills and Agent Robbins, they're nice." She took another deep breath.

"You know Jess, just because you want to be different from everyone else, doesn't mean you had to bring home a CIA detail from your vacation."

The joke fell flat.

"Agent Stills flew home with me. He's a good guy. They're just trying to keep me safe."

Cassie gave a grunt in reply.

"If you're worried about your safety I can ask them what they can do."

"I'm not worried," Cassie said, but the tone she was trying to hide from her sister didn't go unnoticed.

"What?"

Cassie rubbed the back of her neck. "I'm not worried about me, I'm worried about you."

"I'm not worried about me," Jess lied, but Cassie decided to let her sister have the lie. "There is something I *am* worried about though," Jess admitted.

"What are you worried about?"

Jess turned in her seat to give her full attention to Cassie. "Do you really want to help me?"

Cassie raised an eyebrow in answer, so Jess continued, "Can you tell Mom that I'm not getting married now?"

Cassie found a real laugh then and shook her head. "I don't love you that much, kid." She glanced in her rearview mirror and suggested, "Maybe we can get one of those agents to tell her instead. I feel like that falls squarely in the category of 'keeping you safe.'"

Jess sat back and burrowed into her seat. "Actually, that's not a bad idea."

Chapter Four

The coffee pot sputtered its finale as Cassie's recap of Jessica's call and her arrival at the airport also came to an end.

She studied Stills standing across from her as she took a deep breath and confessed, "I don't know why I told you all that."

"People tell me their secrets all the time. I'm very personable," he tried to joke in a monotone voice.

"They weren't secrets," Cassie defended. "They were a series of events. So you would understand what I knew and, hopefully, fill in the rest." Cassie handed over a steaming cup of coffee to Stills and nodded toward the dining table.

Once seated, Cassie glanced toward the hallway that led to the guest room. She was still unable to fathom the strange series of events that had led to the current situation. She was glad Jess was with her, it allowed her to keep a close eye on her. But it was all so surreal. Proof of Jessica's trip was apparent in her injuries. But while she slept, Cassie spent her hours desperately trying to keep her overactive imagination from playing reel after reel of frightening storylines.

"Miss Dodd, the first thing you need to understand is that your sister is safe. Our presence here is simply protocol," Stills began.

Cassie nodded as she digested the information. "Protocol," she repeated, "because no one really knows where Jessica's ex…Thomas Adler…" she swallowed hard, it was difficult to say the asshole's name, "no one knows where he is."

Stills waited a moment before admitting, "Yes. There are some other extenuating circumstances, but Thomas Adler is now at large."

"Jesus, Benji. Don't sugarcoat it," she mumbled.

"Adler worked as a lawyer and, as it turns out, worked in various capacities with the mafia."

Cassie tiredly rubbed her face with her hands, if ever she wanted the succinct truth, Stills had just given it to her. "Jess was engaged to a mobster."

Agent Stills shrugged. "Mob-adjacent."

Cassie raised an eyebrow. "This isn't funny."

"No, it's not," he agreed, but a small smile pulled at his lips; he covered it by taking a sip of coffee.

Cassie wondered if his smile was another attempt to calm her down.

She continued to try to piece together the fragments of the story from what Jess had told her and the bits Stills was willing to divulge. "So, Thomas is a bad guy. Jess found an email on Thomas' computer with a trip itinerary – a trip to Italy. And she...just...followed him?"

Stills nodded. "She showed up in Lake Como, Italy, where our operation was being managed. Parker was informed of her arrival before she could find Adler."

"And that's when the CIA kidnapped her." She gestured toward Stills.

"We didn't kidnap her," he countered.

"You didn't," she snorted mockingly.

"Parker was instructed to keep Jessica out of harm's way until she could return home safely." The explanation fell flat.

Cassie gave a grunt in reply, she wasn't sure his assessment was on the mark. She continued, "Also, apparently there is a side note to this strange story...Agent Parker Salvatore and Jess were married ten years ago? And he just *happens* to work for the CIA looking into Jessica's...Thomas?" This was another part she couldn't wrap her head around. Mainly because she didn't have much information on that front either.

She continued to verbalize the story in an attempt to make sense out of it, "Did I mention that three weeks ago I understood my life?" The question was rhetorical.

"Agent Salvatore having previous interactions with your sister *is* a strange coincidence," Stills said.

"Is he a good guy?" Cassie had as many questions about the events that transpired in Italy as she did about this mystery man, Parker. What information Jessica *was* willing to disclose regarding her trip, left Parker out of the Cliffs Notes. The few times Cassie gently tried to ask about him directly, Jessica's eyes blinked with glassy tears, and she changed the subject.

"He's one of the best men I know," Stills answered.

Cassie kept her voice low as she pointed angrily out the window and demanded, "Then why isn't he out there in that car watching over my sister?"

Stills studied Cassie for a moment before he answered, "Because he's in the thick of the storm. He's doing whatever it takes to track down Thomas Adler and make sure he's brought to justice. That's why he's not out there."

The weight of the announcement hit Cassie square in the chest and pushed her back in her seat. She nodded as the information washed over her. It helped, but didn't take care of the mountain of questions that lingered. She also figured, if she asked Agent Stills to tell her everything, there would be a lot of redactions.

She swallowed hard and quietly asked, "Thomas did that to her? The broken arm and ribs...."

Stills nodded. "There was a fight. We tried to keep Jessica safe, but...as I understand the story, Jessica threw a heavy glass tumbler at Adler, hit him in the head, and angered him."

Angered him. Cassie frustratingly exhaled the clinical explanation.

Stills continued, "By the time we arrived, Adler had abducted your sister."

"Jess said she remembered seeing Thomas kill some head honcho mafia guy?"

He blew out a tired breath. "You aren't supposed to know any of this."

"Yeah, well, here we are buddy." She continued, "So Thomas took Jess to Rome, and that's when she called me." And nothing had been the same since.

"Then you called us."

"Then I called you," she verified with a sigh.

"A true delight." He winked.

Cassie waved his wink away; he was trying to disarm her once more. "So, the way this story tells, it sounds *so* simple. But there's a lot I apparently don't understand. Because if it was simple, I have a feeling you wouldn't be assigned to watch my sister twenty-four seven."

"Is there a question there?" he asked.

Cassie shook her head disbelievingly and annunciated, "Why are you here?"

Stills took another drink of his coffee and studied Cassie over the rim of his cup. She intensified her gaze, a silent challenge. She wasn't going to back down.

Finally, he said, "Jessica is heartbroken."

She shook her head in confusion. "So the CIA have so much time on their hands they watch heartbroken women like some...weird...overprotective 'Big Brother'?"

"Sadly, we don't have a budget for that." He smiled and continued, "We aren't certain of the whereabouts of Thomas Adler. We are here on the off chance he shows up - to cover all bases." He paused, waiting for Cassie to digest the information. She nodded after a moment and he resumed, "Your sister was an asset in our investigation."

Cassie's ire flared, she opened her mouth to yell at Stills, but he held up a hand to stop her. "She volunteered. Jessica *volunteered* to help us. All we asked her to do was be our eyes and ears. She was safe until the night of the fight. She's also one hell of a person, she'll get through all this."

"Well..." Cassie nodded in agreement to the assessment.

"And now I see where she gets it from."

"Really?" Cassie rolled her eyes at his lame attempt at a compliment.

Stills smiled but resumed his account. "Jessica *is* heartbroken, though I doubt she would admit to it. And she's probably going to be battling some post-traumatic stress."

"Post-traumatic stress?" The cavalier way Stills made the announcement heated her anger.

"The body heals easily enough; it's the heart and mind that take a little more time and attention."

This man was concise in his explanation, yet Cassie continually felt off-kilter. And the way he spoke about heartache and post-traumatic stress, it was obvious he was speaking from firsthand experience.

Cassie tried to focus on the bigger issue at hand. "What do I tell my mom?"

"That you are safe." He leveled a calm gaze. "It's my job and I'll follow through to keep that promise."

"For how long?"

"I can't say."

"Can't or won't?"

"Miss Dodd—"

"Agent Stills, I don't need you to manipulate me or my emotions. I need to figure out what story I'm going to tell my parents when I see them and how I'm going to convince them Jess is okay." Saying it aloud dried out Cassie's throat, she had twenty-four hours to figure out how to deal with Barbara Dodd. "The shock of seeing Jess is going to cause problems enough. Piling on the fact that she's suffering from a little PTSD and heartache will not help."

He grunted and sat back in his chair. "Miss Dodd, the situation is that your sister had an accident in Italy. No one needs to know all the intricate details."

Cassie laughed. "Benji, intricate details are *all* Barbara Dodd is going to want to hear."

Chapter Five

Cassie jogged across the street and knocked on the back window of the car as she made her way to the passenger side. Her conversation with Agent Benjamin Stills the previous day had not helped illuminate the situation she found herself in, or help her figure out what they were going to tell their mother. When she told Jess that it had to be done, Jessica asked Cassie to go request Stills' help.

"Miss Dodd…" Agent Stills gave a frustrated sigh as he rolled his window down.

She held up a hand before he could disapprove of her tactics. "I need your help."

"What's wrong?" He was out of the car assessing the area as well as Cassie for a threat.

She adjusted the headband on her head and took a deep breath. "My twenty-four hours are almost up. My mom and dad deserve to know what's going on."

"That is completely up to your discretion."

"Benji…"

He raised his eyebrow.

"Agent Stills…" She hated how much of her vulnerability was showing, but she needed his help. "Jessica and I are driving to my parents' house. You're going to be following us anyway. So maybe you could drive with us…and help us figure out the best way to explain Jessica's current situation to our overprotective parents, who don't see us as thirty-year-olds, but still as teenagers."

"Is that all?" he asked dryly.

"Well, actually..." she shifted her weight and cleared her throat, "Jessica was really wondering, if once we get to our parents' house...you'd do all the explaining." She rushed the last words out.

Stills glanced behind him in the car, at Robbins who was pretending to have not heard everything, and directed his question at his partner, "Your ass is part of this too, what do you think?"

Robbins didn't hide his smile as he told Cassie, "Benji has always had a thing for a fiery girl with gray blue eyes in need of assistance."

Cassie rolled her eyes, she didn't have time for this machismo, no matter how intriguing it was that Stills scowled at his partner in reply.

"Please." She leveled the request at him.

"Fine. When?"

She slapped him on the arm and took a few steps backwards, "We leave in thirty minutes. And hey, I made coffee cake for everyone." She turned then and jogged back to the apartment before he could find a reason that the time frame wouldn't work for him.

"Barbara, sit down," their father, Walter Dodd, said as he ran a shaky hand through his short, salt and pepper hair.

"Cassie," their mother said, hands on her hips, "why are you standing in front of Jessica? I need to talk to her."

The moment they walked in the door and her parents caught sight of Jessica and her healing wounds, all hell broke loose - just as Cassie predicted.

There wasn't time to introduce Agent Stills or get a word in edgewise. Barbara Dodd pulled herself up to her full five-five height and began demanding answers; of course, she didn't wait for the answers, so she began to create her own nonsensical storyline that had everyone trying to unsuccessfully interrupt.

"Jesus Christ, Mom!" Jessica finally screamed, loud enough to get everyone's attention. "Dammit, sit down and take a breath and I'll tell you all about my 'romantic' Italian getaway that was thwarted by a tiny kidnapping and a broken arm."

It took every ounce of control Cassie had to not bark out the inappropriate laugh that wanted to escape. She unsuccessfully hid it behind a cough.

Jessica continued, "Spoiler, I live and everything is okay."

Stills took advantage of the uncomfortable lull to introduce himself, "Hello, Mr. and Mrs. Dodd–"

"This is Agent Benjamin Stills with the CIA," Cassie announced quickly. Stills aimed a sideways glance at Cassie, nodding his appreciation for using his full title.

"CIA?!" her mother screamed and began her litany of demands and hysterics again.

"Mom." It was Cassie's turn to stop the woman; she grabbed her by the upper arms and gave a shake. Cassie stood a few inches above their mother, so it was easy to attempt to be menacing as she looked down her nose and narrowed her gaze.

Her mother stopped and slapped at Cassie's hands. "Fine." She took a deep breath and stepped back. She patted her short, curly hair she kept dyed ash blonde, and then pulled at the bottom of her button-down shirt before taking another calming breath. "Fine. Explain."

Cassie held out her hands, silently begging her mom to understand. "Mom, we aren't being brought home by the cops because we got caught shoplifting. Let him explain everything, then you can ask all the questions you want. And Agent Stills here will let us know what Jessica can, and can't answer." She took a step back toward her sister.

"You were arrested for shoplifting?" Stills whispered the question, intrigued. But the moment was thwarted by Barbara's demand, "Why can't you answer all my questions?"

"Ma'am," Stills smiled apologetically, "we are in the middle of an ongoing investigation. For your family's safety, we need to be careful until we've tied up any loose ends on our part. It's the procedure we follow in such events."

"Are you married?" Barbara asked Stills. The quick shift in conversation made Jessica roll her eyes, but Cassie realized she was very interested in the answer. An unexpected thrill ran up her spine when he shook his head in the negative. "No, ma'am."

Barbara continued, "I am going to assume you do not have any children?"

"No Ma'am," he said warily.

That bit of information, Cassie also found interesting. A curious part of her leaned forward and wondered what other sort of personal information Barbara might be able to derive?

Jessica tried to intervene, "Mom-"

Her mother ignored the attempt. "So you don't understand the protectiveness that comes from being a parent. These girls are my life. You've heard of the tiger mom? I *invented* the tiger mom."

Cassie and Jessica exchanged embarrassed, wide-eyed glances and Cassie found herself biting the inside of her mouth, she was one more weird comment away from breaking down into inappropriate hysterical laughter.

"So Agent Stills, I need a little more to go on other than *procedure*."

Stills was quiet for several long moments. Cassie glanced at him, curious how he was going to proceed.

"You're right. You deserve to hear the whole story. As long as you can promise me, for your safety, and for the safety of all of your extended family and friends, you will keep what we discuss today confidential. If you can do that, I'll forgo protocol."

Cassie shook off the strange wave of attraction that brushed over her skin. "Damn, who knew standing up to Mom would be a turn on," she muttered under her breath.

Jessica caught the whispered declaration and elbowed Cassie. "I told you he was a nice guy."

Sure, he was a nice guy. Nice looking, nice deep voice, nice build, nice eyes...but it would have been a lot nicer if he'd given her the same benefit when she'd demanded to know what was going on.

Their mother nodded her head in agreement. "Alright then." She gingerly sat down on the sofa and gestured for everyone to follow her lead. "Cassandra, for goodness sakes, stop standing guard over your sister. Now everyone, sit down."

Cassie glanced at her father who rolled his eyes at his wife's theatrics, but his reaction was only show for his daughters; there was no denying the tension in his shoulders as he sat down next to his wife on the sofa.

Agent Stills pulled a high back chair from the corner into the middle of the room and settled himself across from Cassie's parents. Jessica sat to his left in a big recliner, Cassie on the edge of Jessica's seat.

All eyes were intent on Stills as he began to speak. "I've been part of a task force that's been working for the past few years to indict members of a well known Italian crime family." He looked around the room to assess how everyone was taking the easy part of the information. He sat forward, his forearms resting on his knees. "Jessica's ex-fiancé, Thomas Adler, was working for this crime family. He helped with the legalities of hiding money offshore and also used his talents to make sure various criminals were never prosecuted."

"Bastard," Cassie hissed. Stills glanced at her with a raised eyebrow; she repeated her opinion, "He's a bastard." She waved for him to continue.

"The man who is considered the head of the crime family we were investigating used Jessica. He had her unknowingly set up several accounts for his fraudulent business."

"Jessica," her mother bit, "why didn't you know?"

"Oh my God," Cassie shot as Jessica responded defiantly, "The point of a fraudulent account is to make sure it looks like the real thing to unsuspecting people."

Cassie pointed at her sister. "She *was* the 'unsuspecting people.'"

Stills continued, "It was this man who set Jessica and Adler up on a date."

"The fairy godfather is the bad man? Luigi?" their mother asked incredulously.

Stills might have been shocked that Jessica's family knew who Luigi was, but nodded at her assessment.

Jessica waved her hand. "People know Luigi introduced Thomas and me, it was part of our...story," she explained.

"Well, while Jessica thought it was a love match, according to Adler, the set up was a test."

"Test?" their mother asked.

Jessica dryly said, "Yeah, the test was to see if Thomas was willing to marry me, in order to pay his dues by keeping an eye on me and do right by 'the family.'"

Cassie reached out and patted Jessica on the shoulder.

"But he seemed so nice," Barbara floundered.

"He *seemed* nice until he tried to kill her," Cassie said.

Walter Dodd, ever the calm and stoic voice of reason, had been intently listening. As the information came, his eyes grew glassy and his lips drew further into a tense line. Finally he found his voice enough and gestured toward Jessica to confirm, "He did this...?"

Stills nodded. "He did. It wasn't supposed to get to the point where Jessica's life was in any danger."

"But it did," Cassie pointed.

Barbara shook her head. "So how did she end up in Italy? Thomas called me and said he was the one who had taken her to Florence for a pre-wedding getaway."

Jessica began, "The day I got my wedding dress, the house we put a bid on was accepted-"

Their mother's eyes widened. "You bought a house with this man? I didn't even know you were looking for a house."

"Mom..." Cassie sighed.

"Of course *you* knew. She tells you everything." Barbara gave an irritated hiss.

"Actually, she doesn't," Cassie bit back.

Jessica's forehead creased at the comment, but she continued. "We were closing on a house," she said loudly. "Thomas left for a business trip. I needed to forward some information to our realtor from his office computer, and I found an email with his itinerary."

Stills nodded. "Adler told Jessica that he was going to New York, but the itinerary she found was for a trip to Italy. She was upset at being lied to and decided to confront him."

Jessica glanced at Stills. "I was more than upset."

He continued, "When Jessica arrived at the hotel where Adler was staying, we intercepted her."

Cassie grunted, "Kidnapped her."

"Miss Dodd," Stills warned.

Barbara rubbed her face. "Wait, the CIA kidnapped you?"

"No," Jess sighed, "I walked into the middle of their operation. They got to me before I could get to Thomas. But it didn't matter anyway. Thomas knew I was in Italy. He was tracking my bank accounts and my phone."

"He was tracking..." Their mother paled.

Stills went on, "A plan was agreed upon where Jessica would help us gather information."

"You used my daughter as a...a...an asset?" Barbara seethed through her teeth.

"It was my idea." Jessica annunciated each word. "They needed someone close to Thomas, and I was as close as you could get."

"Jesus Christ," their father whispered.

"It wasn't that bad. At least, he didn't want anything to do with me that way, nothing..."

"Sexual," Cassie offered.

Jessica frowned. "Physical," she supplied. "It was more like a roommate arrangement. I went to a lot of brunches and dinners and cocktail parties. I wore a bracelet that had a listening device in it. So all I really had to do was stand around. Thomas got to show everyone that he was doing what they wanted, and I kept you all safe."

That was Cassie's breaking point. "You kept us safe?"

Stills confirmed Jessica's explanation, responding, "Adler gave a veiled threat that if Jessica didn't pretend to be the doting bride-to-be, someone in the organization might hurt one of her family members."

"Jessica!" Cassie stood.

"Cassie, sit down," Jess said tiredly. "It wasn't as bad as he's making it sound. He never threatened me, never laid a hand on me. Really, it was a lot of amazing wine and Italian food and waiting around for the CIA to figure out how to get me home."

"If it wasn't that bad, then why-" Cassie cut herself off.

"Why what?" Jess asked.

What she really wanted to say was that if it wasn't that bad, why did Jessica have nightmares and why was she trying to hide her crying? And why did Stills say she was suffering from PTSD? But if her mother caught wind of that...Cassie wondered, what level of mothering was beyond 'all hell breaking loose'?

Cassie shook her head and was thankful for her mother's interruption.

"How did standing around get you hurt this badly?" Barbara asked.

"I drank too much one night, and so did Thomas. I was also at the end of my rope. I decided I'd had enough waiting around..." she trailed off.

Stills continued, "Jessica threw a glass tumbler at Adler and hit him upside the head. Angered and intoxicated, Adler pushed her and she fell on a glass table."

Their father clenched his jaw as their mother pressed a hand to her chest.

"I passed out, and when I woke up, Thomas had taken me to Rome."

This was where things got convoluted. On the ride over, the women asked Stills to leave the phone call to Cassie, as well as Parker and Jessica's relationship, out of the narrative. Those were bombshells for another day. And right now, it didn't make or break the story.

Jessica glanced at Stills who picked up the thread once again. "Luigi showed up at Adler's home to inquire after Jessica's well-being. It was reported that Adler allegedly killed Luigi. In a panic, he abducted Jessica and took her to Rome, thinking to use her as a bargaining chip with the CIA. He would return Jessica in exchange for immunity and witness protection."

If it was possible, Barbara and Walter Dodd's faces had lost even more color.

Jessica continued quickly to get to the end of her story and put her parents out of their misery. "I was done with all the bullshit at that point. I wasn't about to let Thomas use me. Thankfully, the doctor Thomas hired to treat me was a kind man. He helped me get away. He hid a phone for me to use when I escaped. After I got out, I found a taxi driver, called the CIA, and they directed me to a safehouse."

"How did you run away with your arm broken and the pain..." Their father's question trailed off.

"The doctor gave me a shot of painkillers before I left," Jessica answered, she hoped reassuringly.

Agent Stills stepped in to finish the story. "As soon as she was cleared for travel, I accompanied her home. I am part of three teams that will be watching Jessica around the clock until Thomas Adler is captured."

"And when will that happen?" Barbara asked.

"Mr. and Mrs. Dodd, we have our best agents on the case. Adler is out of moves and there isn't anywhere for him to hide." He held out his hands. "The situation your daughter found herself in was unfortunate, but she rose to the challenge and aided in an important operation. Jessica is a hero. That's the tall and short of it." His words punctuated the end of the story.

No one said anything. The ticking of the clock in the living room was the only thing keeping track of Barbara Dodd's speechlessness. Cassie traded silent, shocked expressions with her sister. So this is what it took to quiet the woman.

The stillness was interrupted by Barbara's sudden movement. She stood and tugged Jessica out of her seat with one hand and reached for Cassie with her other, and pulled her daughters into her arms. There was no commenting, no speeches; just a mother overwhelmed by a story and grateful for her daughters' safety.

Walter followed suit; he stood to the side of the triad and pulled Jessica to his side.

After a few moments, their father made eye contact with Stills. "Is she safe?"

"I'm convinced Jessica is safe; our continued presence is just policy," Stills answered.

Their father gave a few more nods of his head while he allowed the information to soak in. "Okay then," he finally said.

"Mom," Cassie said when she pulled away, "we have a few more things to talk about."

"What more could there possibly be?" Her breath rushed out exhaustedly.

"We need you and Dad to do us a favor," Cassie said.

Jess nodded to their mother. "It's going to be the hardest on you."

"What's hard? I don't care, I can do anything," Barbara declared, forcing her shoulders straight.

Cassie gave a dry laugh as Jess cleared her throat. "Mom, Dad, you can't tell *anyone* about this."

Their father grunted. "Who am I going to tell?"

"We're not worried about you," Cassie muttered.

Jess continued, "Mom, we can't tell anyone about anything. We can't tell anyone Thomas was a bad guy or what he did."

From where he was sitting, Stills added, "The story we're encouraging is that Adler changed his mind and the wedding has been canceled."

Barbara crossed her arms over her chest. "I don't like it."

"Mom, that's *all* there can be to this story," Jessica said.

"I don't like it," she repeated.

"You don't have to like it. It's what we have to do," Cassie said tiredly.

Their mother put her hands on her hips. "Can't we say you dumped him?"

"What?" Jessica asked.

"I would rather say *you* dumped *him*. It sounds better. A lot better."

Cassie glanced over at Stills. "Benji, that isn't too much to ask."

He agreed, "That works."

"Of course it does," Barbara affirmed. She took a deep cleansing breath and blew it out with a clap of her hands and changed the subject. "Now, Cassie brought that gorgeous coffee cake, I'll make a pot of coffee and we'll all go sit in the kitchen."

"Mrs. Dodd, I appreciate the offer, but now that I've done my part, I should get back." He gestured to the front window where Robbins was waiting in the car.

"That's the CIA?" Barbara asked.

"Agent Robbins," Cassie offered.

"My partner," Stills confirmed.

Their mother looked between the car and Stills. "Well, you're watching Jessica more closely if you stay; so you'll stay. Cassie will take your little friend some coffee and cake."

Cassie rolled her eyes. "Mom, they're grown men."

"Cassandra."

Stills agreed, "I see your point, ma'am. I'd love to visit."

Jessica pushed her mom. "C'mon Mom, I'll help you start the coffee."

Their father held out his hand to Stills. "Thank you," he said and gave a slight nod, then he too left the room.

Cassie watched them all go and was relieved when the weight she'd placed on her shoulders began to loosen.

"You okay?" Stills asked.

"Are *you* okay?" Cassie gave a dry laugh. "The Dodd family can be a bit much at times."

"So, you bake?" he asked, instead of answering Cassie's question.

She nodded. "It relaxes me."

"Really?"

"Why would I lie about baking relaxing me?"

He gave a slight shrug. "I suppose you wouldn't." He looked over Cassie's shoulder, in the direction the rest of the family had gone. "Miss Dodd, would you agree that since I helped you today, you now owe me a favor?"

Cassie's eyebrows knitted together in question. "What sort of favor?"

"You need to stop bringing attention to the car parked on your street."

She nodded her head once, then had a thought. "But what if I need you?"

He tilted his head. "You need me?"

"You know what I mean..." She waved away the unexpected thrill the misunderstanding brought about.

"You won't need us," he promised.

"But..."

"Tell me about being brought home for shoplifting."

"What? It wasn't..." she saw the twinkle in his eye, "are you trying to distract me?"

"Why would I do that?"

"I don't know..." she tilted her head to the side and studied him, "you think distracting me makes me feel better or more in control or some bullshit."

"I'm merely trying to explain that everything is okay. You don't need to worry." There was that deep dip of his voice that caught her off-guard.

She frowned. "Agent Stills, I've told you before, I don't need to be handled."

"Well Cassandra, what would happen if I confessed that I did indeed want to handle you?" The frown lines that creased his forehead eased and that slight sparkle in his eyes returned. He was flirting with her, she realized, and Cassie liked it. And why not? He was a grown ass, single man and she was a grown ass, unattached woman.

"I don't know Benji, the heat in the kitchen gets pretty hot. You might get burned if you try to *handle* it."

His grin spread and he whispered smoothly, "That sounds like a challenge, Dodd."

Chapter Six

Cassie knew it was Stills on duty this morning. Even though the windows were tinted, she knew he was watching her cross the street. She needed to see the men in the car with her own two eyes. She needed to make sure they were still there. He'd told her not to approach the car, but she was a visual learner, something a counselor in high school told her, and she used the excuse when it suited her. And it suited her now.

She walked slowly, gave a little swing to her hips and acted as if she had all the time in the world to cross the street and approach the unmarked car.

Cassie wasn't surprised when she reached the passenger side and the window was already rolling down. Agent Stills gave, what she had come to think of as his usual greeting - an annoyed look, a nod and the declaration of her name. "Miss Dodd."

"Hey, Benji. I was baking and figured since you liked the coffee cake so much the other day, you'd like some of my world-famous banana bread." She held up two plates with slices of the fresh baked bread, topped with melting butter and a dusting of powdered sugar.

Stills blew out a frustrated breath meant to convey his disapproval, but took a plate and handed it to his companion in the driver's seat, Agent Robbins, who asked, "What makes it world-famous?"

"It's really a banana cake recipe." She winked and handed Stills the other plate then pulled out two plastic forks from her back pocket that were wrapped in napkins, and handed them over. "How ya doing today Benji?"

"Agent Stills," he corrected. "I'm fine. How are you Miss Dodd?"

"My name is Cassie, Agent Stills." She tried to match his tone.

Agent Robbins took a fork, elbowed a frowning Stills and said, "This is all an act, he doesn't mind you."

The scowl increased, so Cassie leaned closer into the window. "Really?"

"Miss Dodd, we've been assigned to keep your sister safe, and I believe I explained to you the other day that it would be in everyone's best interest if you would stop bringing attention to our detail."

Cassie tilted her head. "Benji..." she started.

"Agent Stills."

"Agent," she nodded her head, "you are in a black Escalade with tinted windows and have been parked in roughly the same spot for a while now. Your presence isn't that much of a secret."

"This is good," Robbins said with his mouth full. Cassie smiled and continued her assault on Stills' personal space by moving into the window a bit more; enough to cause his clenched jaw to tighten. At his reaction, Cassie knew this was all for her own entertainment now.

"I'm glad you like it." She turned her head to look at Stills who was pressing himself back against his seat in an attempt to put more distance between them. "What do you think, Agent Stills?"

An announcement came over the radio then, requiring both of the men's attention. Cassie held her hands up as she moved out of the way. "Duty calls."

"Miss Dodd, please don't approach us again," he warned. Robbins elbowed him and he sighed, "And thank you for the bread." He rolled up the window.

"Cake." Cassie corrected her reflection in the mirrored window.

She exhaled a laugh as she made her way back to her apartment, but when her balcony was in view, she lost the quick smile.

She might be pestering the agents, but she was doing it because she needed to be sure of them; sure they were still alert, sure they were still watching the apartment, and sure they could help at any moment if needed.

It seemed a lifetime since Cassie picked her sister up at the airport with the instructions to pretend everything was normal. And in the past few weeks of Jessica's recuperation, all that had happened was that Jess continued to tell Cassie she was fine, even though Cassie could hear her frequent bouts of crying through the thin apartment walls.

Though, if Cassie were pressed to pick a week that had been the most difficult so far, she would choose this past one. Her parents, having been told the entirety of the situation, had *not* made Cassie's circumstances any better. If anything, it had increased both her blood pressure and the number of phone calls she received each day from her mother.

Barbara Dodd's latest epiphany was that *she* should move into Cassie's apartment, declaring it would be the best situation for everyone. To avoid this outcome, Cassie was ready to drop her sister off at their parents' house, until Jess begged Cassie to let her stay.

"Please, Cass...let me get over this on my own. Without Mom. Just...keep her away from me, please. I need this."

Cassie didn't think twice as she agreed to the herculean task. She simply pulled up her responsible, older sister panties to achieve Jessica's request; which required a leave of absence from her job; she'd already been taking sick days and working from home. The second part of the arduous promise, meant that Cassie was intercepting each and every phone call and text from their mother.

But for herself, Cassie made sure as shit that the unmarked vehicle was always, *always*, in her line of sight. If she could see them, they could see her apartment, which meant they could see Jess.

She opened the door to her apartment and went to check on her sister who was still asleep. She backed away and headed to the kitchen.

She had a nice calm life before all this. She and her friends were planning a trip to Baja California, her job continued to be fulfilling, she had a comfortable apartment all to herself, and her family was safe and sound. It was a good life.

Now, she was running on an overload of responsibility and fear.

And baking.

She hadn't been lying when she told Stills that baking was the one thing that had always calmed her down. When she was eleven and the first blushes of puberty were wreaking havoc on her emotions, and increasing the number of arguments she and her mother had, Barbara Dodd taught her oldest how to cook.

Cassie was never sure why her mother put her in front of a mixing bowl, but it did the trick. Ever since then, when the world got on top of her, she turned to the kitchen. Of course, she liked to cook when her world wasn't falling apart; but over the past few weeks, things weren't necessarily stable.

"Stable." She snorted the word. Who knew when things would be stable again?

She reached for her favorite French cookbook and began flipping through the lusciously photographed foods.

Jess always teased Cassie that she was 'stress baking', and maybe she was. But what was wrong with that? Cassie liked the control that came with precise measurements and timing. The repetition of stirring and kneading was a kind of meditation. The heat from the stove and oven were comforting. And the process itself had a beginning and an end. Not to mention how the smell of fresh baked goods filled Cassie's senses and surrounded her with a momentary soothing hug.

Was it any wonder that she was constantly turning to a mixing bowl the majority of the time? It was all she could do to outrun her current worries these days. Baking was more productive than sitting around and pacing and waiting for God knows what.

But the worry only dissipated for a few moments here and there. It didn't seem to want to go away for any real length of time. She wasn't sure when it would, but then again, she'd never been in a situation which involved CIA and possible mob-adjacent ties.

She flipped to the index page and drew her finger down the contents until she found what she was looking for: 'Croissants'. It would take two days to make them. And she would make a double batch.

She read through the recipe and admitted to the kitchen, "I'm going to need a lot more butter." She rolled her shoulders and shook out her hands. Time to get to work.

Chapter Seven

Cassie pulled the door of the apartment shut, double checking to make sure both locks were secure. She stared at the peephole for a long while, then bent to retie her running shoes before straightening for another round of contemplation.

She needed to move; needed a physical release from the stress. Baking could only do so much.

A double batch of croissants, a dozen cream cheese Danish, a two-tiered vanilla cake, and over a hundred cookies had been baked just this week alone. While Cassie's neighbors were thrilled, she was at the end of her rope as Jess continued to languish in a veritable sleepwalking existence.

Cassie lied to their mother when she called, saying, "She's doing so much better and Agent Stills said they are closing in on Thomas. Any day now." It was all wishful thinking.

Today, Cassie tried to concentrate on some mindless work on her laptop while she and Jess watched reruns of *30 Rock*. At noon, Jess muttered she was going back to bed, and Cassie decided to follow through with the plan she'd been struggling to execute. "Jess, I'm gonna try and go for a run."

"You should," Jessica agreed.

"I'm just going around the block. So half the time the apartment will be in sight."

Jess waved to her sister. "Cass, it's fine. I'm fine."

That was the problem, she wasn't. "I'll be gone for like, twenty minutes."

"I'll be asleep, so it doesn't matter. Take an hour." Jess held up her cast. "And later tonight, can we do another round of 'lavender trash bag wrapping' so I can take a shower?"

"Sure."

Cassie watched her shuffle to the back of the apartment.

Jessica was right, she wouldn't know Cassie was gone. And Benji was outside.

Cassie gave the front door a pat, palmed her keys and cell phone and headed out of the building, debating whether or not she should tell Benji what she was going to do. Of course, he would probably be able to guess on her third trip around the block. And he didn't need to be told what she was going to do. She was free to do as she pleased.

But maybe out of consideration, she'd tell him.

When she was down the front steps of her building, she glanced at the car and saw Benji leaning against the back bumper. She'd never seen any of the agents out of the car.

She had her joke about Stills being out of his natural habitat locked and loaded, but when she approached, his normal disapproval had been replaced by something completely different. Her steps stuttered to a halt when she was met by the force of his heightened awareness, which was at odds with the casual way he was leaning.

"Don't stop, come here," he instructed.

Cassie followed the directions, worry slowly plummeting into the pit of her stomach. "What..." she began, but his narrowed gaze stopped her.

"Cassandra, I need you to listen very carefully." She knew when he said her name that way, it wasn't good. She glanced back at the building, but Stills stopped her, hissing, "No. Look at me."

Her eyes zeroed in on his controlled face as her breathing quickened.

"We're going to take a few steps toward the passenger side of the car, you stay on the sidewalk," he instructed.

Cassie did as he directed and when she was near the open window, she heard Robbins speaking in a low tone to someone and the phrase, 'we have eyes on him.'

"You have your cell phone?" Stills asked, but Cassie was staring at Robbins.

"Cassandra," he pulled her back, "do you have your phone?" His harsh demand dried up her ability to speak. She nodded.

"Good. Everything's fine," he insisted, "I just need you to look at me Dodd, focus on me."

Another jerky nod.

"Now, I need you to smile at me while you pull your phone out."

She didn't move, fear was waging war with the calm exterior Stills was displaying while his words were urgent and exact.

"Dodd, you need to smile at me *now*." He smiled at her, coaching her, even though the smile didn't reach his eyes.

She followed his directions, barely able to present a terse smile.

"Good. Now, point toward your right, and look at your phone like you're asking me for directions."

"Benji..." She tried to ask what was happening but it was difficult to form the question as she faked a smile and pointed to her phone. It was like the first time someone asks you to rub your stomach and pat your head at the same time.

"You're okay. You're doing great." His encouragement made her stomach tighten, and she felt clammy, her upper lip broke out with perspiration.

Robbins broke through once more, "Team two is en route now."

The shock was palpable.

Stills' voice lowered as he forcefully demanded, "Look at me Cassandra."

She met his command with wide eyes and attempted to draw as much strength as she could from his measured demeanor.

He pointed in the same direction she had. "You're going to smile again at me as if you're thanking me. Then you are going to head in the direction we're pointing. There is a gas station on the corner, do you know it?"

She kept her head still but darted her eyes to the building.

"It's going to be fine," he said evenly.

"I can't leave her."

"Dodd," his voice commanded her attention once again, "walk slowly to the gas station. Like you have all the time in the world. Once you're there, lock yourself in the bathroom. I'll be there as soon as I can."

"Benji..." She was beginning to shake.

"Go."

She couldn't move.

"Cassie," that caught her attention, "smile at me."

She did as tears formed in her eyes and he pointed down the street once again. "Everything is going to be fine. I'll get to you as soon as I can. Now go."

She walked shakily down the street, fighting every urge to turn and run back into the building to be with Jessica. To save her. From what she wasn't sure, but walking in the opposite direction felt like a complete betrayal. Her throat closed around a sob and ached with fear.

She arrived at the small gas station and pulled together the remaining strength she had left in order to ask the attendant for the key to the outdoor restroom.

She continued to coach herself: *Just get inside. Get inside and lock the door and then you can lose your shit.*

As she walked to the back of the building she was unable to control her shaking. Her hands trembled and it took her three tries to get the key in the lock and open the door. Once inside, she pressed her back against the locked door and slid to the ground. She dropped the key and held her phone up in front of her face, unable to focus on the screen once she had it on.

As her focus on the clock of her home page crystalized and faded, the bright Southern California sunset picture she'd set as her background mocked her. *Remember when things were easier?*

She physically jumped when the minute changed on her phone. "Breathe," she said sternly, but it came out as more of a question.

Still, she watched the phone and inhaled as deeply as she could, then blew out, attempting a slow steady breath. Despite her attempts to calm herself, her breathing was still shaky and often caught on threatening tears.

She thought about calling Jess, but she said she was going to be asleep. So maybe when all this was cleared up, she wouldn't be any wiser about what was happening.

Another minute passed.

But what if Jess hadn't gone to bed? What if she'd gotten up, glanced out the window, saw her and Stills talking…she'd see whatever the 'threat' had seen, she reasoned. "She would have seen me and Benji pointing and smiling."

She didn't need to call Jess.

But she couldn't just sit here and wait. What if something had gone wrong? She needed a plan.

"Stick to the facts," she whispered and then said it again louder, "*facts.*"

Another deep, unsteady inhale and exhale.

"You need a key to get into the apartment building." Fact. "Robbins and Stills are capable." That was a fact. "Superman capable." She wasn't so sure about that but putting it out there made her feel better. "The CIA doesn't hire bums off the street. There's protocol…" An unexpected stressful laugh erupted at the word; stupid Stills. "I locked the apartment door. Both locks. You need a key to get into the building." She nodded her head, yeah, those were facts. Good, sensible facts. "Benji is a badass." Fact.

"Shit." She didn't have Stills' number. She didn't know who to call. Wait, that wasn't true. She opened the history of her phone call log and found the number she'd called obsessively every day until Jess was home. She had that number.

"Okay. Okay." She kept her thumb hovering over the call button as she watched the time in the top right hand corner.

She would wait for twenty minutes. "You can do anything for twenty minutes." Twenty minutes and then she would press the call button.

Two minutes ticked by, her eyes blinked back another attempt at tears. She started another round of shaky breathing accompanied by counting. She wasn't sure what she was counting to, but when she ran she often counted, and somehow the familiar rhythm helped.

One, two, three, four, five…as she watched the clock she would lose her train of thought and start over, sometimes she would start at ten and count backwards.

By some miracle, she reached the eighteen minute mark. She did the math from the time she started looking at her clock until now. Memories of watching the second hand on her clock when Jess had called her from

Italy, flashed. She'd made a commitment then to wait twenty minutes. How the hell did she find herself in the same situation again?

A knock on the door caused her to jump up from the ground; she took several steps away from the door and slapped her hand over her mouth to keep from yelling. She stared down the back of the dirty, yellowed door.

She was trapped. Why did Stills tell her to come here and wait? There was no other way out.

Another knock.

She couldn't find her voice to declare, 'occupied', which should have been obvious to anyone who attempted to get the key from the attendant. But what if the guy Robbins had 'eyes on' had followed her instead? What if Stills had allowed it?

"Dodd." She heard her name echo through the hollow steel door and her knees quaked with relief. She fought to convince herself to move.

Another knock and she finally found control of her muscles.

She swung open the door and the flood of relief when she saw Benji in his sensible tan dockers, copper polo and calm demeanor, allowed the tears to begin spilling.

"Hey," he reached out and took her shaking hand, "it's okay." When her eyes focused on his, he nodded. "You did great."

"I'm hiding in a bathroom." She waved behind her.

"You did exactly what I asked you to do," he reasoned.

She grunted in reply, and when he moved to release her hand, she tightened her grip. He adjusted his hold on her hand. Cassie glanced down at the way his large hand encompassed hers; soothing, reassuring. They didn't move however, she continued to stand inside the safety of the restroom, leaving him on the threshold.

"The threat has been eliminated," he told her.

"Eliminated," she replied with a shake of her head. "What does that mean? Because there's a whole lotta ways a person could interpret that word."

He didn't answer, instead he glanced at their joined hands. Cassie wondered if she should let go, maybe he thought her response to the situation was ridiculous. She tried to pull away, but Stills kept hold of her. "Let me buy you a cup of coffee," he offered.

"I need to get back to Jess." Everything was coming back together now. Whatever threat had been 'eliminated' had to do with Jess and Cassie needed to see her sister with her own two eyes.

"We have agents at the front and back doors of the building. Robbins is with them. She's safe. Let's talk." He gave a slight tug on her hand.

"The key." Without letting go of Stills, she bent and retrieved it. If he didn't seem to mind holding her hand, she wouldn't argue. She needed his unfaltering control at the moment. She took a few more deep breaths to settle her nervous system.

"I'll return the key," he said.

"I can do it," she insisted as they walked toward the front door of the convenience store. She finally pulled her hand away and was stunned by the empty feeling. But she didn't have time to think about that right now.

When she returned, Stills was standing by the passenger side of the black Escalade, holding the door open. She climbed in and pressed her head back against the headrest, closed her eyes and finally released all the built-up adrenaline and fear.

Stills let her cry, reaching out to hold her hand once more. He drove two blocks to an old-fashioned 50s diner. Cassie was grateful he stayed in close proximity to her apartment.

He parked the car, but didn't shut off the engine, giving Cassie time to collect herself.

"This is all adrenaline releasing," she excused.

He squeezed her hand in reply.

"She's safe?" Cassie asked.

He nodded.

"Benji, I need to hear you say it."

"She's safe."

Cassie pulled away from the comfort he offered, wiped at her eyes and took a deep breath.

"Ready?" Stills asked.

"Ready." She got out of the car and rubbed her eyes. "Can I borrow your sunglasses?" She knew how red her face was; every time she cried her whole face became a blotchy red mess; and she wasn't interested in having the patrons stare at her.

Stills passed the glasses that he'd pushed atop his head to her. Cassie adjusted them as they walked inside.

"Two," Stills informed the bored teenager playing hostess, "and a booth in the back, if you don't mind."

Once seated with coffee and water, Stills removed his earpiece, and pocketed it. Cassie took the glasses off and handed them back. "What the hell was that?" she blew out the question.

He opened his mouth, but shut it, thinking better of what he had to say. He glanced around the almost empty diner before he quietly revealed, "We spotted one of Paroni's men. He was casing the building."

He might as well have punched her in the gut. She bent at the waist, placing her elbows on the table and scrubbing her face with her hands.

Stills reassured her, "We apprehended him."

"Don't tell Jess," she whispered.

Stills tilted his head to the side. "We weren't planning on it."

"Okay. Okay." She pushed herself up and glanced out the window they were sitting next to, looking for some semblance of control.

"You're okay too, you know," Stills said.

"Actually," Cassie grunted, "I'm not, Benji."

"I promise you, Cassandra, we've eliminated—"

"The threat, yeah. I caught that the first time," she muttered.

Too many 'what if' scenarios were whipping past. What if Stills hadn't seen the guy? What if the threat had already called someone with a report? What if he worked for Jessica's ex? What if Cassie had stayed home and been kept in the dark?

A waitress returned and asked if they wanted anything to eat. Cassie shook her head.

"We'll share a basket of fries," Stills ordered.

"Cheese on those?"

He nodded. "And a side of ranch."

She left to fill the order.

He leaned forward. "Everything is okay. You and your sister are safe." His sincerity was palpable.

"We can't tell Jess," she repeated.

"Your sister is far stronger than you give her credit for."

Cassie snorted. "You've mentioned that before. Trust me, I know my snorted. "You've mentioned that before. Trust me, I know my sister is a badass; but it's like...lately...she's used it all up." She cleared her throat, how could she explain this? "The reason she's sleeping her days away in my apartment right now, Benji, is because her *badass* tank is empty. She's got nothing left," she insisted.

He nodded thoughtfully.

Cassie continued, "So it falls on me to tap into *my* badass tank and take over for a while."

"And you are a badass, Dodd."

"Benji..."

Stills tapped the table gently with his hand. "We weren't planning on telling her about the man we captured. It wouldn't do any good."

"No, it wouldn't." Cassie pulled the coffee into her hand and cupped it for warmth. "I don't know what to do."

"About what?"

"It's like it wasn't real, you know? You said your presence was just a precaution, but today..." she looked aimlessly into the brown liquid, "maybe Jess does need to know."

"Okay. And what good would that do?"

"I don't know...I don't know." The calm she had fought so hard for since she opened the restroom door to find Stills standing there was slipping. She expelled a deep breath, "Maybe, if she knew, maybe..."

"Dodd," Stills said sternly.

Her eyes cleared and she glanced up, anchoring herself to his gaze. "Let's talk it out," he said calmly, "the pros and cons of telling Jessica about today."

She licked her lips. "Okay. If Jess knows what happened..." she shook her head gently, clearing away the fear and 'what ifs', trying to focus on the facts, "if she knows, it will scare her."

Stills picked up the thread, "Perhaps, if she knew, she wouldn't take any unnecessary risks."

"But she isn't leaving the apartment now as it is, so there aren't any unnecessary risks being taken." Cassie put her cup down and ran a shaky hand through her hair. "Her *not* leaving the apartment is another problem altogether. She's nervous to leave, so telling her would prolong her getting over her shit so she *can* leave and go do normal things."

"If she doesn't know, will *you* be able to act normal around her?" Stills asked. "Or would she pick up that something is wrong?"

"She isn't really seeing me or my life right now." Which, Cassie realized, might actually work in her favor for the time being, "She's really focused on her own problems."

"Not telling her means you have a burden you have to carry alone," Stills offered.

"I don't mind," she was quick to respond. "The problem is that some creep was trying to get to my sister and I can't do a fucking thing about it." She hissed and ground her teeth.

"Now that's *your* problem, something you need to come to terms with."

"*My* problem?" she bristled.

"You are not alone in this," he frowned. "Do you really think we aren't capable of looking out for your sister?"

"No." She gave a sad smile. "Yes," she amended. "I don't know. There is this big sister inside of me that isn't about to let anything bad happen again. Not on my watch. But I don't know what I'm fighting and I don't know how to fix any of it."

Their eyes met, the main question at hand still lingering in the air; did she trust him to do his job?

"I trust you," she sighed. "But I'm also hopped-up on adrenaline and fear right now. I can't seem to calm down, so I don't know what the fuck to think or do." A new thought flashed before her. "Benji, did he see me? Does he know who I am?"

"We don't think so."

"You don't think so!"

"Cassandra."

"Don't Benji, just don't..." She bent back in the booth, pressing the palm of her hands against her eyes.

"We'll know more after he's interrogated," Stills explained.

She attempted to rummage through her flawed reasoning for some solid ground, but when she couldn't she asked Stills, "What should I do? Tell me what to do, Benji, and I'll do it."

He reached for her hands and she gave them without hesitation.

He met her gaze. "You are going to breathe and have coffee. Then we're going to share some fries. Then I'm going to take you home and you are going to carry on the way you have been. We will always be close by. You're going to get over today and move forward. And Jessica will not be told anything."

"Okay," she agreed.

He gave her hands a squeeze. "Okay?" he asked, requiring a more forthright agreement.

She gathered her courage and repeated, "Okay."

He nodded and released her hands. The waitress reappeared with fries and coffee refills. After several bites, Stills continued his instructions for Cassie.

"Dodd, you're going to feel spooked, and that's normal. But in three days, you're going to go to the store or a coffee shop by yourself and you're going to leave your sister at home, alone."

"What, why?"

"Because you need to understand that she will be okay."

Cassie shook her head. "Jess can go with me..."

"Cassandra, in three days you are going to need a break. Why did you leave today?"

She pursed her lips in answer.

He pointed, "You're dressed to go for a run. You needed a break."

"And the lesson I learned was that I shouldn't take a break," she argued.

"Dodd, I understand the urge to stay indoors, close to your sister, but for your own well-being and hers, you are going to have to begin dipping your feet back into reality. To show Jessica she can do it too, when she's ready," he asserted. "So, in three days you're going to go somewhere by yourself for fifteen minutes. Go somewhere close."

She didn't answer him, she didn't know what to say. Right now, the thought of going out and leaving Jess alone....well, she'd already felt that overwhelming sense of betrayal when Stills asked her to go to the gas station rather than return to her apartment.

"Dodd," he whispered her name, "promise me."

She gave a jerky nod of her head.

"Good. Also, as much as I appreciate the baking, you really need to stay away from the car."

She struggled to find the right words as she opened and closed her mouth, then finally whispered through trembling lips, "What if I need you?"

"You need me?" They'd been here before, only this time, his flirting attempt fell flat.

She shook her head and pursed her lips. "No. What if...Jessica needs you? I don't have your number."

"You called us every day for a week," he pointed. "Call that same number. Just tell them your name, they are aware of the situation and who you are."

"Jesus Christ." She glanced out the window as if she could watch her chaotic thoughts buzz around.

"What's going on in that head of yours?"

"I am a researcher, Benji. This is beyond...I was going to go for a run this afternoon. I was going to have a nice, ill-advised, hot midday run to try and relax myself by boosting my endorphins."

"I think you accomplished your goal," he joked.

She snarled. "The boost of endorphins from running wouldn't have left me with all this lingering fear."

"Dodd, you'll be okay."

"Have there been any other incidents like this? Other...people...casing my apartment?"

He didn't answer and Cassie pointed a finger at him. "Not answering doesn't help me calm down."

"This is the first sighting."

She nodded her head.

"Dodd, I need you to do something else for me."

Cassie didn't realize she was holding her breath until he finished his thought, "I need you to trust me. Trust that I can do my job."

"I trust you," she defended.

"Do you?"

She grunted. "Do I have a choice?"

Stills winked as he popped another fry in his mouth. "You got this, Dodd."

Chapter Eight

Cassie hitched her purse higher up onto her shoulder and gripped her keys a little harder in her hand. She glanced in the mirror by the front door but she wasn't looking at herself, she was looking at her sister across the room.

"Is there anything else you want from the store? Chicken nuggets? Jalapeno poppers?" She hoped her voice sounded calm, because her insides were anything but.

"Just Doritos." Jess pointed the remote at the TV and changed the channel.

Cassie rubbed her face with her free hand then widened her eyes at her reflection: *You've got this. You can do this.* She gave a nod, this was no big deal. She could do this.

It had been three days. And for some stupid reason, she decided to follow through with her promise to Stills and leave the house for fifteen minutes. She opened her mouth to ask if Jessica wanted to go; changed her mind, and slipped her purse off her shoulder. She'd stay home. It was a stupid idea in the first place.

She glanced back at Jessica.

He'd asked her to do this. And it was only fifteen minutes.

They were right outside. She had checked for the car before she decided to leave. She also chose nine a.m. because the last time she tried to leave it was noon when the 'subject' had cased the joint.

"Dodd," she hissed at her reflection; a CIA agent said you have to go for a fifteen-minute walk, who cares? "What does he know?" she snarled in answer.

His words rang through her mind: *I need you to trust me.* "And you said you trusted him."

"Who are you talking to?" Jessica called from the sofa.

"My past self," Cassie muttered.

"And what are you telling her?"

"She's ridiculous."

"Ah."

Cassie picked her purse back up and slung it over her shoulder again. "Okay, let's do this."

"What are we doing?" Jessica asked.

"I think I'm taking a well-being break and you're learning how to be alone again."

Jess glanced at Cassie in the mirror and gave her a double thumbs up. "Let's do this!"

You're only going two blocks away.

"So...Doritos?" she confirmed.

"Cassie."

"I'm just checking. I only need a few things. It won't be very long."

"Cassie."

"I might also grab a coffee." She spoke her last minute decision aloud.

"You should."

Cassie crossed the living room to the sliding glass door that led to her balcony and glanced outside to make sure of the surveillance team once again.

"Cassie," Jessica soothed, "we can do this."

"I know. I won't be very long. Where's your cell phone?"

Jessica held up her phone that was sitting on the arm of the sofa next to her.

Cassie gave a curt nod and before she changed her mind again, gripped her keys as she marched across the room, pulled the front door open and closed it behind her.

She locked the bottom lock and then stopped, her hand hovering in front of the top lock. If they needed to feel a sense of stability, as if things were getting back to normal, her *not* locking the top lock was a strange symbol of life moving forward. So she put her keys in her purse and reasoned, if Jessica was feeling unsafe, she could lock the top lock herself. It would be her choice.

Cassie tore herself away from the door and forced her feet to begin walking. As she walked she announced to the hallway, "Well I'm never having kids."

She stepped outside and found a deep breath as she glanced toward the car one final time to make sure it hadn't mysteriously moved. Benji wasn't working today, it was one of the other groups. She willed them to see her and realize that she was leaving, so they would watch harder.

"Watch harder," she mocked herself and rolled her eyes.

She turned her attention in the opposite direction and hugging her purse to her chest, forced herself to begin walking as she continually stated out loud, "Fifteen minutes. Fifteen minutes. You can do anything for fifteen minutes."

She was only going two blocks to the quaint neighborhood store. The A1 Market. It was a mom and pop store that had been around for years, always doing the same thing. But with the regentrification of the neighborhood, the almost obsolete store had been prod into a suddenly trendy one-stop shop. Two years ago they'd expanded, as the son of the owners had attended pastry school in France and returned home with an idea.

He added onto the building and opened a small French style bakery and café called La Petite Café. The coffee was wonderful and the baked goods were something right off the Champs-Élysées in Paris.

She continued to talk herself through the timing of her adventure. The store was a five-minute walk from the apartment, she could easily cut the time in half if she had to run back for any reason. She checked her cell phone, for the seventh time, to make sure the ringer was on. "You are out of control," she chided; but she wasn't listening to herself.

She slipped the phone in her back pocket for easier access and directed herself, "Calm down."

She fought all the nerves vigorously bouncing around in her stomach as she crossed the street and coaxed herself into the café with Stills' lingering words: *Trust us to do our job.*

Shit, it was Stills she said she trusted, she hadn't gotten to know the other agents very well. Maybe she should have waited until he was on duty to take this ridiculous adventure.

"You're fine," she said between her teeth, "just get coffee. Sit for five minutes. Then you can go home." *And be done with this impossible assignment.*

The café had a short line and an overflowing pastry case. She studied the luscious pastries, glazed and packed and preening perfectly for customers. She made a quick decision to have an almond croissant and took a steadying breath.

See, she was doing great. She could wait for the customers in front of her and let herself appreciate the artwork of the pastry case. "Oh, éclairs," she whispered. Tomorrow she'd make some éclairs.

She took two whole seconds of appreciation before she pulled out her phone and checked to see if she had somehow missed a message or call. But what if the ringer wasn't working? She made sure the volume was up on the notifications as well as the media. The actionable step helped tamp down some of her worry.

"Fancy meeting you here." The unmistakable deep voice so close to her right side jarred her out of her phone studies. She turned and raised a surprised eyebrow at the man standing beside her. "Benji."

"Miss Dodd," he greeted.

Cassie was so shocked, she allowed herself a minute to study him. He wore black and white Adidas tennis shoes, faded jeans, and an untucked light blue polo shirt with the top two buttons undone. Cassie swallowed the unexpected disappointment that his shirt wasn't tucked in flat against his abs.

She pointed her phone at him in question. "What are you doing here?"

Stills inclined his head toward the pastry case. "This is one of the best kept secrets in LA. The pastries remind me of Italy."

"The owner is the son...of the grocery store," she lamely explained.

"The grocery store had a baby?" Stills winked.

"What? No. You know what I mean. The owners of the grocery store; their son, studied in Paris." An awkward mingling of worry and awareness of the way his tanned chest peeked out of his shirt was not helping any of her focus.

"Well, the pastries remind me of Italy." He tapped his hand against his thigh.

"*Is* this a coincidence Benji?"

He gave a sheepish shrug just as the young woman at the counter called, "Next."

Stills nodded for Cassie to go ahead of him and order but pulled out his wallet and instructed the cashier, "My treat."

"Benji..."

"Today is the third day. I knew you'd follow through with your promise," he confessed.

That led to a plethora of questions.

A smile flickered across his face, "I just thought I could help."

She turned away from his distracting smile and ordered, "Can I have a small latte and an almond croissant?"

Stills leaned forward and added to the order, "A small cup of coffee, black. A fruit tart and an éclair, please."

"For here or to go?" the cashier asked.

"To go," Cassie said at the same moment Stills answered, "For here."

He raised a questioning eyebrow at Cassie. She squeezed her phone as she said, "I've only allowed myself five minutes."

"Then we'll only stay for five minutes. But we'll stay," he maintained.

She nodded and looked around, as if she could detect any wayward threats lurking nearby. Stills repeated the directions to the barista, "For here, please."

He paid and accepted the numbered placard the cashier gave him, so the server would know where to find them then gently touched Cassie's elbow to move them aside and allow the next customer their turn.

The heat from that simple touch crept up her arm, not only offering reassurance, but generating a surprising electric attraction. She glanced sideways at his hand, his strong forearm; then followed the trail of subdued power that was Stills, all the way up to his studious hawk eyes.

He would know if something was wrong. He could help her if she had to get back to Jess quickly.

"Is your car nearby?" she asked.

"Why? Do you want to go make out?" His voice was silk.

"What? No. What?" She was blushing and tried to hide it by checking her phone. She would text Jess that she might be a few more minutes than originally anticipated.

Stills took the phone from her hand.

Cassie's head shot up. He had an encouraging grin fixed on his lips as he stepped closer toward her, his head leaning slightly. She mirrored his motions, confused, her pulse quickening.

What the hell was happening?

He slipped the phone into the open front pocket of her purse, but didn't move back.

Cassie licked her lips; his eyes drank in the motion. She quietly asked, "What are you trying to do, Agent Stills?"

"I'm trying somethin', Miss Dodd."

The air grew thick. Cassie jutted out her chin, a slight dare. Stills reached his hand up, a breath away from her cheek, when another customer bumped him from behind, shattering the moment and causing his fingers to jab into her cheek.

"Ow."

"Shit, Cassie I'm sorry."

She rubbed her cheek, glad for the distraction, as the man who bumped into them gave his apologies.

Stills glanced around the seating area of the café. "Where should we sit?"

"Outside," she suggested and led the way out a side door that opened to an area walled in on three sides. Each wall boasted lush bougainvillea climbing the full width and height. Box planters lined the bottom, all filled with tall, fragrant lavender.

There was room for ten tables, spaced perfectly for casual visiting, and five large, blue umbrellas offered full shade over the area.

Only one of the tables was occupied, but Cassie still went to the table farthest away so they would have absolute privacy.

"Very nice. I guess I didn't do enough re-con over here." He waited for Cassie to sit down. When she was settled, he took his seat.

"Chivalrous," she commented.

"I'm a nice guy." He leaned back in his chair.

Was he? Although, truth be told when she wasn't worrying over Jess or baking or sleeping, she had a few spare thoughts that had inadvertently turned toward this man. She would be lying if she didn't admit she found him slightly attractive.

Okay, really attractive.

And the ill-timed moments when he flirted with her, trying to anger her or distract her, were so intriguing, she found herself wanting more of them.

But what did she really know about him? His calm demeanor and confidence strengthened her curiosity. Who was the man behind the agent?

"How did you know when I was going to be here? Were you going to wait around for me all day?" she asked.

He shrugged. "I'm pretty good at waiting."

"Kinda like a stalker." She narrowed her gaze.

"I'm trying to be a friend, Dodd."

She grunted in reply and Stills blatantly changed the subject. "So this is the kind of thing you would normally do at nine in the morning?" He indicated the patio.

"It seems like a lifetime since this was part of my normal." She glanced around.

"You'll get back to it."

"Do you have a definitive date for that yet?" She watched his face for any reaction. All she received was an apology.

"Sorry."

Cassie pressed her purse against her body, feeling her phone in the front pocket. She met Stills' non-judgmental gaze. "It's difficult with no one to talk to."

"You've taken on some hefty responsibilities," he agreed.

"Why do you do that?" she questioned.

"What did I do?"

"I'm sure it's part of your training to rationalize the feelings of those you're protecting, but all I can do is sit around all day and try to figure out how to deal with my sister and all this bullshit."

"While not giving away your own feelings," he pointed.

"There it is again." She shook her head. "Benji, I'm sitting on the sidelines here with nothing to do. There isn't one damn action I can take to help anyone. It's left me in a precarious position."

"But that's not true."

"Isn't it?" she asked.

"Why do you think your sister is staying with you and not your parents?"

Cassie held up her hands. "I see where you're going with your reasoning, but I spend all day thinking about Jess and worrying about Jess and trying to figure out how to fix Jess..." Her thoughts were interrupted as she watched the server enter the patio area. "I hate to admit this, but you were right Benji. I needed some time away to remind myself there is life apart from my sister."

The server arrived with their coffee and pastries. After setting everything down she asked, "Can I get you anything else?"

Cassie had a list of things she needed, but instead answered with a polite, "No, thank you."

She didn't want to look yet to see if Stills was doing an intensive study of her, now that she'd said he'd been right.

He took a bite of his éclair and gave a grateful groan. "That's good."

If her decision to make éclairs hadn't been solidified before, it was now.

She cleared her throat. "So these taste like Italy?" she asked and took a bite of her own pastry, finally meeting his gaze.

"Oh yeah." He took another bite.

"Did you get to have a lot of pastries when you were in Italy?"

He gave his professional reply, "I may or may not have been in Italy, Miss Dodd."

"We all know you were," she stated. "Were you able to get out that much? I don't ever see you leave the car..."

"So," he winked, "you keep an eye on me?" He took another bite.

"Someone's gotta look out for you." She returned his wink. "What is Agent Stills' favorite Italian pastry?"

He waited until he chewed all his food to answer. "It was this puff pastry that was filled with cream and folded into a pocket, then deep-fried and somehow, ended up with a sugary caramelized crust."

"What? How have I never heard of this? Do we have them in the states?"

"I haven't found them yet. It's like..." he nodded to Cassie, "I'm no baker, and I don't have much to go on, but I think it is like a homemade toaster pastry if you filled it with cream, rolled it in sugar and deep-fried it."

"What's it called?"

"A sfoglia."

Cassie laughed. "Was that a word?"

"It took me forever to learn how to say it, Parker helped." The name slipped out and his jaw immediately clinched.

Cassie nodded at the name. "You know what the hardest thing to deal with is?"

"I can imagine," he offered.

Cassie shook her head. "This is all such a weird, difficult situation. And then we have the mystery man, Parker. He's like a ghost. Jess won't talk about him. He's nowhere to be found—"

"I told you—"

"I know," she interrupted, "I'm just saying, this is a tough part too. Jessica's heartache is wrapped up in layers of betrayal and loss." She spread her hands out in front of her, as if she had a picture she could lay out in order to explain what she meant. "There's the loss of Thomas, a man she thought she loved, not to mention his betrayal. Then there's the loss of the life she thought she was going to have. I think she feels like she's betrayed herself somehow, for falling for all of Thomas' lies and deceit. And then, there's Parker's betrayal, because even though you've told me he's out there 'fighting the good fight', he's not *here*." She took a deep breath. "I think she feels like she's lost him too." She steadied her gaze on Stills. "Of course, I could be speaking out of turn, and Parker isn't really lost...but his radio silence seems like another form of betrayal."

After a long pause, Stills nodded and agreed in a roundabout way, "Those two have a lot to figure out."

She tried to lead him again. "I would think it's kinda difficult to figure shit out when you're not together."

"I can't divulge–"

Cassie waved his excuse away. "Just in case you had the power to pass on a message, I'm going to go out on a limb and say that message would be something like: *one fucking phone call could change everything.*"

"Noted." He took another bite.

Cassie took a deep breath and reminded herself she wasn't going to deep dive into her sister's 'Parker' problems.

She turned their conversation around. "So...an unpronounceable Italian dessert drove you here."

"That and it helped that it was in close proximity to your place."

"That *would* help." She pressed the purse again.

"Check the phone," he instructed.

"What?"

"Cassandra, you know you want to check it. I said leave the house, I didn't say to put your phone in airplane mode."

She pulled out the phone and checked it, nothing. She double checked the ringtone once more as well.

Stills nodded. "Now, why don't you put your purse on the back of the chair and stay awhile."

She did as he suggested and changed the course of the small talk to something neutral. "You look so normal in your civilian clothes."

"I always have civilian clothes on."

"Well, somehow this is different. More relaxed, it's a good look on you."

He glanced down and brushed the front of his shirt. Then he turned his full attention back to Cassie, his voice dipping into a lower octave as he pointed, "You always look good."

So much for neutral.

She was going to dismiss the comment, but found herself leaning forward instead. "Are you flirting with me, Agent?"

"Not at all."

His answer wounded her.

"I'm just stating a fact, Miss Dodd. I'm not allowed to flirt."

"Protocol?"

"Your sister is part of an ongoing investigation, and your proximity to her makes *this*..." he gestured between them, "difficult."

Cassie was feeling slightly adrift in this conversation. "This?" she asked as she took a sip.

He casually offered, "The undeniable attraction between us."

Cassie choked on her drink in reply.

Stills stood and came to pat her on the back, but she waved him away and finished choking on the liquid for another minute.

When she finally was able to catch her breath, she took another sip in an attempt to clear the obstruction.

"You okay?"

"Do you have normal conversations?"

"You're intimidating," he said.

Cassie shook her head. "What's intimidating? The fact that I bake so I can bug you and make sure you're tending to my sister's safety? Or the fact that I hide in bathrooms when the going gets tough?" He opened his mouth to answer her but she continued, "By the way, what do you mean you're not allowed to flirt? You've been flirting with me every time we see each other. And yeah, maybe it does eliminate the fear and worry for a few minutes...but..." She shook her head as he raised an eyebrow; could he say something now? She decided he couldn't. "And I don't 'always' look good. You've only seen me in yoga pants or running shorts and t-shirts."

"Yeah, I like the yoga pants," his voice softened.

Cassie shook her head, flustered. This man flustered her.

He took a moment before he continued his explanation, "Dodd, you say what you mean. You don't mince words. You don't play games. You own your actions. You are fiercely loyal to family, so I assume that goes for friends too. And you've got balls to take on the CIA."

She grunted. "That right there. That is so off-putting."

"If I seem off-putting, it's only because you are."

Cassie shook her head. "Is this like...when boys pull girls' pigtails cuz they like them?"

"Oh, yeah," he leaned back in his chair, "this is *definitely* like that."

"But because of your work, we can't have an attraction to each other." She circled back around to his original point.

"Well, it's not that black and white. If you were an asset, dating you would be a completely fireable offense."

"But I'm not an asset, I'm the sister of an asset," she pointed.

"Actually, Jessica isn't my asset. She's my work."

"Benji..."

He held up his hand. "My job is to sit surveillance and protect your sister. So right now, she is my job."

"So I'm just a...job-adjacent problem?"

"Dodd," a grin tugged at the corner of his mouth, "you *are* a problem. But a welcome one." He took a bite of his éclair.

Cassie took the opportunity to attempt to diffuse his intensity. "Do you have horrible hemorrhoids?"

He didn't choke, but his eyes sparkled and his gaze intensified as he finished the bite in his mouth.

"It was worth a try," she said. "I'm not going to pretend I understand your job. And from what I can figure, you aren't allowed to tell me much about it." She waited for him to nod his agreement then continued, "So up until a few weeks ago, everything I knew about the CIA I learned from a Brad Pitt movie. But now, from what I've witnessed firsthand, it seems like a lot of sitting around and waiting."

He nodded. "I can tell you that people would be shocked at how boring the job really is. It's a lot of reading through reports and then making educated cause and effect guesses."

"Until someone is lurking and other agents are en route."

"Are you dating anyone?" he asked abruptly.

Cassie shook her head softly. "Sometimes, Benji, it's okay to let someone feel their feelings. I don't need to be disarmed from what I'm thinking about or feeling."

"I realize that, Dodd." He scratched the side of his face mindlessly and confessed, "but I'm actually very interested in the answer to *this* question."

It was her turn to study him intently as she answered honestly, "I see people."

His jaw clenched and he gave a quick nod of understanding.

She liked having the upper hand for a moment. "Benji, I'm single. I'm in my thirties and while I'm not obsessed with finding the 'one', I still go out on dates and see people. But no one serious."

"Playing the field?"

"A girl deserves to have her itches scratched when required." It didn't sound as flirty as she had hoped it would, so she took a bite of her croissant to hide her cringe. With her mouth full she asked, "What about you?"

"Relationships are difficult in my line of work."

"But?"

"I too have friends that can help scratch itches that might arise."

She nodded casually as her subconscious loudly volunteered: *I would love to help scratch those itches.*

She coughed and turned her attention to finishing her food while examining her surroundings. They took awkward turns watching each other until Cassie began to laugh. "This is ridiculous. Tell me about yourself, Benji."

He rubbed his hands together to rid them of crumbs. "What do you want to know?"

"I don't know," Cassie shrugged. "What was the first pet you owned? How old are you? Where did you grow up? Have you ever had your heart broken?" She threw out a few of the questions that had crept in during those worry-free moments when the handsome CIA agent had slipped into her mind's eye. Of course, she steered clear of the one question she really wanted to ask, the juvenile demand: 'Are you really attracted to me'?

He relaxed against the seat as he answered. "I'm thirty-eight. I lived in San Diego until I was eighteen. I enlisted in the Marines when I graduated high school and served four years of active duty. Then, rather than re-enlist, I went to school for computer science. I've had my heart broken, but it was my own fault. My first pet was a goldfish named Goldie; I called it a girl, but I'm not sure anyone can actually tell the difference when it comes to goldfish. She lived for two weeks and when she died, the Tears for Fears song "Shout" was playing on the radio. To this day, I get strangely sentimental when I hear that song." He raised his eyebrow; was she satisfied with his answers?

Cassie clutched her cup with both hands as her insides vibrated with his honesty. A slight bob of her head was all the concession she could muster that he'd shared enough.

"What about you?" he asked.

"What about me?"

"Tell me about yourself."

Cassie sat back, attempting to copy his casual posture. "What do *you* want to know?"

After a long pause, the timbre of his voice deepened as he declared, "I'd like to know what you'd do if I told you my fantasy of taking you camping in Mesa Verde in the Four Corners area so I can make love to you under the stars."

A visible shiver raced up her spine and she pressed her lips together to capture the honest, wanton suggestion. Her cheeks burned and her hands petrified in place.

A grin pulled at the corner of Stills' mouth as he shifted slightly, just a bare inch of movement toward her, his amber eyes intent on decoding any secrets made evident in her reaction to his declaration.

A million smartass comments rippled through Cassie's mind, and a few challenging replies showed themselves as candidates; but first she needed to find the ability to speak again.

Somehow, she convinced her body into action and used the momentum to take a sip of her coffee. Finally, she said, "I don't think that sort of talk follows protocol."

A broad smile accompanied his declaration, "That is the truth, Dodd. But it doesn't change the fact that I'm attracted to you."

"Well..." That answered that question.

"And I think *you* might be attracted to me as well." Time stood still as the glorious lust of a new attraction blanketed Cassie. She released all the bullshit of the previous weeks and leaned into this moment. She might be scared for her sister, but honest attraction was not something she was going to shy away from. "And how do you know that, Agent Stills?"

"I'm trained to notice the little things," he replied.

"The little things."

He opened his mouth to explain, but the words died on his lips.

"Are you blushing, Benji?" She raised an eyebrow. "Or are you nervous to tell me all the little things you've noticed?"

"Perhaps."

"Then let's look at the facts. We both know I moved my computer desk so that I'm in your line of sight and you're in mine."

"Do we?"

"We both know that on the occasion I brought you and Robbins banana bread, I glanced back as I walked away, in the hopes that you were watching me in the mirror."

"I can neither confirm nor deny that fact." He was enjoying this.

She was on a roll. "Is it a fact that you call my sister by her first name?" Cassie asked.

"Jessica?" He frowned at the question and Cassie nodded the verification.

"So that's a fact. But you call me Miss Dodd."

"It's morphed into Dodd now," he pointed.

Her voice shook slightly as she implied, "I think you do that because you need the distance it puts between us. Because you're trying to be professional and I'm..." she lost her momentum.

"A liability." When he offered the definition, the flirtatious air fizzled out of the moment.

She couldn't make eye contact anymore as she agreed, "I suppose that's what I am."

Stills took Cassie's hand in his, stood and pulled her until she too was standing, then he abruptly hauled her body against his with so much force it was a shock when he slowly, ever so slowly, began to move his lips toward hers; his eyes dared her to stop him and at the same time, dared her to meet him halfway.

She held her breath for a mere second then angled her head and moved toward him slightly. It was the encouragement he needed to close the distance between them and seal his lips to hers.

Cassie eased into the kiss, melted against Stills' chest and wrapped her arms around his neck. There was no demand, but there was need. No overpowering, but a giving of himself.

His self-assuredness flowed into the kiss and soothed Cassie. There was heat and promise that scared and thrilled her at the same time.

Then the alarm she set on her phone went off, jarring her out of the kiss.

She glanced at the table where her phone lay, but kept her arms around his neck. Stills continued to hold her around the waist, pressed against him. "You are trouble, Dodd," he said.

"I have to go," she breathed back.

He inclined his head in an attempt to put himself in her line of sight. "What's going on?"

She loosened herself from his grasp, retrieved the phone and silenced the alarm. "That's my fifteen minutes."

She picked up her purse and slipped it onto her shoulder. "I should go."

Stills stepped toward her and pulled the purse back off. "What are you doing?" Cassie asked as he draped it over the back of the chair the way she'd had it before.

"You have time," he declared as he sat back down.

Cassie narrowed her gaze. "You're handling me again."

"Dodd," he gave a gruff laugh, "you have no idea just how much I want to handle you."

She blew out a long breath and rubbed her shoulder. "And you said *I'm* the problem?"

She glanced behind her as if she could see her apartment and her sister's supposed need for her.

"They watch every movement of the people going in and out. There are three back doors that go into your apartment complex. Each one of them has two camera angles watching. One of the agents in the car is always monitoring the cameras."

She swung her attention back to Stills. "I didn't know that. Why didn't you tell me?"

He tilted his head, did he really need to answer her?

She didn't sit down, but she looked at the seat as if she might.

"Your sister's ex-fiancé," he started, trying to speak as covertly as he could in public, "is being sought after by other interested parties. Worldwide."

Cassie frowned. "I should go."

"Please sit down." When she did as he asked, he took her hands and leaned forward, continuing his explanation, "Other people might have come to Southern California on the off-chance that Jessica's ex-fiancé had sought refuge with her." He leveled his gaze, did she understand?

"Oh." She glanced again in the invisible distance toward her apartment. "That's why the lurking?"

He nodded.

"I'm tired, Benji."

He gave her hands a squeeze. "I imagine you are," he responded sympathetically.

The sheer weight of his hands helped ground her.

"The way I see it," he started, "the only thing you can do for your sister is be there when she's ready to talk. And in the meantime, you gotta keep your own sanity about you. You're no good to your sister if you're a mess as well."

"Well, you know us Dodd girls, we're strong-willed messes."

"And smart and bullheaded."

Cassie laughed. "We're always right too, by the way."

"And intrusive."

"Better watch out, Benji; you're really working the sweet talk now." She released his hands and felt better.

"Just take care of yourself, and when she's ready, your sister will follow your example."

"And the PTSD?"

"She'll get through that too."

"How can you be so sure?"

Stills shrugged. "Because I've been where she is," he said matter-of-factly.

"Injured or heartbroken?"

"Both."

Cassie took the last sip of her coffee and nodded. "Can you tell me about it? Your injury?"

"I was shot in the line of duty six years ago. It was what's considered a 'lucky shot'. It went through part of my hip on the left side; a bullet that doesn't stay in the body does less damage," he explained. "It was a rough assignment; physically and mentally grueling."

Cassie didn't like the gut punch of fear that accompanied his explanation. She cleared her throat. "I'm sure the details of said assignment are classified."

"There is a lot of bad crap in this world. There are a lot of bad people," he said. "This is your first taste, and it's Jessica's as well."

"I know there are bad people…" Cassie tried to defend herself, but Stills held up his hand, as if he would like a minute to explain himself.

"I've chosen a work situation that, while sometimes can get inundated with the bad, thrives on the excitement of the chase as well. It's an adrenaline high. I thought I was bulletproof, and I thought I was 'the shit' before I got shot."

"Young and impulsive?" Cassie asked

"Young*er*. And cocky," he offered. "I had a girlfriend I was never around for, who got a lot of apologies and not a lot of attention. When I got shot, I got angry and pushed everyone away."

Cassie itched to ask if the girlfriend was the heartache he had mentioned. But she waited for him to tell the story.

"I did the physical part of rehab, but not the mental part. I returned to work with a grudge on one shoulder while continually looking over the other for the next bullet." He gave a sad smile. "Did you know that stage four brain cancer has the same symptoms as the stress you can be under in this job? Exhaustion, dizziness and headache pain. It's negative information overload."

"I had no idea."

"Eventually, I burned out and was forced to take time off and see a therapist, even though I didn't think I needed to. It turned out that therapy saved my life, changed everything. I learned how to manage my stress and separate the job from my life."

"How do you manage your stress?"

"I walk. I accept my limits. I have rules for myself. I talk to friends, I have fun and I do yoga to unwind."

"Yoga?" She smiled.

"You'd be surprised at how relaxing it is."

"Oh, I'm aware." She nodded. "And these rules fixed everything?"

"They took the edge off. They were just baby steps at first, but they added up over time and the fear disappeared. I figured out how to have a life outside of the job. Even rebuilt relationships with my family."

"And who broke your heart?"

He took a deep breath and gave a mournful smile. "Fifth grade, Elaine Brewster."

"Fifth grade?" Cassie raised an eyebrow.

"Elaine Brewster," he confirmed. "What about you?"

"I didn't know Elaine enough to love her."

"Touché." He laughed.

They allowed the information and lull to soothe them. Cassie studied Stills' strong jawline, not looking away when he winked at her.

"You know Benji, most of the time, I feel like you're trying to control my emotional reactions, which should piss me off. But then, you are so forthcoming with personal information and easy to talk to. And you've got all this," she looked him up and down and waved, to indicate what she was referring to, "going on..."

"I'm sorry, what do I have going on?"

"You're not bad on the eyes," she whispered the confession.

"Neither are you."

"And you kiss me like..." Here, her courage faltered, but Stills had no problem taking over. "You want more?"

"God yes," she sighed. "I want to sit in the back of a car and make-out with you like we're seniors in high school."

"Well Dodd, that is one task I *would* be willing to get back in a car for."

She laughed, torn between throwing herself at him and running away. "This is weird," she gestured between them, "or maybe it's weird that it isn't weird."

"I'd like to ask you out."

"You move backwards - kiss first, then ask the girl out?"

"I'm attracted to you, you're attracted to me..." he began.

"You're attracted to me," she stated, wanting to hear him say it again and again.

"And I want to get to know you," he added.

The notification from Cassie's phone made her jump. She lost her smile and fumbled, reaching for it. After a glance she shakily informed him, "It's just my mom." A tear slipped.

"Okay." Stills took the last sip of his coffee and stood up.

She followed suit then affirmed, "I need to go."

Stills pulled her into his arms. "You did really good."

She let his solid form take all her weight and wrapped her arms around his waist as she tried to stop the tears. Or maybe she'd take this moment for what it was, allowing someone else to shoulder the weight she was carrying. "I don't need to be saved," she mumbled into his chest.

Stills rested his head atop hers and the rumble of his laugh radiated in her chest. "The one thing I know for sure, is that the Dodd sisters most definitely don't need to be saved. They do, however, need to figure out how to accept help when it arrives."

Cassie pulled away. She looked up at Stills, accepting, "I'll take the help."

"Good. Let me walk you home."

"I need to go to the store first."

He nodded. "I've got a few things I need to pick up as well." He gestured for her to go ahead of him as they began their way back inside the café. "This will be good for us. Shopping together, a good test to see if we're compatible."

"I don't know if you're a good idea," Cassie said, but she reached out and took his hand.

He stopped walking and pulled her to him once again, sealing his lips to hers. Cassie angled her head to give him better access. She had wanted to kiss him again; if it hadn't been for the intrusion of the timer she'd put on her phone, they might not have stopped in the first place.

The kiss was strangely familiar, it echoed in her chest and vibrated throughout her body. She gave into it; ran her hands up Stills' back and moaned as his muscles flexed under her hands.

They parted as easily as they'd come together, but this time, they didn't break eye contact. "So..." Cassie started but she wasn't sure what she wanted to say.

"Yeah..." he agreed as he loosened his hold on her.

With little ceremony they fell into step once again, holding hands as they continued through the café toward the store.

To see if we're compatible – Cassie rolled her eyes at the idea but wasn't about to let go of the warm hand sending electric shockwaves up her arm.

Chapter Nine

"I'll tell him," Cassie said.

"Why? I don't mind telling him." Jess tried to push past Cassie, but Cassie pushed back. "I said I don't mind telling him."

Jess stopped and narrowed her gaze on her sister. "Why?"

Cassie gave what she hoped was an ambiguous shrug. "After this past week I figured…I should tell him."

"Cuz you're mad at him?"

"What? No. Why would I be mad?" Cassie shrugged. She wasn't *just* mad, she was furious.

The moment Stills left her on her front porch, after their unexpected coffee encounter, she missed him in a way she hadn't missed anyone in a very long time. She spent the rest of the day reliving each moment, each glance, each kiss. She found herself staring across the room at nothing, absently touching a finger to her lips, still able to feel the ghost-like tingle that lingered hours after their kiss. She was excited to make éclairs, in the hopes that if she ate one and had a cup of coffee, she'd be able to taste him on her lips again.

All the scenarios and fantasies she'd indulged in after such a simple morning together fell to ashes when Stills arrived at her door the next day. He gave Cassie nothing more than a polite nod and the explanation that the CIA had decided it was time for Jessica to be debriefed; leaving Cassie to an overt amount of pacing and worrying.

She spent the day creating outrageous storylines in her mind: What if the CIA had double agents who were *'Bourne Identity'* good and could abduct a woman right out of their offices? What if, while en route, the car was ambushed and those mob-adjacent to Thomas Adler kidnapped

Jessica again? Or what if Thomas had been watching Cassie's apartment too? What if he showed up at Cassie's door?

Actually, that was one of her favorites. Cassie played that one out a few times; it always ended with her taking her metal baseball bat to Thomas' face and genitals, rotating angrily between the two areas.

But as the hours ticked away, agonizingly slow, Cassie's grip on reality was difficult to maintain.

Finally, after twelve hours, Jessica was returned home; pale, her head hung low, looking like she'd been hit by a mack truck. She told Cassie she was going to have to return the following day.

Cassie's frustration turned to anger.

Then two days became three.

And on the evening of the third day, Jessica shuffled into the apartment without a word and went straight to bed; turning Cassie's anger into a heated rage.

"Cassie..." Jessica shoved her sister, trying to get her to move out of her way.

Cassie matched her sister's tone. "Jessica," she rubbed her face, "I think if *you* talk to him he'll spout some bullshit about protocols, but if I tell him, he won't argue with me."

Jessica raised an eyebrow. "You gonna beat up the guy watching out for me?"

"I wouldn't mind having a moment of his time." She slathered the truth sweetly, leaving out the part that she wanted a moment of his time to scream at him for how lax he'd been in his duties to look out for her sister the past week.

Jessica pushed at Cassie again. "Yeah, you are *not* gonna talk to him."

Cassie stepped into Jessica. Using one of her favorite defensive moves from playing soccer she hip checked her sister. Jessica wasn't expecting it so she tripped out of the way.

"I'll be right back. Make sure you have everything ready to go." Cassie was out the door and down the hallway. Behind her, Jessica yelled, "You suck!" That was followed with the instructions, "Be nice!" It was the only 'you win' confirmation Cassie would get.

A flutter of excitement interrupted her anger as she drew closer to the driver side of the car. She shook her head and silently explained to her bodily reactions that they were no longer attracted to Stills. "I'm mad..." she explained to the whirlwind of conflicting emotions.

The memory of him holding her hand while they shopped had burned so easily into her memory that the action was almost erotic. The simple way he'd carried her two grocery bags for her, like they were school kids in the 50s and he was carrying her books home, set up an exciting weight in her chest. Not to mention those kisses, the way his warm hands slipped around her waist, holding her, comforting her, wanting her. That heat seeped into her dreams and she woke with lingering, overheated desires that could only be sated by one man.

Of course, seeing her sister sitting at the table drinking coffee, forehead drawn in exhaustion, her voice hoarse, and her eyes lifeless was also burned into her memory. And that was the memory that presented itself front and center and overrode everything else.

Stills was rolling down the window as she approached, the same deep frown and sigh greeting her. "Miss Dodd." He nodded; only this time, if she cared, there was an added sparkle.

But she didn't care.

"Agent Stills," she returned coolly.

He raised an eyebrow at her greeting. "Everything okay?"

"We're going to our parents' house soon. We have to send out the regret cards today, and cancel the rest of Jess's wedding."

"The regret cards?"

"I don't know, that's what Mom says they're called. There's all this crap to cancel."

"How is she dealing with all of this?"

"My mom doesn't seem to be that upset that Thomas is out of Jessica's life," Cassie bit.

"You know I meant your sister. How is Jessica managing all of this?"

Cassie paused for a moment and studied him before she bit, "Do you really care?"

Stills turned to his partner. "I'll be a minute," he said before he climbed out of the car.

Cassie took a few steps back, folded her arms across her chest and jutted her chin in the air when they were squared off.

"What's wrong?" he asked.

"Nothing. I'm fine. You didn't need to get out of the car, I thought you'd want to be notified as to where we were going and what we were planning and why it might take a while."

Stills frowned.

Cassie matched his look, forcing them into a silent confrontation. His amber eyes narrowed, trying to determine the depths of Cassie's unspoken coolness toward him. She wasn't about to lose herself in the heat of his regard, but she'd be damned if she looked away first. She pressed her folded arms against her chest and raised her eyebrows in question. *Let him look. What could he find?* His gaze dipped to her lips then, almost breaking her. He didn't look away quickly or back up to meet her gaze, but lingered as he wet his own lips.

Cassie's blood heated against her will, her body began tingling excitedly.

"Have a good day." She didn't want to be the first to speak, but she didn't have any other choice.

"Is this because you were left without a detail watching you this past week?" His question broke through the heat, reminding her anger of its place.

"We're going to burn Jess's wedding dress in my parents' backyard. In case you see smoke later in the afternoon."

He nodded his head. "Good to know. Is there any other information you'd like to part with, Miss Dodd?"

"We're leaving in fifteen minutes." She turned to leave, but then thought better of it and turned back around. "*I'm* fine by the way. I continue to be fine. My sister, on the other hand, is the one you should be looking out for," she bit angrily, shoving her hands on her hips.

Stills nodded, finally understanding Cassie's anger. "She had to be debriefed," he excused.

"You drug her over the coals," she pointed.

"It wasn't like that."

"No? What was it like, Agent Stills? When she became pale and her voice grew hoarse and she was clearly worn down, how were you looking out for her?"

He reached through Cassie's personal space and brushed a strand of her hair behind her ear. She pulled away from him. "What are you doing?"

"You have dark rings under your eyes."

"And you smell like you're living in a car," Cassie countered.

He gestured to the car. "I *am* living in a car and it sucks."

"Well," she took a small step away from him, "I *am* losing sleep worrying about my sister and *that* sucks."

"Jess is a fighter, she'll get through this."

"I didn't like you taking her away. I couldn't get to her," she said emphatically knowing how ridiculous it sounded, how childish. But they had all had more time than Cassie to get used to this current situation.

Stills opened his mouth to excuse himself but Cassie continued, "I didn't know how long she was going to be kept. I didn't know how to contact anyone if she didn't return. I hated it."

"Don't you have the head office phone number?"

"I wanted more than that." Cassie didn't like how honest he made her. "I have to go," she insisted.

"You don't have to carry the weight of this burden all alone."

"Yes I do." She swallowed hard and waved a hand and turned to leave again. She hated this conversation. She hated how he saw through her thinly veiled excuses and planted seeds of reasonable thought.

"Miss Dodd..." Stills called her.

She whipped around. "It's Cassie, Agent Stills. My name is Cassie."

His voice was a low whisper when he said, "Cassandra." That deep rumble reverberated behind her ribcage.

It was all she could do to mumble, "We need to get going."

"If you ever need to talk again..." He let the offer trail off.

"I don't need anything." Her power was returning.

"I can't stop thinking about you," he admitted in that same low rumble.

"Jeez Benji, and just what am I supposed to do with that?" She pressed the ball of her hand against her chest, trying to stop the progress of his admission from radiating through her veins. Then she pointed to the earpiece he was wearing. "Won't someone hear you?"

"It's off."

She tried to look around Stills, into the car, but she couldn't make anything out.

"Go out with me."

Cassie gave an unladylike snort and glanced around Stills at the car. "A date. Out in public? Where everyone will see."

"That's how dates traditionally work. Unless you would rather have something more private?" He winked.

"I can't date you," she snarled.

"Why not?"

"I'm mad at you," she said incredulously.

His eyes sparkled. "Give me a chance to smooth things over then."

"Why should I?"

"Because I bet that you haven't stopped thinking about kissing me. And I bet that you've replayed each moment we spent together as much as I have."

"No, I haven't," she lied unconvincingly.

"Tomorrow we have a meeting concerning this detail, and I'll have a better idea of my schedule."

"Congratulations." She needed to leave. Stills had done what he was becoming very good at; calming her down and making her see the forest in spite of the trees. And she didn't want that right now. She still needed to be angry and she wanted to put the blame atop his firm, broad, well-built shoulders.

And his sexy temptations were making her question her anger.

"So what do you say, Dodd? When I figure out my schedule, will you go out with me?"

She turned her back on him and he laughed. Actually laughed at her, so she turned again, pressed past *his* personal space this time and meant to yell at him, but all that came out was one, hissed word, "Maybe." She pointed a finger into his chest.

A slight grin pulled at the corner of his mouth. "I'll take it."

"I'm still mad at you."

"I can take that too."

She attempted to shoot another smartass comment his way, but he took a step toward her; when he was this close, her grip on her anger began to slip. Not to mention those damn eyes were tempting her to cover the last bit of distance that separated them, so that they could melt into another kiss that would ignite electric shocks of desire.

She took several steps backward and repeated, "Maybe."

Chapter Ten

Canceling a wedding wasn't that difficult. Granted, Cassie had never canceled a wedding before, but she had been under the impression it would be a lot more complicated. This assumption probably had something to do with the long, drawn out process of watching Jess buy a dress, and the endless arguments she was privy to between her mom and sister over the 'right' accent color, the invitations, the flowers, the venue and a laundry list of other wedding details.

"You know," Jessica said at one point, "we could just save all of this in case Cassie gets married."

Cassie gave an incredulous look at her sister. "I'm not getting married."

In fact, if she ever did agree to marry anyone, she was going to elope. *That* decision brought the immediate vision of a virile, thirty-eight year old man. Cassie shook her head harder than she needed, to dislodge the face. Scrape it away, like the magical sand in an Etch-A-Sketch.

"Cassie, go check on your father," her mother ordered, probably because all Cassie had done was drink mimosas and add to the growing laughter and raucousness among Jessica's friends.

She had been dreading the day, mainly because she and Jess had no idea how their mother would handle things. But Barbara Dodd had swooped in with overwhelming support of her daughter and righteous indignation toward Jessica's ex.

She bad-mouthed Thomas Adler properly and fussed over Jess' four friends, who had come to help address the 'regret' cards and make other phone calls, all the while peach mimosas flowed freely.

Cassie grabbed two beers from the fridge, opened them and made her way to the living room. "Don't," she warned herself even as she glanced out the large front window to get a peek at the car. She could see a fraction of the front bumper.

"Beer?" she called and her dad nodded, sitting up from his slouched position in his favorite chair. He paid extra for the soccer and European Football packages on cable, which meant, to her mother's dismay, that there was *always* a game on somewhere.

"When was the last time you played?" he asked.

"I don't know...over a month ago now," Cassie replied, waving the question away. Her dad raised an eyebrow; but neither of them needed to reference the reason she hadn't played in a while.

"Who's playing?" she asked, settling herself down and taking a deep drink.

"Serie A, Juventus is playing Fiorentina. It's one to one in the second half." He told her the score even though it was clearly displayed on the screen. "Fiorentina looks good this year."

Cassie tried to ignore the irony of watching a game that was taking place in the city from which her sister had recently returned. The Italian men on the Fiorentina side passed the ball seamlessly toward the goal but then one player kicked the ball too high in a rushed attempt to score.

"Settle down," Cassie told the TV, "you've got the time, take the extra step. That would have gone in."

"It's going to be fun to watch you coach," her dad said.

She laughed and shook her head at the idea. "I watched you coach my whole life, I don't think I could fill those shoes." She glanced out the window again, she could see more of the car from this angle. Sudden comfort was replaced by frustration.

"What is it?" her dad asked, following her gaze.

"I'm just making sure..." Cassie took a moment before she glanced at her father and admitted, "I can't stop looking out the window to 'make sure.'"

"I wish you two would come back here for a while. Until everything is finished," her father said.

"I tried. Jess wants to do this all by herself, she doesn't think she can take Mom's...mothering right now."

He grunted.

"If it helps, he says she's safe." She nodded out the window.

"Agent Stills?"

"Benji," she confirmed. Her insides, the traitors that they were, twirled excitedly just from saying his name.

"I thought he introduced himself as Benjamin."

"He did. He doesn't like being called Benji."

Her father shook his head at the enjoyment he knew his oldest got out of tormenting others.

"He said Thomas…" Cassie paused and glanced toward the entrance to the living room, then lowering her voice she continued, "He thinks Thomas is gone with the wind."

"I think your mother and I would feel better if you both came home," he repeated.

"I know, and maybe we should. But Jess doesn't want to." She cleared her throat. "I don't know Dad, but I think it's better this way. Like, somehow it will help Jess get back on her feet sooner. Besides, it isn't just me and Jess who would move in; we come with a rotation of CIA agents. And there's no way Barbara Dodd would let them sit out there, causing a scene." The image of herself pounding on car windows floated before her. She cringed, *oh God, I am* just *like my mother*.

"You look tired," her dad said.

"I hate feeling helpless," she said on an angry exhale.

"You think *you* feel helpless? I want to find Thomas and kill him." He gave a frustrated grunt. "Of course, that would require me to learn how to use a gun, then buy a gun, then find the asshole…"

"And no longer be a pacifist," Cassie supplied.

Her dad glanced sideways at her. "I think I could give up my pacifist ways for you girls."

"But doesn't that go against the very theory of Pacifism?"

"Smartass."

"I am a product of my environment."

They were interrupted by one of Jess' friends poking her head into the living room. "Cassie, Mr. Dodd, it's time."

Her dad slapped the armrests of his chair and stood up. "Okay. Let's do this."

"What's wrong?" Cassie narrowed her gaze at Jessica, who'd paled continuously throughout the day. Cassie wanted the day to be over with. Another check off the 'To-Do' list of healing. And she wanted to get Jess far away from her family and friends, for their own safety; in case other assholes were lurking nearby.

"Just...wait," Jess said.

The entire wedding canceling party was standing in the backyard. They'd formed a semicircle around Jess' wedding dress that had been hung on a metal ladder over the fire pit. Jessica's childhood friends, turned bridesmaids, were the ones who insisted burning the dress was a good idea. A symbolic cleansing through fire. Cassie didn't necessarily disagree. She was all for symbolic gestures to rid one of past bullshit. Their father, on the other hand, was confused as to why the dress was being sacrificed, rather than returned for a full refund.

Jessica's friends had been part of the Dodd family ever since Jessica brought them home in the fifth grade. They had been annoying extensions of younger siblings at first, but once Jess and her friends got to college, the dynamic shifted and Cassie considered them as part of the family the same way her parents did.

Over the years she played big sister to each of them in one way or another. She'd given sex talks, hangover remedies, and even threatened a high school boyfriend or two.

Any other day, she was glad for the fierce loyalty the girls had for her sister, but today, she wanted them all to hurry the fuck up.

"Let's burn this fucker." One of Jessica's friends stood next to the dress, clicking a crème brulee torch on and off.

"Just wait," Jess repeated.

This was what Cassie was worried about, that it was too much too soon. "What's going on?"

"Nothing."

*Nothing my ass...*Cassie tried to make light of the moment, "Are you worried Benji is gonna come crashing through the door when he sees the fire? I told him we were gonna burn something."

"You told him that?"

Cassie shrugged. "Yeah."

The continued conversation among Jessica's friends railroaded the moment.

"Have you seen how built those guys are?"

"Which one is Benji?"

"The agent that flew home with her."

"The blonde one?"

"No, Benji's got auburn hair." Cassie bit her lip after the detail was out. She turned her gaze away from Jessica, but caught her sister's interested head tilt.

Cassie waved toward the dress, an indication to hurry this along.

"Oh, the one with dark hair is sexy as hell."

"Is he?" Jessica asked after the comment.

"He's nice," Cassie supplied. What was she doing? It was like she wanted these girls off the scent of her man.

Her man?

'Go out on a date with me'. His question floated by.

Cassie cleared her throat and looked to her dad, as if he could speed up the situation. He gave an apologetic shrug in reply.

"Benji *is* nice." Jessica elbowed her sister as the tangent of conversation continued to swirl around them.

"Who's the other one?"

"I'll take any of them. Have you seen the B team? They'd work too."

"You're married."

"So are you."

"Benji stood up to Barbara Dodd," Jessica said and was rewarded when all the women 'oohed' impressively.

Their mother blushed. "Girls," she chided.

"Your mom said they're fans of your baking." One of the friends nodded toward Cassie.

"What?" Jessica asked.

Cassie rubbed her hands together as she said, "I've been stress baking and I'm not going to eat everything myself. And you sleep a lot. So...*one time*, I took Stills and Robbins banana bread."

"You did? When? Why didn't you tell me?" Jessica asked.

"There's nothing to tell," Cassie said defensively.

"So, living together is going well?" a friend surmised.

Jessica glanced at her sister. "Yeah. I like having my big badass sister looking out for me."

If Jessica only knew the half of what looking out for her meant.

Cassie rolled her eyes dramatically and prayed the worry she was continuously steeped in wasn't apparent. "I'm only being nice because of what she's been through. When she's back on her feet with a job, I'm kicking her out."

Thankfully, the questions and side conversations continued at a rapid pace.

"Have you started looking for a new job yet?"

"They were such assholes at your old job."

"What happened to your apartment?"

"The CIA packed it up into a storage unit for her."

"Who knew the CIA had a furniture moving division."

"Can we..." their father interrupted.

"Yes," Cassie agreed.

"Wait!" Jessica scrubbed her face with her hands.

Cassie was ending this, they were needlessly putting Jessica through hell. "Let's go inside—"

"It's not...enough," Jessica announced. "I mean, I got used, cheated on..."

Cassie took a wide-eyed step back from her sister's powerful eruption.

The friends filled in the blanks of how Jessica had been mistreated.

"Beat up." Another friend flicked Jess' cast to make her point.

"Forced to listen to Vivaldi."

"Drugged."

"Exactly," Jess said emphatically, "and all I can do in retaliation is burn a dress?"

"You need another drink."

"No, she needs to burn the dress and then go on a date."

"Yeah, get out there. Put as many guys as you can between you and Dickhead."

"Sometimes it's helpful to jump in bed with another man. I'm not saying it's the right thing to do, it's just helpful."

"I should have had boys," their father muttered.

Cassie hadn't seen this strong side of her sister in so long, she let a laugh wash over her. It was refreshing. She didn't realize how much she needed to see it.

"Jess, it's time," Cassie pushed.

Their dad nodded. "Real Madrid is playing Rayo Vallecano in twenty minutes."

"What's happening?" one of the girls asked.

"We're a soccer family," Cassie offered.

"You don't have to be here, Walter," their mother chided.

Cassie watched her father eye their mom, the understanding of almost forty years of marriage flashed between them. He nodded at Jessica. "Yes, I do."

"Okay, listen up." One of the friends held up her champagne flute in a toast. "We are gathered here today to celebrate our friend Jessica. Sweetheart, you looked gorgeous in this dress but it does not deserve you now."

Muttered agreements and cursing of Thomas were thrown around happily. Yet it was their mother, who held up her glass and loudly announced, "Screw you Thomas Adler you...you dickhead!" That signaled the end of the ceremony.

Cassie laughed and squeezed Jessica's shoulders as the dress burned. It was an awkward sight, watching the synthetic beauty puff black smoke and melt before being engulfed entirely by blue flames. Cassie studied Jessica out of the corner of her eye; she wasn't crying. In fact, Cassie could have sworn that as the dress completely caught fire, Jessica's shoulders straightened.

Chapter Eleven

"**I**'m tired of being tired," Jess said as they walked back into the apartment after the long day at their parents'.

"Anyone would be tired after having Barbara Dodd drive them home because she insisted they had too many mimosas."

"We did have too many mimosas," Jess verified.

"But Benji offered to drive us..."

"Well...at least Dad followed and took her home. I'm not ready for a sleepover with Mom just yet." Jess gave a yawn and repeated, "I'm just tired of being tired."

"Look, you can't use today as a barometer for how things are going. I'm in pretty damn good shape and *I'm* exhausted," Cassie offered. "Besides, it's true what your friends and even Benji keep saying, healing takes time. You're doing great."

"I'm glad it's over," Jessica said thoughtfully, "Cass, you know, when I was finally on the plane to Italy, I wasn't upset because Thomas had lied. I was upset because somewhere along the line, I'd figured out he wasn't right for me. I went to Italy to confront him and then break up with him." She nodded at her truth she was finally able to put into words. "It was just that the second I got to Italy, all hell broke loose."

"I think you might have found more than you bargained for in Italy."

Jessica grunted. "That's an understatement."

"Not the weird CIA-mob crap...I mean, you were given a chance to hold up a mirror to yourself and your life, and you decided to finally take charge of everything."

"You think so?"

"Look, I'm worried about you," and if Jess was tired of being tired, Cassie was tired of being worried, "but...I know you're fierce and you'll be able to find your feet again." Stills' words echoed. "Time, kid. You need time. Personally, that's what I'm having the biggest problem with. I want to fix everything for you. Right now."

"But you can't," Jessica said sadly.

Cassie gave a ridiculous pout. "But I really want to."

"I know." Jessica smiled. "I just want you to understand. I want you to know that *I* was the one to reject him. I'm exhausted and my arm itches really badly under this cast, and the world seems heavy right now...but *I* was the one to reject Thomas. *I* was the one who stood up to him. And *I* saved myself." Her chin jutted into the air.

"You're in charge of your life now."

"Even though my life is a little more wobbly than I'd like?"

And still in danger. Cassie forced the thought away.

Jess went on, "I think it's time to push myself again. I'm gonna call Sara tomorrow," she referred to one of her friends, "and see if she can help me get a job. She's offered so many times in the past, I think I should finally follow up on that. See what she has in mind." The statement came across as more of a question.

"That's a fabulous idea," Cassie confirmed.

Jess stretched and yawned. "I know. But now, I'm going to bed."

"I'm gonna stay up and watch TV for a bit."

Cassie exchanged her wedding canceling clothing for yoga pants, sports bra and a tank top. She grabbed a beer out of the fridge and settled herself on the sofa. She was scrolling through the channels when there was a soft knock on the door.

She froze as fear flooded through her body.

They found Jessica.

The panic stuck in her throat and she quit breathing. Her attention on the door caused it to blur, she had to shake her head several times to find some reasonable mental footing and get the door to focus once again. Finally, she was able to force herself to take a long, deep drink of air and talk herself through some rational thoughts. It was unlikely that the bad guys would be politely knocking on the door, and even more unlikely that the people watching outside would let the bad guys in the building.

That was good. Facts, she was dealing with facts again.

There were cameras and they were *always* watching the cameras. Another fact.

However, it wouldn't hurt to be proactive about her own security. She tiptoed to the door, grabbed the baseball bat she'd dug out of her closet when Jess first moved in and held it loosely as she looked through the peephole.

Stills.

She pressed her head against the door and released a shaky breath. She replaced the bat before opening the door, pressing herself against the edge of it as she said, "You scared me."

He began to speak but changed his mind, his eyes narrowed as he slipped his arm around Cassie's waist and gave a tug.

She floated into his arms in one smooth motion. They hungrily collided before either of them had time to wonder if this was a good or bad idea.

The flood of fear was replaced with want and need; and all of the opposing emotions weakened Cassie's knees as she pressed herself against Stills. He took her weight, tightened his hold as open mouths, heat and soft lips yielded to each other, seeking out all the other was willing to give.

He pushed her into the apartment, but once clear of the closing door, she pushed back so that they fell against the solid wood. She wanted more. More heat, more caresses, more touching. There hadn't been enough touching. His hands snaked their way under the fabric of her shirt, and their warmth radiated into her lower back, kindling her desire. He was the kind of man who could devour her whole, and Cassie was definitely interested in seeing what that would be like.

Somehow, reason floated back between them, pushing them apart. They let the deep passionate kisses burn out, exchanged for lighter, soft nips.

Cassie took a shaky breath and rested her forehead against his chest. She didn't dare notice how well they fit together or how good his arms felt wrapped around her. And she didn't want to admit that she was in favor of forgiving him for this past week's transgressions.

"I didn't mean to scare you," he said softly into her hair as he rubbed her back.

"Well, this is a little scary too," she breathed.

"What?"

Cassie pulled away and looked up at him. "You don't think this physical reaction we have to each other is a bit sudden and strange?"

"I don't quite know what's going on, but we're both unattached, consenting adults." He whispered the confession, "I'm attracted to you, you said you're attracted to me. And I really like kissing you."

She slanted her head and stared at him; she could be certain of him if she could dilate her eyes just right and peer into his soul. "I've never been attracted to someone this quickly," she said. *Or this intensely.*

"Me neither." Stills threaded his hands into her hair and tilted her head back, he lowered his mouth slowly and brushed a smooth, sexy, sweet kiss against her lips. He pulled back and studied her. "I wanted to see how you were."

"You mean, am I still mad at you?"

"That too." He soothed her with another brush of his lips.

"Did you come up here to kiss the mad out of me?"

"If it's working." This time he prolonged the moment, holding back. He pulled away, agonizingly slow. "How are you?" he breathed.

"Tired. Are you on duty?" she asked.

"Just leaving, I told them I would come check on things," he whispered, still not releasing her.

"There's cherry turnovers and decaf coffee," she returned softly.

Stills raised an eyebrow. "Oh yeah?" He let her go, but slipped his hand into hers and led her across the small space to the kitchen. The gesture should have been ridiculous, but the continued connection was needed.

In the kitchen, she finally did drop his hand so she could start the coffee. When she was filling the pot with water, he stepped behind her and pulled her against his chest, and then leaned down and kissed the side of her neck. Cassie leaned into his attentions, but the sound of the bedroom door opening parted them.

They didn't jump, they simply righted themselves and stepped apart in silent agreement. Cassie poured the water and grabbed coffee and filters as she called, "Jess, Benji's here."

Stills growled at the nickname. Cassie grinned and looked over at him. "No one ever called you Benji before?"

"It's Ben now," he offered.

"Was it ever Benji?"

"When I was little," he muttered grudgingly.

"Hi," Jessica was smoothing out her t-shirt when she rounded the corner, "is something wrong?"

"Not at all, I was checking on you after today," he made the smooth excuse.

"He really came for the pastries." Cassie pulled out three plates and placed a fruit stuffed pastry on each.

"I didn't know I was coming for the pastries." He looked over at the frosting drizzled squares, baked to light brown perfection. "Now, I think, that is exactly what I'm here for."

Jessica took a plate as Cassie said, "I'll finish the coffee."

Stills took his plate and made sure to brush his fingers against Cassie's, allowing them to linger a moment. "I'll take yours." He took the opportunity to make sure their fingers met again before walking with Jess to the table.

Cassie touched a finger to her lips, then rolled her eyes and pulled out three coffee cups. *This man.* She found a tray and placed the half and half along with the sugar bowl on it. She paused and shook her head, she already knew he drank his coffee black, did that mean something? *Jeez Cass, it meant that he was a handsome man who kisses well and has the wherewithal to admit that he's attracted to you. Why not know how he likes his coffee?*

"Coffee will be ready in a minute," Cassie said as she joined Jess and Stills.

"Is there any news..." Jess left the question open, not asking after whom she really wanted news about.

Cassie set down the tray and gave Jessica's shoulder a reassuring squeeze. She sat down next to Jess, across from Stills. She was continuing her job as protector, and it was a nice opportunity to take in the man who could kiss her with such abandon one moment, making her knees weak, then become so completely in charge and buttoned up the next.

"The only thing I can tell you is that thanks to the information you parted with this week, we've been able to pick up a few more colleagues of Luigi Paroni and indict them."

Cassie's sisterly instincts pricked. "Because of Jess? Does that mean she might be in more danger?" She was actually asking a different question.

"No." He leveled his gaze at Cassie before turning it toward Jess, "No one is aware of your work with us."

"Except Thomas," Cassie offered.

"And everyone thinks he killed Luigi Paroni," his voice was even, "so he would be stupid to seek help from anyone associated with Paroni." He waited for the information to resonate. Cassie nodded her head as Stills reaffirmed, "Jessica is safe. You are both safe."

Here they were again, she was going to have to continue to trust Stills or make herself crazy with fear.

"I mean it," he challenged her, seeming to know what was going on inside her head.

She let a grin turn the corner of her mouth up. "Okay."

The coffee loudly sputtered the end of its process. Cassie retrieved the pot.

Jess bit into her pastry. "These are my favorite so far," she commented with a full mouth.

Stills took a bite and when the sweet and sour hit his tongue, he glanced over at Cassie. She'd been watching him out of the corner of her eye, curious about his reaction. When she saw his surprise, she felt lit up from the inside.

She poured the coffee but fumbled slightly when she also caught the innocent, sexy way he licked the lingering frosting from his lips. God, what would those lips taste like now? Cherry and coffee and heat and need.

"Cassie." Jess reached out and steadied the cup.

"Oops." She attempted a quick look at Stills, he winked in reply.

They sat in silence, chewing to the sound of the clock until Jessica asked, "So...?"

When she didn't continue, Stills raised an eyebrow in question.

But Jessica's courage faltered. "Nothing," she lied.

Cassie pointed her cup at Stills. "Benji, Jess wants information about the *man*."

"Cassie," Jess cautioned.

"Jesus, Jess. It's okay to ask about him. It's okay to say, Benji, tell me about Parker. Is there or isn't there any news?"

Jess was staring daggers at her sister.

Cassie met her gaze as she began the line of questioning again, "Benji-"

"Agent Stills," he corrected. Cassie turned her frown on him.

"Unfortunately, his whereabouts and work are classified. I wish I could tell you more," he claimed.

"Is he okay?" Cassie asked the question, trying to convey with her pursed lips that he needed to give Jessica *something* to hook her hope onto. If there *was* still hope.

"It's fine," Jess said, "when I left we both knew it was over."

"But it's still okay to ask about him." Cassie nodded toward Stills.

"He's fine," Stills parroted, "safe."

Cassie reached out and gave Jess' hand a pat. "See?"

Jess pulled her hand away. "I'm not a child."

"I never said you were." Cassie returned the same snarky tone.

"You're treating me like a child."

"Well excuse me for caring." Cassie took a bite out of her pastry and angrily chewed.

Jessica stretched her neck before continuing, "I know you care, just stop...coddling me."

"Jessica, I'm not coddling you. I'm trying to figure out what the hell to do for you. What the hell to do *with* you."

"What does that mean?"

"Well, other than one doctor visit, two trips to Mom and Dad's, and three days spent in CIA offices, you haven't gone anywhere else."

"So?"

Cassie overenunciated, "It's been weeks now."

"So?" Jess demanded again.

"You cry in your sleep. You have nightmares every night, you jump when the phone rings, and I'm scared to leave you."

Stills cleared his throat and pushed his chair back. "Maybe I should-"

Jess pointed at him, her own ire up now. "Don't you dare leave. This is just a sister fight. It's no big deal."

"Have another pastry." Cassie stood, grabbed his plate and headed to the kitchen. She tossed a turnover onto it then let the plate drop onto the table in front of him when she returned.

Shoving her hands on her hips she faced Jessica down. "They want me back at work next week. I can't go."

"Why not?"

"Who is going to look out for you if I go?"

"Miss Dodd..." Stills tried but Cassie pointed a warning finger at him.

"I don't need to be babysat," Jess reasoned.

"I think you do."

"Go back to work if you want to. I'll be fine."

"Will you?"

"Jesus Christ Cass, I don't know," Jessica seethed. "I'd like to think I'm going to be okay and all of this will get put behind me sooner than later. Did you ever think that maybe you coddling me isn't helping?"

"Well fuck you very much."

"Fuck you," Jess hissed.

"Jessica! Everything I've done since you got home...I'm...I am trying to keep you safe. I'm trying to make sure you don't feel alone."

"I don't feel alone!" Jessica yelled.

"Then what the fuck is this all about?"

"I'll be fine if you go back to work!"

"She will be fine." Stills took the break in conversation to insert his statement in a calm, even tone.

Cassie gave a brisk wave. "Benji..." she started at the same moment a frustrated Jess said, "He's right."

The two women glared angrily at each other for several long moments before Jess' face brightened with a wide grin.

Cassie rubbed her face with her hands and let out a long deep breath. "God...I needed that."

Jess' face flushed with the heat of the exchange. "Poor Benji, he looks like a deer caught in the headlights."

Cassie shook her arms and whole body as if she had physically released a month's worth of unwanted emotions.

"What was that?" Stills asked.

Jess explained, "Sister fight, we've had them our whole lives. We were in high school when we realized going toe to toe and screaming at each other was liberating. We'd yell and call each other names, then slam our way into our bedrooms. Then after a good cry, we'd find each other, apologize and go hang out."

Cassie took over, "It somehow got all the pent-up shit out of our bones and it always felt good to yell at someone who you knew would still love you in the morning."

Jess stood up. "I'm sorry. I'm really tired, I can't keep my eyes open." She looked at Cassie, asking a silent question, 'would she be okay if she were left alone with Benji?'

"I'll see him out and see if I can get any other information from him." Cassie winked.

Jess took a few steps away from the table, thought better of it and came back and hugged Cassie around the neck. "Stupid bitch," she whispered.

"I hate you so much," Cassie said with all the love in her heart.

Stills took a sip of his coffee and watched Cassie organize herself once more at the table. When the bedroom door closed he said, "I have two brothers."

"Where do you fall in the lineup?"

"Oldest by two years. My brothers are twins."

"Names please."

"Nicholas and Daniel."

"Ben, Nick and Dan. Did you get along?"

"Fought a lot through grade school. I had freshman and sophomore year to establish myself in high school, and then when they became freshmen and I was a junior, we kinda buried the hatchet. Been decent friends ever since."

"Decent?" Cassie frowned at the word.

He pursed his lips as he explained, "My job...I'm not always good at communicating. I've gotten better over the past several years."

"The rules you have for yourself?" she asked.

"Tactics," he supplied the correction, "they help me keep things from getting overwhelming."

Cassie took a bite of her pastry and had to lean forward when some of the filling came dripping out. "Guess I didn't close that one very well."

"These are good." He took another bite and nodded at his assessment. "Everything you've baked has been wonderful. Why aren't you a pastry chef somewhere?"

"I thought about it," Cassie sat back, "a lot. It would be fun to have a little coffee shop and bakery, like La Petite Café. But when you turn something that's supposed to be fun and relaxing into a job, it becomes a job. I wanted to keep having fun."

Stills moved to the seat next to Cassie, picked up her hand and caressed it, studying it. "Where did the genealogy come into play?"

"I shouldn't be surprised," she said, referring to the fact that she hadn't told him what she did for work yet.

"But I'm just doing my job," he said and pulled her hand up so he could brush a kiss across her wrist.

The breath fluttered out of Cassie's pores. "Your job could be considered erring on the side of stalker."

"So, genealogy?" he prodded, releasing her hand but making sure his knee was pressed against hers.

"I liked history so that's what I studied in college. I liked researching. In my senior year, I fell into a job for my professor doing research. She was so impressed with my work, she introduced me to her friend who was getting a company started that analyzed DNA. They were beginning to add elements of ancestral research; I began a sort of internship for the company and never looked back."

"Ancestry Home." He supplied the company name.

"And what is my position at Ancestry Home?" she asked.

"Academic Historian," he said, "which sounds impressive."

Cassie laughed. "What else do you know about me?"

"It's not so much what I know about you, but what I *want* to know about you." He inched closer to her. "For one thing, I want to see what cherry turnover tastes like on your lips."

They were so close, Cassie thought he must definitely be able to hear the excitement that hummed beneath her skin so she conceded, "I was thinking the same thing."

Stills bumped his nose against hers. "Oh really?"

He gave a low groan and claimed her lips.

Cassie thought he would taste like warm pastries fresh from the oven, hot coffee and rugged man. Not only was she right, it tasted better than she imagined.

And then his phone rang.

Stills pulled away from the kiss and pressed his forehead against Cassie's.

"Work?"

"Sorry," he pulled out the phone and answered, "Stills."

She shifted away from him and watched as the cloudy passion that had filled his eyes began to clear.

"I'm on my way," he reported and ended the call.

He held up the phone with a shrug, a silent apology.

"Is everything...are we..." How the hell did she ask this question?

He cupped her face. "It's a technology thing. Everything is fine. I promise."

She nodded. "Want a pastry for the road?"

"If I can't have you, I suppose that'll have to do for now."

Chapter Twelve

"So help me God, Cassie, if you touch my hair one more time..." Jessica snapped.

"Excuse me for trying to help."

They stood with matching defensive snarls in place for several moments before Cassie reached out and pushed a chunk of Jessica's hair behind her ear again.

"Cassie!" Jess hissed as she pulled away from her sister.

"You're going to be late," Cassie defended.

"Then stop...hindering me." Jess hitched her purse up on her shoulder but Cassie caught the way her grip tightened on the folder that held her resume.

"I'll stop. Let's go." Cassie took a step toward the front doors of the imposing high-rise where Jessica was about to have the interview her friend set up.

Jessica shook her head incredulously at Cassie. "You're not going inside that building with me."

"Why not?"

"Like a fucking babysitter?" she yelled as a group of women in tailored suits exited the building.

The two sisters stepped aside, presenting false smiles to the women. The smiles were returned and once the well dressed group was past, the sisters faced each other again, formidable frowns back in place.

Jessica leaned forward and quietly lectured, "This isn't the first day of school. You are *not* taking me in and holding my hand to make sure everything is okay."

But that was exactly what Cassie wanted to do.

"Besides, I'll have Robbins lingering as it is." Jess gestured with her nose to the man standing nonchalantly on his cell phone a few feet away.

"It's just been a big week for you," Cassie gave the lame excuse.

"All I did was get my cast off."

"Well, it was a big deal."

"Monday. I got my cast off Monday. Today is Friday." Jessica's eyes widened in warning as Cassie stepped toward her again, her hand out, about to fix something else. "I'll call you when I'm done. Go have coffee or something."

"Okay," Cassie held up her hands in resignation, "okay."

Jessica pointed to the street once more.

"I said I'll go." Cassie took a step back.

"Thanks for the ride," Jessica checked her anger but added a muttered, "even though I could have driven myself."

Jessica headed inside as another business attired group exited, leaving the door open and giving Cassie the opportunity to call out, "You're gonna do great!"

She caught Jessica's mortified grunt and Cassie aimed a successful smile at the group.

With a deep breath, she took a moment to study her surroundings and decided the coffee shop across the street would indeed be the best place to wait.

As she retraced her steps back to the curb, she passed Robbins and glanced away from him as if something down the street had suddenly caught her attention. Then she worried that maybe it was too much of an overreaction and perhaps she should have given him a polite nod.

"Shit. You're a wreck," she admitted as she craned her neck, squinting at the high-rise, noticing how the reflective film on the windows rejected the bright morning sun. She wished she knew which floor Jess was going to be on.

"She's gonna be fine," she mumbled. "This is good. No problems at all. No one knew she was gonna set up an interview...she'll be fine in there."

"Talking to yourself Dodd?"

The voice made her jump, she whipped her head around and found Stills.

"She'll be fine," she reiterated.

"She'll be fine," he verified calmly.

Cassie nodded, glancing once more up at the building.

"C'mon."

"What?" she asked.

Stills pointed across the street. "That coffee shop has a good vantage point for watching."

She eyed him.

He sighed and put his hand against the small of her back, urging her across the street.

The heat of his hand electrified her spine, she thought she was prepared but the shock was a strange defibrillation to her system, her attention was abruptly taken off her overbearing protectiveness and placed firmly on Stills.

It had been a week since, what she referred to in her mind as, the 'cherry turnover incident'. A week since those explosive kisses. A week since she had been this close to him.

She'd physically gone back to work two days this week, it was all she was able to do at the moment, but it was a move in the right direction. She continued to abide by Stills' request that she steer clear of the unmarked car, which meant there hadn't even been an innocent glimpse of him on her way to or from work.

And she missed him.

They didn't speak as they crossed the street or stood in the mid-morning coffee line. But as they pretended to study the menu, they leaned into each other, touching arms. Cassie reached out her pinky to brush against his and was disappointed when it was their turn; ending the connection.

Coffees ordered, they sat next to the large front window across from each other. Cassie glanced at the building, then back at Stills and asked, "How are you?"

He looked taken aback by the question and a small smile crept onto Cassie's lips. "Have I never asked you that?"

"You've had other things on your mind," he replied, giving her an excuse.

A barista brought over their coffees allowing Cassie time to study him and determine that he looked well rested. So he wasn't losing sleep, which she thought might be a good thing, because if he was losing sleep then wouldn't that mean something was going very badly behind the scenes?

He wore black pants today with a heather gray polo. His sunglasses rested on top of his short auburn hair. His earpiece was visible, though it looked like a wireless earbud. When he picked up his cup, his forearms flexed and she watched, fascinated at how the ripple of muscle movement crawled up his arm and radiated into her chest.

He was attractive, there was no denying that, but at first blush, he seemed average. Like he could easily get lost in a crowd.

"Nondescript." The word slipped out and she hid her mortification behind a long drink of her coffee, turning her attention out the window.

When she was ready to meet his gaze again, she found him patiently waiting for her as he said, "Do I dare ask?"

"You're more than meets the eye," she blew out the confession quickly.

"So are you, Dodd."

"Benji-"

"Agent Stills." He whispered the request.

"How..." she pointed to his earpiece and lowered her voice, "can everyone hear us?"

"Not if I don't want them to," he verified.

She nodded and continued. "How..." she cleared her throat, "when was the last time you dated someone?"

"Two years ago. We went on a few dates, but she didn't know what I did for a living, and my schedule at the time was rather...fraught." He pursed his lips. "Needless to say, things didn't work out."

Her forehead creased with a frown.

"What's wrong Dodd?"

"I just don't understand how dating works for you." She shrugged.

"Well, I find a girl I like that has a lot of fire and sass. Then I let her call me names and try to seduce her in my free time."

"I'm serious." She laughed.

"So am I. Dodd, whatever you think I am, when all is said and done, I'm just a normal guy."

She raised her eyebrow. "How many people are in the coffee shop right now?"

He licked his lips in reply.

She nodded as she further challenged, "How many look dangerous?"

No answer so she leaned forward continuing in a hushed tone, "What's the best way to get out of here if we couldn't go through the front door?"

"You know, anyone with military training would be able to answer those questions too," he reasoned.

She pointed her cup at him. "I'm just trying to make a point about how you might not be *just* a normal guy."

"If you want, we can discuss the existential definitions of what *normal* means," he offered. "But I'd rather point out that I find you fascinating."

"I find you nondescript," she declared, jutting her chin.

Her statement did not have the desired effect, though. Stills' outright laugher was shocking in its warmth and contagiousness. It cocooned Cassie in the moment.

When his laughter settled, he asked an out of the blue question, "Were you a big Halloween kid?"

"Oh yeah. Jess and I used to coordinate costumes and go all out. Our mom let us decorate the whole front yard. Even in our twenties, we'd go to our parents' and decorate and dress up and hand out candy..." Her voice trailed off. She hadn't thought about that in a while. "Jess and I used to do a lot more together." She cleared her throat and asked, "What about Benji, Nicky and Danny?"

"A giant pillowcase each, and we'd race through the neighborhoods trying to fill the damn things all the way up."

"Favorite costume?"

"Obi Wan Kenobi." He gave what was meant to be a 'force' wave with his fingers. "You?"

"The Queen of Hearts," she said excitedly. "Jess was Alice in Wonderland. We spent two months making our costumes that year. They were spectacular. Jess did this whole steampunk version of Alice. I used playing cards for the neck ruffle of the dress and bodice, and tulle for the skirt. We decorated the folks' whole front yard like the scene for the croquet match. Flamingos and all."

"You doing anything this year?" he asked.

Cassie sat back, the excitement fading. "That seems so far away."

"Only a few months."

"Well, the way things are going, I don't think I'll be doing much this year."

"Damn, and here I was with this image of a sexy soccer player."

Cassie chuckled. "What the hell does that even mean? We don't wear short shorts to play soccer, you know. I get all sweaty, put my hair in a headband that's permanently sweat stained and end up with grass stuck to the back of my thighs."

Another genuine laugh escaped. Cassie shook her head.

"When was the last time you played?" He asked.

"You know the answer to that."

"Dodd, you need to get back to your normal life."

"Benji..."

"Hear me out."

She pursed her lips.

"It's time for you to get back to your own life. It's good that you went back to work a few days a week, but next week you need to try and add more days."

"I'm doing my best," she defended.

"Your sister has licked her wounds long enough," he said softly.

"No, she hasn't." Cassie stood up, but Stills reached out toward her, imploring, "Cassie, what are you worried about?"

She looked around before she leaned back toward him and seethed, "Other than her ex-fiancé showing up to kill her?"

"I'm starting to get offended. I thought you said you trusted me." He gestured for her to sit back down. "Please?"

She perched herself on the edge of the seat and mumbled, "You asked me to trust you and I do."

He grunted in reply. "So what are you really worried about then?"

"You're a shrink now?"

There was a long pause before he answered, "I'd like to think I've become a friend."

The honesty deflated Cassie, she slouched and exhaled. "I'm worried that she won't need me anymore and she'll go away and we won't be as close as we've been these past few weeks."

There it was. The truth of it all. While she didn't like her sister's life in danger, she *did* like how close they'd become again.

"When we both still lived at home we were so close, and then we both got our own lives and apartments and…that's life, I get it. I'm not so naïve to think that we were going to spend every second together, but we grew apart over the past few years…and I've missed her."

Stills didn't interrupt as she rationalized her feelings, "Do you know, I feel like if we'd been as close as we used to be, then she would have called me to let me know what was going on with Thomas and *I* would have been with her on that plane to Italy."

"And what would you have been able to do?"

Cassie gestured. "Save her."

Even though admiration for her sparkled in his eyes, he patiently explained, "I'll tell you what would have really happened, Dodd. Our operation would have had two security liabilities and you would have been detained until we sent you both home."

"See," she pointed, "in a way I would have saved her *and* you guys wouldn't have tried to use her as a spy."

"Asset," he corrected.

"Spy," Cassie bit and scrubbed her face with her hands.

"How are you?" he asked.

She squinted at the question and waved it back to Stills like it was a tennis ball lobbed her way. "How are *you* doing, Benji? Really."

"I'm tired, but I'm okay."

"Me too."

His voice lowered as he admitted, "And I think about you a lot."

Cassie didn't have a retort for that.

He let a grin pull at his lips as he emphasized, "*A lot.*"

"But…"

"How do you know there's a 'but'?"

"I've seen movies."

"What does that have to do with anything?"

"When that movie, *The Spy Who Dumped Me*, came out...have you seen it?"

He raised an eyebrow.

"Well, it's about a girl who's unknowingly dating a guy in the CIA and it's a whole adventure...but when the movie came out, I remember reading this interview with an ex-CIA agent and she said how the movie missed the mark on some points, but got other parts right."

"What are you trying to say?"

"I don't know, Benji. I just don't have a lot to go on, I'm tired of saying that I know you can't tell me about your job, but then, sometimes, I think maybe you've already told me too much."

She glanced between Stills and the building across the street. "Is it true that if you go on more than three dates with someone, the CIA does a soft background check on the person you are dating?"

He sat back in his seat and considered Cassie's raised eyebrows for a moment before he said, "You know, it's really a boring job."

She grunted. "Is this another tactic? A way to disarm the civilian?"

"I'm not using tactics on you, Dodd."

"Aren't you?"

"Well," he narrowed his gaze and focused on her lips before meeting her eyes once more, "the tactics I'm using on you are the kind I've been using long before I got into this line of work."

"But are you allowed to like me?"

He blew out a breath. "I'm not in a cult. You're sexy as hell and I'm a grown-up. I'm allowed to be attracted to you."

"But what about falling for..." she sat forward and whispered, "...an asset?"

"Dodd, we've been over this before. You are the sister of *Parker's* asset."

"Fine, fine. I'm not an asset. But I was just wondering if you could get fired for dating me because of all the things you've told me."

"Okay, look, the day you came outside to go for a run while we were in the middle of a situation, I was compromised."

"Compromised?"

"Yes. I watched you walk away and knew I had a job to do but part of me was worried about you the whole time. Did you get to the corner safely? Was someone else that we were not aware of waiting at the gas station? Were you okay?"

"That's why it's not a good idea to get involved with an asset, you're led by emotions then."

Stills nodded.

"I'm telling you, I think romcoms have some of this stuff right."

He grunted. "Yes, when emotions become involved, a person could lose control of their focus. And in the job I do, focus is everything."

"So I need you to stop thinking about me, *a lot*," she parroted his original statement. "Because the way I see it, you need to be one hundred percent focused on Jessica."

"I am," he said defensively.

"Are you?"

"I only think of you when I'm not working," he said roughly.

"Well, you're always working, so that seems like a moot point."

He took a calming breath. "Here's what I want you to understand. This case, involving Jessica and her ex, is going to be over soon." The authority in his voice caught all of Cassie's attention; was he trying to tell her something without really telling her something?

"What do you know?"

"The facts. Things end. This operation will come to an end. And when it does, you and I are going to have to talk."

"About what?"

"Us," he said sincerely.

"Us," she repeated.

Was she ready for an 'us' yet? She'd kissed an attractive man a few times and liked it, and he confessed to being attracted to her. But was she in the mood to hurry up and wait so they could go out? And even if they did go out, his job would be a very large part of their relationship.

"This is a pretty intense conversation for coffee on a Friday morning, don't you think?" she asked.

He held up his hands, an offering that he would back off.

"Why did you choose this line of work?" she asked, blatantly changing the subject.

"I think that might also be a pretty intense conversation for a Friday morning." He shrugged. "Actually, I just like the research aspects."

"Really?" She squinted her eye suspiciously.

"Really. When you get down to it, most of my job is just researching movements and actions of others and putting the pieces together to figure out what they are going to do before they do it."

She gave a 'hmph' in reply.

He repeated her sound.

Cassie tilted her head. "But there's more to it than that, isn't there?"

"Why do *you* think I've chosen this current job path?"

"I asked you first."

"But you have a theory." He pointed with his cup.

"I think Robbins was right, you like saving people. Obi Wan Kenobi always liked a good damsel in distress."

She thought maybe he blushed a bit. "Well, that's not entirely wrong."

Stills looked out the window suddenly and pressed his finger to his ear, nodding at whatever was being communicated to him.

Cassie's body tensed. When he looked back at her and saw her reaction, he soothed, "Jess is done. Robbins is on the move, that's all."

They stood but Stills reached out and touched her hand. "I want you Dodd," he said as if he were telling her he needed to make a phone call.

"Benji," she shook the comment off, trying to ignore how his words vibrated though her blood stream, "you make these declarations. But then you turn on a dime, going from flirtatious to professional. And at some point we both have to get back to our real lives, and I'm left wondering how...*if*...anything is *really* going to happen." She shook her head. "I don't do well with empty promises."

"I haven't promised anything."

And he hadn't.

The truth of it hit her hard and she tried to find solid footing, a way to shrug off the disappointment. "Well," she cleared her throat, "my grandpa always said want in one hand—"

"Cassandra," his voice lowered, "don't try to cheapen our feelings because the timing isn't right."

"You are...an...asshole," she lashed out.

"Because..."

"Fine." She took a few steps away from him, but then thought better of the people lingering and returned to where she wouldn't be overheard.

"I guess I just get to continue to lose sleep thinking about how it feels to kiss you."

"Good."

Her eyes widened in disbelief as she poked him in the chest. "Asshole."

He winked at her as her phone began to ring; seeing it was Jess she answered it immediately. "You ready?"

Stills leaned across her body so she could feel the heat from his chest seep into her own, and whispered into her other ear, "And I'll think about how much fun it's going to be when I finally get to show you exactly how I've wanted you and how crazy you make me."

He pulled away, laughing at Cassie's reaction; she was wide-eyed and appeared to have lost the ability to talk. When she was finally able to find her voice, it came out as a squeak as she relayed to Jessica, "Yes, I'll meet you in the lobby."

Chapter Thirteen

"It's been two months." Cassie shrugged into a lightweight sweater as she watched Jessica from across the room.

"Thank you, Cassandra. I know it's been two months," Jessica muttered.

Cassie frowned. "Don't bite my head off." She tried to be angry, but she was just nervous. Again. Or maybe she hadn't actually stopped being nervous yet.

She spent the last hour, as she dressed, counting the days and weeks since Jessica had returned. Of course, she was also counting the days since the 'lurking' incident had occurred.

She was trying to justify her outing this evening, and while she had thought that doing some math regarding the number of days that had passed would help, it just made her more anxious.

After several days of internal debates, Cassie decided to attend her company's annual anniversary dinner. It was always an entertaining event. They went overboard each year with the theme, decorations, food, prizes and celebrity guests. All of it solidified the family culture her company was known for.

"Why are you in a bad mood?" Cassie asked.

"I'm not in a bad mood," Jessica answered moodily.

Cassie sighed. "Is this about the new job or..." She waited, hoping Jessica would fill in the details. Of course, she hadn't yet, so why would she choose tonight, moments before Cassie was about to leave, to say Parker's name.

"I don't know what you're talking about."

Cassie ran a frustrated hand through her hair. "Jess, I heard you last night. You were having a nightmare and you yelled out Parker's name."

"It's nothing." Jess kept her attention glued to the television. "Like you said, it was a bad dream. They're getting better." Then she added, "I'm fine."

Fine. Cassie snorted at the word, that was the last thing her sister was. "I can stay home."

"Go to your dinner. I need to figure out how to be alone at some point."

Cassie bit her lower lip, that was exactly what Stills had told her needed to happen. She had to start dipping her toe back into her own life, so that Jessica would fight her own demons and venture back into *her* own life.

Cassie had taught Jessica how to roller skate, how to swim and kick a soccer ball. Her mother used to bemoan the fact that Jessica did everything Cassie did when they were younger, always trying to emulate her older sister.

Well, if Cassie ever needed Jessica to follow in her footsteps it was now, because Jessica had been offered a job and she was about to be pushed back into the world, so there would be no more hiding.

Cassie reasoned that her going to this dinner would be another good jumping-off point, for both of them.

"Benji's on duty tonight," Cassie said aloud.

That didn't land the way Cassie hoped it would, as Jessica angrily punched the button to turn the channel as she said, "The only reason they're still here is because there's still a threat."

"We don't know that." Cassie's voice rose on the statement, even though she knew better than anyone there was still the possibility of a threat.

"Really?" Jessica shifted and turned all her attention toward her sister. "The CIA has nothing better to do than watch a thirty-two-year-old who lives with her sister?"

"A thirty-two-year-old digital archivist for Warner Brothers Entertainment who lives with her sister!" Cassie tried a different perspective, mentioning Jessica's new job title.

Jessica jutted out her chin. "Yeah, well..."

"How pissed are you that one of your best friends could have gotten you that job years ago?"

"She said she was waiting for me to realize my potential and use my connections like a good Southern California girl." Jessica rolled her shoulders and then slouched back into her original position.

Cassie examined Jess for several more seconds, then realized all her reasoning tonight was flawed. It was just a company dinner, this was her sister. And she was far more important. She began to shrug out of her sweater.

The action propelled Jess into action. "Oh, no you don't!" She was across the room, pulling Cassie's sweater back over her shoulders. "I'm tired of getting in the way of your life. Like you said," she picked up Cassie's keys and phone and put them in her purse, "it's been over a month. Benji's outside. I haven't been anywhere, but neither have you." She opened the door.

Cassie pulled away from Jessica. "It's not a big deal."

"It is."

They squared off, staring each other down. Finally, Jess gave a sigh and a tired smile. "Go. I'll be fine."

Cassie nodded. "I won't be long."

"I'll be fine," Jessica reiterated.

Cassie pulled her sister to her for a hug. "Okay. Have a good night."

Jessica gave a sarcastic snort and waved toward the sofa. "I'll make sure it's exciting." She pushed Cassie out the door and slammed it in her face before either of them had time to change their minds.

Cassie adjusted her sweater and the contents of her purse, then smoothed her clothing and headed to the parking area behind the complex. But when she got off the elevator, she decided to do what she promised Stills she wouldn't.

She marched across the street, her heartbeat picking up as she neared the car. She hadn't seen Stills since his parting words whispered in her ear about showing her how much he wanted her.

Her mouth was dry and his car door opened before she reached the back of the car.

His frown was evident in the dusky light of sunset. "Miss Dodd."

Goosebumps shivered up her arms.

What the hell?

"Benji, I'm going out tonight."

He nodded, and she didn't feel like she needed to explain any more than that, but she quickly mumbled, "It's for work. A work dinner. They do this big celebration each year." She waved off the words and pointed toward her balcony. "I need you to talk to her."

"What's going on?" He followed her gaze and took several steps toward Cassie.

"The nightmares haven't stopped," Cassie said. "I thought they would. She *has* stopped crying, but now...I hear her yelling in her sleep every night. It wakes her up."

Stills nodded and rested his hip against the car. "It's going to take time."

"It's been...weeks." The excuse fizzled out. "Maybe I shouldn't go tonight." She bit her lip in thought then turned an accusing finger at Stills. "You know, the only reason I'm going in the first place is because you said it would be a good idea for me to start showing Jess how to live again...through my own actions." God she hated how that sounded.

"You look good," he said.

Cassie gave a dry laugh. "Don't."

"Sexy," he amended.

She tilted her head and paused a moment before she gave a slight smile and admitted, "I know."

"No, you don't." He straightened himself and crossed the distance between them, and reached out to brush a hair behind her ear, then whispered, "I'm looking for any excuse to touch you." His hand slowly inched its way down the strand of hair, lightly grazing her ear and then the bottom of her chin. "*Any* excuse."

Cassie swallowed hard and took a step away from him, breaking the intimate connection. "Could you," she had to clear her throat again, "could you talk to her? Please?"

He nodded and the heat between them dissipated. "But Dodd, you need to do a favor for me."

"Stop bringing attention to the car?" she guessed.

He nodded.

"I won't bug you again unless it's important." She took a few more steps away from him, glancing over her shoulder as she began to cross the street.

"Have a good night." His deep velvet voice wafted over her, sending another wave of goosebumps.

She pointed her finger. "Help my sister." She annunciated the command in an attempt to shake off the sexy man who was looking for any excuse...

Chapter Fourteen

"Shit!" Cassie pushed the chair out of her way and grabbed the toe she stubbed, hopping around in a slight circle.

"Now what?" Jess asked.

"Nothing," Cassie jumped around, "just stubbed my stupid toe on the stupid chair."

"Don't do that, it hurts."

"No shit Sherlock."

"God, you have been in a bad mood for the past two weeks. What is going on with you?" Jess stood up and frowned down at her boots.

"Nothing, nothing's going on with me." Cassie sat down and angrily rubbed her toe. That was the problem, the whole of it. *Nothing* was going on with her. She hadn't seen Stills in two weeks. Ever since Jess started her new job, Stills was following her sister. There had been no more lame excuses made just to see her, no more coincidental meet-ups at coffee shops. And since she and Jess weren't keeping the same hours, there were no more incidental interactions either, which meant no more sexy stolen kisses.

Not to mention work had been exhausting. The projects Cassie had worked on from home had been minimal, and she'd allowed too much to build up. On one hand, she was grateful she didn't have a moment to think, and on the other, when she did find a moment, she fluctuated between worrying about unknown threats to Jess, and daydreaming about 'how much fun it's going to be when he finally got to show her exactly how he wanted her.' Both of which did not help her productivity at all.

On the weekend, Cassie had gone to La Petite Café and lingered over a coffee and pastry, willing Stills to join her, but of course, he never did. So she decided to stop acting like some lovelorn schoolgirl. The ball was in his court. He knew where she was.

"Stupid," Cassie muttered again and then stood up, testing her toe.

"I gotta go, how does this look?" Jess asked, standing with her hands out to the side.

"Good. I like the boots."

"Good, because they were a bitch to zip up. The little things still hurt," she admitted.

"What still hurts?"

"Bending over, my hand is still weak and sore...but it's getting better."

"It is getting better," Cassie repeated. "Have a good day. I'm going out to dinner and maybe a club tonight with friends from work, we'll probably leave from there. You'll...will you be okay?"

Jess didn't look at Cassie as she continued gathering her things. "I don't need a babysitter."

"Good, cuz I don't want to babysit you. I'm just asking...this is the longest..."

"Cass," Jessica stood in front of her sister and leveled her gaze, "I'm good."

"Okay then." Cassie waved her sister away.

"Besides," Jess reassured, "the girls are taking me out for drinks after work tonight and someone is always watching."

Cassie ground her teeth as she busied herself with her own clothes. "Okay, I'll see you later tonight then."

"See ya."

Cassie waited for several minutes until she was sure her sister wasn't coming back into the apartment, then took the long way to the edge of the window. She watched as her sister's car appeared and as the Escalade pulled out behind it.

"Stupid tinted windows," Cassie muttered. "Who cares, I don't care." She spent the rest of the day with that mantra playing through her mind, trying to convince herself that she didn't really care. By midmorning she abandoned the mantra and was staring across the room at nothing, touching her finger to her lips, wondering what it would be like when they finally did see each other again.

And that thought gave a sharp twinge in her pelvic region.

The music was loud, the lights dimmed and the drinks her friends had insisted on loosened Cassie up perfectly.

She needed this, she thought, as she danced and laughed with her friends from work. This group of friends had been together for seven years at the same office. She'd been to weddings, baby showers and funerals of parents.

When she confided in one of her friends the reason she had been working from home for so long (obviously leaving out big chunks of the story), the friend insisted that the core group go tie one on and 'get loose'. She couldn't remember the last time she'd felt this uninhibited, this free.

If this had been almost three months ago, she would have called Mark right about now. He'd come lamely flirt and dance with her and then they'd have drunken sex at his place.

"Fuck!" Cassie yelled into the air, but no one could really make out what she had said over the music. The release of pent-up anger and frustration and worry felt so good, she screamed the obscenity again.

She glanced at her friends who grinned and gave her a thumbs up.

"I need another drink." She gestured to her empty glass and headed to the bar.

She ordered and danced to the music while the accommodating bartender saw to her drink. As she danced, a pair of hands slipped onto her hips and rested there. She frowned down at the large hands and turned to find an old friend she'd gone to high school with.

"John?!" she screamed.

"Cassie Kay," he smirked and they hugged like the long-lost friends they were.

"What are you drinking?" Cassie asked and he pointed to a beer that was being delivered.

"Who are you here with?" she asked.

"Some friends, but girl, I saw you and knew we were in trouble."

He carried their drinks and they mingled their two groups together, overflowing between two adjacent booths. Drinks came and went as the thumping intruded and pulled various couplings to the dance floor.

John and Cassie jumped up and down when a favorite song from their high school years played. They sang along laughing, surprised that they still knew all the words. When a particularly sexy song from the late 90s echoed onto the dance floor, they gyrated their bodies together, for old time's sake.

Cassie beamed at John. "You're still all hands!" she yelled. He bumped the side of her neck with his nose and bit her ear playfully in return.

The night flashed forward quickly but the stresses of the past traumatic weeks were released from Cassie's cells. She was an airy, floating version of herself from seven years ago, when she had first met this group of friends, *and* the girl from high school who was excited about all prospects the world had to offer her.

"You're good for me John," she announced in his ear.

He nodded. "You're good for me."

John had always made her feel sexy and smart and funny.

The group dwindled as the evening hours lengthened. There were babysitters to relieve, boyfriends to get home to and adult problems on the horizon for the following morning.

When the bar closed, only John and Cassie remained. He'd promised her friends he would get her home safe.

Cassie pulled out her keys and held them up. "I can't drive."

"Neither can I." John put the keys back in her purse. "But I can Uber." He pulled out his phone.

"How about food? Like old times. Denny's? Oh, Taco Bell," she said, giddy with nostalgia.

"Ugh, they both give me heartburn now." John chuckled.

Cassie sighed. "Me too."

"Donuts?" John offered as he studied his phone and ordered a car.

"Yes! Yum Yum is right down the street."

"I'll have the car pick us up there."

John held her hand as they drunkenly wound their way down the street to the donut shop. They ordered a half a dozen each and stood outside waiting for the car. Cassie talked with her mouth full, asking John about his life. He was working as a graphic artist for some game that he claimed was big. Cassie, having never been a gamer, took him at his word.

They sat close on the car ride home as if the good memories of their developmental years spent together could be communicated through touch.

"I'm so drunk," Cassie said happily. "God, I haven't felt this good in such a long time."

"You're gonna be sick tomorrow," John warned.

"Jess is living with me; she can take care of me." Cassie snorted at the statement.

"Oh, how is little Jess?"

"Not great, but I can't talk about it." Cassie held a finger up to her lips. "It's a secret. Shhhh."

John nodded. "Shhhh."

The driver pulled up in front of Cassie's apartment building. John leaned forward to ask him, "Can you wait five minutes, man?"

The driver agreed and John got out with Cassie. She tripped getting out of the car, John caught her around the waist and she held up her right hand, which still had the bag of donuts clasped tightly. "Safe!"

They laughed as if that was the funniest thing that had ever happened. John twirled her so she was upright and hugged her. "Okay sexy, can you make it from here?" he asked in her ear.

"I'm a big girl. I've got this," she whispered back.

He nipped her ear again and Cassie sighed. "We would have been great together."

Suddenly the world around her spun; she'd been ripped out of John's arms and propelled backwards. It took a good long second for her eyes to catch up to her brain before she realized that the troublemaker responsible for the new position was Stills. He stood between her and John.

"Agent Stills," Cassie drawled drunkenly.

He paid no attention to Cassie but leveled a look at John and evenly said, "You need to go."

Cassie gave a tsk and pushed Stills out of the way, moving back to stand next to John, who was staring wide-eyed at the threatening man in front of him.

"You go Benji. This is my friend. Leave him alone."

"Go," Stills said in a deadly tone.

John glanced at Cassie. "You know this guy?"

She gave a scoffing laugh. "I know this guy."

"You safe with him?"

"He's part of the shhhh." She held her finger up to her lips.

John caught her hand and pressed a kiss on her knuckles. "When you sober up, give me a call." He glanced at Stills again. "Apparently, we've got some more catching up to do."

Cassie smiled and rather liked how Stills' eyes darkened and his frown deepened.

"I promise." She kissed him on the cheek. John turned his full attention to Stills and after a moment, gave a slight bow at the waist before getting back in the car.

Cassie put her hands on her hips and stared daggers at Stills. "You owe him an apology."

"What the hell Cassandra?" He didn't raise his voice, but his tone was formidable.

She blinked wildly and took a step back before realizing she wasn't holding her ground; so she changed tactics and stepped toward him in an attempt to be almost nose to nose. She poked him in the chest with the hand that was holding the crumpled bag of donuts. "You don't talk to me for two weeks. Not a word. I don't even have your number; you know that? If you've been stalking me, then you have my number, but you don't call or text. So don't...what the hell...me." She poked again.

"I've been busy. Working." He enunciated the word.

"So have I." She matched his tone and gave another poke at his chest. She nodded, so happy with how she was holding her own. She turned and headed toward her front door, ready to go home.

Stills caught up to her and turned her around. "So you go out and meet up with another guy? Just because I don't call?"

"Maybe." She shrugged him off and poked him again. "All there is between us is an attraction that has no definition, no labels, no...action..." She frowned, she was not happy about the current sobriety that was setting in. "We're not dating Agent Stills. We aren't even friends really. So...so what if I go have a good night out with friends?" She tried to walk away from him, but turned and made an awkward circle back, poking his chest once more as she glared up at him. "You asked me out on a date and then you never did anything about it."

"I don't like him." Stills pointed angrily in the direction the car had pulled away.

"So?" She walked around him and began to fumble for the keys to the door of her apartment complex.

Stills stopped her again by stepping in front of her. "How good of a friend is he?" he mocked.

"Don't you know who I'm sleeping with? Or are you asking if I slept with John tonight?"

He looked like she'd slapped him, and she liked that power. He was ruining her buzz that she had needed to try and forget how much he had hurt her feelings in the first place. "It's none of your goddamned business. And secondly, this is the twenty-first century pal and I'm a woman with needs..."

She pulled away and tried to move around him but he was in front of her again. "I don't like it," Stills seethed.

"You don't have to like it. You're the agent assigned to watch my sister. That's all there is between us." She tried to pull away from him but overcorrected, and in her drunken state, she began to fall toward the ground.

Stills caught her just in time, pulling her so her back was pressed against his chest.

"Let go," she fumed.

He tightened his grip as she tried to squirm away while again demanding, "Let me go, Agent Stills."

"I don't want to." He whispered the admission in her ear.

Cassie twisted in his arms until she could look up through her foggy drunken state and study his eyes in the light of the streetlamp.

"Why didn't you call?" she asked and was angry that the question got caught in her throat.

"I can't stop thinking about you," he said gruffly, "and it's not good for my job. I thought if we took some time apart..."

"You should have told me." She tried to dislodge herself, but it didn't work. "I live in the apartment you're watching, how is that time apart?" She pushed against him and he still wouldn't let her go.

"I don't know what this is between us, but I can't find you with another man kissing your neck and..." He couldn't finish.

"He always kisses my neck, it tickles," Cassie said and the steely darkness returned to his eyes.

"Did you sleep with him?" The way he asked the question was sterile and by the book. Cassie thought it was probably an agency way to ask such questions.

"I haven't slept with anyone since I met you," she said, then wondered if she should have given him that much ammunition to use against her.

"Were you going to sleep with him tonight? If I hadn't shown up..."

"Probably not."

"You either were or you weren't." He was pushing for an answer.

"I'm not his type," Cassie muttered.

Stills frowned and she rolled her eyes. "Benji, he's gay. He's been gay since the day we met freshman year of high school. He's a flirt and he makes me feel good every time I see him. And tonight, I needed to have fun and feel sexy."

"He's gay?"

"Is that a problem?" Cassie asked defensively.

Stills shook his head. "Of course not." He processed the information a moment longer and said, "I'm sorry."

"You need to apologize to John," she demanded with a slight pout.

"I will."

"And you need to apologize to me."

He leveled his gaze before he said, "I'm sorry."

"You don't get to make decisions about *our* attraction on your own," she said and he nodded his head.

"Okay."

"You should probably ask me out. On a real date."

"I will." He smiled.

She continued her list of things she'd been wanting from him during his absence. "And apologize for making me so miserable these last two weeks." She was glad for the liquid courage rolling through her veins at the moment. "And I'm tired of you keeping yourself in check all the time when you're around me. You said you're attracted to me, so we should be stealing every moment we can get and be making out."

"Oh really?"

"I want to make out like a teenager and sit on your lap and...and...do dirty things."

"Oh, hell yeah." He nodded his head and lowered his head slightly toward hers.

"And one more thing."

"What can I do for you, Dodd?"

"I'm gonna be sick." He did release her then.

She held the donuts toward him behind her back as she bent over the side of the steps to her left and vomited into the flower bed.

Stills took the bag and tossed it onto the steps, then pulled her hair back with one hand while rubbing her back with the other.

"I don't like getting this drunk," she miserably told the flower bed.

"Then why did you?" Stills asked.

She dry-heaved and then stared at the tears that fell onto the ground. "Because I missed you."

She thought she heard him chuckling behind her, but with a stomach empty, a head swirling, and exhaustion winning over, her body gave into a tired blackout.

Chapter Fifteen

"N o." Cassie's voice croaked as she covered her face with a pillow to defend against the jackhammering coming from the kitchen.

"Time to get up sleepyhead, it's noon on a Saturday. I already answered the text from your friend seeing if you were going to the pickup game today. I explained your current situation and she understood," Jess cheerfully informed her sister from the foot of the sofa.

Cassie carefully sat up. With eyes closed she levered herself up onto her elbow. When that worked and didn't feel too bad, she pushed herself back against the sofa in a half-seated position. She stayed there and took several deep gulps of air before pushing herself into a full upright seat, moaning as she finished the maneuver.

Jess brought a glass of water and handed over two migraine pills. "You got up to no good last night," she simply stated.

"How did I get here?"

"Benji."

Another moan.

"He said he would check up on us later today."

Us.

Cassie took a sip of the water, her mouth a ghastly, dry desert. She began to cough and held her head with her free hand as she slowed the coughing. She took the pills and nodded as she took another deep drink of water.

"I stopped drinking like that when I was twenty-five," she bemoaned.

"There's coffee on and I'll make you some toast."

Cassie nodded. She looked down at the skirt that was pushed up around her waist and her shirt that was twisted. She touched her hair that was standing on end.

Jess smiled. "Yes, you look *that* bad."

Cassie gently went into a crouch position, then stood and shuffled to her room to change clothes. She somehow managed to wash her face and brush her teeth and hair; tasks that were all accompanied by groans of pain.

She staggered back to the dining room table, turning off the overhead light before she gingerly lowered herself into a chair. Surprised her head stayed screwed on, her raspy voice whispered to her sister, "I ache all over."

"So it was a drunken "Dancing Queen" sort of night?" Jess joked as she placed a cup of coffee in front of her; Cassie lowered her head so she could meet the cup half way.

Jessica sat down. "Who brought you home?"

"Ran into John Strumm, he got an Uber," she muttered.

"Oh, I love John. How is he?"

"Good, we didn't talk, just danced. How was your night?"

"Action movie night at Sara's. No one wants me watching anything romantic. They're still walking on eggshells, but it was fun. Felt good to do something so normal."

Cassie grumbled and took another sip.

Jess brought the toast over and put it in front of Cassie. "No butter. Just in case."

"My car's at the club," she said.

"We'll go get it later." Jess sat down across from Cassie and beamed.

"What?"

"It's kinda nice being the one who isn't messed up or needs looking after for once."

Cassie picked up a piece of toast and held it in salute toward Jess before taking a bite. With a full mouth she promised her aching head, "Never again."

"I do appreciate it. How you look out for me. You know that, right?"

"It's my job," Cassie said before sipping more coffee.

"No, it isn't," Jess retorted, angered at the sentiment.

Cassie raised her heavy eyes and looked at her sister. "I don't *have* to. But I'm your sister. How old we are doesn't matter. Who's older or younger doesn't matter. I will always be your sister, and that means, no matter what, I'll always be willing and ready to kick the ass of the situation or bully who is making your life hard." She swallowed her tears, blamed their appearance on her current state and added, "And I expect you to do the same for me."

"I would," Jess said softly.

Cassie sat up straight and tested her vertebrae, making sure they were willing to stack atop each other and hold her head up. "Oh," she closed her eyes, "I think I threw up in front of Benji."

"I suppose it was a good thing they were watching the apartment then, huh?" Jess said offhandedly, but it was enough of a spur to kick the memories of Cassie's conversation with Benji out from the fog of her brain and into the sunlight of the morning.

Cassie groaned again and slowly lowered her head to the table.

"He's probably seen plenty of people throw up. I'm sure he didn't mind."

There was a knock at the door.

Right on time.

Cassie kept her head on the table but turned to look at the door, but instead pointed to Jess. "You didn't jump."

Jess began looking around her, as if she was testing her body, then smiled and repeated the claim, "I didn't jump."

Cassie gave a thumbs up from where she was resting her head. Jess stood and twirled toward the door, opening it to find Stills.

"Good afternoon, Benji." The overstated good afternoon was for Cassie's sake.

He held up a bag with the lettering from La Petite Café and a six pack of Gatorade. "I come bearing gifts."

Jess teasingly mocked her sister's hangover, "Oh look Cassie, you were so drunk, he knew you'd need to replace your electrolytes."

Cassie moaned again and pushed her head back onto the top of her bones.

"Coffee, Benji?" Jess asked.

"Please," he accepted and crossed the room to the table as Jess made her way to the kitchen.

He was wearing what Cassie considered his weekend attire: jeans, t-shirt, Adidas and a smile. When he reached Cassie, he glanced toward Jess to make sure her back was to them as she poured the coffee. His eyes sparkled as he placed the drinks and bag on the table in front of Cassie and then brushed a quick kiss across her cheek. "Morning, Dodd," he whispered.

She grunted but felt the lingering brush of his lips against her skin. This time he sat next to her, across from Jessica. A triangle. She fumbled to get a Gatorade out of its packaging. Stills took it from her and completed the process.

Cassie held up her hands. "Morning hands," she explained, realizing that all of her limbs were feeling the effects of the previous evening.

As he opened her drink she looked in the bag, it had her almond croissant and a few other pastries.

"Thanks." She couldn't quite bring herself to look him in the eye. Not just yet.

He slid her Gatorade over toward her as Jess returned with the coffee. "Cream or sugar?" she asked.

"Black," Cassie answered for him. She was busy taking a drink, so she missed the interested eyebrow raise Jess gave her as she handed the cup over to Stills.

"Do you want more, Cass?"

She nodded and Jess went back to the kitchen.

"How ya feeling?" Stills shifted so that his knee would touch Cassie's. She pressed her knee back against his, grateful for it.

"Embarrassed," she admitted to her Gatorade.

"Me too." His admission brought her full attention to his face.

"Here you go." Jessica sat down and pulled the bag of pastries toward her. "You've tried Cassie's pastries, I keep telling her they are just as good as this place. We all keep telling her she should open her own pastry shop." Jess pulled out a chocolate filled croissant. "We're lucky you were on duty last night, Benji. Otherwise it sounds like Cassie would have been sleeping on the front step."

"Jess." Cassie frowned and took another sip of the Gatorade. It was helping, and along with the toast, coffee, water and migraine pills, the initial vice that had been squeezing her head when she first woke was loosening.

"No problem at all," he said and then sat back, "I actually am here this morning with some news. Tomorrow is our last day on duty." He let the announcement settle around them. Cassie glanced at Jessica to see how she was doing with the news, but she saw the same emotions fly across her sister's face as she was feeling them - elation and fear.

He continued his explanation, "The situation has been assessed and due to certain variables, we are assured you are safe and will continue to be safe."

"Certain variables?" Jess asked. "Do we get to know what those are?"

He shrugged. "Sorry."

"So, it's over? Did they catch Thomas?" Cassie asked.

"Unfortunately," Stills began, but Jess finished for him, "It's classified."

"Jessica, you are safe." He said the phrase slowly with every ounce of reassurance she would need.

Cassie began to ask about Parker, "What about—" but Jessica stopped her, "No, it's over. That is all that's important."

No one said a word, it was as if Cassie and Stills had silently agreed to wait for Jessica to process the information and comment first.

Finally, Jessica took a deep breath and smiled. "We get to move on with our lives." She nodded, her smile growing. "I have a new job. You're back to work. In no time at all, I'll move into my own apartment again and...this is good." Jessica nodded her head and looked to Stills for confirmation. "This is good."

"Very," he agreed.

Cassie reached across the table and took her sister's hand. "This is awesome news, Jess."

"We should celebrate," Jess said.

Cassie groaned. "Only if celebrating means soft voices, low lights and no movement?"

Jess laughed. "How do you celebrate the end of something like this?"

"However you want," Cassie said.

"Benji, are you sure?" Jess asked again and he shifted forward in his seat, narrowed his gaze and said, "Completely and utterly."

Jess nodded her head. "It's going to take some time to get used to everything being normal."

"Baby steps," Cassie offered, "little things every day will build up over time." She dared a sideways glance at Stills as he raised an eyebrow at her advice.

Jess grunted in reply. She took a deep breath and let it rush out of her, as if she hadn't been able to breathe that way in a long time. It felt so good she did it again and this time the tears began. She stood up and stared down at the table. Cassie reached out for her hand and Jess smiled. "I just need a second, okay?"

Cassie nodded. "Take your time."

"Just...I'll be right back," Jess said and retreated to her bedroom.

Cassie watched her and bit her lip; it was Stills now, taking her hand, that brought her back into the moment. "She'll be okay," he reassured.

Cassie didn't feel completely convinced. "Is it true? It's over, she's really safe now? Did they catch Thomas?"

"Cassandra..."

"I know, classified." She licked her lips. "What will you do? Do you have to go somewhere else?"

He smiled. "I have some desk work to finish up over the next few weeks, but I've put in for a transfer."

Cassie's stomach churned at the idea; of course, it could also be the residue of the previous evening. But what the hell did that mean? Transfer.

Stills amended his explanation, "I'm looking into a more permanent desk job. Here. In the Los Angeles area."

"What?" Now it was butterflies that erupted in her stomach and lightened her head. "Jesus," she pressed a hand against her side, "my body is in no shape for all these bits of news today. It's reacting to everything. Very dramatically."

"Good." He flashed a satisfied grin. "Where's your cell phone?"

Cassie pointed to the coffee table and watched him retrieve it.

He was going to stay in the LA area. Did she dare assume it was for her? She felt another twist and twirl of her sensitive stomach.

He handed the phone to Cassie. "I think it's time we had each other's numbers."

She opened her contacts and added his number under 'Agent Stills', then sent him a text so he'd have her number.

He grinned as the notification sounded and he took out his phone and began typing.

She raised an eyebrow at the continued typing. Her stomach bounced at the prospect and did another somersault when the notification sounded on her phone. She opened the message:

Agent Stills: I missed you too. I bought a lot of cherry pastries the last two weeks, just trying to relive how it felt to be with you and how it tasted to kiss you. Nothing worked. Dinner, next Friday?

"Next Friday?" she asked.

He frowned. "Work is going to be busy, a lot of debriefings. It's the soonest I know I'll be able to get away," he said apologetically.

She smiled and began typing; Stills tried to look over at her screen but she pulled it away. Her finger hovered over the send button, what was she getting herself into?

Cassie: Only if the evening can finally end with more than one kiss and you can promise me that I'll wake up the next morning with chapped lips and butterflies all day.

Stills read the text and Cassie watched the smile that spread across those sexy lips, the sparkle she knew as trouble in his eye. His strong jawline clenched as he replied:

Agent Stills: I want you on my lap, my hands in your hair, your lips on mine, and the heat building between us so much our bodies burn.

"Jesus," Cassie whispered.

"What?" Jess asked.

Cassie was overly grateful she was hung-over in that moment, because her reaction to that text was wreaking havoc with her whole nervous system. A blush was creeping over her body, her eyes were wide with the audacity and need in the text, and her mouth had gone dry.

"You okay?" Jess frowned at Cassie.

"Just overheated," she said and was glad when Stills began coughing to cover up a laugh.

"I should be going," he stood up, "if you need anything Jessica, just call."

"Call?" Cassie asked with a frown.

"I have Benji's number in case of an emergency," Jess explained as if Cassie was out of her mind.

A pang of jealousy erupted but was doused by Stills' explanation. "My work phone. It's monitored by the agency, just in case there is an emergency that I can't reply to."

Cassie raised an eyebrow. "Good thing someone like our mother never got that number. Can you imagine the embarrassing messages she might have sent?" Of course, by her mother, she actually meant herself.

"Have a good day, ladies."

Jessica walked him to the door while Cassie sat where she was glued, but she watched Stills cross the room. When Jess pulled the door open, he took the opportunity to wink at Cassie and mouthed, '*I can't wait.*'

Cassie didn't have time to reply.

She glanced back at the message.

I want you on my lap, my hands in your hair, your lips on mine, and the heat building between us so much our bodies burn.

Oh, God.

"Let's go get your car, we need to get groceries and I feel like I want to go tell Mom and Dad it's all over in person," Jess said.

Cassie closed the screen on her phone. "I'm too hung-over to see them today. Can't we get my car first, and then you do the rest by yourself?"

"Please?" Jess asked.

Cassie looked down at her clothes, she had a sports bra on and yoga pants. "As long as I don't have to change and we do everything quickly."

"Deal."

Cassie grabbed another Gatorade and stood up. "I just need my purse and flip-flops."

In the hallway that led to the elevator, Jess said, "So it's finally over."

Even in the throes of a hangover, Cassie felt the stress slipping off her own shoulders.

Chapter Sixteen

As Jess started her car, Cassie fumbled through her purse for her sunglasses; the late afternoon sun was showing off and she wasn't in the mood. Where was the hazy sunshine when you needed it?

Sunglasses in place, she tried to lean the seat back, but her head and stomach retaliated. "Nope." She righted her position. Her body was heavy and achy. Her stomach muscles hurt along with her legs and hips. Some of that was the dancing, some of it was being sick.

"I should have gone and washed out the flower bed," she muttered.

"What?" Jessica asked.

"I threw up in the flower bed outside the apartments, like a college freshman." The least she could do, as a somewhat responsible adult, was take a bucket of water to the area.

"I'm sure it will still be there when we get back."

Cassie rolled her shoulders, and gingerly tilted her head from side to side then sat back. As thick as her bones felt, and as fuzzy as her head was, her spirit felt light. She felt content, that was for sure.

The previous evening had done what she'd needed it to do, released some serious tension. She needed to scream, sweat, drink and let go of repressed emotions. And she needed to see Stills jealous. And hear him apologize.

A thrill ran through her body, but she wasn't sure if it was the loss of electrolytes or that damn text message that caused it.

She opened her phone and read it again, this time she felt the echo of the message between her legs. She gave a chuckle and closed the phone.

"What?"

"Just a smartass remark about being hung-over from one of the girls I play soccer with."

"About how you should know better?"

"Something like that." Cassie stared out the window and touched a finger to her lips.

"It'll be nice to get back to normal," Jess said.

Cassie glanced at her sister and watched her for a few moments, was there a 'normal' for Jess? She might have had the chance to close the book on Thomas, but there was another chapter that was still wide open. "What about Parker?"

Cassie caught the way Jess tightened her grip on the steering wheel and clenched her jaw before she asked, "What about Parker?"

"I think—"

"He hasn't tried to contact me. The paperwork for the divorce went through before I even left for Italy. There's nothing there."

"Okay," Cassie held up a hand, she would drop the topic, "okay."

Jess blew out a frustrated breath, "There never was anything there. It was just a drunken mistake and then an angry mistake...Parker Salvatore was a mistake."

"I'll take your word for it."

"Yeah, you will. Because he's an asshole," she shot.

Cassie bit her lip, she probably should just leave the conversation, but her need to lighten the mood and make things better forced the next comment out; "You really do have a type, kid."

Jessica's eyes widened and she shot daggers at her sister. "I don't have a type. And don't call me kid." Then they both melted into laughter

"No, there were plenty of guys between the first asshole and the second one," Cassie soothed.

"It wasn't that many."

"Jess," Cassie shrugged, "I'm trying to help. I didn't mean it for real, you know that."

"Do you think I should go jump in bed with someone?" she asked.

"Like your friends suggested?" Cassie shook her head. "No. Not yet."

"Why not?"

"Jesus, Jess. I don't know...I'm not your keeper, if you want to go sleep around, go sleep around!"

"I didn't say you were my keeper," Jess mocked, "but you sure have been enjoying the position lately."

"I haven't been your keeper, I've been your protector." Cassie pressed her fingers to her temple. "Jess, I can't fight right now. My head can't take it. We'll have to do it later."

"Fine," Jess hissed.

"Fine." Cassie matched her tone.

They marinated in their own misunderstood anger for a few moments, heightening the tension in the car. But as Jess raced the other Southern Californian drivers from red light to red light, the strain slipped out of the cracked windows. After several blocks, Cassie said, "A lot's happened since you called me all hopped up on Italian painkillers."

"I was out of my mind," Jess admitted.

"You were amazing."

Jess digested the compliment before commenting, "I never meant to scare you that much."

Cassie thought about that night. "Do you know, after I gave you Stacie's number, I waited twenty minutes then called her myself. I talked to Benji for the first time that day."

"What? Why didn't you tell me?"

"What was there to tell? Besides, when you finally got home, you had a lot on your plate, so to speak."

"But you talked to Benji? How? What did he say?"

"After you hung up, I waited twenty minutes. It was agony, watching the minutes ticking by. Then I called the number I gave you and Stacie's husband answered. I explained I was your sister and that you'd just called me. He'd just had the same weird conversation with you that I did, so he was more than happy to give me Parker's number."

"Amedeo gave you the number?"

Cassie grinned as she raised an eyebrow. "I was a bit hysterical. And possibly demanding action, and probably cussing. A lot."

"So you called Parker."

"Yes...no - he didn't answer."

"Gyeser Prime, how may I direct your call?"

"Parker Salvatore." Cassie spat the name as she paced through her apartment. Her sister's voice was still fresh in her head, 'I'm on drugs', 'Parker's my husband'.

She'd called Stacie, and her husband, Amedeo, had answered. Cassie explained who she was, and he'd told her what Jessica had told him, that she needed Parker's number and she'd sounded weird. Cassie didn't have too much time to explain either as she was losing her grip on her vocabulary and her senses; she didn't know how much longer she could hold onto the minor bits of sanity she had left.

Amedeo gave Cassie the number he had 'in case of emergencies' and told her that Parker's last name was Salvatore.

"Mr. Salvatore's office," a woman answered.

"Yes, my sister just called you, looking for Mr. Salvatore..." Cassie hissed the name, "and I need to talk to him now too."

"I'm sorry ma'am, Mr. Salvatore is away on a business trip, I could schedule you a meeting for two weeks from today."

"My sister just called and said she's in Rome and her fiancé killed someone and the CIA is involved and she's on drugs and that Mr. Salvatore was her husband." Cassie was trying not to yell, but it was really difficult, so she settled on overenunciating, "Now. I don't know what's going on or why she'd call this number, but it means that even in her altered state, she thought the person on the other end would help her. So I need *you* to do the same thing for *me*." So much for holding it together. She pulled the phone away and yelled the last part at the black screen, "I have a right to know what the fuck is going on with my sister!"

She watched her sanity slip, unobstructed through her fingertips, to be promptly replaced with fear.

After a long pause, followed by an inconvenienced sigh, the woman on the other end of the phone tersely said, "Please hold."

Static classical music began to play and Cassie rolled her eyes. "You better hurry up," she told the music. "I am freaking out here."

It took four minutes.

"Hello, this is Benjamin Stills, I understand you have some information regarding Jessica Dodd?"

"Damn right I have some information, she's my goddamned sister and she just called me and told me she's in Rome and she has broken ribs and a broken arm and that her fucking fiancé killed someone and the CIA are involved and she's married to some guy named Parker Salvatore and she's on drugs. If that isn't enough information for you, I can tell you where she was born, went to school, the name of our first dog, her social security number and our mother's maiden name." Her voice rose as she made the list. She took a shaky breath and declared, "I am a mess here, man. I need someone to help me."

"I understand ma'am."

"Oh, fuck, no. Don't you dare." That lit her up. "You do *not* understand, and I do not appreciate being *handled*. And my name is Cassie, not ma'am. And I have every right to be upset, and I have every right to know what's going on."

"Unfortunately, the information you are asking about is classified..."

"No!" She took a deep breath. "Benji? Is that what you said your name was?"

"Benjamin," he corrected.

"Benji, are you CIA? What's going on?"

Another long pause made Cassie groan. "Do they teach the long pause in CIA school or something?"

"Ma'am..." he started.

"Cassie." She bit the correction.

"Miss Dodd, your sister *is* in Rome. Agent Salvatore is en route to her as we speak."

"Holy shit." Cassie wasn't sure she really wanted all of that verified. "Holy...shit."

"Miss Dodd, please calm down."

"This *is* calm, Benji. What...what do I do? What can I do? Are you sure she's okay? She said her ribs were broken. She sounded so weird." A sob threatened but Cassie swallowed it.

"Miss Dodd, your sister is safe. So the first thing I need you to do is take a deep breath."

She took a deep breath and let the air rush out of her lungs. "I don't like being handled, Benji."

"I understand, take another deep breath for me."

She did as instructed and when he heard her exhale, he said, "Unfortunately, your sister was caught in the middle of an ongoing operation. She was kept under close surveillance until we could safely get her home."

"Well it sounds like someone failed at their job if she's calling me to get in touch with *you*, don't you think?" The breathing stopped helping.

"All I can tell you is that she is safe now. I promise you."

"I don't know what that means," Cassie said.

"Breathe."

"Don't tell me what to do," she demanded even as she was doing what he told her; three more deep breaths - in...and out...

"You're okay. We are doing our job. Jessica is safe," he reassured her.

"Benjamin Stills?" Cassie repeated his name.

"Yes, ma'am."

"You get my sister home in one piece," she demanded, "or I will find you and rip off your fucking head."

"I promise. She'll be home soon."

"What else can you tell me? I don't know how I'm going to do anything while I worry about her."

"Miss Dodd, I need you to trust me."

"I don't know you!" The hysteria hadn't gone far.

"I realize that, and I realize I'm asking a lot from you. You are going to worry, and that is completely understandable. How about this, as soon as we can, we will allow your sister to call you."

"Okay...okay." That was something. She could try to work with that sort of promise.

"I need you to do something for me. I am going to have to ask you not to disclose any of the information your sister has told you, or the information I've verified, to anyone else. For your safety and your family's safety."

Cassie sat down heavily on the sofa, she could manage being in trouble, but her sister and her parents? "Are *we* in danger?"

"The intel we have suggests you and your family are in no danger whatsoever."

"But Jess is."

"No, Agent Salvatore is expected to arrive at her locale any moment now."

"Can you call me and tell me when he's gotten her and she's safe?"

"She's already been taken to a secure location."

That was something wasn't it? Cassie took another deep breath. Nope. "That's not enough."

"Miss Dodd, I will call you personally as soon as I know for sure that Agent Salvatore has seen your sister and verified she is secure."

"She's not an item, Benji, she's a human," Cassie said, but the statement caught in her throat and turned to a sob she couldn't swallow this time.

"I realize that. I apologize. Miss Dodd, what do you normally do when you're stressed out?"

"What?" She shook her head at the strange turn in the conversation.

"When you're overwhelmed and stressed out, what do you do?" he repeated the question.

"I bake. Or I run."

"Good. Then what I want you to do is take your phone and go for a run, as fast as you can," he said.

"What?" This idiot was out of his damn mind.

"Right now. Go for a run. Running will reduce your body's stress hormones, I'd be willing to bet your adrenaline is running on overtime right now. If you run as quickly as you can, the endorphins will help you calm down."

"I don't need a PE Lesson Benji, I've played soccer my whole life. I know all about this crap."

"What position?"

"What?" What was happening?

"What position do you play?"

"Left full." She frowned. "Why are you asking me this? Shouldn't you be dealing with Jess and all this shit?"

"Run, Miss Dodd," he instructed.

"Run," she repeated.

"As fast as you can."

"And you'll call me back?"

"Take your phone, and I will call you as soon as I can, Miss Dodd."

"Okay, okay. And Jessica's been taken to a safe place and she's fine, right?" In her current, frazzled state, Cassie needed to repeat the information to make sense of it.

"Yes, I am certain that she is safe and in no danger."

"Are you going to get in trouble?" Cassie asked, now that she had a plan and something to do and someone who was going to keep her informed.

"For what?"

"For giving me information that you shouldn't have?"

"I haven't given you any information that would jeopardize our operation," he said.

"Oh."

Another long pause. Cassie looked around her apartment.

"Miss Dodd, are you alright?" the agent asked.

"I'm a fighter Benji, I can deal with this." She made the comment more for herself.

He gave a slight chuckle then. "If you are anything like your sister, then you most definitely can manage this and anything else that comes your way."

"Is that code for stubborn?"

"Yes ma'am."

Cassie was caught off-guard by an escaped laugh. It must be fear-induced. She shook her head and admitted, "Jessica *is* stubborn. We're *all* stubborn women in my family."

"That's good," he said. "I promise Miss Dodd, I will call you as soon as we have confirmation. Now, do what you promised me. Go run. As fast as you can."

"Agent Benjamin Stills." Saying his full name lit Cassie up from the inside and she shivered from the effect.

"You okay?" Jessica asked as she plugged her phone into the charger while waiting for the light to turn green.

Cassie cleared her throat. "It's just leftover residue from last night."

"So did Benji tell you anything?"

"It was weird. He was so calm. The more I yelled, the more patient he got," Cassie said.

"Isn't it annoying?" Jessica added. "But he's so...nice. He's been nice throughout this whole ordeal." She cleared her throat. "So you yelled and he got patient and told you to run."

Cassie laughed. "Then he promised he would personally see to your safe return home."

Jess shook her head in wonder. "And he did."

"And he did."

"How were you after that?"

Cassie grinned. "I might have called the CIA number every day for more information. A very nice woman who had the same temperament as me gave me daily updates. They were lame. 'Your sister is safe. She's in a safe location. Her wounds are not life threatening. As soon as she is cleared, she will call you.'" Cassie gave the monotone impersonation. "But you know, it helped."

"You didn't tell anyone?" Jessica asked.

"Who was I going to tell? Mom and Dad? The CIA isn't equipped for that sort of onslaught. And have you ever asked yourself why you got on that plane and chased Thomas down in the first place? You get it from our mother." Cassie explained, "It was the same reason I got on the phone and started demanding answers - *every* day."

Jessica groaned, "Oh, God."

"Yup," Cassie rubbed her head, "Barbara Dodd helped make us the amazing women we are today."

"Jesus, Cass, we can't ever tell her."

"Of course not. Who knows what she'd do if we acknowledged that we are strong *because* of her, not in spite of her."

Cassie's phone beeped and a ripple of excitement rolled through her. She didn't even need to look, she knew who the text was from.

Still, when she opened her messages and saw it was from 'Agent Stills', another visceral reaction played with her nervous system. She used the name as a joke, but it was obviously backfiring.

Agent Stills: Glad I got to see you today, Dodd.

The message was so simple and so needed.

"Who's that?" Jess asked.

Cassie wasn't ready to confess that she and Stills had more going on than anyone knew. She wanted him to herself for a while. She wanted to explore the attraction with just the two of them, no onlookers, no opinions.

"More ribbing," she lied.

Chapter Seventeen

T he mornings began with texting.

Agent Stills: Good morning, Dodd.

Cassie: Good morning, Benji.

Agent Stills: Agent Stills.

Cassie: Is it still 'Agent Stills' if you aren't protecting us anymore?

Agent Stills: Benjamin?

Cassie: What are you up to today?

Agent Stills: Classified.

Cassie: Of course it is.

Agent Stills: How about this, the things I'm thinking about you aren't classified.

Cassie rolled over onto her back and blew out a breath, reading his text again until it was ingrained in her senses.

Agent Stills: What do you have today?

Cassie: Finishing up a large research project for a source that is classified. But it's difficult to work on.

Agent Stills: What makes it difficult?

Cassie: I can't stop thinking of you.

Agent Stills: Good.

Cassie: You're getting in the way of my job.

Agent Stills: It's only fair. You got in the way of my job for weeks.

Cassie: Good.

Agent Stills: I miss your pastries.

Cassie: That probably shouldn't sound as dirty as it does.

Agent Stills: I can make it sound dirtier.

Cassie: I have to work, you've already done enough.

Agent Stills: I miss you. How's that?
Cassie: I miss knowing you were just outside.
Agent Stills: Is everything okay?
Cassie: Yes. I just kinda miss you too. That's all.

Cassie's alarm went off, she dismissed the button on her phone and wondered if she was ever going to sleep again. She was living in a blissful twilight reality, where she couldn't really concentrate on anything except a building excitement of the coming date night.

The current project she was trying to finish was difficult to concentrate on because most of the time, while pretending to work, she caught herself staring off into space as she relived the handful of kisses she and Stills shared; the way his hand felt holding hers; the way her body fit tucked against his; how his chest felt when she rested her cheek against it...of course, this new texting situation was exciting as hell and she loved how all of the new relationship exhilaration made her feel alive.

The physical reaction she had to Stills was as frightening as it was electrifying. It was like riding a roller coaster, wrapped in bubble wrap, while Enya played.

She laughed at the analogy and thought, when she finally decided to come clean and tell Jess she had a big ol' crush on Benji, she'd share that one.

But not yet.

Cassie was going to get time alone with this man first. Then she was going to date the crap out of him. Then he was going to make good on all his enticing promises, especially that one about making love to her under the stars.

Then she would think about telling her sister she liked someone.

Stills texted in the mornings and called her before he went to bed. She lay awake at night waiting for the calls to come in. And he always called, even if it was one in the morning on a school night.

And Cassie's body would contract and pump adrenaline to all her limbs when she saw his number light up the phone. She'd answer and hold her breath, waiting for his tired whisper of, 'hey, Dodd,' which both soothed and thrilled her to the very marrow of her bones.

She stretched her body from the tips of her fingers to the bottom of her toes, breaking up the imbedded emotions Stills caused by just texting.

Cassie: My alarm just went off. I need to get ready.

Agent Stills: Okay. Two more days.

Cassie: Can't wait to see you.

Agent Stills: Me either. Have a good day, Dodd.

Cassie: You too, Benji.

Chapter Eighteen

"Cassie Kay!" John declared as he met Cassie walking out of her office building. They were meeting for lunch because it had been good to see him the other night and because she needed a confidant. She was feeling compelled to gush about a man and since John had come face to face with Stills and he *did* tell her to call him...it only seemed right.

"How are you?" she asked as he pulled her into his arms for a hug, picked her up and twirled her around. She slapped at his arms. "I'm too old for that."

"Nah. Never." He put her down and gestured toward the Mexican restaurant across the street they'd previously decided on.

He linked his arm in hers and leaned his head toward her. "Is there a chance that some tall drink of water will come out of nowhere and assault me, just for being this close to you?"

"I hope so."

John laughed. "Oh, baby girl, me too."

Seats taken, orders given and drinks delivered, John leaned across the table, his rapt attention on Cassie. "Tell me everything."

She ran a hand through her hair. "I don't even know where to begin."

"Name?"

"Benjamin Stills. Benji."

"Age?"

"Thirty-eight."

"How did you meet?"

Cassie expected the question, but she was blindsided by the weight of it. The truth of how she met Stills gave away his position with the CIA.

And shouldn't that be information that Cassie protected? Other than her family, she wasn't going to be able to tell anyone the real story.

So how could she tell it?

"I met him through Jess." That was a good place to start, and it was a fact, wasn't it? "He and I talked on the phone first." Another fact. "Then, a few weeks ago we finally met in person." Fact.

John wrinkled his nose. "Cassandra Dodd, you've always given a play by play so much better than that." He lowered his voice, "Not to mention the fact that the other night, you said Jess moved in with you because of a secret, and *then* at three a.m., a man you referred to as 'Agent' whipped you out of my arms and looked super jealous and super official."

A smile tugged at the corner of Cassie's mouth. "I wasn't sure how much you remembered."

"Oh honey, I remember everything about that strapping hunk of a man. Six three, muscles straining beneath a polo, a shame about the Dockers, eyes on fire for you." He ended the description and narrowed his gaze. "Now spill."

Cassie licked her lips. "Jess got herself in a little trouble, Agent Stills," she looked around and leaned closer toward John, "is with a certain three letter organization and has been keeping an eye on her. I really did meet him because of Jess. Before she moved in with me, I really did talk to him on the phone. Then, once Jess *did* move in with me, I met him in person."

"Ohh, did our little Jessie get herself involved in some sort of espionage?"

"I can't really talk about the details."

"That's fine," he waved the excuse away, "I just want all the *agent's* details."

Cassie was giddy. "Oh my God, John. He's killing me. Every damn time he touches me, electric currents hum all the way up my arms." She held out her arms toward him as proof. "He kisses me and I cling to him because my knees won't hold me up. And I never did believe in the idea of soul mates, or that we were all separated at some point and have been wandering around trying to find our other half. But I feel like I've known him my whole life..."

John shivered. "Yes. *This* is what I wanted to hear. He's strong too, the way he pulled me away from you, oh."

"He's not condescending, and he's manly, and he tastes like fresh baked...life." She didn't have all the words to explain how he made her feel. "I love flirting with him." She blushed. "Do you remember when we were younger, how we had our first crushes and we felt all giddy and wanted to explain how every moment made us feel but we didn't have the words because we were awkward, weird teens?"

He nodded encouragingly.

"That's how Benji makes me feel."

"Benji." John frowned.

"He hates it when I call him that, but it's become a nickname and I think he's coming around."

"Oh, what does he call you? Honey, sweetheart? He looks like a guy who would say," he deepened his voice, "hey baby I want you so bad."

She bit her lip before saying, "He calls me Dodd."

He gave a disappointed grunt.

"It's sexier when he says it."

"So he's a man of mystery and danger."

"No mystery. He's pretty straight forward." Even as she said it, the blatant declarations of the past few weeks caught on the edge of her throat. "It's all so adult and honest."

"Examples please."

"He tells me he wants me and can't wait to be with me. No games. No beating around the bush...just...honesty."

"You haven't done it yet?"

"We haven't even gone on a date yet," she complained.

"What are you waiting for?"

"He's been on assignment and we keep getting interrupted..." she muttered.

"But Jess is the assignment and she's living with you?" he asked skeptically, attempting to verity the details.

"Well, yes." She leaned forward in her seat. "There have been some really hot, unexpected kisses. And a lot of those turned into weird conversations."

"Honest, adult conversations?"

She nodded.

"Oh, you've got it bad." He pointed.

Cassie shook her head. "You have no idea."

"But honesty is good for you," John said, "you've never been the kind to play games. Hell, remember when we were freshman, at the end of the year dance, you sashayed right up to Matt Eidel, told him you liked him and asked him to dance."

"He was so stunned, he didn't know what else to do but agree to dance with me." She laughed, still embarrassed and emboldened by a story that was a summation of her developmental years. "But when the song was over, he high-tailed it out of there."

"Girl, that's because you are *a lot*."

She rolled her eyes. "Thanks."

"You know what I mean, this isn't news to either of us. You're a strong woman and not a lot of men know what to do when confronted by a sexy, badass strong woman."

"Well this one seems to have the staying power." The words flew out of her mouth, and she and John both stared wide-eyed at each other. "I mean…I hope he does," she corrected.

"Start from the beginning, tell me about every conversation, every kiss, every touch, everything!" John demanded just as their food was brought to them.

Cassie took a deep breath, trying to find the straight line of the story. John hung on every word, wiggled in his seat when she described the first kiss at the café, and pressed the back of his hand to his cheek when she told him about Stills finally asking her out and how many more days she had before the date - and the fact that she didn't know how she was going to make it.

By the end of the story and their meals, John sat back and eyed his long-time friend. "But…" he questioned.

"But what?"

"Cassie, there's a 'but' in this story."

She slouched down in her seat. "Is it that obvious?" He didn't answer, just gestured for her to continue. "Well, his job might not be the best."

"Ah, our secret agent man *does* live a life of danger."

"I don't know. Maybe...he says its not bad, mostly research. But he's been shot before. I don't know. I don't want a project like that in my life."

"A project?"

"Worrying about him all the time."

John sat back in his seat and after a moment he said, "If anyone is equipped to love a man who has a dangerous job, it's you.

"Who said anything about love?" John raised his right eyebrow as Cassie laughed. "I'm in lust. I'll admit to lust at the moment."

"Fine, but Cassie, I could die tomorrow in a car accident. An earthquake could take out friends and family any day. Would you agree, that you can't live any sort of a life, if you are always worried whether or not someone you love is going to die?"

"I understand what you are saying, but his job puts him in more...precarious situations than our jobs put us in," she argued.

He nodded. "Baby girl, didn't the three letter organization train this man?"

She rolled her eyes.

John waved. "Of course they did. And he's been doing this job for a while now?"

Cassie nodded and muttered, "And he was in the Marines for four years."

"So what's the problem?"

"What if something happens to him?"

"What if something happens to *you*?" John retaliated. "Cass, you gotta live your life. Death is coming for all of us. You can either keep yourself locked up behind closed doors and worry, or go out and get yourself a slice of that fine man and laugh and dance."

She pointed at John. "This is why I called you."

"I know. I am very wise."

Chapter Nineteen

"Are you sure it's okay if I go?" Cassie asked Jess for the fifth time.

While they had been on their own for a week, Cassie still had bouts of worry when it came to leaving Jess alone. Cassie knew they were unfounded worries, but leaving her sister alone in the evening hours, reignited old, irrational childhood fears - Brothers Grimm type fears of dark forests, dangerous witches and lurking threats.

The only distraction she had from her ridiculous fears was the anticipation of seeing Stills again. She couldn't wait to be in his arms. Couldn't wait for his heat to encompass her and for the crescendo of all the virtual flirting she'd gone through to materialize. Just wondering when they might get to explore more intimate facets of their need for each other, sent a thrill up and down her spine.

"I can cancel..." Cassie lied.

"No. Go. We need a break from each other," Jess assured Cassie for the fifth time. "I've got a pizza coming. I've slept without a night-light for two nights in a row and when someone knocks on the door now, I don't jump."

Cassie studied her sister, really studied her. She was looking and acting a lot more like herself again. "If you're sure."

"I'm sure. I've got my chick flick attire on." She gestured to her yoga pants and oversized 'I love LA' t-shirt.

"Very chic."

"I have three movies lined up for my pizza date. Now go have fun with Mr. Mystery Man." Jessica waved her off.

Cassie almost told Jess she was going out with Stills, but changed her mind. Not yet. She also wasn't sure how to explain the natural, seamless progression of their attraction to each other. How in one moment they were just two strangers, but with each interaction, slowly and smoothly, without any pretense or stress or shock, their attraction grew.

She rolled her eyes at her thoughts. That's how you'd describe it. So if she wanted to, she could explain it. She just didn't want to.

Tonight, she was anxiously excited for this very natural step of seeing where dating would take them.

"Okay, have a good night," Cassie said. She stopped at the mirror by the front door; leaned close to make sure her mascara hadn't clumped or left gritty residue and then ran her fingers through her shoulder length hair. Finally she stepped back to make sure her cotton, knee-length, sleeveless black dress hung just right.

Jess appeared behind her in the mirror. "This guy must be something."

Cassie bit her lip.

"Just tell me who it is?" Jessica pleaded.

"I'll tell you later."

"Why?"

"It's just a date, Jess. It might not work out."

"Then why are you so nervous?"

"I'm not nervous," Cassie lied.

"Fine. Don't tell me."

"I won't."

Jess smiled and pushed a strand of hair back from Cassie's face. Cassie pulled away from her and Jess laughed, then reassured her sister. "You look great."

"Okay." Cassie made sure her phone and keys were in her purse, then folded a lightweight, white sweater over her arm and turned toward Jess. "So...okay?"

Jess rolled her eyes, took Cassie by the arm, opened the door and propelled her out. "Have fun."

"I'll try," Cassie called over her shoulder as she headed down the hall.

She'd asked Stills to wait for her at the corner. He'd grudgingly agreed.

The magic hour was upon Southern California. The last hour of light drew long shadows of palm trees and lamp posts across the streets. Neighbors were taking dogs for after work walks. A young couple, strolling hand in hand, smiled at Cassie as she turned right and headed for the corner.

Then she saw him.

Standing against the passenger side of his car, sporting black pants and a button-down white shirt, top button undone, and the long sleeves rolled up to his forearms. No Adidas this time.

Cassie gripped her hands into fists to keep from pressing them against her chest.

His grin grew when he saw her, capturing her in his trajectory, pulling her in.

Cassie floated toward him. He might have moved, but she wasn't certain. One minute they were so far apart, and the next, she was in his arms, pressed against that white shirt, looking up into that sexy smile as it descended upon her.

They laughed against each other's lips and tilted their heads to get better access, but the more intimate position caused Cassie's breath to catch. She pulled back slightly and nipped at his lower lip while she tried to control her breathing. Stills wanted more of her. His hand slipped into her hair, and steadied her head as he tilted his own to fit their lips together.

Cassie ran her hands over his shirt, up the length of his back and into his short hair. A low moan erupted somewhere in his chest and echoed its way into hers, sending a shiver throughout her whole body.

Cassie didn't hold back the tremble, but it was the tremble that brought Stills' attention back to their surroundings.

He pulled back slightly, but allowed his lips to linger over hers, hovering; just in case. Cassie crossed the distance that was so minute and so agonizingly far; igniting another slow, soft, enticing kiss. Then, somehow, she found the same control Stills had moments before and pulled away. Her breathing, which she had fully sacrificed in exchange for his taste, began again.

"Hi," she whispered.

"Hi. You ready?"

She gave a slight nod and allowed her hands to retrace their original path, from his hair back down his back, over his shoulders and down his arms until her hands were on top of his forearms. She hadn't been given this much time to study the little things, like the veins in his forearms, or the dark hair that covered his olive skin.

Stills let her explore. Her attention followed the line of buttons on his shirt, her fingers itched to begin removing that long line of obstacles. As her gaze drew lazy circles on the exposed skin of his chest, she licked her lips. Whatever was happening, she didn't care. She saw a twitch out of the corner of her eye, his erratic heartbeat pulsing in the vein in his neck. "Am I doing that?" she breathed.

"My heart's been racing since I got out of the car to wait for you."

A smile pulled at the side of her mouth, she wasn't sure she'd ever had that kind of power before and she liked it. "Good."

He stepped away from her and broke the spell they'd been under. "We should go." They walked back to the car, Stills held her door.

"Where are we going?"

"It's a surprise," he said as the door closed.

As he walked around the back, Cassie did press a hand against her chest this time. "Good Lord," she whispered.

She'd worried that the build-up to the date would be more exciting than the actual date itself. The text messages that kept her blissfully sidetracked and daydreaming had set up some very high expectations. She was worried this tension and attraction might have all been a reaction to stress-induced fear and the excitement of irritating a real-life CIA agent.

But holy hell, the first kiss alone displaced any and all worries.

He drove through downtown Los Angeles in the dusty-orange evening light. The beginning glow of neon helped brighten the gray architecture.

"I never picked you for a Volkswagen SUV sort of guy," she said, mainly to make conversation. Her excited nerves were firing strangely throughout her bloodstream when he let go of her. It was one thing to be texting or angry at him or sitting close enough to touch and kiss him, but the distance, even this slight, made her nervous.

"It looks new." She bit her lip and gave herself a silent lecture to stop.

"I'm not in town a lot, but I like to be able to go camping and hiking in my free time, this is a good car for that sort of thing."

"You like camping?" she asked.

"Do you?"

"I asked you first."

"I do. It's relaxing to get away from everything."

"I love backpacking and hiking and camping," Cassie smiled. "I just don't get out enough. I don't have too many friends who like it."

"Where do you like to go?"

"I used to go backpacking around Idyllwild a lot in college." She mentioned the small mountain town, east of LA in the San Jacinto Mountains then her memory flashed, remembering Stills' confession: 'I want to make love to you under the stars'. Jeez, maybe this conversation wasn't the soothing topic she'd hoped it would be.

"That's a nice area. I've done a few trips there myself," he said.

Cassie cleared her throat and continued to turn the tide of conversation more to the innocent 'get to know each other' type. "What was your favorite camping trip?" She turned slightly in her seat and studied the side of his face, lit up by the dashboard and the neon glow of the city.

Damnit. That might have been a wrong move as well.

"One summer, I went with a friend and we spent six weeks hiking the Camino de Santiago," he answered.

"No way..." Cassie said excitedly, "how was it? Wait, is that considered camping? I thought there were a lot more hostel stays on that trail?"

"We stayed in hostels and camped, a lot. So it counts as a favorite camping trip and a favorite hike as well." He shook his head recalling the fond memory. "It was the trip of a lifetime. We met a lot of interesting people, had a few spiritual experiences, and cried and laughed to the point of exhaustion." He glanced at Cassie. "What was your favorite?"

She answered quickly, "The Grand Canyon. I went with two friends, we were young and stupid and underprepared. We arrived on the south rim and it was snowing. We found a place to camp for the night, and the next morning, packed up and spent the next four days hiking. One day down, one up to the north rim, the next day down again, and the last day back to the south rim."

"I've never been to the Grand Canyon. I've always wanted to try to hike it."

"Oh, you have to. It was so fun. Exhausting, the continuous down was just as difficult as the continuous up. I lost three toenails that trip." She wondered if she should have shared that detail, but felt like he would understand and not really care.

"I get it. Our feet, after six weeks..."

"A mess, huh?"

She was about to ask him more about the Camino de Santiago trail but he pulled up in front of a large looking house, partially hidden by trees, that had been turned into a restaurant. The entire front of the building and surrounding trees were covered in twinkle lights. Not a Griswold Christmas Vacation sort of covering, but the kind of lighting used when attempting to produce a fairy dream. Entwined lights played hide and seek among the façade, twinkling and winking promises of romance between overgrown branches. A glimpse of more lighting and glittering from within beckoned diners to enter.

The entire scene stole Cassie's breath and the only word she could conjure was, "Oh."

"Le Stelle," he said the name of the restaurant as he pulled the car to a stop at the valet stand, "have you ever been?"

Cassie slowly shook her head as she watched the way the lights played with the various trees and the ivy-covered building front. "I didn't even know it existed."

A valet was at each door, and Cassie accepted the hand of the man helping her out, glad for his presence because she couldn't take her eyes off the romantic scene before her.

She felt Stills' hand slip into the small of her back, warming her and sending chills all at the same time. She continued to try and make sense of the rapid emotions. Stills felt so familiar and yet she almost felt broken for the amount of time she'd waited for this moment of familiarity she never knew was missing.

"You okay?" Stills asked.

She beamed a reassuring smile in his direction, there were no words to express what she was feeling.

They walked into the corridor where giant chandeliers sparkled and demanded attention among lights that were strung the width of the entire ceiling. Cassie whispered the obvious, "It looks like stars." She was simply taken aback by the dazzling dreamy scene unfolding before her.

Stills leaned forward and whispered, "That's what they're going for, le stelle means the stars. In Italian."

They arrived at the host stand. Stills gave his name and a waiter was snapped to attention. He gestured for Cassie and Stills to follow him and preceded them into a room with a vaulted glass roof, two more hanging chandeliers, and all the overgrown trees protecting the glass roof with their stretched out branches, were showing off their entangled, glimmering lights.

There were sixteen tables in the room, all set for two, all made private by large potted plants and squat palm trees throughout. The waiter led them into the seclusion of the back corner. The white tablecloth brushed the floor; a flameless candle and a vase of intricately arranged white roses adorned the table, and just to the side, a pedestal with a chilled bottle of prosecco.

"Oh, my..." Cassie wondered if she would ever be able to form a coherent thought again.

Again Stills leaned forward, he smelled of light aftershave, breath mints and masculine confidence. "Do you like it?"

She turned to him, her eyes alight. "I love it. I'm just...I'm overwhelmed. This is amazing. It's too much."

He pulled out her chair and after she was seated, he leaned down and brushed a kiss along her neck. "It's not enough," he whispered seductively.

"You are dangerous," she said as he made his way to his own chair, which he pulled closer to hers before he sat down.

"Your menus." The waiter gestured to the simple menu, one elegant printed page fitted into a black placard at their place settings. "I'll give you a few moments and return to take your order." He then opened the bottle of prosecco, poured two glasses and left with a slight nod.

Stills held up his glass toward Cassie, she grinned and mirrored the action. Then he lost his grin and she thought the beginning of a blush was forming. She raised an eyebrow in question and he laughed softly. "I was going to be smooth and toast your beauty or how you make me feel...but it seems like it's not enough now." His vulnerability flashed.

Cassie glanced around her and finally nodded. "To magic," she offered. Because the moment she walked out her door this evening, with the way the sun was setting, to the first glimpse of Stills and that kiss, along with the twinkling garden that had grown up around the restaurant draped in lights – it was magical.

"To magic," he agreed and tapped his glass to hers.

The waiter brought an order of bruschetta, set the plate down and left.

Cassie picked up one of the red topped toasted breads and took a bite; it was just tomatoes, olive oil, basil and garlic but something had happened in the simple mixing of the ingredients, they morphed together into a divine exploration of spice and taste. Of course, it could be the evening, the restaurant or the company; or the fact that her stomach continued to build with butterflies and excitement at each passing moment...either way, it elevated the simple bruschetta.

"What are you in the mood for?" Stills was looking over the menu. Cassie perused her own menu and shook her head once she was halfway through. "All of it," she laughed, "it all looks good." After another moment she decided, "I think the Bucatini all'Amatriciana." She read the description again: bucatini pasta, pancetta, onions, plum tomatoes and a touch of spice. "Oh yeah, that's the one. What looks good to you?" she asked the menu. But when Stills didn't answer, she glanced over to find him looking at her; his eyes had gone dark and sparkled with that intriguing mischief. "*You* look good to me," he said softly.

Cassie reached out her hand, meaning to touch the side of his face, just to touch him, to feel if he was real, if this was really happening, but he intercepted her hand, took it in both of his and brushed a kiss against her palm.

"I don't know if I'm ever going to get used to that," she whispered.

"Good."

The waiter arrived and Stills reluctantly let Cassie's hand go.

"And what may I get you this evening?"

Stills gestured for Cassie to go first. When she was finished he ordered. "I'll have the Burrata e Aragosta."

"Will there be anything else?" the waiter asked.

"The Antipasto Le Stelle?" Cassie looked at Stills. "Do you want to share that?"

He nodded and gave their menus over to the waiter.

Cassie sat forward, resting her chin in her hands on the table. "No one has ever brought me somewhere this romantic before."

Stills grunted in reply to her statement. She tilted her head toward him. "What?"

He moved his arm around the back of her chair, pressed his knee against hers and said, "I'm glad I'm the first man to do something this romantic, and at the same time, I'm disappointed no other schmuck saw you were worth this."

"Schmuck?"

He took a sip of his prosecco. "I'm secure enough to admit I don't like the idea of other men having taken you out. But I'm not stupid enough to think it didn't happen."

"Are you asking me for my dating history?"

"Not tonight."

"What if I want to know your dating history?"

"Do you?"

Cassie knew that he would tell her anything she asked; unless it had to do with a classified operation, of course.

"No, because I found I was particularly jealous of the schmucky Elaine whats-her-name."

"Schmucky?"

"Schmucky," Cassie verified.

She took a sip of prosecco and glanced around the room, it was difficult to keep her eyes from the star lit, enchanted forest she was basking in. "You know," she said, "I would have been just as happy with a picnic on the beach."

Stills glanced around the room and raised an eyebrow. "Really?"

She laughed. "If I wasn't aware that a place like this existed, then yes. But now..." she waved a hand at the opulence, "I'm ruined."

"Good."

She was being wooed and it was working. She was being romanced and she liked it. She pulled the vase of flowers forward and smelled the roses, they were fragrant and gorgeous.

"I didn't know what kind of flowers you like. But I think of you and I think of white roses."

"You know, historically, white roses are a symbol of purity and love. But, traditionally, when a person gives you white roses it means you just want to be friends."

"Oh thank God," he muttered, "I was really trying for a neutral romantic gesture."

"I'm sorry, I just know too many weird little historical facts."

He cleared his throat and said, "The lady at the flower shop said that they can also symbolize new beginnings and respect."

"Oh, even better." She took another deep breath of the fragrant stems. "I love them." She shifted and leaned toward Stills, he smiled at her movement. "Hey Benji?"

"Yes, Dodd?"

"I'm gonna kiss you now." She followed through with her declaration and the electric shock that waved its way through her spine made her want to climb onto his lap, hold on tight and let the powerful attraction take over.

She forced herself to pull away, shaken by the reaction. "I don't know if I'm ever going to get used to that."

"I know what you mean."

She cleared her throat and took a sip. "So Benji...what's...your favorite place you've ever been?" She wanted to know all about him, but there were so many questions and she wasn't sure where to start, because in all reality, she just wanted to kiss him until she was physically worn out.

"Mesa Verde." It was like he had the answer locked and loaded.

"Is that in Colorado?"

"Southeast Colorado. Have you been?"

"No, but I've spent some time in Utah; Zion and Bryce canyon. Hiking."

"That is some beautiful country too."

"Have you been?"

"I have."

Cassie opened her mouth but then thought better of her comment.

"What?" Stills encouraged her by pressing his leg against hers.

"Didn't you tell me…" she shook her head and took a sip of her drink, then she continued, because why not? "You wanted to take me there? To Mesa Verde?"

"Hell yes." His voice lowered and he moved toward her as he said, "I believe I told you on our first meeting, that I wanted to take you camping in the four corners area and make love to you under the stars."

The whispered confession brought about a growing need for a moment that had been promised twice now. She had to clear her throat several times to find her ability to speak again.

"You okay?"

Cassie laughed nervously. "I think I felt that comment in my bones." The first time he made the comment, it unnerved her, now it radiated just beneath her skin.

"Me too," Stills said.

"It's so tempting to make plans." She had to fight slightly to continue her honesty. Since she met him, neither had played games. It was like an unspoken agreement. And it was refreshing as hell, but it also required a bit of courage that Cassie continually had to call upon. "I want to make plans with you, Benji, but past experiences and human nature…" she trailed off.

"I get it," he nodded his understanding, "what if we get hurt again? But, Dodd, you know as well as I do, nothing in this life is ever guaranteed."

"So what does that leave?"

"Trust," he said simply.

"Trust," she parroted.

"And romantic dinners."

"And stars."

"And stars," he agreed.

"Who are you?" Cassie asked.

He leaned across the space between them and brushed a kiss across her lips. "The one you've been waiting for."

She let him kiss her but then pulled back and gave him a suspicious study. "Are you?"

"*I* think so."

There was a moment or two she thought she could overcomplicate what it was between them, try to define it and talk it out more. But the ease and the attraction was simple. So why not let it be?

She was open to speaking her mind, and allowing him to speak his. Even if it *did* quicken her heart rate most of the time. He wasn't pushy or chauvinistic. He wanted her but he asked her questions that showed he was also interested in her ideas and experiences. He was interested in Cassie as a whole. And that's what a woman should have in her life.

Their meals were delivered, and after they'd taken their first bites, rolled their eyes into the back of their heads with the wonder of the flavors and insisted each other 'try this', Stills asked, "What's your favorite place?"

Cassie shrugged. "I'm not sure, I haven't been everywhere yet." She laughed. "My dad says that. But of the places I *have* been, Paris was beautiful. Years ago I went on a European tour with some friends."

Stills narrowed his gaze. "But that's not your favorite."

"No, it wasn't. A few years ago, I was hiking in the Olympic National Park," she began, "I'd gone on a four day backpack trip with some friends. It wasn't an ideal trip. It rained on and off the whole time. It was cold, you know how the cold can get to you when it's humid and damp?"

He nodded. Cassie smiled, of course he understood.

"We decided to skip our last night and go home, so we had to cover more miles than anticipated. We hiked at our own paces along the trail, which meant we were alone most of the day. It was the sort of day when you just put your head down and put one foot in front of the other, you know?"

"I do."

Cassie held her hand out. "Marines?"

"Yes," he said.

"So you most definitely have been in that kind of moment."

He nodded.

"Well, it wasn't a grueling hike, no altitude change, no hills or steep inclines, it was just long. When I'd gone three fourths of the way, I looked up and I was at a waterfall. The whole forest was overgrown and looked like something out of a *Jurassic Park* movie," she smiled, "and there was this lush waterfall and a small bridge. I sat down and watched the water, and the clouds parted and rays of sunlight fought their way through the branches here and there. The only sound was the rushing of the water. I couldn't even hear my own heavy breathing, but there were a few birds I could hear." She looked across the room as if she could still see the moment, still touch it. "I was exhausted, but it was that good exhausted where the adrenaline has kicked in and you feel light and excited. That moment, that place, that *peace*...it was beyond words. And I think of it every time someone asks me about my favorite place."

Stills pushed through her memory, ran a hand into her hair and tugged her gently toward him. She smiled, and wondered if she hadn't just mingled two separate moments divided by space and time, into one.

She jumped into the deep end to swim around, not caring what might come next; drowning in the unnamed emotions that were budding and blooming between them.

When dinner was over and they both sat in satisfied stupors, the waiter brought over dessert menus. "I can't," Cassie looked disappointed, "I want to, but there's no more room."

"To go? Maybe we'll want something sweet later?" Stills offered.

Cassie nodded, and they decided on Tiramisu and the Torta Di Cioccolata, a flourless chocolate cake.

The waiter offered coffee, but Stills declined. When the waiter left, he said, "I have an idea for coffee later. If that's okay?"

"I don't think you're ever going to beat this." She gestured to the restaurant.

"I'm gonna try." He winked.

Chapter Twenty

Even though the traditional 'go-to' for date night was to head to the movies after dinner, or the theater or a concert; Stills kept clear of all those.

He drove to The Grove - a highly decorated, self-contained complex of lights and stores.

They parked and companionably walked hand in hand to the elevator.

"Are you nervous?" she asked as they got into the elevator. He was about to answer when a family with four kids interrupted, the raucous crew chattering simultaneously. The father insisted everyone remember that they'd parked on the purple level, while the mother issued threats about staying together or they'd never leave the house again. Neither had the attention of any of their children who were all busy arguing over arbitrary childhood things.

Stills and Cassie were pushed to the back of the space, frozen in a paused moment of conversation, giving them time to contemplate each other. Cassie grinned as she reached out and touched his ear where an evident closed earring hole was, raising an eyebrow in question. He shrugged, the smile radiating into the flecks of green in his eyes, so apparent in the fluorescent light.

One of the excited kids bumped into Stills, pressing him into Cassie. The parents profusely apologized, and while Stills and Cassie waved off the intrusion with a smile, they didn't separate. Stills moved his hand around Cassie's waist and pulled her closer to his side.

After the family exited the elevator, they followed, continuing the comfortable contact as they leisurely strolled toward the glowing hustle and bustle.

Stills finally admitted to his motives. "I thought we could just walk around and talk. Get to know each other, and the shops might bring up things for us to talk about. And we'd get a chance to see what the other likes..."

For the first time since she met him, he truly faltered.

"I like it," Cassie soothed.

He cleared his throat. "I'm not trying to be cheap or unromantic...I just..." he ran a hand through his hair, "Jesus, this seemed like such a good idea on paper. But executing it seems lame now."

Cassie stopped and turned so she was completely encompassed within the circle of his arms, she reached up on her tiptoes and placed a sweet kiss on his lips, then slowly lowered her body down, pressing against his full length as she did.

"Books first." She gestured with her head toward the two-story Barnes and Noble across the palazzo where each store entrance faced.

The tension eased from his shoulders, he nodded, "I feel like I'm back in high school on a first date again."

"What did you do on your very first date?"

"Movies."

"And what did you take the young lady to see?"

He fidgeted before muttering, "*Psycho.*"

Cassie barked out an unexpected laugh. "Alfred Hitchcock? You took your first date to see Alfred Hitchcock's *Psycho*?"

"I thought she'd be scared and uninterested and that would lead to a more intimate date." He scratched his chin sheepishly.

"And is that how things went?"

"Her two friends met us at the theater and sat between us and talked the whole time. I ended up paying for two tickets and popcorn and drinks and nothing happened."

"No kiss goodnight?"

"Her friends drove her home."

Cassie pursed her lips.

"It's funny now," he said. "I've gotten over the disappointment of it all. It's okay if you laugh."

"I think I feel bad for little Benji."

"Well, it helped me learn how to do things a bit differently over the years."

"Upped your game, have you?"

"And was your first date all romance and flowers?" he asked.

"We went to a drive-thru, then watched *The Princess Bride* at his house. Then he drove me home. I don't remember what we talked about, but I remember sitting in front of my parents' house listening to the soundtrack from the movie and willing him to kiss me."

Stills raised an eyebrow in question.

"The only move he made after we'd listen to a few songs was to get out of the car and open my door and say, 'well, goodnight.'"

"Smooth," Stills said.

Cassie smiled. "So far, you're leaps and bounds beyond some of the first dates I've had in my life."

"Good, because you're the kind of woman a man should have to go to leaps and bounds for."

Unsure how to reply to such a declaration, she continued the path of executing Stills' plan. They walked and shopped and talked.

The next three hours floated by seamlessly, and too quickly, much to Cassie's surprise and frustration. She wanted more time. So much more.

Cassie bought the newest Carl Hiaasen book. Stills hadn't read the author so she suggested one for him to read first. "Only if you're really interested, he's just a fun read. Quick and entertaining. His books won't change your life, but you'll feel better for living in his world for a while," she explained. "And better for knowing that someone who can entertain like that lives in our world."

"I trust your judgment."

They grabbed several magazines. "My guilty pleasure," Cassie said of the *Country Living* and *Southern Living* magazines she picked out.

He held up a copy of *WIRED* and *National Geographic.* "We've all got em, Dodd."

They went into a toy store and exchanged stories about siblings ruining their favorite childhood possessions. "I had to share my toys, of course," she said.

"Of course."

"Jess cut the hair off a lot of my Barbies. Gave some mohawks, some buzz cuts...I was mad at her for so long after that."

"Nick and Dan used cherry bombs to blow up this Crossbow and Catapult game I got one Christmas. I loved that game."

Cassie walked into Crate and Barrel, a store she typically loved to browse, but a few feet in, she shook her head, retraced her steps and gestured for Stills to follow her saying, "Nope." He followed her quick exit asking, "What's wrong?"

"That store is a little too domestic," she muttered. He raised an eyebrow and she waved. "I saw a cooking store over there."

"Isn't that domestic?" he asked.

"Not if it's for baking purposes," she said over her shoulder, walking excitedly ahead of him. She turned and grinned, holding out her hand to get him to hurry up.

"Baking purposes? Like banana bread, cherry turnovers and coffee cake?" He course-corrected and caught up to her.

"Maybe."

Cassie walked in and took a deep breath, it smelled of spices and fresh baked bread. There must have been a cooking class earlier in the evening. She loved cooking stores. It was as relaxing to her as baking itself. She touched a few objects, and then lovingly picked up an embossed rolling pin with a paisley print.

"What is this for?" Stills asked, reaching around her body to study the object as well as continuing to keep the intimate connection between them.

"Once you have your cookie dough rolled out, you use this to roll the design onto the dough. Then you cut out shapes and they all have this really cool design."

"I eat out a lot," he said. "I don't get a lot of home-cooked meals."

"You mean there isn't a full kitchen in the backseat of your spy car?"

"It's a lot of sandwiches and whatever is easy to grab. So, I have to admit, I've really enjoyed the things you've made."

Cassie twisted in his arms. "Even though the baked goods came with a side of harassment?"

"Maybe *because* they came with a side of harassment."

"Yeah," Cassie whispered, "I knew you liked a challenge."

"You aren't a challenge. You're just...strong. Stupid men don't understand strong women." He grinned.

It was on Cassie's lips to ask him how well he understood strong women but she decided to go a different route. "So, on our next date I could cook for you?" she asked. "Like, a whole home-cooked meal? The whole shebang and you wouldn't hate that?"

"Not at all. That sounds really good." He let his arm slide down her arms, then took the rolling pin from her hands, righted himself and headed toward the checkout.

"Benji..." Cassie caught up to him in an attempt to stop him from buying the item.

"Dodd," he returned, "do you have one of these?"

"No," she muttered.

"Is it something you've always wanted but never bought yourself?"

"Yes." She sighed and nodded. "You know what? I'm going to let you buy it for me." She reached up on her toes and brushed a kiss on his cheek.

He snaked his free arm around her waist and pulled her against him as he lowered his mouth to her ear, "Do you know how badly I want you right now?"

The air left the store, customers faded away and the salesman who had asked if they were ready to check out became a distant memory.

Then those eyes, the steamy, gleaming, amber flecked eyes darkened, and he muttered an expletive, "Fuck." And time started again.

Cassie blinked several times at the reaction until she realized it was his phone ringing that had brought about the profanity.

"Stills," he answered, then mouthed 'sorry' to Cassie. She nodded, it was okay, and turned her back to give him some space and told the cashier, "We'll just be a moment." She stepped to the side for any other customers who might want to pay.

"What? How?" his voice raised.

Cassie whipped back around. She couldn't read him, his damn calm countenance was still firmly in place, even though his words were angry.

She gestured toward the door, did they need to go? He nodded sadly but pulled his wallet out and handed it to Cassie. She shooed the wallet away and gestured to the counter. "I don't need it."

He covered the phone. "Please, I want you to have it."

Cassie didn't argue. Stills pointed that he would be outside.

She was worried by the call that had him radiating his professional calm and anger all at the same time. So with one eye on his parting form, she gave half of her attention to the cashier as she handed over the first bank card in the wallet. "Let's try this one."

With the receipt in the bag and the card returned to the wallet, Cassie left the store and found Stills tucked between the buildings. He was near the employee entrance, where he wouldn't cause a scene and where he could concentrate. He was listening intently but when he saw her he gave a quick smile and then gestured toward the parking garage. She handed over his wallet, he put it away and suddenly demanded, "I'm an hour out. Do *not* make a move without me." He hung up.

He took Cassie's hand and didn't necessarily run, but there was a definite increase to their pace.

She wanted to ask him what had happened, who was on the phone. But the last time she was in the middle of a situation that seemed this dire, she found herself freaking out alone in a gas station bathroom.

Her heart began pounding erratically, and the fear she tried to explain to John crept up beside her. It was one thing to be wooed on a date and forget what he did for a living, it was another thing to be on the receiving end of phone calls that ruined the most romantic night of her life. The truth was a bright florescent light on the facts. This man had a dangerous job. Was she prepared for that? Was she willing to ride the roller coaster of 'worried sick' and 'thank God he's safe' until he had to leave again?

"What happened?" She forced the question.

There was a long pause. She knew this time, the pause meant he was thinking over the pros and cons of telling her what was going on, and that worried her even more.

"Thomas Adler just fell into police custody," he said.

"What?" The force of his confession struck Cassie, she released Stills' hand and froze in shock. She was sickened with fear and overwhelmingly relieved at the same time.

"Cassie?" He reached out to help her.

She shook him off. "How?" She attempted to catch a breath and steady her whirling thoughts.

Stills pressed a hand to her lower back. "I have no idea, but he was reportedly walked into a police station and handed over with the instructions for the CIA to be contacted. He's in county lockup right now."

"Holy shit." Cassie nodded a few times, it was difficult to focus, but she knew Stills had to go. She forced her shaky legs to walk. "This is good, right? Is this good?"

"Yes, very good."

"Okay, that's good. Okay." They reached the parking garage and she pointed, "I'll get an Uber, you need to go."

Stills stopped and turned all his attention on Cassie. "He's in jail." He leveled a gaze at her until she gave a brisk jerk of her head that she understood. He took a deep breath that Cassie mimicked.

Stills smiled. "Dodd, he can wait; *you* can't."

"But neither can your job," Cassie argued.

His voice lowered, "My job can wait the time it takes for me to make sure you get home safely."

She tried to break the tension. "This isn't the 1950s, Benji."

She only had a moment to watch that playful grin that pulled at the corner of his mouth before he pulled her fully into his arms and crushed his lips against hers. When she was good and kissed, when the argument was kissed out of her, he pulled away and met her gaze. "I am *not* ready for this evening to end," he said in way of explanation. "I don't want to stop touching you and holding your hand and stealing sideways glances at you. So we can use the time it takes to get you home to continue to enjoy each other's company."

Cassie thought perhaps she would have agreed to anything in that moment. She was drunk off that kiss and his words.

They entered the elevator and Stills announced, "Besides, bad guys enjoy waiting in jail cells."

Cassie didn't expect the nonchalant joke and laughed. "Well, if they like waiting…then this turd can wait forever as long as I'm concerned."

"That's my girl." Stills squeezed her hand. "You bought your fancy rolling pin?"

"Yes, thank you." She held up the bag as proof.

"You'll make me cookies tomorrow?"

"Do you want cookies tomorrow?"

"Why would I buy you a cool baking tool if you weren't going to experiment for me right away?" he said as they reached the car. He took time to hold her car door.

"Experiment for you, huh?" she asked when he got into the car.

"We're talking sugar cookies, right?"

"I might have a good recipe." She laughed and tried to sift through the turbulent roll of emotions she'd been taken on so far this evening.

"Do you want to call Jess and tell her?" Stills asked once they were on the road.

"Do you have any more information other than the fact that Thomas has been arrested?"

"No."

Cassie thought for a moment then said, "No, I don't think she needs to know right now. I don't know what good it would do to tell her if there isn't anything to really tell."

They were silent as Stills maneuvered the car through Friday night traffic. At a stoplight he took Cassie's hand in his.

"Are you worried?" she asked.

"About what?"

Cassie shrugged. "I don't know, is there anything about to happen that will be dangerous?"

He pressed another kiss against her hand. "No. This is the least dangerous part of my job there is."

She nodded absently, hating the thrown away admission that '*this* was the least dangerous part of my job'.

"Did you have a good night?" Stills asked, his seldom seen vulnerability winked at her.

Cassie cleared her throat and packed away the worry, she'd deal with that another time. "Eh, it was okay."

He raised an eyebrow in question and Cassie laughed. "Jesus, Benji, I'm kinda worried that you've set a precedent of how I'm supposed to be treated now and I'll never be the same again."

He squeezed her hand. "Good."

As he pulled down her street, she unbuckled her seatbelt and when he slowed the car, she was opening her door before he came to a complete stop.

"Dodd?" He stopped her.

She glanced at him questioningly. "Don't you have to go?"

He put the car in park in answer, opened his door and walked around to help her out. The moment she was close enough, she knew what was coming, so she wrapped herself in his arms and offered her lips to him.

There was no hurry or speed, just steadiness. A slow, deep kiss filled with promises.

"What are you doing tomorrow?" he whispered as he moved from her lips to her neck.

Cassie exhaled, leaning her head to the side so that he had better access. "Making cookies."

"I need to see you tomorrow," he said desperately.

"Okay."

"I'm not sure when I'll have time."

"It's Saturday. I'll be around," she assured.

They reluctantly parted. Stills took out the bouquet of flowers and handed them to Cassie after she took out her keys.

"They really are beautiful."

"So are you."

She shook her head and glanced up at the window of her apartment, then back at Stills. "You'll really be okay, right?"

"Yes." His steely gaze sealed the promise. She needed that confidence from him.

She nodded and again, looked back at her apartment. "If I tell Jess...what *should* I tell her?"

"That it's over. For real."

Chapter Twenty-One

Cassie dreamily zig-zagged her way to her apartment. In one arm she carried the vase of flowers, in the other her rolling pin. A jumble of alternating emotions flitted about. She felt light and giddy, dizzy and worried, sexy and grounded.

"Benji." She whispered his name to feel it form on her lips, to hear it echo in the busy space between her ears. And because the time since he last pulled her into his arms was so recent and yet so long ago. And because the whole situation was a complete revelation.

She'd been dating on and off for years. Her mother referred to her as a late bloomer, but she liked to think she knew who she was and what she was about, years before she decided to start dipping her toes in the dating pool. And the dating pool was difficult. She'd had some serious relationships, some fun ones; but she'd never been in a hurry to settle down. Despite her mother and grandmother's continual urging to 'find someone nice' before it was 'too late', Cassie wasn't concerned. She decided a long time ago to allow life its ebb and flow.

She wasn't hitting the streets searching for her M.R.S degree. She'd always thought that life would fall into place as needed, when the time was right. After all, life was a great adventure, there were chances to learn new things around every corner. That had been the motto she lived by.

Sure there had been heartaches and struggles, but the opportunity for growth always intrigued her. It was why she was so good at her job; she loved to hear about the lives of others, to see how they learned and how they conquered difficult times and celebrated the good ones.

She wondered if, when, she found someone intriguing she felt a connection with, would it be a lightning strike that hit her over the head?

Would she know right away? Would it be a sort of Hollywood love story? Was there such a thing?

Enter Stills. The man and the feelings she had for him had crept up on her. Slowly. One smile, one conversation, one kiss at a time until moments like tonight, when he pulled her into his arms and kissed her, erupted with unforeseen power.

Those moments brought bolts of energy that created a skin of static; sensitive to the touch, longing for an uncommunicable culmination that had been built on a mountain of tiny little exchanges.

She rolled her eyes at the fantastical thoughts and pushed open her apartment door; dropped everything but the flowers on the entry table.

Jess was sitting at the dining table.

"Honey, I'm home," Cassie said as she performed a comical, dramatic twirl with her flowers to the table. But when she arrived, something was wrong.

"Oh shit, did you already hear?" Cassie asked and sat down next to her.

"Nice flowers," Jess said absently then frowned. "Hear what?"

"That Thomas was arrested. They got him, Jess. He's in jail," Cassie said emphatically.

Jess gave a dry laugh. "He might be in jail right now, but a few hours ago, he was in that very doorway, kidnapping me again."

"What?!" Cassie stood up with a scream and looked at the front door as if she could still find Thomas hovering there. "How did he get in? You have to have a key to get into the building!"

"He probably picked the lock, or someone held the door…"

Cassie retrieved her phone, she would call Stills.

Jessica continued, "He came to the door, with some big lug. They took me to an Olive Garden."

"What?!" Cassie screamed the question, turning all her attention back to her sister. She shook her head incredulously and repeated, "What?!"

Jess continued her dazed telling. "I thought I was going to die; when Thomas and this big goon kidnapped me and forced me in the car, I thought, this is it. But then he pulls up in front of an Olive Garden. The three of us go inside and we're shown to a private room in the back, and there's Luigi Paroni."

"What? The main mob boss guy? But he's dead." Cassie felt like she was going insane, and she sure wished she had a different question or another word other than *what*. But seriously - "What?!"

Jessica's voice was hollow, but the sentiment dripped with sarcasm as she explained, "So Luigi tells Thomas to apologize to me, which he does, and then the big goon grabs Thomas and takes him away. Luigi owns twenty-three Olive Gardens, by the way. So he feeds me dinner and tells me his life story and turns out, he was playing some fucked up puppet master in *my* life over the past year. He *knew* Parker was CIA and that we were married. He was trying to set Thomas up, or set up Parker or set me up... but he really likes me because I remind him of his daughter. The dead one."

"What the fuck?!"

"Cassie, stop yelling!" Jessica's eyes cleared as she yelled back at her sister.

"I'm confused! This is so...when I stop being confused, I'll stop yelling!"

"Stop it now." Jess rubbed her face with her hands.

"Are you okay?" Cassie knelt in front of Jess, took her hands and began studying her from head to foot to make sure there weren't any visual signs of trauma.

"Cass, stop. I'm fine. Luigi Paroni asked me to forgive him. And he's the one that turned Thomas into the CIA." She continued the highlights of the evening.

Cassie shook her head and moved to sit down heavily in a chair. "Holy shit."

"How did you know about Thomas?"

"Stills...called me," she lied.

Jess gave a humph in reply and continued, "Well, after a crazy conversation, Luigi explains everything, which I still don't think I fully understand. But he asked me what my favorite part of Italy was."

Cassie snorted and sarcastically answered, "Not being kidnapped." Because after hearing about Jessica's ordeal, the one thing Cassie would have liked best about being in Italy was not being kidnapped.

"Right? Well...I actually told him the cappuccinos were my favorite thing; and the next thing I know, he's taking me to Bed, Bath and Beyond to buy me all this espresso stuff. Then we stopped at the store on the corner to buy milk, and when we came back here, he taught me how to make the perfect Italian cappuccino."

"What the fuck?" Cassie looked at the table then; two cappuccino cups sat in matching saucers, rings of dried espresso and milk caked onto the sides.

"Want one? I can teach you," Jess offered, obviously still in shock from the whole evening.

"Yes." Cassie really was curious about how to make an Italian espresso in the comfort of her own home, but at the same time, she didn't know what to make of the night Jessica had been through. She cleared her throat and suggested, "And maybe you should start your story all over again."

Jess nodded and took a deep breath. "Okay, but seriously, these are pretty good. You're gonna love this."

Cassie followed Jess into the kitchen and interrogated her about Luigi and her evening. But she also paid close attention to the new skill she was being taught.

Cassie watched as Jess put espresso in the stovetop espresso maker and heated milk in a stainless-steel pitcher. She then took the top of the container that looked like the top of a French Press and used it to foam the milk. During this whole process, she attempted to reassure both Cassie and herself, "Luigi said I'm safe, Parker is safe, our family is safe."

"That's good, isn't it?" Cassie asked hesitantly.

Jess tapped the steel pitcher on the counter.

"Why are you doing that?" Cassie asked.

"To get the air bubbles out?" Jess reasoned. "Luigi said a lot of stuff tonight and I'm still trying to wade my way through it all. Even the reasons for doing things to make the damn cappuccino."

The stovetop espresso maker sputtered, Jess took it off the burner and poured two equal amounts into each of the cups that Cassie had washed while Jess talked. Jessica frowned at her sister after the liquid was distributed. "It's not decaf."

Cassie snorted. "Do you really think we're gonna be able to sleep tonight?"

"Touché." Jess topped the espresso with the milk and then added a little foam.

Cassie pulled out two apple cider donuts she'd made the day before and recalled the desserts sitting in the back of Stills' car. "Damn. That would have been good," she muttered.

"What?" Jess asked.

Cassie waved the thought away.

Jess brought the drinks to the table. Cassie took a sip and closed her eyes. "Oh my God, this is amazing."

"Right?" Jess took a sip and then murmured, "He kissed me goodbye."

"Who, Thomas?"

"No, Luigi."

"Like a kiss on the cheek sort of kiss?" Cassie frowned.

"No, like the way a man kisses a woman kinda kiss."

"What?!"

"Cassie, stop yelling."

"Stop telling me the strangest story I've ever heard and I'll stop yelling!"

Jess rolled her eyes, but she was finally smiling. "I kept asking him, Luigi, if I was safe. He kept telling me he wanted to explain and I kept asking him if everything he said to me he felt comfortable for the CIA to know, because while I wasn't working for them in an official capacity, they seemed to like asking me a lot of questions." She paused and took a sip of her coffee.

"And he said?" Cassie prodded.

"That I was safe." Jess studied her cup. "I asked him if I was the kind of safe that meant, one day, he'd show up on my front porch and ask me for a favor."

Cassie sat back, pouted her lips and did her best Marlin Brando impersonation from *The Godfather*, "Someday, and that day may never come, I will call upon you to do a service for me. But until that day, accept this justice as a gift on the day of my daughter's wedding." She brushed the underside of her chin with her fingertips.

Jess rolled her eyes. "That was awful...but yeah, I kept asking him if I was going to owe him a favor and he continued to say the slate was clean. So...I'm just going to have to take his word for it."

"Get to the kiss," Cassie said excitedly.

"We talked about...life, really. Just little things, and once we came back to the apartment, it was more of the same, and then he excused himself and said he needed to go. He kisses me the traditional Italian way..."

"What's the traditional Italian way?"

"Both cheeks, oh, and in case you ever have to do it, go right first. I got all confused the first few times."

Cassie frowned, she didn't think the story could get any stranger. "Okay, right first. So he does the Italian cheek kiss thing, then...?"

Jess laughed. "He kissed me full on the lips. Like this really tender, sweet kiss."

"Oh my God! What did you do?"

"Nothing! It was weird."

"So he just kisses you and leaves?"

Jess took a sip of her coffee, but Cassie saw the blush creeping up her cheeks. "What?"

From behind the cup Jess cringed and said, "I asked if it was the kiss of death."

Cassie laughed. "Was he offended?"

"No, he did this suave, male, Italian thing where he brushed a hand down the side of my cheek and said, 'sometimes, amore, a kiss is simply a kiss.'"

"Whoa." Cassie took a bite of her donut and shook her head, staring in disbelief at the lingering strands of the story her sister had just shared.

Jess sighed. "So how was your night?"

"Not nearly as eventful as yours," Cassie shook her head in wonder.

Jess pointed to the flowers. "That seems eventful." Jessica's phone rang then, she glanced at the caller ID and said, "Benji."

Cassie felt a pang of jealousy but knew this was a work call; protocol.

Jess answered and put him on speaker phone, "Hey Benji."

"Hello, Miss Dodd." He was operating by the book, but being called 'Miss Dodd' was Cassie's pet name. She licked her lips and took a deep breath and reminded herself not to be so ridiculous.

Stills continued, "You will be happy to know that we have Thomas Adler in custody and a stack of information that will put him behind bars for a long time. You are safe."

"Cassie told me."

There was a long pause and Jess frowned at Cassie, so Cassie called out, "Hey Benji, I told Jess you called and told me already and that you'd call when you had more information."

"Ah."

Cassie wanted more than that, but she knew he was surrounded by other agents and after all, this was a work call. Cassie also thought he needed to know the other piece of information Jess hadn't offered yet. She mouthed 'tell him' but Jess shook her head and flared her nostrils.

"He stopped by here, Benji," Cassie supplied.

"Who stopped by?"

Jess stuck her tongue out at Cassie and sighed as she said, "Thomas came by, kidnapped me and took me to the Olive Garden."

"I'm sorry, what?"

Cassie flicked her sister's shoulder. "See, it sounds crazy."

"Luigi Paroni was the one who turned Thomas into the CIA," Jess explained.

There was a very long pause, a muffled sound on Stills' end of the phone. When he returned he said, "Jessica, we need to debrief you."

"No."

"It isn't a question," he said apologetically.

Cassie saw the exhaustion on her sister's face. "Benji?" she started.

"Miss Dodd," he replied, with what sounded to her, like a smile in his voice.

She hid her own smile. "Can you interview her over the phone?"

Another muffed conversation and then Stills was back. "We can send an agent to your residence to take your statement. That's the best I can do."

Cassie shrugged, it was better than nothing.

Jessica mumbled, "Fine."

"Alright, expect Agent Robbins within the hour. Have a good night, ladies," he said but didn't wait for either of them to answer.

"Let's watch a movie," Jess said. "And eat Doritos and ice cream."

Cassie wanted to hear the whole story again, one intricate detail at a time, but Jess was going to have to rehash her whole night as it was, so she decided she could wait. "Doritos and ice cream!" she agreed.

They watched the first half of *Girls Just Wanna Have Fun*, both in the mood for the simplicity of their childhood and not in the mood for a high-speed action movie or an intense romance. Agent Robbins showed up, and after a few moments of small talk, Cassie excused herself and went to her room.

She got ready for bed but couldn't sleep. Her mind was running rampant, fueled by espresso and the preposterous story Jessica had related, both of which overshadowed the best date night of her life.

Even though quiet contemplation was not an option, the one thought Cassie didn't mind playing over and over again was that it was finally all over.

She took several deep, calming breaths and allowed that truth to seep into her veins. When was the last time she'd been able to breathe like this? Completely, without all the harsh edges of worry surrounding it.

She should call her parents. Just to say the words aloud - Jessica was safe. She looked at the clock, two-fifteen a.m. She wouldn't wake them, the news would keep until morning.

Finally, Stills began to creep into the cracks, where the worry had lived, as she found herself able to concentrate on replaying the evening in great detail in her mind. She couldn't help but touch her lips when she relived each kiss. Her hands tingled when she thought about holding his. Before the phone call, he'd been attentive and relaxed. She wanted to tell him so much, and she had so many questions for him. She wanted one on one time with him for as long as she could get it, to ask him everything and find out everything.

She pulled out her phone:

Cassie: I know you're going to be working late, but I miss you already. Thank you for a gorgeous dinner and the opportunity to get to know you better. Let me know when you have time tomorrow, can't wait to see you.

She turned off her light and lay on her back as her mind and the shadows played games, neither interested in letting her fall asleep. And maybe that was because she knew what was coming. She smiled when her phone notified her of an incoming text.

Agent Stills: It was all my pleasure. I can still taste you on my lips. Sleep well, Dodd. You have some serious baking to do for me tomorrow.

She thought her face might crack from the pressure of the smile, her body radiated excited pulses and she tensed all her muscles at once, an attempt to hold tight to the feelings and let go of the strain.

She reread the message several times, and somewhere between memories of kisses and listing questions she wanted to ask him, sleep claimed her.

Chapter Twenty-Two

"Tell it again." Cassie stood by the stove where the cookies were baking. She had pulled out a set of Pac-Man cookie cutters she'd received as a white elephant gift, and was practicing rolling out sugar cookie dough with the paisley roller before cutting out the shapes. When Jess saw what she was doing, she shook her head and muttered, "Pac-Man never looked so good."

Jess was using her newly acquired cappuccino making skills as she filled Cassie in on the debriefing. Her clinical, exhausted telling wasn't what Cassie wanted. She waved her spatula at her sister. "Tell the good part."

"Why? It was scary and Thomas is in jail."

"Not that, the conversation with Luigi."

"I told you all this."

"Jessica. We had a *Godfather* in our home. A real life, being watched by the CIA, Godfather. I don't know about you, but I feel like we could start selling tickets. Come learn how to make an Italian cappuccino the way Luigi Paroni taught us. People will pay to see all sorts of roadside attractions," she reasoned. "Also, I wasn't there; so I have to live vicariously through you."

"Jeez."

Cassie prompted, "At least tell me about the kiss again."

"This isn't healthy."

"Jessica!" Cassie demanded.

"Cassandra," Jess mocked and then gave in. "Okay, so he does the Italian cheek kissing thing and then he plants one on my lips."

Cassie laughed and clapped. "And you really asked him if it was the kiss of death?"

"Well, what the hell would you do? Some...man who is supposedly the head of the Italian mafia kisses me...I have no measure of what that means, so my imagination went straight to *The Godfather* movies."

Cassie pressed her hip against the counter, she had kissing on the brain. "He was good, huh? Like, you didn't see it coming but he had age and sex appeal and know-how on his side?"

Jessica licked her lips and tried to hide a smile. "How do you know he has sex appeal?"

"That's a yes," Cassie pointed, "I mean the guy even knows how to make an exit." She did a horrible Italian impression and repeated Luigi's parting words, "'Sometimes, amore, a kiss is simply a kiss.'"

There was a knock on the door. Cassie raised an eyebrow. "He's back to tell you he can't live without you."

"Not likely," Jess said.

Cassie did a melodramatic twirl toward the door with her arms open wide. "I'm coming my love, I'm coming."

"Cassie..."

Cassie opened the door theatrically, what did she care if one of her neighbors thought she was crazy, she was trying to embarrass her sister.

As she flung the door wide, instead of a neighbor, she found herself face to face with the strongest, most handsome man she'd ever seen. Stout was the first word that came to mind. Broad was the second.

She was having trouble finding her voice and felt her eyes widening as she continued to study the body building hunk in front of her. When she was finally able to squeak out a few words, all that she could produce was a long drawn out "Oh, my." She no longer wanted to embarrass her sister. She straightened herself and smoothed a hand over her hair. She grinned, waiting for him to explain who he was and what he wanted.

"Jessica?" he finally asked in a thick Italian accent.

Cassie heard her sister's muttered curse. Apparently, she knew who this was, which caused Cassie's eyes to widen even more. She swung the door open all the way, and gave a game show gesture as she revealed the strapping man behind door number one. "Jessica, I believe it's for you," Cassie gave the man another once over, "I *wish* it was for me."

Jessica shuffled across the room, and stood close to Cassie, her arms crossed over her chest. Cassie was curious about the frown plaguing her sister's features, as well as her proximity. Cassie's body tensed; was this man a threat? But then Jessica took a step toward the Italian Adonis and demanded, "What the hell are you doing here?"

He didn't say anything, and shifted from foot to foot. Jessica stood stock still and waited. Cassie was impressed, her little sister had this kind of power over a hulk of a man? She really had changed. But Cassie couldn't stand the mystery any longer. "Aren't you gonna introduce me?"

Jessica sighed and said, "Cassie, this is Carlo."

Cassie's eyes did another impressive pop upon hearing the name. Carlo had been a slight blip in the storyline of Jessica's Italian adventures thus far. All Cassie knew was that there had been an 'inside Italian agent' named Carlo who'd helped keep Jessica safe. Cassie formed her own vision of the man - imposing, dark hair, a greasy mustache and average build. But *this* man should have been described in detail. Jessica should have never skimmed over him. Cassie considered Jessica; what else was her sister keeping from her?

"*This* is Carlo?" Cassie verified.

"Carlo, my sister, Cassie," Jessica muttered again.

"Carlo," Cassie said his name slowly, "yes, please. The lady will take one." She held out her hand and fluttered her eyelashes.

Carlo frowned.

Finally Jessica asked, "Is everything okay?"

He shook his head in answer. Cassie lost her flirty smile when Jessica paled and her hands gripped her arms where she had them crossed. Cassie put a hand on her sister's shoulder, letting her know she was right here.

Jessica's voice was a whisper when she asked, "Parker?"

"He's fine," he grumbled, "it is me. I am not good." This big strapping man was not good? Cassie had so many questions, but she wasn't sure she would be allowed to ask any of them.

After a few moments Jessica made her decision, she released her clenched arms and waved in to the apartment. "Well, I suppose you should come on in."

Cassie pressed herself against the open door as he passed and asked, "How did you get in the building?"

He shrugged. "The door was standing open."

Jessica turned to her sister. "This building has pretty shitty security."

"Do I smell coffee?" he asked as he filled up the space that seemed larger with just the two of them. Cassie thought Carlo could make a lot of things look miniature.

"Espresso, cappuccinos," Cassie smiled, "it's how we do things around here."

Carlo raised an eyebrow.

"You want an espresso?" Jessica asked.

He nodded and sat down at the kitchen table, helping himself to the last apple cider donut. After two bites he held it aloft proclaiming, "This is good."

"Thank you, I made it." Cassie sat down across from him and marveled, "You are so...solid."

"Don't you have a date you need to get ready for?" Jessica urged.

Cassie got a text from Stills saying he had time around one in the afternoon to get together. She told Jessica she had a date, continuing to keep the 'who' out of the description.

"I can't go anywhere until my cookies are finished. But I think I should cancel because of what keeps going on around here." She winked at Carlo.

Carlo's frown deepened.

"Don't cancel on my behalf or the fact that the Italian senate seems to be popping in uninvited."

"Right?" Cassie said.

"Go on your date."

"I have time." Cassie continued to leer at Carlo.

"It's almost 12:15," Jessica informed.

"I'm aware of the time, what I'm not aware of is *this* part of the story." Cassie smiled. "You barely touched on the part he played."

"Cassandra..." Jessica gave a frustrated grumble.

"Fine." Cassie stood up. "Fine," she repeated, heading toward the kitchen, reaching out to touch Carlo's shoulder as she passed him.

"Oh my God, leave him alone." Jess swatted Cassie's hand as they switched places.

Cassie held up her hands and admitted, "I'm sorry Carlo. I've just never seen anyone with so many muscles before this close." She didn't try to hide the trace of awe in her voice.

Jessica set the coffee down in front of him and Cassie listened closely from the kitchen. The cookies were ready to come out of the oven, but it would be a few more seconds before they could be moved to the plate. She moved slowly, so she wouldn't miss anything over any noise she made.

"Why the hell are you here and how did you find me?" Jessica asked.

The hulk of a man answered, "CIA. I need to talk to Parker."

Cassie froze with the cookie sheet in her oven mitt hand.

"He's not here," Jessica said, the steel in her voice evident from the kitchen.

"What do you mean? He's been back for three weeks. I thought...I couldn't find him at his house or work. I thought..."

"Excuse me?" Jessica hissed.

Cassie dropped the cookie sheet and stormed out of the kitchen pointing a spatula at Carlo. "He's been back for three weeks?" she parroted.

"What?" Carlo looked confused.

Jessica over annunciated her question, "What do you mean he's been back for three weeks?"

Carlo's frown deepened. "You haven't heard from him?"

"No, I haven't heard from him." Jessica stood up angrily and began to clear the dirty dishes off the table, Cassie stood out of the way as she watched her sister react to the news.

"Not that I care!" Jessica yelled as she rounded the corner into the kitchen and began throwing dishes in the sink. "I mean, fucking Thomas stopped by last night and abducted me again to take me to a strange dinner with Luigi Paroni, but I'm fucking fine."

Cassie's eyes widened as she watched her sister dump half a bottle of dish soap into the sink and then throw the bottle in too. She yelled at the wall in front of her, "Three weeks!?"

Carlo stood up and glanced at Cassie. "What does she mean Adler was here? He's been arrested."

"Everyone seems to know that little bit of information," Cassie said blandly.

Jessica came out of the kitchen and pushed past her sister, hands on hips as she faced Carlo. "Thomas was arrested right after he abducted me. Again."

"What are you talking about?" Carlo asked.

"Luigi made him do it," Cassie offered.

Carlo shook his head. "What?"

"He taught her how to make the cappuccinos, by the way. Just last night." After watching her sister face down this brute of a man, there was no question that Jessica's badass tank was on its way to being refilled. And witnessing it firsthand now, Cassie actually found herself able to relax the last threads of anxiety she'd been holding onto. Because, truth be told, she was beginning to enjoy this confrontation a lot more than she should. Although, the fact that Parker had been 'back' for three weeks and hadn't contacted her sister didn't sit well with Cassie. Granted, it wasn't sitting well with Jessica either.

"Luigi...Paroni was here?" Carlo asked.

"He kissed her," Cassie offered.

"I thought you had a date to get ready for," Jess snapped.

Cassie held up her hands and backed off, making her way to the bathroom, being sure to be as quiet as she could. She quickly wet her toothbrush, added toothpaste and stood by the open bathroom door brushing her teeth ever so slowly.

"Are you okay?" Carlo asked.

"Three fucking weeks!?" Jessica yelled. "Luigi said I was safe and I could visit any time. I bet I could get in touch with him and he'd pay for my trip. Cassie!" Jess screamed for her sister to return. "Want to go on an all-expense paid trip to Italy with me?"

Cassie took a few steps into the hallway with her toothbrush in her mouth. "Yeths," she agreed, "wish him?" She pointed to Carlo.

"No, with Luigi," Jessica corrected.

Cassie left the toothbrush in her mouth and gave two thumbs up in reply before disappearing again. She quickly rinsed her mouth and returned to the hallway.

Carlo was stumbling through an apology, "Jessica...I thought you knew. I'm sorry...I...Luigi turned Adler in?"

"Apparently the CIA have people in his organization and he has people in the CIA and it's a fun little cat and mouse game, but he's old now and his guilty conscious is getting the better of him—"

"Jessica!" Carlo raised his voice as he called her name, finally getting her attention.

"What?" she bit.

There must have been another standoff because it took a few moments before Jessica conceded and asked, "Carlo, what's going on?"

Cassie tilted her head as far as she could without being seen from the small hallway and heard the big man passionately breathe the name, "Alessandra."

Cassie raised an eyebrow and whispered a question to the hallway, "Who the hell is Alessandra?"

Chapter Twenty-Three

Cassie arranged the cookies on the plate, making sure the top layer had one Pac-Man chasing the three different ghost designs. She thought they looked like those decorative renaissance dog paintings, strangely fancy.

She wrapped the plate in plastic and put it by the front door. She arranged another plate of cookies and put them on the table. "These are for Carlo when he gets out of the shower," she called to Jessica who was sitting on the sofa, fuming.

Jessica grudgingly agreed to let Carlo stay with her and Cassie. He asked to take a shower, and Cassie wondered if he did it to give Jessica time to cool off.

Cassie had asked her if she was okay several times and she'd just laughed and said, "I'm more than okay."

Cassie bit her lip and then asked once more, "Do you want to talk about it?" She knew she didn't, but she thought she'd try.

Without turning around, Jessica declared, "I'm done talking."

Cassie held up her hands and retreated to the kitchen. After she loaded the dishwasher and saved the bottle of dish soap, there was a knock on the door. Electricity fired through Cassie's body. She glanced at the clock; she had fifteen more minutes and Stills promised he'd wait outside again.

Jessica shot off the sofa and yelled, "If this is one more bad guy I'm gonna take a baseball bat to someone's balls!"

Cassie was personally rooting for another bad guy to be standing at the door, or at least a neighbor; for real this time.

Heart thumping loudly, Cassie tried to make her hurried gait seem casual. Jessica beat her to the door; Cassie held her breath and pursed her lips when her sister announced, "Hey Benji, fancy meeting you here."

"Miss Dodd."

Cassie muttered obscenities under her breath and patted her hair in place. So this was happening. She couldn't really see any way around it.

"Who let you in?" Jessica asked.

"Excuse me?"

"I think Cassie needs to move, the security around this place sucks."

He raised an eyebrow and explained, "The door was propped open. Someone's moving."

Jessica gave a grunt then said, "I gave Robbins my statement last night, was there something I missed?"

"No, we've got all the information we need on that front. I'm here to pick up Cassie."

"What?"

Cassie forced a smile as Jessica slowly turned and stared daggers at her.

"What's going on?"

"Let me just...grab my phone." Cassie excused herself from the momentary standoff. She could feel her sister's ire along with an amused Stills standing behind her.

Cassie crossed the room to the dining table, an obvious avoidance tactic, but Jessica followed despite the hint. "You're dating Benji?"

"One date. We're not...dating. I mean, it was a date. It just happened. It's nothing...I just wanted to date him without the third degree." Cassie flinched as she fumbled through the explanation. Today of all days, she knew Jessica would not take well to the withheld information. Jessica's red face was proof that she was not happy about the lying and she was also looking for a scapegoat for her anger.

"I knew it!" Jessica pointed accusingly.

"No you didn't."

"Yes. I did. I knew something was going on. You always said his name so...weird."

"You didn't know anything," Cassie insisted.

"When did you even have time to...get to know him or get asked out? That's who you were with last night. Why didn't you tell me?" she demanded.

Cassie rubbed the back of her neck. "Because..." She thought about trying to make an excuse, but decided screw it, the old Jess was back, she could handle a little honesty. "You were heartbroken. It didn't seem like the time."

"I'm fine," Jessica spat.

"Well a few weeks ago, you weren't," Cassie tried to calmly explain, "and when you first got back, you were upset...and you slept a lot..."

"What do my sleeping patterns have to do with anything?"

"I was worried." Cassie raised her voice and then tried to control her anger again, *one* of them needed to be rational, and between Thomas, Luigi, and now Carlo showing up with news about Parker...Jessica was obviously not fit for the job.

"Look...I just...I would harass Robbins and Benji in the car to make sure they were still there," she admitted. "And I liked him. And he liked me." She nodded, were they done here?

Jessica shook her head, the hurt obvious on her face. "I don't understand why you didn't tell me."

"Because..." Cassie hissed and then quietly added, "I...*really* like him, okay?"

"What the fuck?" Jessica seethed the comment.

Cassie narrowed her gaze at her sister. "Fine, you want to know why I didn't say anything? Because of Parker." She said his name loudly. "The secret *husband* we're not allowed to talk about. Ever. I know your heart is breaking. And I know what it's like when you're feeling that shitty and someone else around you is really happy. It doesn't help. So I kept it from you."

"Well." Jessica crossed her arms over her chest.

"And now we find out this asshole has been back in town for three weeks and hasn't contacted you. That's bullshit. You're angry and rightly so. So today of all days, I *definitely* didn't want to get my..." she shook her head as she searched for the words, "my new boyfriend smell all over you."

Jessica snorted. "New boyfriend smell?"

Cassie rolled her eyes. "It's part of Bath and Body Works' new fall line."

The tense moment broke and fell to pieces around them. "I'm sorry," Cassie said.

"I'm angry," Jessica confessed.

"I know."

Jessica studied her sister. "So you *like*-like him?"

Cassie felt the girlish blush color her cheeks. "Something like that." Then she leaned closer to Jessica, whispering, "Want me to ask him about...him?" Although, she had already planned on asking Stills about Parker the moment they were alone.

"Ask him about what?" Stills called from across the room.

"Nothing," Jessica hissed.

Cassie glanced back at Stills and then down the hallway. Then she smiled at her sister as she declared, "Jess has a male visitor. He's in her shower."

"Cassie!"

"Really?" Benji tilted his head.

Cassie continued, "A big, strapping, hunk of a man."

"Jesus Christ," Jessica moved out of Cassie's way, "go on your *date*." She waved.

Cassie brushed a kiss on Jessica's cheek. Jessica pushed her sister away and wiped her cheek dramatically with her hand.

"Please leave." Jessica muttered.

Cassie walked the slight distance to the front door, put her phone in her purse, slung it onto her shoulder and handed the plate of cookies over to Stills. "As ordered."

He looked down and grinned. "These are cool."

A thrill tingled up her spine. "I like the rolling pin," she said.

"Do you?"

"We have to go." She opened the door and pushed Stills out. "See ya, Jess."

"What's going on?" he asked when they were halfway down the hallway.

Cassie linked her arm into his. "Oh Benji, we have so much to talk about."

Stills allowed Cassie to hurry him out of the complex. He noticed how she glanced over her shoulder several times at her balcony once they were outside.

She opened her mouth to speak, glanced back again, shook her head and continued down the block. Finally, she stopped her quick pace and turned her full attention to him.

Stills moved toward her but she put up her hands against his chest to stop the kiss she so desperately wanted. That would have to wait. "If you kiss me, I'm going to forget everything we need to talk about."

He didn't pull away, but stopped his advances. "Is that a problem?"

She pushed at his chest, but he felt so solid and warm under her hands that they lingered of their own volition. "Yes. You'll sidetrack me if you kiss me."

He began to inch closer to her. "And that's a bad thing?"

She pushed him gently and asked, "Benji, where the fuck is Parker Salvatore? We know he's been back here for three weeks."

That was enough to stop his advances.

"That's what I thought." She wasn't sure how she felt about him keeping this information from her. Granted she hadn't told her own sister she was seeing Stills, but that was different, wasn't it? Unless Parker didn't want Jessica to find him. Maybe the relationship really was over and they were both better off without each other. Maybe it had been a fling and the heightened emotions of a dangerous situation was what had kept them glued together for a time.

"Cassandra..." he sighed her name. An apology, maybe. A request for her to give him a chance. An appeal for her to be patient.

"Agent Stills."

He leaned forward and brushed a kiss on her cheek, lingering.

She pulled away slightly.

"Okay Dodd, how about if we go have coffee at our café?" he asked.

"Our café?"

He inclined his head and grinned.

"Fine," she agreed. They could hash this all out over coffee.

She began to walk and after several steps realized he hadn't moved.

She looked back at him. "What?" she asked while finally taking a moment to truly look at him for the first time today.

He had on the same clothes from the previous evening, and from here, the slight black rings around his eyes spoke of his exhaustion; not to mention the worry lines creasing his forehead.

"Have you slept yet?" She retraced her steps, reaching out to cup the side of his face.

He leaned into her hand and a soft smile smoothed out some of the tension. "No," he smiled, "I just needed to see you before I went to bed."

Cassie leaned toward him and kissed him gently, it was sweet and she felt Stills sigh his relief as they kissed.

When they pulled away, he rested his forehead against hers. "Thank you for the cookies."

"You haven't even tasted them yet."

"You've set up an expectation when it comes to your baking, I kind of assume good things."

She grunted in reply.

Stills righted himself. "You don't mind walking to the café, do you?"

"Not at all."

She reached for the plate and asked, "Do you want me to carry the cookies?"

He pulled the plate to his side. "No, their mine."

She smiled and linked her arm with his instead and they began to walk. "How are you? You should have told me you hadn't slept yet."

"You get used to the hours, but like I said, I wanted to see you first," he said.

"Have you..." Cassie shook her head at the question and decided against it. After the previous evening, Cassie wanted some reassurances, but not about how Stills felt about her; she knew he was just as enthralled with her, as she was with him. It was the job and the 'everyday' life that crept in at moments like this that bothered her.

What did it mean to be with a man who had a job like his? Because even though Jessica wasn't allowing anyone to talk about Parker, there were several times Cassie watched her sister unawares, and saw the worry mingling with the heartache.

"Have I ever what?" Stills interrupted her worried internal monologue.

Cassie muttered, "I know you like me."

"Do you?"

"Of course, and I know that *you* know, that *I* like you."

"Well, now I do."

Cassie's eyes gleamed, "I was wondering, if you've ever felt this way before. Has there ever been anyone else you felt like you had to see after a long day, before you went home?"

He didn't answer right away, but took a few reflective moments to gather himself. He squeezed Cassie's arm with his as he began, "There were women I had in my life when I needed a release," he said, "but none of them were women I was desperate for. None of them made me feel like I would be okay if I could just see them." His voice lowered, "The list of women isn't that long, by the way. This is just a tough one to explain."

"I don't think I need you to explain," Cassie said. "I think I understand."

"Do you date a lot?" he asked.

"I've had a few serious boyfriends that lasted a few months until..." She waved the past away. "I've never really made dating too complicated. There's the heartache sometimes, but mostly..." she swallowed, "Benji, I've never reacted to anyone the way I react to you and no one has ever made me feel the way you do."

"How do I make you feel?" he whispered as he leaned into her.

She pushed him slightly. "You crept up on me and now I don't want to get rid of you."

"I think you were the one who crept up on me."

Cassie laughed. "It wasn't hard, you were parked in front of my house."

"Protocol."

They fell silent as they drew closer to the café. Benji broke that silence, stating, "It's strange. We haven't defined anything yet."

"We haven't finished a date yet," she pointed.

"I'm sorry about that."

Cassie shrugged. "I really do understand. There are just some weird insecurities running around with all this newness."

"Insecurities?" He stopped and studied Cassie.

She smiled and tried again, "That might not be the right word. This..." she gestured between them, "is so...straightforward. No games. And I'm really enjoying that part, but I'm also enjoying the girlish crush part, like waiting for a text..."

"Or getting light headed just thinking about you," he added.

Breathing became difficult. "Maybe that's your lack of sleep talking."

"No," he gazed ahead, "I think you hit the nail on the head. I feel like my first hormones just started working overtime and you're in the way."

"Is that a compliment?"

"A big one."

An unseasonably cool ocean breeze lifted Cassie's hair off the back of her neck. Stills' even breathing soothed her, and the warmth of his arm against hers felt different than most other men's warmth. They had all been lame placeholders. As she thought about it, no one felt as real as Stills did. Had she been allowing only phantoms into her life, until Stills came along?

She was leaning into all the feelings and emotions and the moments she and Stills had spent together, and she wanted to lean in a little more.

"Are you really trying to change how you work?" She started with the question she was most desperate to have answered.

"Yes."

"What does that look like?"

He thought for a moment and smiled. "Promising someone I can take them on a date then following through with the whole evening. Home-cooked meals. Sunday morning hikes and more stability than I've had in years."

She allowed her other fear to slip out in the form of a question, "Will you resent someone later, if you change things for her and it doesn't work out?"

"Life is about taking chances, isn't it?"

Cassie grunted, her own life views winking back at her. "What if you get bored?"

His amber eyes tried to deduce what was worrying her. "Life is the biggest adventure, Dodd."

Cassie grinned. "Isn't that from a movie?"

They arrived at the café, Cassie took the plate of cookies and kissed Stills on the cheek. "I'll go find a seat. Vanilla latte please."

Cassie found 'their' table open. "Our table," she whispered, realizing they'd only known each other a handful of weeks, "and not even one full date."

Chapter Twenty-Four

S tills arrived with two drinks and an almond croissant, he slid the treat toward her. "I'm not sharing my cookies."

"Of course not."

He moved his chair so he was sitting next to her and reached under the plastic for a cookie. Cassie sipped her drink, and watched his reaction. She knew the cookies were good. It was an almond sugar cookie recipe that was a bit sweeter, so they didn't need frosting and they paired perfectly with coffee.

"Oh, man." He closed his eyes after the first bite, then popped the whole cookie in his mouth and fished out another.

Cassie didn't know she could ever have this much fun feeding someone.

"Okay, you've had a cookie and I kissed you and we talked about our lustful adult relationship. Where is Parker?"

"Lustful adult relationship?"

She leveled her gaze, asking again, "Where is Parker Salvatore?"

Stills sighed. "Dodd...it's just...protocol," he started as Cassie held up her hand to stop him.

"Agent Stills, I don't care about protocol. What the *hell* is going on? My sister is in love with this guy and he has abandoned her for almost three damn months."

He took another cookie out, but Cassie prevented his hand from reaching his mouth. She raised an eyebrow and threatened, "I'll never bake for you again."

"That's rough," he admitted. "Was there really a man in the bathroom?"

"Yes. And he really was a big one."

"Is Jessica seeing someone else?"

"Where is Parker?"

Cassie watched him weigh his options, finally conceding. "He's wrapping up all his open cases and working on a transfer so he can have a safer job. He wants to marry your sister, for real. He's in love with her."

Cassie slapped the table. "Hot damn!" The coffees wobbled and Stills caught them. She leaned forward and frowned. "Then why didn't the idiot call her? Or tell her any of this?"

Stills reached out a hand and brushed the hair off of the right side of Cassie's face. "Sometimes a man wants to be worthy of a woman."

"Ah, Neanderthal reasoning."

Stills laughed. "Cassie, who was in the bathroom?"

Her grin cracked as she excitedly announced, "Carlo."

A slight raise of an eyebrow was the only tell-tale sign that he was surprised, but Cassie locked onto the reaction. "I know, right? Last night it's Thomas and Luigi and this morning it's Carlo. Have you met him?"

"I may have had the occasion."

"What does he do? He has so many muscles."

"Should I be jealous?"

Cassie screwed up her lips. "Are you that insecure and stupid?"

"No." He waved the idea away and she knew it was the truth, Stills was stalwart and sure of himself. He continued, "Do you know why he's here?"

"Yeah, I overheard him telling Jess that he needed to find Parker because of someone named Alessandra." She reached out and grabbed Stills by the forearm and gave him a shake. "Benji, who is Alessandra?"

A smile tugged at the corner of his mouth, but instead of answering, he pulled out another cookie.

"Benji!" she tried again. When that didn't work, she changed tactics. "Who is Alessandra, Agent Stills?"

He winked and with his mouth full said, "Parker's sister."

Cassie sat back. "Oh my God! This whole damn thing has soap opera possibilities."

He wiped his hands on his pants as he finished chewing and reached for his phone. Grinning, he asked, "You wanna have some real fun?"

She nodded excitedly.

Stills dialed a number and when the phantom on the other end answered, he stated professionally, "Yes, this is Agent Stills, I need to speak with Agent Salvatore."

Cassie grabbed his forearm again and shook it. She knew when the call had been answered because Stills winked at her.

"Hey Salvatore. I have some information I thought was pertinent to you." His controlled, unemotional 'Agent' voice took over. "I just came from Jessica Dodd's current residence, and there was an unidentified gentleman suitor on the premises."

Cassie heard the angry reaction echo out of the phone. She clapped a hand over her mouth to keep an excited laugh in.

Stills relaxed the straight-laced agent act, "I don't know what to tell you Salvatore, just that things seemed really cozy."

Another explosion of questions and accusations from Parker.

"I'm certain it wasn't the sister's boyfriend. Cassandra Dodd herself said that the man in the shower was Jessica's. I just thought you'd want to know. It looks like you might have lost your window, buddy."

Cassie heard the loud expletive. Stills frowned at Cassie and held out the phone. "For some reason he hung up on me."

"That was incredible!" Cassie jumped out of her seat, sat down on Stills' lap and kissed him.

She meant for it to be a quick little peck, a reward, an uneventful moment. Instead, it was electric heat and explosions.

Stills had infiltrated her emotions and now every touch was voltage and lightning. She held his face in her hands, tilted her head to the side and swept her tongue inside his mouth, taking all his secrets and giving all of hers.

He tasted like almonds and coffee, the ocean breeze and late August. He tasted like possibilities and hikes and future plans and laughter and twinkle lights.

He twisted the back of her shirt in his hands and moaned into her mouth and Cassie took all of him.

Somehow, they arrived back on earth and found the ability to separate from each other.

"I think I'm mad at you for not telling Jess that Parker was in town," she confessed, her forehead pressed against his.

"It wasn't my secret to tell."

"I don't know. Maybe they needed the time apart. She's so mad at him and so in love with him."

"I think a fire was definitely lit under his ass today." Stills reached around Cassie and picked up his cup and took a drink of his coffee. She moved to get off his lap, but he repositioned her so they were both comfortable.

"I'm sorry," he apologized.

"Well, if it happens again, then we're going to have to have a long conversation about trust and honesty and all that crap."

"Dodd, my job doesn't lend me a lot of honesty," he said seriously.

Cassie nodded. "I've been thinking about that a lot too. Last night, after you got that call, I knew you were safe. I mean, you were just going to a police station and you were able to tell me about Thomas because I'm on the outskirts of this whole situation. But I started thinking about how it would be if you just had to leave with a promise of 'I'll be safe'. I'd be left with no way to know what was going on, where you were or when you'd be back."

He agreed, "It's a lot to ask of someone. Especially a new girlfriend."

"I'm your girlfriend?" she joked sarcastically.

"I want you to be," Stills said, but a shadow of vulnerability flashed.

"Okay. Cuz that's what I want too."

"Thank God." He sealed the conversation with a kiss, sweet and soft.

Cassie nipped several times at his lower lip then said, "Benji?"

"Do you think you could ever call me Benjamin?"

"It's so formal," she said, leaning back so she could focus on his eyes, "and I see the sparkle in those eyes; *you* are not a straight-laced Benjamin." She tilted her head, deciding, "And you aren't a stoic Ben, either. I mean, maybe when you have to be, but that isn't who you are." She traced his jawline with her finger. "You're Benji."

"Cassie..." he tried to argue his point but she put her finger to his lips.

"Benji..." She reached over to her purse and rummaged around until she pulled out a folded piece of paper. She looked at him sheepishly and swallowed hard before reading it: "Benji. You have good words to say about everyone. Although you often know more than you will say, you are discreet in your choice of friends. No matter what happens to you, you land on your feet and easily leap obstacles in your path. You believe in yourself and are at peace within. Benji means son of the right hand." She blushed and let her summation rush out before she lost her momentum. "Benji is more powerful, and you know it."

He reached for her hand and gently pulled at the piece of paper, she fought a quick internal battle before releasing it.

"What is this?" he whispered as he reread what she'd written on the paper.

"I work in the genealogy field. Names are important. Just the naming of a person has a story. I've always loved finding out what a name means, because it's often another window into someone's life."

"What does Cassandra mean?"

She puffed up her chest and grinned as she said, "To excel, to shine."

"Damn," he whispered.

She saw the awe in his eyes and allowed herself to bask in the rays of it. He wouldn't change her or pressure her. He was the kind of man who would stand next to her, not try to lead. Oh sure, he'd challenge her, but that was going to be half the fun. Because she knew she would challenge him right back.

"What do you think Parker is up to?" Cassie asked.

"If I were him," he reached around and grabbed another cookie, "I'd be on my way to the apartment."

"Really..." She bit her lip and leaned closer to him. "Hey Benji, wanna go see what kind of fire you lit?"

"Hell yes," he said with a mouthful.

Chapter Twenty-Five

"I assumed you liked to bake pastries and cakes, but you said last night that you cooked other things too?" Stills asked as they slowly walked back to her apartment. He cradled the cookie plate with one hand, while using the other to pull Cassie's hand to his lips.

"I do like to cook," she shrugged, "I just tend to bake a lot more when I can't control...certain situations." She elbowed Stills.

"Are you trying to control me?" he asked.

"Situations," she corrected. "Jess calls it stress baking. But I also bake when I'm happy."

"What else can you make?"

"What do you have in mind?"

"Meatloaf," he said longingly.

"Meatloaf," Cassie repeated.

"I haven't had a really good meatloaf in a long time. Do you make a good meatloaf?"

"The best."

"You're pretty sure of yourself."

"I've been cooking my whole life." She smiled. "So...if there's meatloaf, then I'd have to make mashed potatoes to go with it of course."

"Yes, you would. Do you make good mashed potatoes? I had a cousin once who invited me over for dinner, served potatoes that he basically boiled and mashed. He didn't even have butter to put on them."

"Eww. Well, compared to that, I make amazing mashed potatoes. And I'd probably make a veggie medley to go with it."

He winked. "I *am* a veggie medley sort of guy."

"With cheese on top?" she asked.

"Parmesan," he supplied.

When they reached her building and found the front door still propped open, Cassie looked around and frowned. "What the hell is going on?" If someone was moving, then they had finished. There was no moving van or residents in sight.

"I think the landlord is relaxing security again," Stills said. "Someone from my agency *might* have told him we were with the city and insisted that he take the safety of his residents seriously. I cannot confirm or deny that a few warning letters were sent when we saw the door being continually propped open."

"What?"

He gestured for Cassie to go ahead of him into the building. "It's been a few weeks since he's received any notices, so that's why he's probably become lax."

She shook her head, not sure what to say to that.

"How much notice do you need to make me dinner?"

"Well, first, I think I'd like to know what I get in return for making you dinner."

The response was everything she wanted it to be as he snaked his arm around her waist and pulled her slowly against his hard, warm body. She thought the green flecks in his eyes attempted to hypnotize her, or maybe she just wanted to be hypnotized by them. He brushed a kiss across her lips and when he pulled away she sagged against him. "Fine, how soon can I make you this dinner?"

"C'mon. Let's go see if Salvatore showed up."

Cassie was making a mental grocery list as they rounded the corner of her hallway, but standing in front of her door was Jessica and her mom, mouths agape, staring into the apartment.

Elation from Stills' kisses turned to worry as she sped up her pace. "Mom?" Cassie called.

"Cassandra," her mother greeted her, but her attention zeroed in on the hand Cassie was holding. She tried to pull away, but Stills kept tight hold of it.

She swallowed and licked her lips, this was it.

"Mom," Jessica said, "you remember Agent Stills. He was in charge of the surveillance team and now he's Cassie's boyfriend."

Cassie shot daggers at her sister.

"Mrs. Dodd, how are you?" Stills dropped Cassie's hand to shake her mother's. Barbara accepted the hand, but looked between Cassie, Jess and Stills with dazed eyes.

"What is going on?" Cassie asked again as she narrowed her gaze on Jess' face and raised her voice at what she saw, "Do you have a black eye!?"

"Why do you always yell everything at me?"

"I was gone for like, ten minutes!"

Stills leaned forward to study Jess' eye when a crash from inside the open apartment door drew everyone's attention. He moved in front of all the women, his instinct to keep them safe kicking in. What he saw was Agent Parker Salvatore throwing a punch at the hulking Carlo.

He looked over his shoulder and shot a grin at Cassie. "Looks like Salvatore showed up."

"And Carlo from the...the Italian CIA..." Jess offered. "Of course, Cassie probably already told you he was here," she said with mild irritation.

"Yes, I did. Now tell me how you got a black eye in the ten minutes I was gone! Because it seems like I can't leave you alone at all anymore," Cassie said incredulously.

"What does that mean?" Jessica shot.

"What's going on?" Stills' attempt at interrupting didn't work.

"I try going on a date and you get kidnapped again, and now *this*," Cassie said in frustration, dramatically gesturing at her sister's face.

"You were kidnapped?!" their mother yelled.

Another crash brought a momentary pause to all the arguments.

"What is happening?" Cassie asked, finally focusing on the scene playing out in her living room.

"Well," Jess linked arms with Cassie and her mother, "Carlo is in love with Parker's sister and she made him come all the way to LA to ask Parker for her hand in marriage. I don't think Parker likes the idea."

Carlo pushed Parker into the wall and Cassie cringed as several pictures crashed to the ground with the sound of breaking glass.

"Excuse me." Stills put the plate of cookies down in the hallway before inserting himself into the middle of the brawl.

Cassie took a step toward him, to tell him to stop. She opened her mouth to yell for him to be careful but the words dried up when he stood on the outskirts of the two fighting men and began to tell them to settle down.

"What in God's name is going on?" their mom demanded.

Neither one of them answered her question. Instead, Cassie asked Jessica, "That's Parker?"

Jessica gave an exhausted sigh of affirmation.

Cassie laughed off the worry and pointed, trying to follow Parker with her finger. "Mom, that guy that's fighting, not the really built guy, but the other one. That's the guy Jessica was married to."

"What?!" Mom screamed.

Jessica pulled her arm away from Cassie and snarled, "You're dead to me."

"I wasn't ready to tell anyone about Benji yet," Cassie defended.

"Then why were you holding his hand?" Jess asked.

"I'm a grown ass woman, I can hold a man's hand if I want to."

Jess shook her head as if she were trying to dislodge the past few months' worth of craziness.

Cassie watched Stills attempt several times to defuse the situation, but the only reply he was given was angry yelling and accusing finger pointing. He gave up and threw his own punch that landed across Parker's jaw. Cassie ground her teeth, her whole body stiffening as if she were the one who had been punched.

Jessica waved. "This is mostly testosterone now."

Cassie shook her head. "Being kidnapped has changed you."

"Tell me about it."

Their mom pulled off her purse then and threw it at Cassie; squared her shoulders and marched into the apartment, inserting herself into the middle of the brawl.

"Mom!" Cassie and Jessica shouted at the same time. They took a few steps after her to try and stop her but were struck dumb when their mother yelled from her inflated five-five height, "Gentlemen. That. Is. Enough!" The authority with which she screamed might have had the ability to stop a runaway train.

Stills stumbled a few steps and stopped at the same moment Parker and Carlo's eyes cleared.

Cassie never felt so much pride, embarrassment and admiration in her life. She grinned and looked at Jessica who was shaking her head in wonder.

Now that their mother had everyone's attention, she continued, "You will conduct yourselves accordingly." She crossed her arms over her chest. "Agent Stills?"

He had gathered himself enough and was grinning at Barbara Dodd. "Yes ma'am."

"You are dating Cassandra?"

Cassie knew that look her mother was giving, she was assessing Stills for boyfriend material. Cassie elbowed Jessica. "This, *this* was why I didn't want anyone to know."

Jessica elbowed back. "You outed me. I don't care."

"You were married. I've been on one date," Cassie hissed.

"Girls." Their mother stopped the whispered argument.

Stills stood at attention while Barbara Dodd studied him. "Yes ma'am, I am dating Cassandra."

"Well, Walter and I are so grateful for all the hard work you put in, watching the girls and keeping them safe."

"It's my pleasure." He smiled.

"I don't know how I feel about your job, but you look better than most of the men Cassie's brought home in the past." She turned and winked at Cassie who frowned in reply. She was suddenly seventeen again, bringing home her first boyfriend, mortified and strangely worried that her parents wouldn't like her choice.

"Were you in the middle of a date?"

"Yes ma'am. Cassie wanted to come back and see...well," he gestured to the other men as he confessed, "I called Salvatore. And we were curious if he had shown up."

"Mom..." Cassie started.

"Cassandra. You and your boyfriend go and continue your date."

"Mom–" Cassie tried again.

"Cassandra." Her mother hissed her name which didn't leave much room for argument.

Cassie looked at Jess wide-eyed, what could they do? Jess shrugged in reply. The only thing left to do was shove her mother's purse into Jessica's arms.

Stills held out his hand to Barbara. "I apologize for this," he waved behind him. "It was nice seeing you again Mrs. Dodd."

She nodded her head and Cassie saw the light of an idea forming in her mother's eyes. She reached for Jessica's forearm and squeezed, cringing before their mother could voice her idea.

"I'd like to get to know you better. So how about tonight, at seven? Come to the house for dinner."

"Mom," Cassie hissed.

"Seven p.m.," Barbara Dodd narrowed her gaze and pointed a finger at Cassie, "no excuses."

Cassie knew that her mother had sunk her teeth into an idea and there was no amount of arguing or 'excuses' that could get her out of it. Jess shook her head, what could they do?

"Cassandra." Her mother pointed out the door.

"It's my apartment," she reasoned.

"Cassandra," her mother said sternly. Cassie had officially been excused. She leaned toward Jess, demanding, "Call me...if you can. When you can."

Stills was behind Cassie, she picked up the plate from the hallway, and without a word they matched each other's speed as they collectively held their breath and comments.

Once outside, they looked at each other dumbfounded. Cassie blurted, "That was one hell of a fire you lit under his ass."

"No shit." He smiled but rubbed his hand.

Cassie took his hand with her free one and studied it. "Are you okay?"

"It's not the first time I've punched someone, it won't be the last," he said, but he didn't pull his hand away.

"Soak your knuckles in Epsom salts and then ice, it'll be sore for a day, but you'll live," she said.

He raised an eyebrow at the unexpected instructions. "Have you doctored a lot of hands?" He turned his hand over and began to rub hers.

"I've played as a fullback on soccer teams since I was twelve. I have a way of bracing myself when I go for a ball that makes other girls bounce off of me." She licked her lips. "On several occasions, some of the girls got pissed and started throwing punches. So, I might have had to throw one or two of my own in retaliation," Cassie admitted to his hand.

Stills tilted his head. "Intriguing."

Cassie met his gaze then. "You think so? My mom thinks it's barbaric."

"I think I find it strangely attractive."

She grunted in reply.

"So, we have a dinner to go to." He took a deep breath, but the exhale came out as a yawn.

"Benji, you're exhausted. You need a nap first."

"I'm fine."

"We have about five hours. That's time for a nap. But," she looked up at her apartment, "it looks like I'm coming with you, as my apartment is occupied."

"I've dreamed of sleeping with you in my arms a lot." He meant for the comment to be sexy but he began yawning at the end of the sentence.

Cassie laughed and patted him on the back. "Alright, Casanova, let's go."

"We need to go to the store before we go to your parents' house," he said as he opened the car door for her.

"I don't like this dinner idea." He shut the door but when he climbed in, Cassie continued, "I'm not prepared for the coming interrogation."

"I'm good at interrogations."

"Yeah well, this interrogation is going to be all for me. And it won't necessarily be verbal. A lot of visual cues...that's what Barbara Dodd will be inspecting."

"What kind of guys did you used to date?"

"One guy!" She threw her hands up in the air. "One guy rode a motorcycle and then they all became bad seeds."

Another yawn.

"Are you okay to drive?"

"I'm okay."

"What do you need at the store?"

"I need to buy flowers for your mom," he said as he pulled into traffic.

Cassie shook her head and groaned. "Oh, don't do that."

"It's protocol, Dodd. Always take the mother flowers on the first visit."

Cassie sighed. "Eww...my mom is going to like you."

Chapter Twenty-Six

"**Y**ou okay?" Cassie asked as she stood behind Stills. He unlocked his apartment door, but had yet to turn the knob and open it.

He glanced over his shoulder. There was an indecipherable look on his face, and Cassie wondered if it was worry. She found herself enchanted at the idea, it felt like discovering another side of him.

She elbowed him and tried to ease him by joking, "Are you a slob?" Actually, she was pretty confident he was the kind of guy who kept his life quite tidy.

He found whatever courage he needed to finally push the door open. He stood to the side, allowing Cassie to enter. The entryway was a long hallway containing a closet and a half bath to the left, then at the end, it gave way to a large open concept kitchen, dining and living room area. On the opposite side of the great room, she saw another hallway that must lead to the bedroom.

"It's very white," Cassie surmised quickly, then cleared her throat and corrected, "it's very clean."

Clean and minimalist.

"I don't spend a lot of time here," he excused.

The kitchen boasted two appliances: a toaster and coffee maker.

The kitchen table was a worn, functional light wood number that could seat four, but only three chairs surrounded it. In the middle was a stack of obvious fast food napkins; the logo for Subway visible on the top one.

She walked through the space, continued until she was running her hand over the arm of the heather gray sofa; it felt so new, she expected to see a sales tag still intact.

There were two mismatched lamps, a wood and wrought iron coffee table, and a flat screen TV that was small by current 21st century standards.

The only other items in the sparsely decorated space were two pieces of art. One hung on the wall of the dining room area, a slender watercolor of the Eiffel Tower done in various hues of blue. The other hung over the sofa, a print with a forest of lush green trees, jungle-like undergrowth and a trail leading to a misty waterfall.

Cassie stood in front of the print.

"I thought about that when you told me about your favorite place," he was leaning against the kitchen wall by the entryway, watching her while she took in her surroundings.

She kept her attention on the print as she asked, "Where is it?"

"The Blue Ridge Mountains. It's called English Falls."

"Gorgeous." She took a few more moments of silent reflection before turning her attention back to finish her inspection of his apartment. "No framed family pictures," she gestured. "You know Benji, they say that's the first sign of a serial killer." She shot him a mischievous grin.

He pulled his phone from his pocket. "Check my online photos folder. My brothers and my mom share all sorts with me. There is also a treasure trove of incriminating pictures you might enjoy."

"Really?"

"If I recall, the most recent are pictures of my whole family and me in matching reindeer sweaters as well as matching tutus. My niece had a ballerina party and insisted we all wear them."

"Oh, we're going to have a fun 'show and tell' one day."

He put what remained of the cookies on the kitchen counter, but kept his distance. If Cassie didn't know any better she would have thought he was nervous.

"It's nice." She nodded her head as she gave another glance around the length of the apartment.

Stills smiled. "It's a bed," he admitted, "it's not a home."

Cassie licked her lips.

They were caught in an uncomfortable lull of conversation.

Hell, Cassie thought, they were caught in the lull of their budding relationship. Jessica was finally, truly safe, which meant the part of his job involved in watching over Jess was finished. His words from the day at the coffee shop played through her mind, *one day this will all be over and we'll get to see about 'us'.*

"Everything's over now. For real, right?" She felt like she needed to hear the words, so she reiterated, "With Jess. It's all done."

"For real this time. Everything is over," he confirmed.

And whatever was going on with Parker was figuring itself out, so Cassie no longer needed to hold fast to any worry concerning her sister. She had thought when the time came, the stress would just slip off her shoulders and she would seamlessly move on with her own life, but it didn't seem to be that easy. However, having yet another confirmation caused some sort of melting, and the worry that did evaporate, was replaced by exhaustion.

Stills asked, "You okay?"

"I'm relieved."

He nodded, still immobilized. Cassie allowed herself to study him, take him all in.

"Finally alone." He had read her thoughts.

"Really alone," she whispered. Her anticipation and excitement of this moment that she'd waited months for made her speechless.

The fading stress was replaced with want. Each breath, each heartbeat was need and desire that began in her stomach and twirled as it grew larger and larger, encompassing every part of her. This man, standing across from her, allowing her the space to gather herself, was attracted to her. He wanted her. And damn if she didn't want him.

The tiny tinge of need was churning now, a riptide flowing through her. Stills clenched his hands, drawing her attention to his strong, taut forearms. Her skin itched to have those hands on her. She was certain he could hear her changed breathing, the rhythm of it had become quick and shallow. The air in the apartment thickened, her chest constricted and this was just from being in the same space as him and wanting him.

A slight tug at the corner of his lips was the only indication she was given that he knew what she was thinking, and that maybe, he was thinking the same thing. She let her gaze rest on the strong veins in his tanned throat and was rewarded with a visible quickening of his pulse.

She met his eyes and smiled, but she didn't want to move, not yet. She was basking in the effects speeding through her bloodstream. She was savoring her yearning. If she moved slightly, just a fraction, she knew they would crash into each other; a combustion of forceful desire.

Then, Stills yawned.

The spell they'd been under fell like fine dust particles to the ground around them. Cassie laughed until she began yawning as well. She shook it off and pointed to herself. "I'm letting go of stress finally. You're exhausted."

"I am," he said sadly.

"You should probably go to bed."

"I should."

The unspoken 'but' hung between them. Finally, Stills broke through the exhaustion and the lull, effortlessly crossed the room toward her; without the awkwardness or build-up, he pulled Cassie into his arms and placed a chaste kiss on her lips. "I want you so badly, but I'm so tired."

"I understand."

"Lay down with me?" He quickly mumbled the request.

Cassie glanced at the hallway off the living room that led to the bedroom, cocked her head to the side and asked, "Aren't you worried you'll be tempted to start something once we're in bed together?"

"I'm planning on it." He grinned and took her hand.

His room boasted a king size bed, one nightstand and the other kitchen chair.

His confidence faltered when he neared the bed.

Cassie squeezed his hand. "What's going on Agent Stills?"

"This wasn't how I wanted to get you into bed." He whispered the confession.

Cassie released his hand and pressed herself and her lips against him. He smiled at her advances, and when she pulled away to look into those intriguing amber eyes, another yawn. Cassie grinned and pushed him so he fell into a seated position onto the bed with an 'umph'.

She sat next to him and began to take off her shoes. He followed her lead, and pulled out his wallet and cell phone, placing them on the nightstand. Cassie stood back up and moved so she was standing in between his legs. He reached for her, his hands splayed on her hips, then wound their way up her back, and the warmth on her skin sent shivers. She cupped his face and tilted his head slightly to the right, then the left. His eyes were properly bloodshot now. The black rings that worried her were a shade darker. His lips seemed fuller however, and their attraction to each other was definitely unfettered. But his exhaustion was evident.

She nipped at his lower lip, but he stopped her playfulness and deepened the kiss.

This, Cassie thought, she wanted this endlessly. She liked being wanted this much. She liked wanting him this much. She wanted to climb on his lap, and drown in his lips and let the friction between their covered bodies escalate and intensify until they were undone; out of their minds with passion.

Somehow, she pulled herself together enough to end the kiss. She pressed him away from her. "You're dead on your feet."

"I know."

"Lay down, Benji."

He did as instructed. Cassie climbed over his prone form to the other side of the bed, eliciting a grunt when her foot hit his thigh.

"Jeez, Dodd."

She arranged herself with a few exaggerated movements until she was on her side, her back to Stills.

When he didn't move, she reached behind her, grabbed his arm and pulled. He gave his own overexaggerated rumbles of arrangement until he was pressed against her, pulling her so each inch of her back and legs were tucked against the front of his body.

His hand snaked over her stomach, and she pulled his hand to her lips and kissed it, then held it to her chest. "Go to sleep, Benji, we have time for the rest later."

He kissed her neck. "Just let me rest for twenty minutes." They did a strange dance of trying to get organized once again, with arms and legs tucked just so. Cassie knew the moment he had fallen asleep - his breathing evened out, steady, deep.

Cassie thought she wasn't going to be able to sleep at all. She was too excited. She wanted to wake him up and demand he not sleep until she was sexually satisfied. She wondered how that hidden passion he kissed her with would translate between the sheets.

She truly thought they'd figure it out this afternoon, and she saw the yearning in his eyes, but she also knew she wanted *all* his attention, not a fraction of a man who was beyond exhausted. She wanted all of him, unbound, uninterrupted, unexhausted.

Her stomach fluttered at the idea and she wiggled herself against his warm body. It felt good to be in his arms, she knew it would. She let her thoughts rummage around; so much had happened in the past few months. Hell, so much had happened in the past two days.

She had been running on worry and adrenaline for so long, that she was nearly blindsided by this attraction. She wouldn't say that Agent Benjamin Stills was someone she'd been looking for, but she'd be lying if she didn't admit, he was exactly what she needed.

Chapter Twenty-Seven

C assie's phone woke her up. She had set it next to her head before they fell asleep. She fumbled with the phone, blinking the screen into focus. It was Jess.

"Hello?" She whispered the greeting.

"Are you on your way?" Jess asked.

"What?"

"Cass, it's six-thirty. Your mother's command dinner will commence in thirty minutes."

"Shit." She hung up the phone without any goodbye and nudged Stills, who had begun to wake up when he heard her talking. "Benji, we have thirty minutes to get to my parents' if you want to make a good impression."

He rolled himself up into a seated position on his side of the bed and rubbed his face with his hands.

"It'll take twenty minutes to get there," she said. "I don't think we have time to get flowers."

"What's better? Late with flowers or on time without?" he asked as he shuffled to his closet, pulling off his wrinkled shirt.

"On time, no flowers," Cassie stated. She rolled herself off the other side of the bed and stretched as she watched Stills' shirt slip to the floor. "Whoa," she whispered, her arms freezing in the air at the top of the stretch.

He turned at her muttered outburst.

The front was better than the back. Gravity pulled her arms down to her side and she licked her lips at the unexpected attractiveness of his form.

He liked her reaction and his eyes darkened.

Cassie shook her head, pointing. "*You*, put a damn shirt on. Right now." Her throat had gone dry. "Good lord..." she scoffed and took a step toward the wall, trying to put more distance and obstacles between them than just the bed.

"Come here." His voice was velvet.

She shook her head, grinning, trying to plug her bugged out eyes back into their sockets. "If we're going to be anywhere on time, you *have* to put a damn shirt on."

A smile broke apart any exhaustion that had been on his face before. "Come here," he repeated.

"Can you stop if I do?" she asked.

He shook his head no in reply, so she stood her ground and pointed to his closet. "Put on a shirt then."

Cassie's phone rang again and she was thankful for the flimsy excuse that pulled her attention away from the temptation across the room.

Jess was calling again. "We're on our way," Cassie answered.

"Do you need anything from the store?" Jess asked. "I'm buying vodka, cranberry juice and beer."

Cassie laughed. "A merlot please. Oh, and can you get a bouquet of flowers for us and leave them in the usual place if we don't get there in time."

Jessica agreed, then hung up.

Stills had finally pulled on another shirt, so Cassie felt confident enough to retrieve her shoes. She glanced down at her own wrinkled clothes and smoothed a hand over her shirt, it would have to do, there was no other option.

"What's the usual place?" he asked, sitting down next to her and pulling on his own shoes.

"In our high school and college years, we created a sort of secret hiding place. We hollowed out a bush to the left of the house. It was the perfect place for hiding things like stolen bottles of vodka from the old man's liquor cabinet, or, a gallon of milk when we needed to prove we'd gone to the store rather than meet up with a guy at the park for twenty minutes to make out..."

"Clever girls."

She winked at him.

"How much time do we have?" he asked.

She glanced at her phone. "Twenty-two minutes."

"I'll make it in eighteen." He put his phone and wallet back in his pants and held his hand out to help Cassie up.

"And what will we do with the other four minutes, Agent Stills?"

"Fog up the windows in front of your parents' house."

"Hell yeah."

Stills pulled up to the front of the house, hurriedly put the car in park, and unbuckled his seatbelt before Cassie could react.

He leaned over the center console, framed her face with his hands and adjusted his head, grinning as he slowly lowered his lips to hers.

She smiled into his mouth and tried to let her passion express what she wanted to do when he'd had his shirt off and she'd seen his well-formed back and chest. Hell, she suddenly wanted to lick him all over and touch every damn inch of him. She moaned her frustration and need into his mouth and he deepened the kiss.

"We don't have to go," she whispered into his mouth.

"Yes we do."

"No, you were looking out for Jess. You already look like a good guy, we can ditch this dinner." She'd taken her seatbelt off so she could meet him halfway. "Just one more kiss and then drive back to your place."

He groaned at the tantalizing idea when a loud tap on the passenger side window stopped their advances. They pulled away, their eyes trying to find each other in the dim dusky glow of the setting sun.

Another knock drew frowns and they glanced at the intrusion. It was Jessica, a Cheshire grin in place.

"There are too many distractions lately," Cassie muttered.

A knock on the driver side window pulled Stills' attention to Parker Salvatore.

"Benji, all you have to do is start the car and drive," she whispered.

He squeezed her hand in reassurance but she knew they were going to a dinner where she would have to answer questions about a relationship that she'd barely dipped her toe into.

"Fine," she muttered as she opened her door, "but you owe me."

Jessica obstructed any reply Stills might have given her by pointing out, "Those windows were starting to get foggy."

"I could have done better if you hadn't interrupted." Cassie righted her clothes and ran a hand through her hair then frowned as she studied Jessica's face. Her eye was swollen and had already turned a dark shade of purple. Cassie took her sister's chin in her hand and tilted her head to the side to get a good look at the shiner in the light, then sighed. "Like you needed another black eye..."

Jessica pushed Cassie's hand away. "I'm fine."

"Are you sure?" Cassie glanced at the man talking to Stills. "You're *really* okay?"

Jessica slapped the large bouquet of flowers against Cassie's chest. "I said I'm fine." She cleared her throat and hid a smile. "And he apologized."

"And you accepted his apology?"

"The jury is still out," Jess said, and when her eyes darted to Parker, Cassie realized whatever questions and insecurities Jess had about Parker Salvatore and their relationship had been answered.

Jessica continued her explanation. "I made him call his mother and tell her we'd gotten married ten years ago in Vegas as a joke. His *Italian* mother," she stressed.

"Is that important?"

"Have you heard the stereotypical crap about Italian men being mama's boys?" Jess asked. Cassie shook her head no in reply. "Well," Jess continued, "it's a thing."

"So how did his mom take the news?"

Jess frowned. "I'm not completely sure, I don't speak Italian."

Cassie laughed and shook her head, God she felt good. Light, even.

"What's happening with Benji?" Jess asked.

Cassie glanced over at the men making their way around the car. "I couldn't tell you. We keep getting interrupted."

She overheard Stills ask Parker, "Are you angry with me?"

"Naw, you saw your shot, you took it," Parker replied.

"You waited too long," Stills said as he made his way to Cassie and slipped his arm around her waist. She handed him the flowers.

"Thanks for picking up the flowers, Jessica."

Jess nodded as Parker made his way to her side and mimicked Stills' gesture, slipping his arm around Jessica's waist.

Cassie felt strange. Just last week, she and Jessica were single and fighting over what movie to watch while they ate Chinese take-out. She glanced over at Stills before Jessica caught her attention.

"Cassie, this is Parker Salvatore," she introduced.

Cassie raised an eyebrow at Parker's outstretched hand. She took it as she concluded, "The husband. You know, you've got a lot to make up for."

She glanced to see if her sister would intervene, but she had that look Cassie knew all too well. The one that implied 'my big sister is gonna kick your ass'.

"I know," Parker admitted.

Cassie dropped his hand and pointed a finger of warning directly at his chest. "If you hurt my sister again, I'll have you taken care of."

Jessica covered her laugh with a cough.

"And don't think I can't do it," Cassie gestured her head in Stills' direction, "I know a guy."

The front door opened then, and standing on the porch was their mother, grinning and waving. "Come in, come in," she called.

The quartet faced the front porch. Jessica leaned toward Cassie and whispered, "This is *not* a good idea."

Cassie would rather have woken up and started something with Stills, but as the realization washed over her that she wasn't the one who had married a man and lied about it for ten years, she began to think that she might actually enjoy this evening. She may only have to answer a question or two about Stills, but that was nothing compared to the explanations required by their mother about the recent revelations of Jessica's relationship.

Cassie gave a devilish grin. "Oh, I beg to differ. This is gonna be the most fun."

Chapter Twenty-Eight

As they reached the front steps, Cassie and Jessica both shuffled, trying to let the other go first. Cassie finally pushed Jessica in front of her toward the bottom of the three steps that led to their childhood home.

Cassie winked at Stills then watched Parker present himself to their mother. She was brimming from the excitement of holding court.

"Hello Mrs. Dodd," Parker held out his hand, "pleased to see you again." In his other arm he held a paper bag weighted down with several bottles of liquor. She took his hand and then leaned in and offered her cheek in greeting.

Jess glanced back at Cassie and mouthed, '*What the fuck?*'

"Call me Barbara," she instructed Parker, "after all, it seems like we're family now."

Jessica and Parker, having passed the welcoming committee, moved on so Stills and Cassie could enter.

"Mrs. Dodd." Stills handed over the bouquet of flowers.

"Oh, they are so beautiful," she gushed and Cassie figured her mother's dream of having her two girls attached was putting her in a good mood. "Call me Barbara." She offered Stills the same opportunity to kiss her cheek.

Cassie raised an eyebrow at her mom. "Been drinking?" she teased.

"My house is full, let me enjoy this." She flicked Cassie's arm.

That was exactly what this was, her mother had always wanted a big family and a house full of people she could dote on. It came across as intrusive and overbearing, and deep down, Cassie admired her mother for wanting the very best for her children.

Inside, the house was warm and smelled like pot roast and baked bread. The windows were open, letting in the evening breeze as Mozart played from the speakers in the living room. A thousand childhood memories washed over Cassie. It had been a long time since she felt this comforted and excited by her childhood home. It damn near felt like Christmas morning. And she knew a lot of it had to do with the man standing next to her.

"Cass," her father called as he came into the kitchen where everyone was congregating.

"Hey Dad," she patted him on the back and gestured toward Stills, "you remember Agent Stills? We've been on one and a half dates. We don't know what this is, but we like each other."

As Stills shook Walter's hand, her father commented, "Well son, one and a half dates? In the book of Barbara you're practically engaged."

"You've never faced any bad guy as cunning or as scheming as my mom," Cassie said.

"I heard that young lady." Her mom tried to chide her, but the smile on her face was boundless.

"Thank you again," Walter said with a glance toward Jessica.

Stills nodded and pulled Cassie to his side. Since she wasn't hiding it anymore, she figured he wasn't going to hide his feelings toward her either.

Carlo was standing over the stove stirring a pan. Cassie glanced at her dad and asked, "What did I miss?"

"Well, seems like your mom made a new friend, took him around town and played tour guide. Then they came home with groceries along with the announcement that your sister was married, and that we're all having dinner."

Carlo pulled out the spoon he was using and studied the white sauce before taking a bite. He nodded his head. "It's ready."

"He cooks?" Cassie asked Stills.

"He's an enigma." He shrugged just as Jessica called them to the kitchen counter where she was pouring drinks.

"What do you want?" Jess asked them.

"Wine," Cassie answered as Stills nodded toward the six pack Parker was pulling out of the bag.

"That's quite the shiner, Jessica," Walter called.

"It was an accident," Jessica reassured.

"Accident?" He glanced at Cassie for confirmation.

Cassie nodded. "It was a hell of a day, Dad."

"I guess. Everyone is covered in bruises." He nodded toward Parker and Carlo.

"There was a fight," Cassie began, but he held up his hand and responded, "Your mother already told me." He turned his attention to Stills. "I grew up with brothers, so I thought girls were going to be these soft, fragile things. But this one," he gestured to Cassie, "started playing soccer and came home with broken bones and black eyes. That one," he nodded to Jessica, "came home with crashed bicycles and wounded animals..." He shook his head in wonder as he trailed off.

Barbara moved around to the side of Carlo. He took another spoon out of the drawer and offered her a taste of the white sauce he was making, and as she licked the spoon clean, she rolled her eyes heavenward.

"Dad..." Cassie gestured to what was happening.

"When she showed up with the big guy, she started cooking and made him sit in the living room with me; we spent two hours talking about Italian soccer."

"Then she made him cook?"

"He offered." He scratched his chin. "It's been an eventful day. I still don't think I have all the details right." They watched Carlo help take the roast out as her mother directed him on where to put it.

Cassie skeptically looked at what was going on in the kitchen. "I think it has to do with Italian men and their mothers?" She guessed at the respect Carlo was giving their mother based on Jessica's prior comments.

Her dad grunted. "Well, the other thing I want to know about is this Parker. What do you know about him?"

Cassie glanced at Stills, it was his turn to answer. "Sir, he's a standup guy. I trust him with my life. Other than a youthful indiscretion," he raised his eyebrow as he referenced the 'mistake' marriage between Parker and Jessica, "he's usually honorable and hardworking."

Parker caught the end of the character reference as he walked over to hand Stills a beer. He added, "And I'm in love with your daughter, sir. I would do anything for her." He held out his hand. "I'm Parker Salvatore."

"Call me Walter." He shook the young man's hand and then gave a laugh. "I've never been surrounded by so many well-mannered young men before. These two haven't always brought home the cream of the crop."

"Dad." Cassie rolled her eyes as Jess defended, "They weren't all bad."

"Please tell us about all of them and spare no detail," Stills instructed.

Jessica brought Cassie a glass of wine. Cassie tapped her glass to her sister's tumbler of vodka and cranberry juice.

The pot roast was plated and Carlo set it at the table. "Mangiamo," he said.

Cassie pointed to the far side of the table where Stills should sit, with Parker and Jessica directly across from them. Carlo sat next to Jessica and their parents completed the family table by each taking their place at the head. Both ends were considered the 'head' of the table, not a power play so much as an equality decision that had been made years and years ago.

"Carlo made the cheese sauce for the vegetables," Barbara offered proudly, as if Carlo was her protégée.

Steam rose into the air from the large plate of roasted vegetables, as well as the pot roast. There was a loaf of fresh baked bread, not homemade, as their mother had found a frozen dough at the grocery store years ago and never looked back.

A large salad was presented, and all the accoutrements a person could want filled in the remaining spaces on the table: butter, olives, dressings, and jam for the bread.

"It looks wonderful, Mrs. Dodd," Stills said.

Cassie glanced sideways at him. His eyes were alight and she guessed he was under the same spell given off by the warmth of the house, the family aspect, and the home-cooked meal he so coveted.

Their father cleared his throat. "If I may", he held his glass of wine aloft and looked around the table, his gaze fixing on his wife at the other end, "it would seem we have all been through a difficult time these past few months. But tonight, we are blessed to have our daughters home, our Jessica safe and sound, and the ability to thank the men who made that happen." His voice cracked slightly as he cleared his throat once more. Cassie, sitting to the right of her father, reached out and patted his shoulder. He nodded. "We are grateful and happy to share this meal with you all."

"Cin cin," Jessica said.

"Cin Cin?" Cassie asked as everyone touched glasses together.

"It's Italian for 'Cheers,'" she explained.

"Well then, cin cin," Cassie added.

Dishes of food were passed around, the sound of silverware scraping against plates and questions of 'could you please pass' filled the awkward beginnings of the meal. Cassie was glad her dad had put on the radio, the music helped smooth out the usual discomfort that came with a new group of people getting to know each other.

"So what did you do today?" Cassie asked Carlo.

When he glanced at her, she cringed; the angry welt on his cheek, that was turning purple, was more prominent in the overhead lighting. It didn't seem to bother him as he explained, "We went to see the famous stars. We saw Sophia Loren's star."

"You took him downtown?" Cassie asked.

"He's a tourist," their mother said. "We went to Grauman's, but they've changed their name to the TCL Chinese Theater."

"So, you two patched things up?" Cassie waved her fork between Parker and Carlo.

"He's in love with my sister," Parker explained.

"I asked Alessandra to marry me. She sent me to Parker for his permission," Carlo told his plate.

"She sent him on a heroic quest," their mother explained.

Parker laughed. "I think she did. She's a force to be reckoned with."

Jessica glanced at Carlo. "You met Alessandra for the first time when I was taken to her house, right?"

He nodded.

Jessica continued her line of questioning. "So, you've known her for three months and you proposed?"

"When you know, you know." He shrugged and pointed his fork at Jessica. "You knew Salvatore for one day before you married him, you don't get to make judgements."

"Way to go Carlo." Cassie laughed.

Jessica shrugged off the comparison and instead said, "Cass, you would love Alessandra."

"She was the 'safehouse' where Parker sent the taxi, right? And she's a doctor?" Cassie thought that one of these days, now that Thomas was behind bars, and the head of a crime family had come clean as to his motives behind his actions, and her sister wasn't heartbroken, it would be interesting to hear the whole story. Chronologically.

"Batman had a good costume," Carlo interjected.

Cassie frowned in confusion as her mother translated, "Oh, he was enthralled with all the people who were dressed up in front of the theater. Of course, do you know, not one panhandler tried to approach us?" She pointed a fork at Carlo. "He is very handy."

"Mom," Jessica muttered, "he's not an accessory."

"I didn't say he was, I said he had a good day. And we had ice cream and coffee and talked about his Alessandra and he even called her," their mother said triumphantly.

Cassie turned her head slightly and said to Stills, "Benji, what would it take to get video of my mother's day out with Carlo? I feel like I need to see the tape."

"Cassandra." Her mother laughed.

Cassie sat back and studied Parker. He had a few bruises on his face, where Carlo and Stills had gotten in their punches. His sandy brown hair was slightly mussed, and he had the same dark rings around his eyes as Stills. His broad shoulders pulled at the fabric of his wrinkled shirt which sported a small stain. He sat close to Jessica, glancing at her often out of the corner of his eye, obviously head over heels enthralled with her. But what was most intriguing was the way he exuded a shroud of protectiveness around her.

Cassie smiled. "So Parker...I'm sure I'm not going to embarrass you any more than my mother has already, so if I may ask, what are your intentions toward my sister?"

Before he could answer, Stills elbowed Cassie and whispered, "I thought you weren't ready for all the talk of relationships and intentions?"

"Jessica has been pining on my sofa for the past three months, and as the older sister who's kicked several guys' asses for less, I think it's only fair I get to ask," she defended.

"And just whose asses have you kicked?" Stills' eyes sparkled at the prospect.

Parker answered, "I love her."

"Ma sei troppo stupido," Carlo muttered.

Cassie raised an eyebrow in question. "He was too stupid to tell her the truth of it," Carlo said in English.

Parker explained, "I was trying to wrap up my current investigation and transfer to a desk job so Jessica and I could be together without any more threats, and so that she wouldn't spend all her time worrying."

The reality of the familiar situation dried Cassie's throat out.

Their mother intervened, "Do you love him, Jessica?"

"I've agreed to go out on a date with him," Jess answered.

"We're still married," Parker offered.

"We'll see," Jessica replied.

"Well, when you're ready. We can always have another wedding," Barbara said.

"Barb," their father warned.

She jutted out her chin. "Just for family."

"You're still married?" Cassie asked.

Jessica sighed. "Apparently, he stopped the divorce from going through. I just found out today."

"Interesting."

Jessica rolled her eyes and tried to hide her smile behind a bite of her dinner.

Cassie knew her sister still loved Parker. And as she watched them interact she saw what she wanted as well; the man sitting next to Jess couldn't get enough of her, and her sister was happy and at peace. Cassie thought that one day, she'd point out to her sister how she'd thought Thomas wasn't good for her, but not today.

"He told his mom about the marriage," Carlo said.

"Is that a big deal?" Cassie asked, as it was the second time it had been brought up and she was confused. Was there a weight to it that she wasn't understanding?

Carlo and Parker both grinned at Cassie. Parker explained, "Italian men and their mothers are a very important relationship. She runs the house, has the last say, and if you are keeping secrets from her and she finds out, it could be as bad as disownment from the family."

"And these are just normal Italian people we're talking about, not mob people, right?" Cassie inquired.

"It's all about respect and coddling," Stills offered.

"It's not that bad," Parker muttered as Carlo added his own disagreement, "It's not coddling."

"What did your mom say?" Cassie asked.

Parker licked his lips. "It seems my sister had already told her."

Jessica began to laugh. "Alessandra told their mother but also said that she was sure Parker would be calling her soon to get her blessing and come clean."

"Alessandra." Carlo grunted the name.

Cassie was fascinated by the love she saw in the big man's eyes as he shook his head, he wasn't surprised that Alessandra had told her mother, and he was possibly a little proud of her too.

"What's Alessandra like?" Cassie asked.

"The complete opposite of Parker," Jessica said. "She is much shorter and has brown hair and eyes. She's super smart...a force."

"Smart is the opposite of me?" Parker asked.

"She is a powerful woman," Carlo finished the assessment.

"You aren't that smart," Stills added, "you waited too long." He gestured to Jessica.

"Well..." He agreed with a nod to the statement.

The room fell silent as seconds were passed around, accompanied by the sounds of silverware scrapes.

When Cassie finished her wine, Stills asked, "Do you want more?"

She felt a slight thrill at his attentiveness. "Please," she replied.

"I'll grab it." He stood and asked, "Anyone else?"

He poured more wine for Cassie, her parents and Carlo.

Parker broke the silence. "So Stills, it would seem you figured out who the firecracker on the other end of the phone was."

"What?" Jessica asked while Cassie's eyes widened, she turned an interested gaze on him.

Stills licked his lips and Cassie thought she saw a slight blush tinge his cheeks.

"What's going on?" their mother asked.

Parker was all too happy to explain. "Mrs. Dodd, Jessica called her sister to help find my phone number. And the call upset Cassie. So as I understand it, Cassie called the number she gave Jess and was quite demanding and...vocal in her need for information."

"Good girl." Their mom nodded her head.

"I was in rare form, using all the tools you taught me, Mom," Cassie explained.

"Stills took the call. Later, he told us that Jessica's sister was pushy and demanding."

Barbara Dodd's grin widened, and she winked at Cassie.

Parker continued, "Then you called her a firecracker. And everyone who heard the comment thought it was *interesting*, because Stills is a no-nonsense, straight-laced, calm as the day is long, sort of man. So the term 'firecracker' didn't seem to fit."

Stills didn't have a chance to answer, Cassie laughed. "But I *am* a firecracker. What can I say?"

"So Stills, since I'm part of the family now, I think it only fair I get to ask, what are *your* intentions?" Parker gave a wicked grin, and Cassie thought she saw both of her parents sit forward slightly in her peripheral.

"One and a half dates." Cassie stressed the number of dates she'd been on with this man who made her body sing and her heart race and her damn mind drift into continual daydream-like states.

Jessica laughed.

Stills sat back and contemplated his audience before admitting, "I like her. *A lot.* We're going to finish the other half of our date one of these days, and then have a few more, and see where this goes." He raised his eyebrow in Parker's direction, was that good enough?

"So Parker. Do you follow soccer?" Cassie knew how to get back at him.

"I follow Serie A." He stated the name of the top tiered professional soccer league in Italy.

"SSC Napoli," Carlo said disgustedly, referring to the team Parker supported in the Serie A league.

Cassie's grin grew, this did not bode well for Parker. If he wanted to impress her father, he had picked the wrong team.

Parker shook his head and pointed a fork at Carlo. "This coming from a man who supports AC Milan."

Cassie glanced at her father, who sat back in his chair and beamed. He might not like the teams the men supported, but the idea of having people to talk to about the sport he loved would be a welcome luxury.

Cassie pointed her fork at Parker and explained, "Dad likes Fiorentina."

"Oh, Dad! We drove past where they played," Jessica exclaimed.

The weight of where her sister had been and the reason, made everyone quiet for a moment.

Carlo shook his head, breaking the silence. "Fiorentina and Napoli are filled with players who have square feet."

Walter and Parker started talking all at once, defending their teams and placement in current ranks.

Cassie glanced at her mother who was grinning at her father.

"Can you pass me the pot roast?" Stills asked Cassie.

She handed it over. "How's your dinner?"

"Home-cooked," was his reply.

Cassie smiled. "You know, I think I'm jealous. I wanted to be the first to make you a home-cooked meal."

He leaned over, kissed her cheek then whispered, "We've got time, Dodd."

"Benjamin, tell me about your family," Barbara instructed.

Stills' voice began to mingle with the rest of the conversational buzz. As soccer and stats were discussed between the other men, Stills chatted with their mother about his brothers, his three nieces and two nephews, and his parents, all of whom still lived in San Diego.

Cassie glanced across the table at her sister. They both shook their heads in disbelief, the silent communication they'd developed over the years as siblings, related in that one action.

Cassie pointed toward Parker with her chin, then gave into a shrug – she liked him. In turn, Jessica raised an eyebrow in the direction of Stills and winked.

Once the food and two bottles of wine were polished off, the men stood and helped clear the table. Cassie shook her head and wanted to explain about expectations that were being set into motion, and then she thought of the hidden restaurant wrapped in twinkle lights that radiated romance.

Cassie's dad patted his wife on the shoulder. "I'll go start the fire pit," he said.

"Why?" Cassie asked.

"Carlo has never had s'mores. Your mother thought we could make some for dessert and have our coffee outside." He gave off the gruff exterior of not liking the idea, but then added, "The winds have died down and it is a nice night for a fire." Even he was having an entertaining night and didn't mind extending the visit.

"You like these guys?" Cassie asked.

"We'll see." Her father flashed a smile. "The music stopped, go put something on and flip the switch." He was referring to the outdoor speakers that were programmed with the stereo system in the living room.

Cassie was just going to put on more Mozart, but she realized she was feeling nostalgic. She wanted something different. She held out her hand on her way to the stereo and traced the records lined up in the entertainment center. She wanted to hear something that resonated with what she was feeling. A releasing, a sense of home, a longing for Stills. The feeling that for these five minutes, all was right with the world.

She looked through the vinyl, each record she pulled out held a different childhood memory. She carefully pushed them back in until she found the one she was looking for. She slipped out the vinyl, careful to palm the record. She opened the lid of the player, slipped the record onto the notch, and steeped herself in the emotions brought on by a set of familiar actions. She set the needle on the song she wanted and turned the volume up slightly, then pressed the input button that would turn on the outdoor speakers.

As the piano solo of the song began, she felt the coming words deep in her chest. And as if she pulled him to her, Stills' arms slipped around her waist and his lips found her neck.

A song that meant so much when she came home each Christmas from college was given another layer of meaning in this moment.

She turned in his arms, and as the slow downbeat of the song started, he began to sway with her. Cassie ran her hands up his chest, then linked them around his neck. The room was dimly lit, but Cassie could still see that enticing glint in the depths of those eyes that she so desperately wanted to spend days getting lost in.

They fit their bodies together, swaying to the music, a first dance. Unexpected, yet as seamless as everything else that had happened between them.

She wondered, could it really be this easy? Then immediately thought, why not? Not everything has to be difficult. She closed her eyes and let it all wash over her - the music and the wine and the strong male scent of the man holding her. Wave after perfect wave.

In the living room of her childhood home, where she learned how to walk and live and love, she was being held in the arms of a man who challenged her, made the mundane flourish and going for coffee at the corner bakery an adventure

Chapter Twenty-Nine

Carlo studied the burning marshmallow skewered atop the metal tongs he was using.

Stills asked, "Do you like burnt food?"

When Carlo replied "No," Stills leaned over and blew out his marshmallow flambé.

Jessica instructed, "Take your time, don't put it straight in the fire, just...heat it."

He pulled it off and popped the gooey mess into his mouth anyway, then gave a grunt as he replaced it with another. This time he was careful to keep it farther from the flame.

"What is a marshmallow made of?" he asked.

"Sugar and gelatin?" Barbara answered with a question. "Have you ever made homemade marshmallows Cassie?"

"No, but that sounds right. I think it's the way you cook the sugar and add the gelatin that gives it the fluffy texture."

"Gelatina?" He looked to Parker for clarification as he pronounced the similar sounding Italian word. □

"I think so," Parker offered.

The soft breeze made the fire a welcome heat. Cassie sat next to her sister, elbows touching like they used to when they were kids; a subconscious assurance. Across from them were the men, Parker, Carlo and Stills. Their parents sat between them all.

The companionable conversation continued. Carlo asked questions about American ingenuity and culture, all of which Barbara Dodd was only too happy to explain and give her opinion on.

"So, no marshmallows in Italy?" Cassie asked.

Parker answered, "Sometimes you can find a bag of the small ones in specialty stores, but they aren't really a big thing."

"When do you eat marshmallows the most?" Carlo asked.

"When you go camping," Cassie answered. "Do they have camping in Italy?"

Jessica rolled her eyes. "Of course they have camping, it's not another planet."

"But it *is* another culture," Cassie reasoned.

"Sì, I don't mind camping, but it is not my favorite," Carlo said as he followed Stills' actions, placing his browned marshmallow on top of a few chocolate pieces between two graham crackers.

"Cassie loves to camp – we went way too much when we were kids," Jess complained. □

Their father gave a gruff laugh. "Jess, we went camping maybe five times."

As the talk of camping evolved into favorite trips and who liked it and who didn't, Cassie attempted a covert glance at Stills. He had been watching her, maybe waiting for her to look at him. A smile was ready for her and she knew he was thinking about the things he told her he wanted to do with her under the stars.

Cassie was glad she was seated in front of a fire, the heat masked the blush creeping up her chest and burning her cheeks. The fever that radiated through her, along with the need for him to make good on his promises, made her shift in her seat.

He winked at her and she grinned before she looked down, pulled her marshmallow off the flames and assembled her dessert.

"Oh, the coffee!" their mother remembered.

Jessica, having finished her s'more, dusted her hands on her pants and volunteered, "I'll get it."

"I'll help," Cassie said around the bite she'd just taken. Together they headed into the house, though when they reached the back door, Jess stopped and glanced back at the group. "Do you think they're okay?"

"They're in the CIA." Cassie took another bite.

"Yeah, alone with our parents."

Cassie pushed her with her hip to continue into the house.

"I can't believe this night," Jessica said. "When you woke up this morning, could you have ever imagined…?"

"Yes," Cassie said with confidence.

Jess gave her an incredulous look, and Cassie sighed. "Yesterday you were kidnapped *again*, so I can pretty much believe anything at this point."

"Mom is in heaven," Jess said as she retrieved the tray they'd used for years to bring coffee to the table when they ate outside in the summer months. She put it down and pointed to Cassie. "I can't believe I didn't notice how hot you and Benji are for each other. He can't keep his eyes off of you. And you look like you want to mount him."

Cassie coughed around her full mouth, when she cleared her throat she pointed a finger at Jess and replied, "I *do* want to mount him." She took another bite.

Jess' mouth curved into a smile, she leaned her hip against the counter. "Where did he take you on your date?"

"Le Stelle." Cassie over pronounced the restaurant name as she was still chewing. She raised an eyebrow in silent question, had Jessica been there?

"Never heard of it. Is it nice?"

Cassie shook her head. "Not nice, it's freaking magical. Downright…mag-i-cal. If you go, it'll ruin everything you ever thought about romance."

"Romance, huh? I thought you'd just been on one and a half dates?" Jessica mocked.

"That man does something to me," Cassie admitted.

Jessica nodded. "I know what you mean."

"I like Parker, but is he trustworthy? Honestly?"

"Cass, he pisses me off. His hair always looks like he just woke up. He challenges me. He can't keep a shirt clean to save his life. He speaks Italian," her smile grew as she listed her grievances, "and his Italian accent is sexy as hell. He speaks his mind. He's bullheaded. He makes my pulse quicken when I see him. And you should have heard what he's been doing the past three weeks." She shook her head in disbelief, "He really did change his whole life for me."

"And in return, what does he want?" Cassie hated how cynical it might have sounded, but she would always be her sister's protector.

"A chance." She held up her hands. "He said he wants to be worthy of me and wants me to give him a chance to prove it." She tried to make a joke of what he said he wanted, but Cassie heard the words catch in Jessica's throat; her sister was in love. Truly. Jessica continued, "He wants an apartment in Florence and a house in the states. And he wants me to set the pace."

"What does that mean?"

"I told him I'll date him, but for about ten years or maybe twenty before I make any real decisions about our relationship."

"And yet here you are, in your childhood home, for a last-minute family dinner. *And* he keeps insisting you are both still married."

"Well, we are. But it doesn't mean anything." Jess got the creamer out of the fridge. Cassie grabbed the sugar and spoons. They added them to the tray as well as seven coffee cups, precariously stacked. Jess took the tray and Cassie carried the coffee pot.

It had been a long day for everyone, the wine and spirits had loosened everyone's bones and the coffee was a warm comfort that finished off a strangely thrown together dinner.

Cassie and Jessica were proud of their parents. They always had been, even though they acted as if their parents were too much at times. When various friends came over to the house over the years, especially during high school, Barbara and Walter insisted everyone sit down and eat dinner together; and while eating, their parents would ask questions of their friends, always interested in the answers and the young people's views. To this day, their mom and dad continued to be surrogate parents to many of their friends.

Cassie and Jessica had friends who always commented that they felt like the Dodds actually saw them and cared. And that was the point; they did care.

That element was alive and well tonight, and Cassie hadn't been aware how much she'd missed it. It had been a long time since Cassie was able to have a dinner that consisted of the warmth of family and not a multitude of questions as to how she was choosing to live her life. Her mother's constant inquiries always left Cassie feeling the need to defend and over explain her life choices

If the past few weeks had done anything, it had reconnected Jessica and Cassie and built a bridge between Cassie and her mother. She understood the woman's worrisome ways more than she ever had before.

Barbara was sad to see everyone go but understood. "Carlo is going to stay with us tonight," she informed the girls.

Jessica directed her question at Carlo, "Are you sure?"

"Your mother is taking me to Santa Monica Pier and the tar pits tomorrow," he answered matter-of-factly.

"She is?" Jessica asked.

"He is leaving the day after tomorrow, I thought he should see a few sights before he leaves. But he has to work in the morning first," her mother explained.

Jessica looked at Cassie who pursed her lips and shrugged.

Parker explained, "Since Adler is in custody and we worked so closely with Carlo's agency in Italy, they wanted him to...assess the criminal."

"Assess the criminal?" Jessica frowned at Parker.

His face softened. "Amore, Carlo is going to interrogate Adler. Is that better?"

She nodded and looked at Carlo asking, "You'll be okay?"

Cassie grunted. "Are you really worried about this huge, hunk of a gorgeous man?"

"He's sensitive," Jess defended.

Carlo frowned while Stills and Parker coughed suspiciously at the same time.

"Be careful tomorrow." Jess said, "and have a good night." She leaned in to kiss him on each cheek, and he seamlessly mirrored the process.

Cassie was continually surprised by such moments; they were a visual aid to verify just how much Jess had transformed. Not a drastic transformation, just more assuredness, more confidence.

Parker and Stills thanked Barbara and Walter, both properly gushing over the food and shaking Walter's hand.

"C'mon son," Cassie's dad slapped Carlo on the back, "we'll watch the highlights from today's games."

Jess pulled Cassie aside when they reached the sidewalk in front of the house. "I'm going to sleep at Parker's tonight."

Cassie grinned. "I figured."

"Just for tonight. I'm still planning on living with you until I can find my feet completely in this relationship and get a few paychecks from the new job."

Cassie glanced at the two men and pulled Jess a bit farther away from them. "Jess, I've missed you."

"I'm right here." Jessica frowned.

"No, the past few years." She licked her lips as she found the words to explain. "I've missed you. I feel like we got lost doing our own thing, and we lived so close but never made time for each other." A tear formed and Cassie brushed it away.

Jessica took her sister's forearm and said, "It's okay. I get it."

Cassie continued, "This is mostly the wine I think. I just wanted you to know that you can take your time. I'm not ready to see you go just yet."

"Then I'll take my time," Jess assured, linking Cassie's arm in hers and heading toward the cars just in time to catch Parker shaking Stills' hand while he asked, "You're headed in?"

Stills nodded and that strange feeling of slipping control was a splash of cold water in Cassie's face. What did that mean, he was headed in? Now? When did that happen? Had he known all night he was going to have to go back to work? Did he know when he picked her up this afternoon, when he texted that he was desperate to see her, did he know then he was going to have to go back to work?

Why was she so upset by this news?

"See you tomorrow," Parker said.

"Jessica." Stills nodded his head in 'good night'.

She smiled at him and took a deep breath. "See ya around, Benji."

Parker held out his hand to Cassie. "I'll try my best to do right by her."

"I'll be keeping an eye on you," Cassie said, but she wasn't very interested in him right now.

Stills held Cassie's car door, and after he'd started the car, he let his hands drop from the steering wheel.

"You okay?" Cassie asked.

He glanced over at her, but his eyes were on the house. Then he reached out and brushed the side of her cheek. "I haven't had a nice time like that in so long. I've been working for about two years straight..."

"I'm really glad. I was worried Barbara Dodd would be too much tonight," she said with relief. It was easier to talk about her mom for another few seconds instead of asking about his work schedule.

"She was fine." His fingers trailed a path into her hair. "I enjoyed dancing with you."

She nodded her head because her throat was restricting her ability to speak without too much emotion.

"I want you," he whispered and she reached out and took his hand and held it in her own.

"You have to work?" She finally forced the question out.

He sighed. "I meant to tell you, but I think I just wanted tonight to feel normal. Like we didn't have a time limit, or need to hurry for any reason."

"How much time do you have?" Cassie asked but she didn't give him the chance to answer. "Benji, I don't want you to go to work, and I'm pissy that you didn't tell me, and if I'm honest, I'm not sure why I'm getting worked up," she said, then leaned her head back, took a deep breath and blew it out.

"This is new," he affirmed, "you want me all to yourself." His voice lowered with the explanation.

Cassie gave a sad smile. "Aren't you full of yourself?"

"I want *you* all to myself," he confessed.

"Worrying like this is new too. I worried about Jess, but now...your job *is* rough, isn't it?"

He pulled his hand from hers and scrubbed his face. "You aren't supposed to know what I do for a living," he started. "Most of the people I've dated in the past never knew. My family doesn't really know."

"But..."

"It's for their safety, so I think that's why I had such a good time tonight. Your family knows." He shook his head. "Dodd, if you and I end up being more, then sometime down the road there is a class you will be encouraged to take. It's called Living and Managing Cover for Spouses."

Cassie's eyes widened. "Really?"

"It helps spouses so they don't inadvertently expose their husband's or wife's job."

Cassie didn't know what to say, Stills shifted in his seat so he was facing her. "I know this is scary and a lot to handle–"

"Kiss me," Cassie whispered.

"What?"

"Agent Stills. Kiss me," she demanded.

He didn't wait for her to repeat herself a third time, but leaned forward, cupped the back of her head with his hand and pulled her to him.

She took all the comfort he offered. She gave reassurances she wasn't even sure of herself. When the momentary passion flamed, before it burned more, Cassie pulled away and said, "It is a lot. But I'm pretty tough. If you're willing to help me and be patient, I feel like we can get through this."

"Jesus." He studied her in the yellow light given off by the street lamps. "Cassandra Dodd, you are...amazing."

"I know."

His face lit up and he reached for her again, cupping her face in his hands. "You know, your sister and her boyfriend have interrupted us every time we've been together."

She tilted her head in thought. "They have, haven't they?"

"Yup. Your sister and her boyfriend are ruining our relationship."

"So it's their fault I can't get in your pants." She grinned.

He moaned and nipped at her lower lip. "Dodd, I can't tell you how much I want you to get into my pants."

She gave a sad sigh then asked, "How soon do you have to go in?"

"Soon. Too soon, but I have a plan." It was more of a question than statement, did she want to hear his plan?

She squared herself to him. "Okay, what's the plan?"

He kissed her cheek and sat back. "What do you have going on at work this week?"

"We just finished a big project, so just typical things right now. Nothing too difficult."

"Can you take Tuesday and Wednesday off? Maybe Thursday?"

"Hell yes."

He smiled. "I need to get a few things organized at work. It's going to take tomorrow and Monday, but if you are willing to wait, then on Tuesday afternoon, I want to pick you up and take you somewhere special."

"What should I pack?"

"Is that a yes?"

"What do I need to pack?" Three uninterrupted days with Stills. Her whole body radiated with delight.

"I'll text you that later."

Cassie studied him for a minute. "What time do you have to go back?"

"In an hour."

"It takes twenty minutes to get to my place," she said.

"Twenty minutes to get to work from there."

"Benji, I really need to fog up these windows."

He was putting the car into drive. "Hold on Dodd."

Chapter Thirty

The phantom melody of the song that Cassie had played earlier in the evening hummed through her. Her lips were good and chapped, thanks to the heady make out session she'd just had, and she felt so light she floated her way to her apartment.

She was halfway down the hallway when she stopped and pressed her hand to her chest. Everything ebbed and flowed through her like a wave, and Stills' kisses reverberated in her body and weakened her knees.

Cassie opened her apartment and turned on a light. Someone had cleaned up the mess from the fight, the contents of the frames that had been wrecked were on the dining table.

She dropped her purse and keys on the table by the front door and slipped out of her shoes. Then she floated to her sofa and sat down with her cell phone.

The apartment was still. All of the comings and goings lately made it feel alive, but Cassie found herself welcoming the temporary quiet. □

Her phone beeped and she knew it was Stills:

Agent Stills: I can still taste you.

She fell onto her side. "This man," she whispered, and just like that, she saw the truth of the situation she was in. The reason Benjamin Stills was so different, the reason this already felt different than any other relationship she'd ever had; he was a man. A man who knew himself. A man who wasn't scared of a strong woman and didn't need a mother. He wasn't a project. When she told John that Stills was a 'project', she didn't mean it. Stills wasn't the kind of man who needed to fix anyone. Sure, he liked to help, but not fix. He was a man who knew what he wanted and Cassie burned with being wanted. And she wanted him.

She texted back:

Cassie: I don't know how I'm going to make it without seeing you for two days.

Agent Stills: Me neither. I'm walking into the office now. Have a good night, Dodd.

Cassie: You too, Benji.

Chapter Thirty-One

C assie made it through Sunday - barely. She tried not to check her phone obsessively, but she checked her phone obsessively.

She sent her own message halfway through the day when she realized she was a woman who wanted a man, and so far they'd both been receptive to honesty.

Cassie: We haven't even slept together yet, and I can't stop thinking about you. You're in the way of my thoughts.

She knew he would reply when he was able, but the quickness surprised her.□

Agent Stills: When I say I want you, I hope you know what I want to do is lay you down, strip you naked and kiss every damn inch of that soft skin, and let my fingers memorize every curve and make sure the smell of you and the taste of you is on my lips and in my memory forever.

"Jesus." Cassie drew the word out.

She glanced around the room, she was not going to make it through the day if those were the kinds of texts he was going to continue to send. She finally made a decision to go run. She put on a sports bra, a crappy t-shirt, running shorts and tennis shoes.

Cassie: Going for a run.

Agent Stills: Need some endorphins?

Cassie: I need something, but since I can't get to it just yet, I'm hoping running will work.□□□□□□□

And as she ran she laughed, because the last time she had to go a week without seeing him, she worried that the building attraction between them would fizzle out once they actually spent time together. But that theory was proven dramatically wrong. So this time, her subconscious was excited to reach for the stars as she imagined what it would be like to be 'memorized' by him. And as she ran she fantasized all sorts of scenarios, which wasn't difficult, especially when he texted her sexy things about being naked under him.

Jessica returned home around four with a far-off look in her eyes. Cassie was jealous. And entertained.

"Did you get *any* sleep?" Cassie asked.

"None." Jessica tossed herself on the sofa and sniffed the air. "What am I smelling?"

Cassie waved a hand. "Garlic and sundried tomato bread, apple streusel muffins and garlic knots."

"So would I be correct in saying that this is now 'pent-up' baking?" Jessica lifted an eyebrow.

"Shut up." Cassie threw the spatula she was washing at her sister.

Jessica was slow to block it, and it thwapped her on the arm. "Ow."

"I'm not sorry," Cassie said. "I'm also jealous. Did you know that Benji and I figured out the reason we haven't slept together yet? It's because you and your husband keep getting in the way."

"Boyfriend."

"Hmmm."

"But I thought you'd only been on one and a half dates." Jessica yawned.

"Well, we got to know each other a few more times in between the bona fide dates."

An hour later, Barbara Dodd and Carlo arrived. They had been to the pier, the tar pits and gone to In-N-Out Burger for lunch. Carlo's flight was at seven a.m. the next morning, and he wanted to say his goodbyes.

Barbara patted him on the back as she touted his accomplishment, "He ate two burgers and animal fries. He likes American hamburgers. I tried to get him to go show those men at muscle beach a thing or two, but he was right when he said they needed to be on top of their own world."

Cassie glanced at Jessica, *who the hell was this woman?* Jessica explained, "I'm telling you, it's an Italian thing. Italian men are respectful of mothers."

"And can apparently handle them," Cassie said.

"Girls, I'm a fun person, did you ever think of that?" She nodded between the two of them. "Carlo also gave me the rundown on your young men."

"*That's* why she likes him so much." Cassie waved her mom and Carlo over to the table. "I made bread, muffins and garlic knots, what'll it be?"

"Oh, honey. Why are you stressed? Is it because Benjamin had to go to work last night and left you alone?" Barbara asked.

Cassie glanced at Carlo. "Did you tell her that?"

He shrugged. "Of course."

"Well, I'm not stressed," Cassie said as Jess corrected, "She's sexually frustrated."

"Jessica!" Cassie yelled.

Jess told their mother, "But apparently I'm the one to blame."

Cassie changed the subject. "Mom, apple streusel muffin?"

"Yes, and do you have coffee? Carlo, you should try one of these muffins, Cassie is very good in the kitchen."

Carlo nodded. "I had the biscotti, the cookies she made the other day. They were very good."

"I can't cook," Jessica said.

"I know. It's a shame," he said sadly.

Cassie smiled at the downtrodden demeanor of the man when he made the comment.

Jessica gave a frustrated grunt. "In Italy the mama's boys also judge a woman on whether or not she can cook."

"So I'm like...a ten in Italy?" Cassie surmised.

Jessica pointed a finger at Carlo. "I might not be a good cook, but I know how to make Italian coffee now. So you want an espresso?"

Carlo smiled at Jessica. "Sì."

"Just regular coffee for me," their mom said.

"Barbara, when you and Walter come visit me in Italy I will introduce you to the Italian espresso," Carlo promised.

"You're going to Italy?" Cassie asked as she placed a sampling of her current baked goods on the table.

"Well, Carlo and I have gotten along so well and your father just took to him...Carlo said that he would take Walter to a soccer game if we visit. I think it would be a hoot to go to Italy."

"A hoot," Jessica muttered.

"Mom, Jessica being kidnapped has changed you." Cassie sighed.

Her mother waved the comment away. "No, I'm just so happy. I saw what happened last night. You and Jessica have found the ones you've been looking for and who have been looking for you. Carlo has too." She paused. "Look you three, I'm not saying it's going to be easy, lord knows love isn't easy..." she shook her head and got a far off look in her eye, "but all of you have found your way to this next level of life, and I'm *excited* for you."

"Because you want grandchildren." Jessica sighed as she placed a small espresso in front of Carlo and took her seat.

"I'm going to tell you two something." She made sure each of her girls was giving her their full attention. "You do *not* have to have kids. I mean it. You don't even *have* to get married, or if you want to get divorced, go for it." She waved her hand and Cassie and Jess exchanged an entertained look. Their mom continued, "What I want is for you to feel powerful and happy. I wanted you both to have the kind of love that makes you a better version of yourself. It doesn't matter how long you love either. Sometimes, being in love for fifteen minutes can empower a person for the rest of their lives."

"Who are you?" Cassie asked.

"And what have you done with our mother?" Jess added.

Carlo held up the muffin. "This is good. And your mother, she is very wise."

Barbara patted Carlo on the back. "I can't wait to meet Alessandra."

Monday, thankfully, was a busy day at work. Cassie put in her vacation request, which was instantly approved by her boss and longtime friend. It didn't hurt that when asked what she needed the vacation days for, Cassie grinned and said, "I need to go see about a man."

Midmorning, she was thrown off task when a message came in:

Agent Stills: Good morning, Dodd.

Cassie: Hiya, Benji.

Agent Stills: Did you dream about me last night?

Cassie: You have to be able to fall asleep in order to dream.

Agent Stills: What's wrong?

Cassie: I kept feeling these phantom caresses and couldn't stop reliving a number of kisses.

Agent Stills: I'll replace each of those phantom caresses with the real thing. I dreamt about you writhing under my hands last night.

Cassie: Dear God, I'm at work.

Agent Stills: Me too.

Cassie: I don't think you're blushing though.

Agent Stills: No, but I can't get you off my mind.

Cassie: Go do some work, this is going to take me the rest of the morning to get over.

Agent Stills: I have a packing list for you, but if I tell you what you need, you'll have an idea of what I want to do with you (and to you). So I texted Jess and asked her to pack for you.

Cassie: Hmmmm.

Agent Stills: Have a good day, Dodd.

Cassie scrolled through her contacts until she found Jessica's number:

Cassie: What did Benji tell you to pack for me?

Jess: Nice try.

Cassie: If you love me, you'll tell me.

Jess: I don't love you.

Cassie: JESSICA! TELL ME!!

Jess: No. Oh, I'm drunk with power now.

Cassie: Fine, I'll just look in the bag tonight.

Jess: Can't, it's already been delivered to him.

Cassie: Then I'll figure out what's missing from my stuff.

Jess: I'm one step ahead of you, I packed two different kinds of bags.

Cassie: You've changed.

Jess: Dinner at Pomodoro's tonight?

Cassie: Why?

Jess: I got a gift card for doing a good job. I think it's supposed to be like a gold star for sticking with the new job or something.

Cassie: Yay, gold star dinner!

Jess: The one on Roosevelt. Seven?
Cassie: K. Just do me one favor?
Jess: I'm not telling you anything!!!

Cassie liked the excitement of the building passions that encircled her. She took another run after work before she had to meet Jessica. When she got out of the shower, she laughingly sent a text to Stills.

Cassie: I've run a personal best two days in a row now. I either need to never see you again and train for a marathon, or be in your arms ASAP!

He didn't answer until she and Jessica were halfway through dinner.

Agent Stills: Tomorrow, I'll pick you up at four p.m. I'll be the one trying his damnedest to not throw you on the ground and have his way with you.

Cassie: I'll be the one sweating profusely from an intense run.

A flush crept up her face as she set her phone down. "Dear God this man...what am I going to do until four in the afternoon?"

"So you really haven't slept with him yet?" Jessica asked.

Cassie pressed her water glass against her cheek. "No. But it needs to happen soon. I don't think I can take the flirting much longer."

"I never pegged Benji for being...sexy." Jessica tilted her head in contemplation. "He seems so even keeled and calm. Kinda boring."

"Yeah, it's that even keel that makes him a man who knows *exactly* what he wants. And he asks for it. And talks about it." She rolled the cup across her forehead. "And that's what is burning me up from the inside out."

"Wow."

"Tell me about Parker," Cassie said.

Jessica sat back. "What do you want to know?"

"Everything!" Cassie said emphatically. "It's finally just the two of us. No one barging in. No mob bosses. No fears. No brokenhearted crying. So now, it's just you and me, with time. Tell. Me. Everything."

Jessica grinned. "It was the best of times, it was the worst of times."□

Cassie groaned.

"Call me Ishmael," Jess started again.

Cassie reached in her glass, got her fingers wet and flicked the cold water at her sister.

"Fine, fine." Jessica wiped her face. "The day I bought my wedding dress, Stacie, my old college roommate called and ask what happened between Parker and me in Vegas, at her wedding. Ten years ago."

"What did happen?"

"I was twenty-two. I was drunk. We were all drunk. He was handsome. We flirted all weekend. We got married. As a joke. And after that weekend I never gave him another thought and actually forgot all about him until Stacie called me. Do you know, I hired a lawyer to file divorce papers and when I finally tracked Parker and saw him again, all the memories from that lost weekend came rushing back. It felt like I was hit by a brick wall."

"So that's when you decided to break things off with Thomas?"

"No," Jessica's eyes glinted, "I hated Parker the first three or four times we rekindled our...mutual acknowledgment of each other. Especially when I found out who he was working for and who Thomas was working for. All I wanted to do at that point was forget all men and come home."

Cassie took a drink of her water and listened to her sister's tale of trying to keep her sanity while in a very precarious situation; how she tried to soak in a little of the Italian culture in the Tuscan countryside. "I mean, I was there. Life is short, so I thought I should enjoy it," Jessica admitted.

Of course, Cassie's favorite part was how Jessica began falling for Parker all over again. □

Cassie picked up her water glass and again, pressed it to her cheeks as her sister ended the very stale story of her and Parker's reunion.

"God, you're even telling it blandly but it's still hot."

"You need to get some." Jess pointed.

"I need Benji, *bad*."

They both began to giggle and Cassie put her hands together in a begging gesture. "Where is he taking me?"

"You'll love it," Jessica said, then mimed the zipping of her lips.

"Dammit."

Chapter Thirty-Two

C assie blinked her eyes wide open at five a.m. exactly. She was excited – 'Christmas morning' excited.

"So much for sleeping in." Sleeping in had been the key element to wasting time before Stills picked her up. But going back to sleep wasn't going to work.

She stretched her limbs, thought about taking another run, then gave a grunt of laughter. "Don't waste all your energy. You might need it for tonight."

She shuffled to the kitchen and decided to call her mom. She was supposed to take Carlo to the airport, even though his flight was at seven, he'd need to be dropped off earlier.

Her mother was just arriving at the airport when she answered.

"Cassandra," Carlo said over the speaker phone of the car, "you will come visit me in Italy."

"You know Carlo, I just might take you up on that." She wished him a good trip and invited her mom to breakfast. "Since we're both awake you might as well come over after you've dropped him off."

Thirty-five minutes later her mother arrived. The coffee was ready and Cassie was finishing the bacon. "Over easy eggs, Mom?"

Barbara nodded and sat down at the table. "I love when you cook for me. I feel so spoiled."

Jessica shuffled to the kitchen. "I thought I smelled something good." She got a cup of coffee and made her way to the table. She gave her mom a pat on the back in greeting, sat down heavily at the table and asked, "Did Carlo get off okay?"

"Yes. He's such a nice boy."

"He's so big," Cassie said as she brought two plates to the table.

"You get used to it," Jessica said.

"You do get used to it," Barbara agreed. "Do you have any more of those muffins?"

Cassie brought them out along with butter and her own plate.

Jessica took a deep whiff of her breakfast. "I'm going to miss your pent-up baking. And why am I smelling cookies?"

"White chocolate macadamia," she muttered. "You can put some in your lunch. Mom, take some for you and Dad."

Cassie moved her food around her plate, and then sat back and rolled her coffee cup between her hands.

"Are you nervous?" Jessica asked.

"What does she have to be nervous about?" her mother asked.

"Benji is taking her on a surprise three-day trip."

"Oh, that's nice. Where are you going?" Barbara asked.

Cassie raised an eyebrow as Jessica laughed. "It's a surprise." She shot the comment at her sister, and then continued, "Benji hasn't told her yet, but he told me so I could pack for her."

"Oh," their mother sighed, "that's romantic."

"I'll call you later today and let you know," Jessica promised their mom. "So, are you nervous?" she asked Cassie again.

Cassie glanced at her mom, then pursed her lips. "Yes and no," she said honestly. "We've had so many conversations and some really nice moments together, but we haven't been able to actually…see any of those moments through." She directed the next comment at their mom. "My sister, her boyfriend, and their problems keep interrupting us."

Jessica grinned. "Well, you'll have plenty of time over the next few days."

Cassie didn't say anything, just studied her cup.

"What is it?" her mom asked.

Cassie laughed and tried to make light of the moment, "I don't want to talk about wanting a man this desperately with my mom."

"Why not?" She looked between her two daughters and then leaned forward, pointing her fork at them. "I know you think I'm a bit much at times, and a crazy, overprotective, judgmental mom. But I'll have you know, I'm also a woman. And I met a man a long time ago who made my heart race and I couldn't think of anything else all day long. And we sprinted to be with each other."

"Please be someone other than Dad, please be someone other than Dad..." Jessica chanted.

Cassie laughed. "The flirting is killing me. And intriguing me. And I'm so nervous when I'm *not* with him. I was nervous before our first date, but then when I saw him, it all melted away. All the insecurities and questions and 'what ifs' just left. I see him and I'm sure about everything again."

Barbara patted Cassie's hand.

"Is it disappointing when the desperation goes away?" Cassie asked their mother.

She raised an eyebrow. "Who says it goes away?"

Jessica groaned.

Barbara laughed. "It becomes something different. The energy moves around the relationship. It doesn't go away, it just morphs into different areas."

Cassie opened her mouth, but for the moment, she was truly at a loss. □

Barbara continued, "Besides, neither of you have anything to worry about. I watched those two men, Parker and Benjamin, and how they are with you. They are desperate. Now, as a mother, I want to have old fashioned values and hope that they are being gentlemen. But then I think of your father and when we first met...and well, it wasn't any wonder you were a surprise to us Cassandra."

"Benji's a good guy," Jessica declared, in an attempt to change the subject. Cassie laughed at her, and Jessica softened, admitting, "A really good guy."

"They're desperate for us, huh Mom?" Cassie asked.

"Infatuated," she insisted.□

The oven timer went off and Jessica stretched and yawned. "I'd love to stay and hear detailed accounts of Mom and Dad's sex life, but thankfully, I need to finish getting ready for work."

"I suppose I should head home," their mother acknowledged, feeling that her work here was done.

"Wait, I'll give you some cookies." Cassie went into the kitchen and pulled out the large cookie sheets.

Her mother followed her into the kitchen. "What are you really worried about?"

Cassie waved the cookies with an oven mitt. "His job," she exhaled.

"That is a tricky one. I find that there are two men in my family's life now that have, potentially, dangerous jobs."

"You have two men in your family now? Mom, I just started dating–"

"A mother knows when she's just met her future sons-in-law."

Cassie gave a humph in reply, then after a moment explained, "Did you know they both put in for desk jobs? I don't know what that really means, or what the difference is, but Benji said that the job he is transferring to has more stability."

Barbara smiled. "I've got tough girls. I'm a tough mother myself." She winked at the joke she made. "I say we all take a few self-defense classes and live our lives."

"That simple?"

"Cassandra, you've never been one to make life more difficult. Let go of the worry. Have fun."

"I just want to have sex with the man first. Before I go making any more plans," Cassie laughed as she finished the sentence.

"That is a good place to start." Her mom grabbed one of the cookies and took a bite. "Oh, these are good."

Cassie put a few on a plate and wrapped them in plastic. She handed them over, but her mom put the plate down and tilted her head to the side. "What else is going on with you?"

Cassie laughed and shook her head. "You have superpowers, you know?"

"I do."

"Well," Cassie crossed her arms over her chest and confessed the other thing that had been bothering her a lot more than it should, "I had this fantasy that *I* would be the one to somehow kick Thomas' ass."

Her mother pinched her lips together with her fingers to keep from laughing and hid her mouth. Cassie swatted the air between them. "I know it's juvenile. But damnit, I'm the big sister."

"Oh honey, this isn't like the boy you beat up for Jess when she was in eighth grade."

"You knew about that?"

Her mother scoffed, "The things you two think I don't know, that I *do* know, could fill a book."

Cassie grunted. "I just thought...I beat up her bully in eighth grade, and kicked Drake Stopper in the balls for making fun of her in high school...I kinda thought I could up my game and kick the shit out of Thomas."

"I think we all wanted to kick the shit out of that man."

"But it was *my* job," Cassie muttered.

"Who said it was your job?"

"You. *You* did." She held out her hands. "You've been telling me to look out for my baby sister my whole life."

"Yes, when she was seven and you were ten and you were both skating in the front yard. I never said you had to save her from the mafia."

"Well..." Cassie shook her head and tried to hide a smile, "I feel like I should have."

Her mom pulled her in for a hug and kissed her cheek. "Oh Cassie..." she pulled away and narrowed her gaze, "thank you for taking care of Jessica. I'm sorry you didn't get a chance to...take a penalty kick on Thomas' balls."

Cassie barked out a laugh. "I'll get over it."

"I know you will. Have a good time with Benjamin." She picked up the plate of cookies and as she headed toward the door, yelled her departure to Jessica.

"Bye, Mom." Jessica peeked her head out of the bathroom.

Cassie went back to the kitchen and looked at the time, *again*, even though not even a minute had gone by since she last checked. Seven thirty-three a.m.

She finished washing dishes, and then pulled out several containers. She divided the bread, streusel muffins, garlic knots and cookies. A total of eight containers in all. She rolled her eyes at the physical display of her repressed baking. But Stills would love it.

When Jessica was ready for work, she came in and grabbed her to-go coffee cup and filled it up as Cassie explained, "If you don't stay here the next few days, can you be sure to take the rest of this stuff with you? If you and Parker don't want it, can you take it to work?"

"Sure." She turned Cassie around and squeezed her shoulders. "Have fun," she insisted.

"Where am I going?" Cassie imitated her tone.

Jessica laughed and kissed her cheek. On her way out the door she loudly announced, "And most importantly big sis, get some!"

Cassie looked around the apartment and then at the time once more. The minute hands were stuck in tar. She was going to have to go for a run.

"How did my life go from helping my broken sister to having my whole family suddenly knowledgeable about the ins and outs of my sex life?" She muttered the question to herself as she dressed in her running clothes. Then she answered herself, "Because you keep offering up the information, ya moron."

She walked up to a dirt running trail that had been built near her apartment. She stretched and then began to jog slowly, loosening up her muscles. A mile in, she stopped and looked at the stopwatch she'd brought. She was going to get a real time today. She set herself, hit the start button and began running.

She kicked her heels behind her, felt her legs engage with the action and the wind against her face. Her breathing was a quick in and out hiss, her lungs burned and she smiled. She picked up speed and counted the way she always did when she was running and tried not to think of anything else: One two three four. One two three four.

She saw the mile marker and pushed herself once more. One two three four.

She hit the mile marker, clicked the stopwatch, then slowed her pace. She was sucking wind as she continued to jog and get her breath back. She ran another quarter mile before she stopped and looked at the stopwatch. She gave a barking laugh when she saw the time. She'd shaved thirty-five seconds off her mile just in the past few days.

She turned and jogged back to the apartment, smiling at her recent accomplishment.

Chapter Thirty-Three

assie glanced at herself in the mirror. She wore jeans, and a tank top with a sweater over it. She also had a pair of shorts and a light rain jacket in her book bag. Even though Jessica had already packed for her, she wanted to be ready for anything. She slipped on a pair of stylish walking shoes as well.

She ran a hand through her shoulder length hair and licked her lips, leaned forward and checked the mascara she'd applied.

Her hands were shaking. She picked up her phone and looked at the time, *again*. Two minutes to four.

The knock at the door made her jump. "Someone needs to start locking the front door to this damn building," she muttered, then took a deep breath. She was about to collect herself when she realized that would be an impossible task.□

She swung the door open and grinned. "Hi."

Stills was through the door, closing it, and in one blurry movement pulling her into his arms and pressing her against the wall opposite the mirror in the small foyer. □

They crashed, tumbled, and slammed into each other. Cassie gave a low moan as his tongue swept through her mouth. She hung onto him for dear life as he clutched her to him. She was starved for him and he gave her everything she needed.

They turned their heads at the same moment and knocked their teeth together. Cassie pulled back slightly, laughing and winded. "Ow," she let out.

"I'm sorry." He cupped her face and studied her for damage.

She touched her finger to her top teeth and shook it off. "It's fine."□

He took a deep breath. "Hi," he said and gave her a quick, chaste kiss.

"Hi." This was the moment, when all the worries floated away and she was connected to him again. She grinned and asked, "Where are we going?"

"To the car." He winked.

She rolled her eyes. "Fine, then let's go to the car."

He didn't let her go, and she wanted to tell him to take her, right now. To rid them both of their clothing and take her to bed.

"Can you wait?" He whispered the question, reading her mind.

"No. Can you?" She grinned, her breathing labored.

"No."

"So what should we do about this?"

He took a step back and held out his hand. "Have a really sexy, uncomfortable drive?"

She groaned but followed his lead. She picked up her purse and book bag, then motioned to the reusable bag. "Can you get that?"

"What's that?"

"Well, obviously I've been doing some baking," she muttered.

He looked in the bag. "Oh good. I was going to ask you to bake me something, but I didn't want to be presumptuous."

"Well, you got garlic knots, rosemary sun-dried tomato bread, apple streusel muffins and white chocolate macadamia nut cookies."□

He looked back at her living room.

"What?"

"Maybe we stay here, get naked and then eat..." he suggested.

Cassie shook her head. "I was promised a surprise, I'm gonna get a surprise."

He groaned, but nodded. "You're right," he kissed her cheek, "thank you for baking for me."

In the car, he took her hand and brought it to his lips for a kiss. "Ready?"

"Yes, just hurry," she insisted.

He pulled into late afternoon traffic and onto the freeway.

Stills drove east which didn't really mean anything. Cassie figured she'd begin to see signs of their destination eventually and all she could rule out now was the beach. Maybe.

"How were your last two days?" she asked.

He smiled. "Difficult."

Cassie's stomach clutched but she didn't have time to ask him what he meant before he explained, "I couldn't focus on anything. I kept picturing this sexy golden haired woman with red highlights and dreaming of making love to her."

"Oh good, it was that kind of difficult. That makes me happy."

"I know you baked and ran?" he said, voice slightly rising with the suggestion that her last couple of days had also been 'difficult'.

She grinned. "I shaved thirty-five seconds off my mile, I just timed myself today."

"So, did you decide if you're in training, or are you throwing it all away for sex?"

Cassie looked at him and thought about the suppressed emotions she'd been dealing with due to his text messages and saw exactly how she was going to handle this situation. "I need you inside me Benji. I need to have at least twenty orgasms before tomorrow morning."

His face paled as her grin grew. She felt powerful until he pulled the car over to the side of the road.

"What are you doing?" she breathed excitedly.

The moment the car was in park and the hazard lights on, he leaned over and began kissing her, his hands roaming this time to cover her breasts. He moaned into her mouth and she returned the purr of want.

"We're never going to make it." Cassie laughed. He caught the laughter with his mouth.

A police siren brought them out of their reprieve.

"God...damnit." Stills looked in the rearview and saw the officer waving them off the side of the road. Stills waved that he understood.

He put the car into drive and pulled back into traffic.

"How far is it?" she asked.

"Two hours," he said miserably. "It seemed like a good idea when I came up with the plan."

Cassie wondered if she could suppress her need for just two more hours. "What are we going to do?" □

"Do you get the feeling that once we scratch this itch, it's just going to make things worse?" he asked.

Cassie nodded her head. "Oh yeah. We've got future problems." She reached into the back seat and took out the top container, which was the one with the cookies. "Here, in the meantime, have a cookie."

He accepted it and took a bite. "White chocolate macadamia?" he recalled.

"Yes," she said, pulling a cookie out for herself. □

"What are you doing?" he asked and pulled the cookie out of her hand. "You said these were for me."

"I said I did some baking."

"For me," he said with his mouth full. "I can't wait for the whole meal."

"We could have stayed at your place and I could have made that happen."

Stills shook his head. "Not a chance! With our track record, who knows who'd show up or call or create a new way to interrupt. I wanted to get away from everyone."

"Probably the best course of action," she agreed.

They fell silent and Stills turned on the radio, they agreed on an 80s rock station. He drove through the city and changed freeways, heading north. "Vegas?" she guessed.

He raised an eyebrow. "No, but I could change plans."

"Nah, my sister already did the Vegas thing." She bit her lip. "I'm just trying to get an idea of where we're going."

He pulled off the freeway and Cassie hadn't noticed any signs for anything suspicious. When he pulled into a coffee drive-thru she grinned. "Are you trying to throw me off the scent?"

"Just want coffee." He shot a knowing glance her.

"Oh, I never told you," she said excitedly. "Did you still want to take me to the four corners area?"

"It's been a dream for a while now," he confirmed.

"I was just assigned a new job that is going to require me to do some research in a small mining town called Eden, Colorado. It's only two hours from Mesa Verde."

"What kind of research?"

"Well, the thing is, their archives aren't online. I talked to the head curator there, and she's going to try and help me, but if I could get a road trip out of it..." She shrugged. "I'm not sure how your time off works, but..."

"Do you have a deadline?"

"It's going to be a pretty intensive project. I don't have all the details yet, but it will probably take about eighteen months once I've started."

He smiled. "You sure you want to go on a road trip with me, Dodd?"

"Benji, there are all sorts of things I want to do with you."

"I'll figure it out. I never use any of my vacation time, so I'm sure I can come up with something."

"You get vacation time?"

"Dodd."

"What, I wasn't sure the CIA accrued vacation days."

He shook his head and smiled. "We're making future plans," he said with confidence.

"Oh, I *know*." She smiled as he handed over her latte. □

Back on the road, content with coffee and cookies, he pulled off the main freeway, continuing east. Now Cassie knew she could narrow down their destination. They were headed into the desert, and the highway they were on would eventually take them to Palm Desert.

She watched as the mountains grew out of the desert floor, shades of late August Southern California bloomed, browns and yellows and peach, stretching into the sky as the sun continued its golden arching descent behind them. The desert floor was alive with the shadow of a few moving clouds overhead, and the changing light.

She thought they might be headed to Idyllwild, but he passed the exit that would have taken them there.

"So not going there." She gave him a sideways glance, and saw a smile tug at the corner of his mouth.

He continued toward Palm Springs but asked, "Dinner first?"

"I could eat, but Benji..."

"Yes, Dodd?"

"Can we just grab fast food? If dinner isn't part of the plan, can we do something fast?" She was done waiting, she wanted him, nothing else.

"This one time, it's completely acceptable."

They went through an In-N-Out drive-thru. Shakes, fries and cheeseburgers purchased, Stills pulled back onto the freeway. Cassie put the tray of fries between them and wrapped Stills' cheeseburger in a napkin before handing it over.

"I like this," he took the burger, "Robbins and Salvatore never wait on me like this."

"I'm not waiting on you," she said as she handed him a napkin.

"They never think of me to the point that they wrap my sandwich in a napkin, how's that?" he corrected.

"And you do nice things for them?" she asked.

"Well, they aren't as pretty as you."

Cassie frowned, they were now heading out of the Palm Springs area. She wondered if he was just trying to throw her off, until he pulled onto a smaller two lane road. At that moment, she knew exactly where they were going.

"Oh." She felt the anticipation of what was coming throughout her whole body.

"I figured you'd know once I started driving this way."

"It's been so long since I've been here," she said as they passed the sign welcoming them to Joshua Tree National Park.

"Me too. I...we're camping. Is that okay?"

"Of course it's okay." She leaned forward in her seat as she watched the blooming sagebrush draw long shadows in the sand and curve and grow their way into the namesake tree of this valley. The Joshua tree, with outstretched arms at so many different angles, were twisted trees reaching up into the desert sky, offering reverence to the Great Spirits.

As they pulled up to the entrance gate, the sun was beginning to dip behind the mountains, stretching its last rays of golden-yellow and blue hues across the desert. Stills paid the fee then continued to drive.

Since Cassie had visited before, she knew there were nine campgrounds spread out within the large acreage of the park. When Stills didn't pull off at the first entrance, she knew he was going deeper into the park. They didn't pass the normal traffic that existed on the weekends on the road that circled the park. "Slow because it's the middle of the week," Cassie said.

"And the end of the season," he offered.

Her stomach did a Swan Lake twirl and leapt at the thought of the campsite to come and the man next to her. She also knew she was about to see just how quickly she could get a tent set up.

The dusky blue sky extended and curled into the distance, tucking in the hills and growing boulders. Wispy white clouds mirrored the stretching length of the sky and floated slowly, taffy pulling themselves into a yawn across the vast blueness.

Stills slowed and pulled into the Hidden Valley campground, driving around several loops until they reached their campsite. They only passed two other groups of campers on their way in. Cassie knew this wasn't the most popular campground because it was further into the park and more secluded.

He pulled all the way to the back of a loop, where no one else was and found a spot to park the car. Giant boulder formations strained into the air, making rounded, jagged stacks and a natural half circle around the campsite - complete with picnic table, water spigot and grill. Joshua trees made a drunken line up into the dusty sand between the boulders. But what caught Cassie's immediate attention was that there was a tent already set up, a very large tent adorned with twinkle lights on top and a glow from inside. She shot a smile of question over at Stills.

"I know a guy," he admitted. "He lives in Palm Springs and he owed me a favor, so he set this up for me."

Cassie climbed out and closed the door, leaning her hip against the car as she stared in wonder at the shadows of the boulders and the softly lit campsite.

Stills came around behind her, slipped his arms around her waist and rested his head on her shoulder. "This is amazing," she breathed.

"You haven't even seen the inside yet."

She grinned, wriggled out of his arms and pulled him toward the tent with her.

"Wait."

"What?"

"Give me your phone," he gently demanded. She handed it over and he tossed both phones into the car, declaring, "No one is going to bother us."

She pulled him toward the tent; it had a screened in four foot long porch entry that led into an impressive eight foot high main room that could have easily slept ten. The 'door' into the main room had been tied back for the sake of aesthetics.

"Jesus, Benji."

There was a rug and a small table set up in the entrance area, a bottle of prosecco was wrapped in an ice bag in a bucket and two champagne glasses. She shook her head and was drawn to the large internal area of the tent. It had been set up with another rug, and against the far side was a queen size bed. She assumed it was an air mattress. It had been covered with a maroon comforter, matching pillow shams and two fluffy white throw pillows. There was a small table set up next to the bed with a vase of white roses. Three lighted paper lanterns hung from the ceiling, and the same twinkle lights that made a ring outside the tent, were mirrored inside. The top cover of the tent had been left off, so that the mesh panel would allow the camper the perfect opportunity for an unobstructed view of the stars.

Cassie turned and shook her head. "This is…amazing …obscene." She shook her head in disbelief. "Who is this guy who owed you a favor?"

"He's an interior designer." Stills hadn't moved from the entrance where he stood watching her as she explored every little detail. His eyes were growing dark, the intensity building, and it radiated all the way through Cassie.

They stood watching each other, taking each other in for a lifetime. There was no need to hurry now. There was finally time. Plenty of time.

She slipped off her sweater and tossed it on the bed. When Stills stepped out of his shoes, she noticed he'd worn his European slip-ons. She slipped her own off with a grin.

Stills reached for the zipper that closed out the entrance of the tent and any unexpected eyes.

The first step he took toward her was a force she felt throughout her whole body, she met him halfway and again they crashed into each other.

His hands found her hair, and she wasn't interested in petting, she had hours and weeks of build-up to release. She pulled his shirt out of his pants, and began to unbutton it, once she had the shirt pushed off his shoulders and down to his forearms, she pulled away so she could see his chest. He didn't look this muscular when he had a shirt on.

She splayed her hands across his chest and slowly let them soak up his heat. Stills let out a groan-hiss. Cassie ran her hands up his strong shoulders and down his forearms; capable, large forearms. She worked her way back up, only this time she didn't stop at his chest, but lowered her hands against his ribcage and then down to the button on his jeans. She began to unbutton the top button when Stills' hands stopped her.

He had his own plans, he pulled the bottom of her tank top up and drew it over her head. Then he slipped his hands down her naked ribcage to her jeans, unbuttoned them, slowly slipping them over her hips. He sucked in a breath. "Good Lord."

She wore a matching black lace bra and underwear. She grinned and finished the job she started, unbuttoning his pants and slipping them off.

He wore tight black boxer briefs. Cassie raised an eyebrow and grinned. "I was wondering..."

He brought her back into his arms and she went willingly, savoring the heat of their exposed bodies, the feeling of warm skin against skin. □

Stills picked up her leg, pulled it around his waist, and then went after the other one. They pressed their lips together, tangled tongues, heat building. He lifted her, her legs firmly wrapped around his waist now, and then turned and lowered her onto the bed. Cassie gasped when her back hit a real mattress.

"A real bed?"

He blushed. "I didn't want the first time to be on a blow-up, I was already hedging my bets on a tent and camping..."

Cassie stopped his worried explanation, reaching up and pulling his head to capture his lips with her own.

The desert hummed around them as wind blew gently through the rocks. Hidden birds spaced out their calls to each other. Cassie felt the ancient hum in her bones, of course it could be the crushing passion, but she liked the idea of great ancient spirits of previous lovers dancing joyously, welcoming her.

Stills' mouth worked her into a frenzy while his hands memorized every inch of her. He removed her bra and burned her skin with his mouth, kissing a trail down her stomach and slowly peeling off her remaining clothes. She tried to help him, but he took her hands and pushed them out of the way; he wanted to do this alone. She balled her fists into the comforter and when his trail of kisses landed in her most private of places, she came undone. She had wanted his mouth on her, his hands, all his attention, and she wasn't disappointed.

He worked steadily, pulling moan after moan from her, building a fire in her that encompassed her entire being. Arching off the bed, her hands linked behind his head and she called out her release.

Stills' own need moved his body up Cassie's, his dark eyes drew her in, sparkling with the same lust filled desire she ached with. He'd given her just a taste, and she wanted more. So much more. She wrapped her legs around his hips and pulled him toward her.

He reached between them and positioned himself. Cassie arched, trying desperately to hurry him, pull him into her. But Stills was agonizingly slow as he smoothly, fully filled her.

He gasped, "Holy shit." He was wholly inside her, entirely pressed against her.

"What?" she moaned, arching again and giving a slight rotation of her pelvis. She wanted movement, she was full but she knew there was more.

He pulled out and pressed into her again and all reasonable thought was abandoned.

She pulled on his head and claimed his lips, and as he built a rhythm she tried to keep time, but it was like holding on in a storm. Her accelerated heartbeat and moaning mingled in chorus with Stills' as the gusts of wind hissed and birds became more boisterous, agitated, excited.

Moans, grunts, groans and an intense building of sensation. A need to take more and give more as they clung to each other in the hurricane. Their bodies became slick and her legs slipped from around his waist, so she planted her feet on the bed and used the leverage to press up and meet his thrusts. He let his body weight fall against her chest, then reached beneath her, gripping the soft, thick flesh of her hips, using them to move quicker and steadier within her. Cassie burned with longing as his chest pressed against her, and his warm, large hands simply squeezed her. She felt the power of him in how he held her, the wantonness she created in a man with her body. She was possessed and alive and her desire for more continued to grow and double and ascend.

She found her voice somehow, and demanded more. The growl erupted deep in her throat, or maybe it began in Stills' diaphragm; they were one now, working together toward a common goal; working toward release; toward relief. □

She was traveling, moving forward, the precipice within her grasp. She moved faster, trying to meet the rhythm that had turned staccato, with all the wrong downbeats, frenzied.

Then the explosion, the tiny quake that began at her core and radiated outward. She clung to him as he began a renewed rhythm, working toward his own release, joining her, colliding with her one last time, holding them both in limbo as he filled her and the stars exploded, surrounding them in particles of light.

They held onto each other as the storm passed, and she held him within her as long as she could.

They were a tangle of quickened heartbeats and legs and arms that had melded together and become one. As the evening desert sounds returned, they separated back into two entities, each with their own torsos and limbs.

Stills lifted himself off Cassie and shifted so he lay on his side next to her. She rolled over and mirrored him, but remained close, so that their legs touched. He brushed a strand of her hair back from her face and gave a slight shake of his head.□

"I didn't expect it to be that good either," she whispered. "I mean," she drew a circle on his chest with her hand, "I thought it would be good, and fun...I knew it would be fun...but..." She sighed and her body shivered.

"Are you cold?" he asked and put an arm over her shoulder, ready to reach for the comforter.

She shook her head. "Just an aftershock."

His hand brushed down her arm, to her thigh, and up her belly.

"Give me five minutes," she breathed. Stills raised an eyebrow in question, and she licked her lips, confessing, "Oh, I want to do that again."

His laugh was a grumble in his chest. "Hell yes," he exclaimed, leaning forward to capture her mouth in a kiss once more which began to flame the heat all over again.

Chapter Thirty-Four

"I'm hungry." Cassie yawned and felt her body ripple beneath her. Her nakedness felt like a luxury now, as if she'd been brought back into her body by this man.

"I have a cooler in the car." Stills traced the line down her hip to her knee with his hand.

"Someone should get that."

"Yeah."

"But they would have to get dressed." She rolled onto her back and hoped the pose she was striking was sexy, but then, she didn't care, because after the past two hours she felt like the epitome of sexiness.

"Then I'll go," Stills rolled off the bed, "no way in hell do I want you covered up."

She nodded in agreement as he pulled on his boxer briefs and slipped on his shoes.

"That is a good look," she joked.

"It's dark, and I'm not in the mood to have to remove too much clothing again."

Cassie smiled up at the night sky that winked at her through the mesh. She wondered if anyone had heard their various bouts of love making that would have echoed off the boulders that hugged them in. At the thought, though, she realized she didn't really care.

Her body was liquid and devoid of all the stresses that had plagued her over the past few months. Hell, maybe she was devoid of every stress she'd ever had.

Stills made several trips emptying out the car. He put the cooler and food bags, along with their bags, in the tent. A propane stove and two gallons of water he left outside.

He brought two sandwiches, a bag of chips and the prosecco to bed when he had finished.

"I guessed what you would like," he said as he handed over a sandwich to Cassie. "I went with turkey, provolone, veggies and ranch."

"Perfect." She pulled herself up into a sitting position and began unwrapping her sandwich as he poured them each a glass.

"I love this," she said.

He looked up from the simple job of pouring two glasses and saw the awe in her eyes. "Good," he said.

They didn't move, just looked across the small distance at each other, and seeing each other in the dim light of the tent, naked, fully vulnerable and open to each other was more intimate than any moment they'd shared so far.

They settled into the hum of the desert, settled into the moment, and settled into each other's gaze. Time floated, lengthened, twirled in on itself and finally collapsed back into reality.

"Of course," Cassie said after she took a bite and pointed the sandwich at Stills, "it could just be the huge release of endorphins."

He nodded in appreciation of the joke and handed her a glass of prosecco, tapped his own against it and toasted, "To a remarkable woman."

"To a pretty amazing man," she said back.

They napped. Because what they did could not be considered sleeping. They talked, slept and then inevitably, someone moved and passions were reignited. They took turns memorizing each other's body, taste and textures.

The stars grew in brightness, the desert sounds calmed into a smooth wave of wind - no hum of a city, no intrusion of light. The night cooled the land and eventually forced them under the covers. □

Cassie saw the first blush of dawn on the edge of the sky and rolled over. "Benji..." she whispered as she brushed her hand across his chest. He smiled, his eyes closed. Just that smile, just the feel of his warmth under her hand, radiated to her core and ignited the longing again. She thought she had sated the yearning each time they came together, but she ached with the need of him. Of wanting him inside her.

She moved her hand down and found him hard. She thought she needed to thank pent-up sexual desires. She moved over his body, straddling his legs, and she positioned him inside her and let herself slip down the length of him. A sigh of relief and fulfillment and desire mingled until she wasn't sure where one emotion started and the other left.

His hands slipped up her thighs, to her hips and side, then cupped her breasts. Cassie smiled into the dim light, seeing his eyes flutter slightly as he pushed himself upward, moving deeper; she took him all in.□

The urgency was gone, taken by exhaustion perhaps of finally having burned away all the need that had built up over the past few weeks.

She felt powerful atop him, she moved her hips, ground herself against him and felt ripple after ripple of sensitive flesh react to him.

She lowered her torso and he hugged her to him. Propped on her forearms she set the pace, slid him in and out and felt full and complete with each new thrust. It didn't take long for an orgasm to ripple through her body, she clutched him and pulled him in as deep as she could while she rode the wave of pleasure.

Stills pushed them both up into a seated position, and she thought he meant to roll her over onto her back, but the position brought them so close, they stayed. Tangled, wrapped around each other, his hands splayed across her back held her in place as he dipped his head to her neck- she offered all of herself to him.

He came then, his teeth brushing her skin as he filled her, and her legs clutching him, again, pulling him deeper.

They stayed connected, seated together. She still wanted to contain him, hold him and stay in place, so she tightened her legs around his waist. She put her head on his shoulder and let her hands study the warm muscles of his back, and in turn, he reciprocated the gesture.

Somewhere, from the floor of the tent where all the clothes had been discarded, a cell phone alarm was chiming.

"What is that?" Cassie asked his chest.

"A wake-up call," Stills said.

"I thought you left the phones in the car."

"I needed the alarm," he told the side of her neck.

"I thought we were on vacation."

"We are, but this is for the next surprise I have planned."

"I don't know if my body can physically handle any more of your surprises," she whispered.

"Probably not, but wanna give it a try?"

"Probably," she parroted. "What do I need to do?"

"Well, Dodd, first we need to get dressed."

She nodded as he helped her to the edge of the bed. He stood up and pulled her into his arms, but she swayed a bit and gave a half grin. "You've turned me into Jell-o."

"A comment like that does a man's ego good, you know."

"Hiking attire or fancy breakfast?"

"Comfortable clothes and slip-on shoes," he instructed.

She unzipped her bag and began to laugh at the plastic baggie just inside containing a piece of paper, adorned with only a smiley face. Stills looked over her shoulder. "What is that?"

"It would seem that my dear sister thought we would be having a lot of sex." The baggie contained a box of feminine wipes, acidophilus pills and cranberry pills.

"What are the pills for?"

Cassie licked her lips and thought about not answering, but this man had spent the entire night exploring every inch of her body. "If a girl has a ton of sex, when she hasn't had that much sex in a long time, they can help maintain pH levels and such in said girl's body."

"How did your sister know we were going to be having a ton of sex?" Stills asked.

"She said it was the way we look at each other." Cassie pulled on her yoga pants and was finishing up with her sports bra when she looked over at Stills.

"Yeah, like that," she said out of breath, "we look at each other like that."

She was wrapped in his arms, tilted back slightly, his lips claiming hers. His alarm went off again. He pulled away. "Back-up alarm," he muttered.

"This must be some sort of surprise."

"It's just...cool." He gave the only clue and finished dressing.

Back in the car, the slight dawn was ushering the stars from the sky. Cassie's skin vibrated, her insides hummed and she felt completely relaxed. Stills kept one hand on her thigh as he drove back out of the park, then he started following GPS down a twisting road.

He slowed when they reached a small shed-like building with a parking space in front. □

"We're here," he said.

Cassie glanced around, there were no other buildings, just this one strange shed. "Is this where you tell me your deep dark secrets?" she joked.

He grinned, climbed out of the car and came around to get Cassie. Then he opened the trunk and took out a duffle bag. Cassie tilted her head in question. He winked at her but didn't head to the shed. Instead, he pointed to a man-made trail that started beside the shed.

He held out his hand for Cassie and she gladly accepted it. The trail was wide enough for both of them, but the dawn only allowed enough light to see several feet ahead. Cassie couldn't imagine what could be so cool out in the middle of nowhere.

But a grouping of trees, that looked suspicious in their structure (as if they'd been planted together), along with bushes that filled the spaces between the trees, was at the end of the short trail. Stills led her into an oasis where a rock lined pool sat in the morning air, steam rising into the cool crisp dawn.

"What..." Cassie couldn't believe it. Where had this come from, who'd made it? A soft babble of water entered from a pipe at the back of the pool, and over the edge, at the opposite end, the water spilled out into a river of its own making. Cassie knelt next to the water and dipped her hand in; it was a hot spring. "Are you kidding me?"

Stills put the bag down and pulled her back into his arms, kissing her gently, an offering, as if this was all for her. He began to pull her shirt over her head and followed with her pants. She let him undress her as she studied the surrounding area.

"I take it this is pretty private?"

"Oh yeah." He stepped back and removed his own clothes. Cassie glanced down and saw that he was already hard for her, and smiled. Again, she was filled with a strange wave of power.

She stepped into the pool, finding it hot and comforting. It elicited a groan of joy from her lips.

Stills placed their towels and a few bottles of water near the edge, then followed Cassie into the large man-made hot spring tub in the middle of nowhere.

Cassie's muscles released any last trace of tension that might have remained, and gasped as she lowered herself into the water. She was sore and well-loved, and yet, she still throbbed for more of him.

Stills was behind her, releasing his own moan of satisfaction at being consumed by the hot spring.

Cassie wrapped herself in his arms. Looking over his shoulder, she saw the dawn light illuminate the San Jacinto Mountains of Palm Springs and witnessed the first blush of the splendid desert coming back to life.

"Benji..." There was a question wrapped up in his name.

"My friend, who owed me the favor and set up the camp, suggested this as well. He said at sunrise it was particularly romantic and made the reservations for us."

She felt him hard against her. Cassie couldn't figure out how to explain how he made her ache for him. She went against everything she knew about water and sex and fitted him inside her.

"Dodd..." He tried to stop her.

"I just want to feel you."

He lowered his forehead to hers and blew out a breath. "I can't touch you without wanting to be inside you," he admitted.

"Good." She gave his favorite clipped answer.

The sun rose and painted the desert with soft brown hues and brought with it a cool breeze. The sounds of Cassie and Stills' slow love making were captured by the breeze and added to the many voices and stories that had come before them, knowing those sounds would fall into the sands, distant memories of the desert for those that would follow.

Chapter Thirty-Five

"Who will pack everything up?" Cassie asked as she took one last glance at the place that was as close to heaven as she'd ever come.

Stills was backing out of the site, it had been a glorious three days but they needed to head home.□

"My friend."

"What kind of favor does he owe you?"

Stills didn't answer and Cassie glanced sideways at him. "The answer is set in too much reality for right now, huh?"

He nodded once.

"Okay then, you'll tell me later." She waved and glanced back once more. "Have I told you how much fun I had?"

Their time had been divided between hiking, sleeping and making love. Stills cooked for her; pancakes and eggs in the morning, sandwiches for lunch, and he'd hired a catered dinner. They'd arrived back to the site from a sunset hike to find two women cooking and the picnic table transformed: white linens, candles, and a gorgeous modern table scape set up so that it was part of the surroundings. The women made a Southwestern dish, and Cassie sat next to Stills and ate, relishing the way he spoiled her.

Was it only last night that they'd had that dinner? Now, they were approaching late afternoon and it was time to drive home. Time to resume their lives.

But what did a work week look like with Stills in her life? The need for him that had grown by leaps and bounds over just three days...how was she supposed to focus now? And did this mean they were going to spend nights at each other's apartments until they decided they wanted more? Did she want to live with him? She wasn't in the mood to be away from him right now, that's for sure. She silenced her mind's questions, recognizing that this was the first blush of a new romance; this was lust and wantonness. She needed to savor it for now. The rest would figure itself out. □

"Tomorrow night, you need to come over for dinner." She decided to fight her slight worry about what the future held by actually making plans.

"Hell yes."

"I can finally cook a whole meal for you."

He reached his hand over and put it on her thigh and gave a squeeze. "I honestly can't wait."

The desert was sleepy again, coming fall months would bring a more dramatic temperature change between night and day.

Cassie slouched down slightly in her seat, laid it back a bit and held Stills' hand on her thigh.

He turned on an acoustic radio station and she meant to take comfort in the final glimpse of the San Jacinto Mountains towering, unwavering in the distance. So crystal clear. The palette of desert brown, beige, peach and gray mingled, creating a dreamy magnificence. But in the midst of her contemplation, her eyes fluttered shut and she fell asleep.

"Dodd, we're home." Stills was brushing the side of Cassie's face.

She blinked her eyes open, they were heavy with the exertion of the last three days. She smiled and leaned toward his hand.

A low laugh came from his chest. "We're home."

She forced her tired eyes open. The car had stopped. She let everything come into view then and gave a disappointed groan when she saw her apartment building.

"What?"□

She sat up and rubbed her face with her hands. "I didn't mean to fall asleep."

"It's okay."

She tried to hide her disappointment as she honestly admitted, "I didn't want to miss anything."

"You didn't, you missed some traffic on the 91 freeway, but that was about it."

She shook her head. "This sounds ridiculous, but I didn't want to sleep. I wanted another two hours with you, talking and just being with you."

His smile softened. "We have plenty of time."

She nodded. "But I wanted more."

"I get off tomorrow night at five-fifteen. I'll head right over," he assured.

Cassie nodded and bit her lower lip in thought.

"I know that look, Dodd. What's going on?"

"I'm just trying to figure out how to get myself in a bit of a pickle so that your job will be to park your ass on my street all day again."

He kissed her nose. "Don't do that. I'm in a new department. It wouldn't be me watching you."

"You switched jobs already? Why didn't you tell me?" He gave that apologetic look and she held up her hand. "It's classified," she mocked, imitating his deep voice.

"Well…" He shrugged with his hands.

She yawned and stretched, glancing at the time; it was seven-fifteen. "Come upstairs for a while?"

He quickly agreed.

Cassie thought they might both be floating. Endorphins in their bodies were working overtime so much that they were even blacking out during various mundane parts of the walk to her apartment. Because one second they were in the car, the next, she was unlocking her apartment door with Stills nipping her neck from behind, his hands on her hips, holding her the way a man holds a woman he's been intimate with.

She smiled and pushed open the door.

Then, like a bucket of ice water, reality greeted them.

Jessica was standing with her hands on her hips in the middle of the living room, Parker across from her, his arms folded over his chest, a grin on his face, obviously entertained by the showdown that was going on.

"Oh good, you're home," Jessica said. "Did you love it?" she demanded angrily.

Cassie frowned. "Yeah, it was amazing," she said slowly.

Jessica held up her hand. "I bet you have so much to tell me; but you got home just in time. You'll never believe what's going on."

"Is it any more preposterous than what's been going on over the past three months?" Cassie asked.

Stills put her bag down and closed the door, then nodded his greeting. "Salvatore."

"Good week?" Parker asked.

Another nod was the only answer he received.

"Your mother," Jessica spat, and Cassie knew this was going to be a problem as they only used the term 'your mother' when Barbara had done something disruptive, "talked to her new BFF Carlo, and somehow, the man convinced her to call Parker's mom."

"Does your mom speak English?" Cassie asked.

Parker shook his head, his grin still in place. "Nope."

"And now, the Salvatores are coming to visit our parents," Jessica said dramatically.

"Cool," Cassie responded. "What's the problem? Wait, if Mom doesn't speak Italian and Mrs. Salvatore doesn't speak English, who translated? And can we get a transcript of that somewhere?"

"Stupid Carlo helped." Jessica snarled and continued, "Oh, and get this, they want to meet the whole family." Jessica then over annunciated, "And, they are staying with our parents!"

"So?"

"Mom is thrilled." Jessica snorted.

"Oh." Cassie gave a laugh and when she looked at Stills, who had raised an eyebrow in question, she offered, "Jessica is going to have to stay married. And probably have a real wedding."

"Not if she doesn't want to," Parker announced. "I made Jess a promise, I wouldn't force her to do anything she doesn't want to do. She wanted to date and take it slow. That's what we're doing. My parents coming to visit won't change anything."

"Yeah, well, you don't know Barbara Dodd. You've had one meal- you think you know, but you don't," Jessica explained.

Cassie nodded in agreement. "You're going to be planning a real wedding on day two of your parents' visit."

"Exactly! Thank you." Jessica turned toward Parker and pointed a finger. "I *told* you, this isn't a good idea."

"Amore, do you want to go and file for a divorce?"

"Yes," she nodded and then sighed, "no."

Stills leaned toward Cassie and whispered, "Your sister and her boyfriend are ruining our free time again."

Cassie laughed, and Jessica frowned at her.

Stills brushed a kiss against her ear, then whispered, "Wanna have some fun?"

"Hell yes." She gave his favorite answer.

"If it will help the situation at all, maybe Cassie and I can take some of the stress off of you." Cassie was smiling up at him, curious about where this was going. But she trusted him. She had fun with him. She was ready for this ride, wherever it led.

"And how the hell are you going to do that?" Jessica demanded.

He pulled Cassie to his side and shrugged. "We're getting married. That should take your mom's attention completely off your shoulders."

"What?!" Jessica screamed excitedly.

Cassie's eyes widened as she turned toward Stills. A mix between audacity and shock and entertainment did an impressive tango; she narrowed her gaze. "I'm not a Cartoon Princess, I don't marry the first man that takes me camping."

He winked at her. "We'll see."

Simply Protocol Trivia

1 - Did you know that In-N-Out has a secret menu? Items that aren't on their main menu board? One of the most popular is **Animal Fries**. It's a stack of fries smothered in melted cheese, grilled onions and In-N-Out's secret sauce.

2 –Distance. So, I don't know if you know this or not, but in Southern California, no one describes destinations by how many miles away a destination is. It's all measured in time. I know, that from my childhood home in Southern California, it took roughly forty-five minutes, without traffic, to get to the Los Angels airport. I have no idea how many miles it really is.

3 – Sfoglia (pronounced: sfow·lee·uh) has many different definitions, the best one for our purposes is 'puff pastry.' The different definitions are the reason when you go online and start to look up sfoglia, the results are many, and quite varied. But I swear, when you go to a café in Italy, the name plate on my favorite pastry is **sfoglia**. Granted there are many different fillings...but look, I love them and I have yet to find a good recipe or their like in the states. So here's a picture of them. (That might look weird in the print copy of this book, but I don't care.)

4 – I have personally never liked the density of banana bread, so I started using the banana cake recipe from the *Better Homes and Gardens New Cookbook*. I do have an extra ingredient and step I use...but if I told you, it wouldn't be special. Maybe one day, when we're having a coffee together, I'll tell you.

5 – As a writer, I've found that I know a little bit about a lot of things. I've heard other writers say this before too. It's because for so many of my books and stories, I end up doing just enough research to make the story viable and the situations believable. Ironically, I write completely unbelievable situations.

When I started writing my book *Big Trouble in Little Italy*, I needed to do research regarding the CIA. (Thankfully, the same research was needed for *Simply Protocol*.) I called a friend to ask her a few questions because at the time, she was my closest source. You see, at one time she looked into becoming part of that organization. And I, myself, do not know any CIA agents.

When I was leaving a message for this friend, a few thoughts came to mind. The most intrusive was this: everything I know about the CIA (and other spy organizations) I learned from a Brad Pitt Movie. (I loved this message so much, I put the line in this book.)

So for your entertainment...

The Top Ten Things I Learned About Being A Secret Agent From All Those Brad Pitt Movies:

1) There is always an asset, a commander, an operation, and an overly intelligent, handsome, street-smart man at the center of it all.

2) Every life or death situation has just enough time for a funny comedic quip.

3) Assets are put into harm's way, but only in foreign, romantic locales.

4) In order to be a good agent, you have to have been a boy scout.

5) The really good agents are mysterious men who have been stand-offish to *everyone* they've ever met and worked with. However, the love of a damsel in distress makes them an open book.

6) Agents always drink really cool, trendy alcoholic drinks.

7) For any mission, "all you need is a stick of gum, a pocket knife and a smile."

8) The trunk of a car is a perfectly acceptable place to have a duffel bag full of guns.

9) It's always a good idea to hide foreign currency, passports, and a gun in several different safety deposit boxes all over the globe.

10) Apparently, only the good guys know how to hit the target.

Thank you and good night.

T hank you for reading! I hope you enjoyed the time you spent getting to know Cassie and Benji. But wait, there's more! How about a sneak peek at the next book in the Simply Trouble Series:

Worth the Trouble

Carlo Moretti, an Italian intelligence officer, is asked to look after Doctor Alessandra Salvatore, a co-worker's sister. It's a simple babysitting job. A job that turned out to be a hell of a lot more complicated than he ever imagined.

HERE'S A SNEAK PEEK AT
BOOK 3 IN THE
Simply Trouble Series

WORTH
the
Trouble
NICOLE SHARP

Chapter One

“A lex, sit down. Your pacing is giving me a headache.”
Alessandra, Alex to her American doctor colleagues, abruptly stopped and knelt in the dirt next to her friend. “Is it getting worse, Maggie?” she asked in her thick Italian accent.

“Only when you pace.” Maggie attempted a smile but it turned into a grimace; she touched her fingers to where her dishwater blonde hair was matted around the temple, where the blood had dried. She rested her head against the cave wall as Alessandra pulled the lantern they’d been left with closer to inspect the purple-black hematoma. She held up a finger in front of Maggie’s eyes, and urged, “Follow the finger.”

Maggie pushed Alessandra’s hand away. “You and Sabrina have already done that. We all know it’s not a concussion. It just aches, like I’ve been hit upside the head with the butt of a gun.” Which she had been. “How is Sabrina?”

“Sabrina is fine,” announced Sabrina, the other woman occupying the small cave with them. She was sitting across from them, several steps away, her back pressed against the opposite wall where she braced her left arm against her side, which she’d fallen on when being directed into the cave.

“Oddio.” *Oh my God.* Alessandra stood and began pacing again as she ran her hands through her short, unruly black hair to get the mess away from her face.

“Alex ...” Maggie muttered.

“Everything is going to be okay. I’ll get us out of this.”

“We don’t even know where we are,” Maggie whispered.

“It will be okay. We’ll be okay,” Alessandra insisted.

"Yes, because we haven't done anything wrong," Sabrina hissed, changing her position in the hopes of somehow getting comfortable.

"And we're working under the international humanitarian law, they can't just ... keep us here," Maggie added. "Their attack is going to be seen as a war crime."

Sabrina caught a sob before it could manifest into something more, the weight of their situation thickening the air in the cave. "Maggie, you signed the same waiver we did. Just because we're doctors in Venezuela doesn't mean everyone is going to abide by the law. These men want cash. Simple as that."

"Basta." *Stop*, Alessandra said as she halted in place and took a deep breath. "I know for certain we are going to be okay."

"Then why are you pacing?" Maggie asked.

"Because his wife is pregnant. He cannot leave her *now*," she hissed.

Across the darkness, Maggie gave a questioning look to Sabrina.

"Are you having trouble with your English?" Sabrina asked. "You got hit pretty hard in the head as well."

"My English is very good. And my head is very hard." Alessandra gave a wave of her hand and a gruff laugh.

Sabrina sighed exasperatedly. "Well, my Italian dear, we are having trouble understanding who is pregnant and why it matters to us here in the middle of nowhere, in this cave, where we've been kidnapped."

Alessandra stopped pacing and crouched between her friends. "Mio fratello, my brother ..." she lowered her voice as she whispered, "he works for the CIA."

"CIA?" Sabrina breathed out, matching Alessandra's whispered tone.

"Yes. He will hear about our capture and he will save us ... perché lui è stupido." Alessandra took another lap around the cave, accompanied by Maggie's moan, a reminder that she needed Alex to sit down.

Alessandra sat next to Maggie, reached out and absently patted the woman's hand.

"What is stupid?" Maggie asked, referring to the Italian word she'd understood.

"My brother. His wife is four months pregnant. He will come save us, but it's going to upset her. And he shouldn't be leaving her upset."

"Don't you think she'll be upset enough if she finds out you've been kidnapped?" Sabrina asked.

"*When* ..." Maggie amended, her voice shaking, "when they find out."

Sabrina whispered, "Sure they'll find out, but that doesn't mean anyone's coming to help us any time soon."

Maggie contradicted, "We're doctors in the middle of a jungle. We're a pretty valuable commodity. Didn't you see how many sick people are in this camp? We're going to be put to work."

"It won't be as long as you think." Alessandra's smile could be heard in the dim light of the cave. "My brother will know very soon ..." She rolled her pant leg up, turning it inside out, and pulled on a small area of fabric that had a secret velcroed pocket. From that, she produced what looked like a flat battery, the size of a quarter.

"What the hell is that?" Sabrina crossed the small distance and picked up the lantern to get a better look at the device.

"When I told my brother I was coming to Venezuela for several months with Doctors Without Borders, we argued for days. Finally, he gave his consent, which I didn't need, and this tracking device, in case of an emergency." She held the device loosely in her hand.

Maggie's eyes widened as Sabrina blurted out in a loud whisper, "For Christ's sake Alex, I believe *this* is the damn emergency."

Alessandra pressed the button and held it for several seconds until a red light began to flash. She put the device back in the pocket. "He will come for us and leave his pregnant wife worried and alone." She shook her head. "Oddio, Jessica is going to want to talk about all of this. Because she's as stubborn as he is."

"Jessica being your brother's wife?" Sabrina asked, sitting back down, creating a triangle.

"My sister-in-law," Alessandra confirmed.

"You're older, aren't you?" Maggie guessed.

Alessandra frowned, but nodded her head. "Yes, why?"

"You act like the older sibling. Taking charge, worried about us, bossy..." Maggie laughed but it turned into a groan.

Sabrina cleared her throat and gave a hopeful whisper. "But he'll come for us, your brother? He'll come?"

Alessandra gritted her teeth as she answered, "Yes. He'll come for us."

"How long do you think it will take?" Maggie asked.

Alessandra shrugged. "A couple of days?" A sob escaped Maggie's throat, Sabrina moved next to her and squeezed her shoulder.

"I'm just hurting." She tried to excuse her tears.

"Maggie is correct," Alessandra clutched her friend's hand, "we were brought here to work. We will just keep our heads clear and do what we have to, but we'll be ready to run when he shows up."

Maggie audibly swallowed, then let her whispered words tumble out. "Because in a few days your brother will be here to save us."

"Yes."

And for the first time, since they had been roughly excused from the hospital they were volunteering, by the militant men who now held them captive in the middle of the jungle, there was a glimmer of hope.

Thank you!

Another book, another long list of spectacular people who helped me get to this point.

Always, there is the unwavering belief my parents have in me. And you might be asking yourself, did I pull from their personalities to create Barbara and Walter Dodd? Oh, hell yeah!! My dad loves soccer, my mom is powerful and they did indeed make various visiting friends sit down at the dinner table to eat together and visit.

Krista Harper at Happily Ever After Required, was an amazing cheerleader of a book coach, helping me keep my shit together as I moved forward along this publishing path.

Ariane Kimlinger of Owl Focus Editing, my friend and grammatical guru. I owe her all the cappuccinos! She makes me laugh and keeps me grounded and sounding good when I do the writing thing. (I won't let her edit this sentence – so it's not her fault.)

A. M. Rasmussen, once again brought my imagined book cover to life to continue making my dreams a reality. These covers are true pieces of art. I can't wait for the collection to grow!

My sister, Katie, who I can't thank enough, but she knows that.

My early readers for this book, who ended up taking on more than they imagined. It was a learning experience and a weird process this time around. So with all my heart, thank you for sticking with me: Michele, Crystal, Ashelee, and especially A.J.!!!!

The weekly support and inspiration I receive from the network of amazing indie authors at TIRAA (The Independent Romance Author Association) has made all the difference. (If you're looking for a community to help on your own writing journey, wherever you find yourself, come check us out.)

Now a list of names....

Amy, Gina, Jewell, Shannon, Sophie, Colin, Cameron, Jeremy, Alison, Barbara, Amy B., Valerie, Cher, Lindsay, Vanessa, Fatima...and all the others who I'm forgetting...I hope each of you know how much you mean to me and how much your love and support fuels me!

And to you, my reader, thank you for taking a chance on this book. I hope you enjoyed your time spent with Cassie, Benji and the Dodd Family. If you like reading the fun behind the scenes stuff and want to be notified about my upcoming releases and other information you won't find anywhere else, why not sign up for my Newsletter?! You can find the sign up at NicoleSharpWrites.com

Legend has it that Nicole Sharp was born to hippies during an ice storm in Stone Mountain, Georgia. While confirmation of said events cannot be agreed upon, one fact is for certain, it was a Tuesday.

By age twelve, Nicole was sure of two things: 1) She wanted to be a writer and 2) She wanted to travel. She begged her parents to allow her to voyage alone to exotic lands. They permitted her to go from California to Boise, Idaho to visit a great-grandmother.

After muddling through her college years, Nicole graduated with a Bachelors in History (think Greeks and Romans). Why not study English if she wanted to be a writer? There were better stories in history class.

Nicole is Italian. According to Ancestry.com it's a rather low percentage, but she feels she is at least 51% Italian. She's visited the homeland a handful of times, studied the language and loves the Italian cappuccino.

Nicole's first concert was to see the bluegrass group The Seldom Scene when she was a fifteen-year-old, thanks to her parent's bluegrass phase. However, she never admits it, and instead tells everyone that They Might Be Giants, whom she saw in college, was her first real concert.

Her first car was a yellow Chevy Celebrity and her favorite job was working as a docent at a museum in an old Colorado mining town. She has written extensively about both.

Visit NicoleSharpWrites.com for more entertainment.